Ren has always wanted to leave, to escape his quiet village life. He wakes up from gold-tinged dreams with his heart pounding and a yearning for something he can't name, can't hold. He longs to experience something magical just once in his life.

Nico's monsters don't lurk under the bed. They walk in daylight. They haunt him every day of his life. He's possibly the strongest magician of his time, yet he's trapped. All he wants is an out.

At a magical carnival in the middle of a forest, Ren and Nico collide. They've been on this collision course their entire lives, always hurtling toward each other. For both men, escape is now. They have no choice but to flee together. Monsters and betrayal hunt them across strange lands. They find themselves on a journey to save each other—and possibly the world. All they have is one another, Nico's magic, and a lifetime of half-remembered dreams. But finding each other, finally having someone to rely on, might be the strongest magic of all.

HE DREAMS

MAGIC

Emme C. Taylor

A NineStar Press Publication

Published by NineStar Press
P.O. Box 91792,
Albuquerque, New Mexico, 87199 USA.
www.ninestarpress.com

He Dreams Magic

Printed in the USA
First Edition
October, 2019

Print ISBN: 978-1-951057-74-9

Also available in eBook, ISBN: 978-1-951057-67-1

Warning: This book contains mention of off-page rape and depictions of graphic violence.

For my mom, who gave me a home full of pens and notebooks and always encouraged me to use my imagination.

And for my cousin Julie, who spent countless childhood summers helping me fill all those notebooks with stories.

Chapter One

REN

The lake was on fire. Ren dipped his oars into the water and swept himself closer to the blaze, each stroke an exultation. He'd been waiting months for this, counting down the hot summer weeks to autumn and rain and flames.

He was ready to throw himself into the burn.

The fire came on time, as it did every year. The first rainstorm of autumn brought them down from the sky. Or so the story was told. Ren couldn't quite bring himself to believe they rode through the skies on storm clouds and dropped to the ground between thunderclaps, stealing their impossible power from the lightning.

Then again, they were magicians. Anything was possible.

Ren's village, Klein, lay huddled in the dark at his back. On the opposite shore, half the forest flickered red. The low clouds caught and held the glowing light from below. The spectacle could be seen from every village in the surrounding valley, a beacon: come, step into the heat, play with us, burn with us.

For the first time in his life, he was going to see it up close. From the quiet safety of Klein, the spectacle always gave the impression of a town set aflame. So near to it, it wasn't like that at all. More like the whole world had ignited. His fingers around the wood paddles twitched with anticipation. This was it. Finally. *Finally.*

By the time Ren reached the middle of the lake, half of it alight, a bright crimson flared across the surface and leaped like waves in wind. Reflections set the rest of the lake ablaze so that it seemed to Ren he was sitting in the very middle of the conflagration. So far, he had avoided the areas of the lake that had caught flame.

Magic. God, yes. He could practically taste it in the air, and he wanted more of it. He'd dreamed of magic for years, a gold thread of it always in his mind's eye. Since childhood, magic remained a ball of yearning lodged in his chest. Ren had to see it for himself. Touch it. Experience it. He wanted to drink it, have it sear his throat.

For years, he'd heard whispers of this from people in nearby villages, those who had gotten close to it over the years.

Those who'd walked through it—and come out on the other side.

Ren paused in the middle of the lake to take it all in. He would be seeing fire in his dreams that night.

His turn had come to walk into this wild world.

He dug his oars into the lake, his reflection rippling away from the boat with each stroke. Ren pushed himself closer to the ruby burn, a moth drawn to the dangerous lure of light.

REN REACHED THE very edge of the inferno. He sat near it for a while, swaying with the water's rhythm against his boat, watching the play of light over the surface. He knew he had to pass through it, but it rose up like a wall in front of him, more intimidating than he'd imagined. He glanced behind, where his home lay tiny across the lake, asleep in the dark.

No, there would be no going back now. He took a breath and hunched low in the boat as he rowed himself into something he'd been waiting for all his life.

He kept his eyes closed, pure instinct, which was why it took him such a long moment to realize he wasn't burning. No heat against his skin, no pain, so he squinted one eye open and then the other.

The fire swirled all around him, engulfing his boat, yet there was no smoke and only enough heat to warm the chilly night. He breathed in embers that flooded his throat with the flavor of smoke. Tendrils brushed against his skin like a warm blanket, ran hot fingers through his hair. None of it hurt, which seemed to be an encouraging sign.

A laugh of pure relief escaped. Of course he wasn't in agony. He'd never heard of anyone dying in it, and surely that would have gotten around. Still, it was one thing to hear about magic and an entirely different thing to face a fiery wall of it. Wisps of orange-red danced around him. He touched his finger to one, and it wrapped its dry warmth around his wrist, up his arm, and then dissipated in black dust. Ren flexed his hand, staring at his unharmed fingers in wonder. He wished he could capture a bit of that magic, take it home with him. He'd put it in a jar on the nightstand next to his bed and keep it as a night-light that would smolder eternally.

Ahead lay a narrow, unnerving tunnel, just large enough for Ren's boat to glide between the flames. He followed the tunnel to shore, a wild swirl of red-gold tingeing the world the whole way. He was light-drunk, giddy, and luminous from its glow.

REN'S BOAT BUMPED against the shore. The downpour intensified, stinging his face and pitter-pattering in the nearby trees as he dragged the boat ashore and found a spot for it on a bank just above the water. The Summer God always passed quickly in the night, leaving the door open for the God of Autumn to sweep in with her windy tumult. Ren adored this time of year. He loved change, and he welcomed the return of each God.

Behind Ren, the lake lit up the night like a giant torch. Ahead, the sway of light beckoned to him. Fire, fire, fire on every side. It stayed always in his sight, a red jewel just beyond reach.

Ren didn't walk far into the woods. One moment, rain dripped down his face. Then he blinked, and having crossed some invisible boundary, another world enveloped him. The soggy forest had transformed into golden light, crowds, laughter, and spices. It flickered around him, a swirl of excited chaos. He had stepped into a warm, sparkling globe.

He stood in the middle of it for a long moment, jostled by eager magic-seekers, impossible to take it all in at once.

Ren's mind latched on to one thing: he'd found the carnival he'd longed to see since childhood.

Being inside of it was nearly more than he could handle. The night spun in rich colors. Ren thought he might throw up, which wasn't exactly the reaction he'd imagined.

All the colors, the lights, the laughter, the shouts, the warm wonder turning the air into a golden mist that hung in the trees, the vividness of this carnival in the middle of a dark forest—all of it caught Ren up in its arms and made him drunk with new sensations, with new sights. Which could be the only explanation for why he stumbled through this spellbinding world, damp leaves and dirt crunching beneath his boots, light-headed as he turned back and forth. He gorged himself on the atmosphere until his stomach tumbled nauseatingly and gold sparks edged his vision. Was he in some wild dream?

There was too much to see, and it would be gone by morning.

Amidst the beautiful mayhem, he recognized many people from neighboring towns, though they were all mesmerized by the ambience too. He didn't say hello to the familiar faces, and they didn't say hello to him. His people took a strict stance against magic, but their neighbors did not share that rule. He'd missed out on this beautiful, unearthly wonder for so many years.

It didn't matter. Tonight was for exploration, of new things. Finally, Ren could share in the spectacle too. This world was his for the night. He just needed to slow down. *Breathe.*

Rows and rows of little makeshift buildings and stages lined the path, with treats to eat and buy and delight in. Ren didn't know where to begin.

Flames whirled in the trees, some as small as fireflies, little embers glittering throughout the forest. Others were so large they rippled up and down the tree trunks and skimmed across the limbs, leaping from one tree to the next. Men and women in black danced through the branches alongside the flickers, as nimble and flexible as the light. Empty air seemed the same as solid ground to them.

Magic saturated the air. Ren imagined he was breathing it in, letting it coat his lungs.

He could think of nowhere he'd rather be. Certainly not home in bed, locked behind the safety of his door, windows shuttered, like the rest of Klein.

Ren stopped on the pathway to drink it in. The feverish atmosphere swirled around him. He couldn't pick out individual parts of the carnival, only the colors and laughter, the jostle of people and the newness of it all. If asked later to describe any particular aspect, he thought he probably wouldn't be able to do it. Perhaps that was why he'd only been able to get vague bits and pieces from friends in other villages. No one ever seemed to remember details. This ephemeral world was a fever dream.

Intoxicated, he tipped his head back, motionless in the midst of the sweet sensory overload, studying the undulating mist and the dancing sparks tangled together in a jumbled golden weave in the trees above.

"Move! Move!" someone shouted from behind. Dreamy, Ren turned around in time to see one of the aerial acrobats soaring down from the branches straight into his path, flames streaking out behind him. A smear of red and black coming at him. Ren fumbled, wobbling first left and then right. He couldn't figure out which way to move. It was all too sudden and there was too much of everything. It was too late anyway. There were only seconds to spare. They were already on a collision course—the flying man and Ren and the flames. What an entanglement.

The impact of the man's body slammed him to the ground, knocking the air out of Ren's lungs as he hit the dirt and skidded, leaves and twigs doing nothing to cushion the crash. Ren's head snapped back, and his skull bounced off the ground, setting off sparks of his own, none of them magical this time. Everything flashed white, black, and then the night slowly blurred back into existence.

Ren found himself flat on his back, the other man's weight resting almost comfortably on top of him. His whole world narrowed to red, red, red, a bleary blob blocking out all else. The fiery backdrop didn't help. The man grunted out a surprised breath.

It took another few breathless moments for Ren's head to finally clear. He focused on the other man, had to blink hard twice to make sure he hadn't slipped into a dream. He was kind of unbelievable. For a second, there was nothing but his hair. They were pressed together, and his hair was all in Ren's face—hair like flames, wild and bright, and just as untamable, a deep auburn unlike any color Ren had ever known. The man lifted his head from Ren's shoulder, blinked back at Ren, wide eyes catching and mirroring the light of the autumn night in a way that hid their color.

"Oh," Ren breathed out.

"Oh damn," said the other man in a silken-smooth voice that made Ren freeze.

Ren couldn't breathe the sticky-warm air, couldn't move a muscle. *Oh. Gorgeous man, you can land on me anytime.*

The man jolted, his whole body jerking away from Ren. He put his hands to the ground and pushed himself up and back, almost frantic in his hurry to part them. Flustered, he stumbled to his feet, just as shaky and unstable as Ren.

Ren cleared his throat, preparing. "Look," he said, climbing to his feet as if uphill through mud, "that was my fault. I was too busy staring around to see you coming at me like that. I didn't mean to get in your way. I apologize for—"

"Forget it," the man said over his shoulder. He was already walking away, his hair a bright jewel fading into the fiery night.

Ren stared after him. It seemed rude to crash into someone and then simply walk away.

"Hold on!" Ren said, jogging to catch up to him.

The other picked up his pace, so Ren did the same to match him, an easy feat with his long legs.

He didn't spare Ren a second glance. "Don't worry about it," he said into the night air.

"Just wait a moment, will you, please?" Ren hooked his hand into the bend of the man's arm. For the reaction that small gesture got, Ren might as well have grabbed a totally different body part. He jerked free of Ren, reeled away, and put distance between them.

It was such a clear gesture to Ren: *Don't touch the goods, villager.*

As though there were only a certain type of person at a certain level who could touch someone like this red-haired gem, and maybe Ren wasn't at that level. He wasn't used to such a clear brush off. It wasn't a good feeling.

Ren brought out his most charming smile. "I feel it's only right to buy you a drink after taking you down like that." He gestured to a passerby giggling into a huge mug. "They must have drinks here, yes? Let me make it up to you."

A perfect bright eyebrow lifted. "You want to drink Quavar? Aren't you a little young to be up this late drinking?"

That caught Ren by surprise. His height paired with his shoulder width usually outweighed his, admittedly, baby face. Maybe it was his shaggy brown mop. Too boyish. He'd been meaning to cut it but kept forgetting.

"Don't worry about that," Ren said, pushing his hair off his forehead as if it would make all the difference. "I'm plenty old enough." Which somehow came out sounding childishly defiant. *Damn it*. Where was his game tonight? Had it been knocked out of him when they'd hit the ground so hard?

Both brows lifted that time, two elegant arcs. "I've never seen you here before. I just assumed you'd snuck out of bed and crept over from that village across the lake. Shouldn't you get home before your parents wake up?"

It wasn't even said cruelly, which made it worse. This fiery-haired, pretty little jerk of a magician was starting to tickle a nerve.

Ren paused as he drank in the man's face in one quick, furtive sip. He wore a strange, sheer opalescent makeup that shimmered across his cheekbones and made him look kind of absurdly amazing. Dark outlines around his eyes too. Ren had never seen a man in makeup, but the extravagant atmosphere made it perfectly believable it had borne this glimmering creature. And there was no denying he looked great in it. *Otherworldly*. Maybe Klein was right. Maybe these magicians did drop from the clouds, having spun from other planets. With this brilliant man before him, Ren could almost believe it.

Ren refocused, crossed his arms, and offered a languid smile. "I can't be as young as you're thinking when we both know I could probably snap you over my knee."

The man stared at Ren. The indefinable eyes widened a bit. Firelight flickered in his irises.

A too-wide grin, tight at the corners, strained across the man's mouth. It came too late. It was awkward and overthought, and it stoppered Ren's words in the back of his throat. He didn't know how to respond to a pasted-on smile like that.

"Fair enough," the man said. The smile sharpened into something that could bite.

Yikes. Walk away, said a voice in Ren's head. *Just walk away.*

Damn the little voice. He didn't walk away. He *couldn't*. All the Gods help him, Ren didn't walk away. He wasn't quite done. And it was hard to walk away from someone—someone who looked like *that*.

Ren had never realized he could be such a shallow thing. May the Gods forgive his superficiality just this one night.

"Do you really believe I'm too young, or are you just trying to get rid of me?" Ren asked.

Ren received a long perusal from beneath a sweeping shock of bright hair. "Would you bug off if I said it was both?"

"If that's what you truly want, then, yes. But...one drink? A drink and no regrets."

The smile Ren got in return was a curious thing, a flash of teeth, there and gone. There was nothing genuine about it. "What could I possibly have to regret?"

"Waking up in the morning and wondering about the memories I might have given you tonight."

The man's eyes tipped upward, briefly. "That was nauseating. Is that the best you've got?" He released an immensely unimpressed sigh. It was so histrionic Ren got the impression it was affected, as though they were on a stage acting out their parts. Unfortunately, Ren hadn't gotten the script.

Ren resisted the urge to move closer to him. He stood a slight distance from Ren, a remote dream in the flickering light, wavery and indistinct.

Gently, Ren said, "But you're still standing here."

The smile, dangerous and unreal, was gone now. With a sense of unfamiliarity, the man said, "You're so confident."

Ren let his laugh escape. He gave an exaggerated gesture down his body as if to say, *Why wouldn't I be?*

Before his hand even fell back to his side, he was immediately annoyed with himself. What was he doing, flashing this shiny, over-the-top swagger?

At the moment, he wasn't confident. He was forcing it, overdoing it, thickening every gesture, every vowel with his desire. He didn't want this lucent man to think this was who he was. It was unnatural, unlike him, and he knew it. It was just that, tonight, it leaked from his pores, as irrepressible as sweat.

He thought the man would walk away from him now. Ren deserved it. *He* would walk away from himself right now if he could.

His companion scanned around them and said, surprisingly, "Fine. Then get me that drink."

Ren remained composed. He was, despite the skepticism, an adult. Turning back to the tantalizing pandemonium around them, he said, "Which drink would you like?"

"Quavar. It's the only drink served."

"There are no other choices?" In a place like this, how could there only be one choice in drink? He'd been expecting all kinds of unworldly wines and champagnes flowing through the crowds.

"Trust me. It's enough."

"We'll see."

"A beverage connoisseur, are you?" The man started walking. He seemed so sure of himself, someone who knew exactly where he was going, that Ren followed him without question. Side by side, they fell into an effortlessly synchronized step, though Ren noticed his companion kept a careful, measured distance so that their shoulders never came in danger of bumping, their hands never close enough to brush.

Ren shrugged. "You could say so. When I was young, I helped at the local vineyard."

"Ah." He nodded as if it told him something about Ren. "A wine man. I've always enjoyed a good glass."

"Nico!" someone shouted from high in the treetops. They both peered up, Ren in wonder at the height and the way the owner of the voice seemed to float upside down in the tree limbs without care or concern. "How long are you taking?"

"I'll be back up in ten."

The other man gave a casual wave of his hand.

"Nico," Ren said thoughtfully, smoothing the name over his tongue as he watched the aerial acrobat backflip away through the air.

"Yes."

"That has a nice ring to it."

"Glad you approve," Nico said in a way that made Ren check whether or not he was joking. Studying Nico's deadpan countenance, he still couldn't tell.

Nico led them through laughing, jostling people; through light flares; through air that sizzled and sparked with enchantment. Everything smelled strongly of strange spices, earth and warmth, the slight musk of so many bodies. They stopped at a large wooden hut that looked like it grew straight out of the side of the tree it was next to. Logs framed an open window. A head full of fluffy white hair popped out of it with a sound of surprise.

"Nico! Taking a break already?" He glanced past Nico to Ren. "You found another one? So soon?"

"I'll take two, Ian," Nico said.

"I bet you would love that."

Ren's mouth opened as he watched their faces. He soaked in the salacious insinuation. It had poured easily from the old man's mouth, and that just made it seem dirtier. Ren thought he must have misunderstood.

Nico ignored the old man's bizarre flick of interest up and down his body. "The drinks," he said, voice hard. "Now."

The man didn't seem to be so much as checking Nico out, as checking *on* him, making sure he was sound. There was an odd air of propriety to it. Ren shifted his feet uncomfortably.

Ian's eyes flittered past Nico to Ren. "You've found yourself a big one for your little stroll tonight," he said, an odd, underlying hiss to his voice. A knowing grin formed around his eyes and melted down to his mouth. "Are you up for it, Nic?"

Nico remained impassive. "The drinks," he said, a careful flatness to his tone.

"Coming right up, sweet prince." Ian's tongue curled around the *s*, dragging it out.

Ren said, "Is that your uncle or something?"

Revulsion flashed over Nico's face. "No," he said.

Through the window, Ren observed the old man take down two saucer-sized mugs from a shelf that held hundreds more of the same. He dipped the mugs into a gigantic barrel, scooped a viscous liquid into each, and handed them, nearly overflowing, to Nico.

"How much?" Ren asked.

The grin gleamed at him. "We don't take money, son. Enjoy your night." He gave Nico an exaggerated wink and disappeared back into the dark depths of the shop.

Ren turned to Nico. "The whole point was for me to *buy* you a drink." He let some exasperation slip into his tone.

"We don't sell anything here."

"Then how do you make money?"

"We're not here for money." Nico took a careful sip of his drink. The mug was nearly the size of his head. He grimaced, swallowed, and held the other mug out to Ren. "Try it."

"Your wince isn't exactly a glowing endorsement. Should I be scared?"

The brows lifted. "Don't you like adventure?"

"Depends on the adventure."

Ren took the mug from him, but Nico slipped his hand away too quickly for their fingers to touch, and Ren found himself disappointed by the obvious distance Nico kept between them. Maybe there were some people he couldn't win over. That hurt to admit. So far in his life, his father had been the only person who had ever disliked him. Ren didn't want to add Nico to that brief list.

"Maybe a drink infused with six different kinds of magic is a little too adventurous for you." There was a challenge in Nico's voice. If he was giving Ren his biting smile as he said it, it was hidden behind his mug as he brought it up for another sip.

Ren sniffed the drink, the steam lifting a scent of spice. "I live for adventure."

Nico lowered the mug and, yes, there was definitely amusement lingering around his mouth, though not quite a smile. "What sort of adventures have you been on?"

"Well," Ren said. "This one. Here. Tonight." He grinned at Nico, raised his mug, and took a large gulp of the mysterious liquid—and choked. He must have inhaled some of the fire in the air as the drink seemed to scorch through his chest and straight into his stomach. Unlike the mystifying blaze all around them, this one actually burned. He doubled over, heaving.

"Oh hell!" Nico hovered closer, warmth on Ren's left side. "You're supposed to sip it at first."

Ren shook his head and tried to breathe past the sensation of his throat melting. He wanted to say *Thanks for telling me*, but he couldn't manage words at the moment.

"Hold on!" Nico's presence at his side faded into the crowd.

Innumerable minutes passed. By the time Nico reappeared in front of him, Ren was sitting on his rump on the ground, with no memory of having sat down. He saw Nico through a bleary haze of heat, his face and throat throbbing.

"Drink this," Nico said, in what Ren considered an inappropriately unconcerned voice, and thrust a cold drink into his hand.

If Ren had been clearheaded, he'd have made a cheesy, grinning remark about what had happened the last time Nico offered him a drink. But his mind was currently floating somewhere in the treetops. He downed the cool drink. Ice water rushed over his throat, soothing as it went down. Ren remained on the leafy ground amidst passing legs, with knees tucked to his chest, drinking until he finished the whole cup.

"Do you need more?" Nico asked. Arms folded across his chest, legs crossed at the ankle, he leaned against a nearby tree, the picture of casual, his mug on the ground at his feet.

Ren cleared his throat. "No."

"One cup of water usually does the trick."

"Wait. You mean this happens often?"

"Of course."

"And you didn't think it would be a good idea to warn me before I drank it?"

Nico gazed at him. "I thought you wanted adventure."

High in the trees, the air dancers were engaged in an entirely different world apart from that on the ground. A glow pulsed overhead near Nico, heat tendrils swirling like fingers of golden smoke above his head, sending firelight dancing over his unreadable face.

Ren pushed himself back onto his feet, taking his time brushing leaves and dirt off his pants. "Well, then. Damn you, you magical bastard."

"Here," Nico said and reached for the mug on the ground next to Ren's foot. "I'll get rid of it and get you something a little less...adventurous. Water seems to be more your speed."

Ren snatched up the mug before Nico could get to it. "No. I'll just drink it slower."

Once again, Nico's gaze settled on him, gleaming and unreadable. "Some people can't handle Quavar. It's potent."

There was that sound of challenge again, and Ren enjoyed a challenge. Grinning, he brought the mug back to his lips. "I promise you, I can handle just about anything." Including the mocking way said magical bastard's lips twisted as he watched Ren go in for his second try.

He took a cautious sip. It seared his lips, burned across his tongue, but he pushed it down his throat anyway. It slipped all the way down his esophagus and heated his stomach. He swallowed his own saliva several times to get the lingering effects of the Quavar off his tongue and rasped out, "Delicious."

"Pace yourself or you'll be drunk in five minutes."

"Maybe I want to be drunk now," Ren said, smirking. He wasn't even sure what he meant by it, except that maybe he wished they were both drunk so he could see Nico's lithe limbs loose and willing. It was, indeed, potent.

"Just wait until your parents smell that on your breath."

Ren took another sip, touching his tongue to the surface of the drink. It tingled. "Exactly how old do you think I am?"

"Eighteen. Maybe nineteen."

Ren stopped a giggle from working its way out of his mouth. A giggle would do nothing to prove he was a mature adult. Maybe that Quavar stuff did have a strong bite, in more ways than the obvious heat-burn. Ren usually wasn't a giggler. Coughing to cover the almost-giggle, in a voice rough with held-in laughter, he said, "Add five years."

Nico gave him a sidelong look. "Really?"

"Really." Ren sipped his drink, though it singed his tongue. "And I'm not going home to parents, so you need not worry about it."

"I'm not worried."

"You can cast your spells on me," Ren said, grinning over his mug, "and I won't even tell my mother on you." He regretted saying it five seconds later when Nico turned away, his patience a fleeting thing. An immensely awkward silence closed them up in a little bubble as carnival goers giddy with wonder streamed past.

"How old are you?" Ren asked just to change the subject.

"Also not an adolescent," Nico said with a distant tone. Perhaps his mind was in the canopy, flying, free.

Flirting usually came to Ren so easily—until now. He wanted to blame his fumbles on the drink, but he couldn't. It had everything to do with Nico being so near and the way the actuality of him overflowed Ren's senses. There was something about Nico that set off a yearning in Ren, like waking from a dream that he couldn't hold on to, wanting something he couldn't name. Ren couldn't get over a reality where someone like Nico truly existed.

Nico's sharp profile was lit from behind as he observed something or someone in the distance, a glow of gold and ruby spotlighting his pensiveness. Ren had the hot urge to capture the fleeting expression on Nico's face. He wished he were an artist, if only to paint Nico in that moment.

Nico said, "Do you always stare?"

Ren came out of his stupor. He hadn't realized he'd been staring.

"I think the drink might be getting to me," Ren said, a weak excuse.

Nico ignored that, too preoccupied with the crowd and the world above in the canopy, his attention an ephemeral thing Ren couldn't seem to capture. "I need to get back to my show."

Nico walked away without another word. The sheer abrupt rudeness of it was like nothing Ren had ever seen. Hadn't they been talking? Sort of?

No one in Klein would have ever done such a thing. Were these magicians really so different from his own people? So openly rude? Or was it just this one?

This was his night away from the home, the night he had been planning for months. Maybe years. Maybe since the first year he'd noticed the riotous glow in the woods across the lake, and his mother had sat him down and told him everyone was forbidden from going to the spectacle in the woods, that it was much safer to shutter the windows and bar the doors against it. Many in Klein believed the carnival troupe might have dark connections to the Autumn God, that they could use the God's power to twist the weather patterns and help bring down the gloom of the cool rainy season.

Ren didn't care. Even as a child, he'd always had one thought. *But what if I'm missing out? What if there's something at the carnival I need to see?*

Besides, Ren thought of autumn as his season, and he thrilled to the idea of his Autumn God in cahoots with magicians to weave storms. The season of mystery, when the town hushed up, kept its secrets and suspicions held tightly to its chest. He wanted to discover secrets. Starting, perhaps, with Nico—this enigma. He needed to touch his fingertips to Nico, satiate his curiosity against Nico's skin.

"You," Ren said when he reached Nico's side. Some of the liquid in his mug sloshed out onto his shoes. "Did I say something to offend you?" Nico's pace slowed. He kept a small distance between them, as though reluctant to let Ren near. "Please tell me if I did."

Nico stopped so abruptly that Ren spilled more of his drink on the ground. He licked some off his fingers, and this time, it almost tasted pleasant. Its warmth had a soothing quality, despite the sizzle in his throat. The way Nico followed the curl of Ren's tongue over his fingers answered at least one question for him, and the relief of that realization made Ren a little giddy. It appeared Nico wasn't utterly disinterested in men.

They were standing closer to each other than they had yet, so close Nico was forced to tilt his face up to him. Ren was nearly a head taller, and Nico's eyes were level with Ren's chin. And, yes, maybe Ren liked that a little. Or a lot, actually. Since age sixteen, he'd been taller than nearly everyone. He'd always had to tip downward to look at people, but he hadn't really thought about it or taken such a thrill from it until now.

"I have a job to do," Nico said, his regard sweeping up from Ren's neck, to his chin, to his mouth, and finally meeting his gaze. "You seem like a decent man. Go home."

"What?" Bewildered, Ren pulled back. "Are you kicking me out of the carnival? I just got here. Wait. Can you even do that? I don't think you can do that."

Nico's focus slipped away from Ren's face, skittered to the people nearby as he spoke. "It's not worth staying. Go home."

"I've already found a reason to stay longer."

"No," Nico said with force, "you haven't. Don't say that." His mind was clearly elsewhere, and that really got to Ren, as though he were so unimportant he couldn't even be spared any consideration as he was being rejected. Nico could at least look at him as he gave him the brush-off.

Ren snorted. The disappointment bubbled up, unavoidable, uncontainable. "You're kind of an asshole, aren't you? Why is it that people like you so often are?"

Finally, Nico abandoned the crowd around them, facing Ren warily. His shoulders were up, making him seem smaller. Softly, barely loud enough to be heard over the carnival noise, he said, "People like me?"

Ren swept a hand through the air, a gesture that took in all of Nico's body. "Ridiculously beautiful people." At that, Nico's mouth twisted into a familiar exasperation that told Ren he'd heard it before. Of course he had. Didn't beautiful people always know they were beautiful? Fine. Maybe Ren wasn't worthy of a magical creature. Nico was a dream man, not a reality. But it still *hurt*. He looked at Nico, and that hurt too. "All you had to do was tell me you weren't interested right away," Ren said, more softly. "It's all right."

"I did," Nico said. "You wouldn't let me walk away."

"Simple and straightforward," Ren went on. "Say it to my face. It would've been a letdown, but it would have been quicker."

"That was a little hard to do with you following me through the crowd. Should I have kneed you in the balls and then walked away?"

Ren ignored that. "Now I've spent more time with you, and it makes me want— It makes me wish..." *I had a chance.* It made him feel so spoiled, so entitled, so pathetic. He couldn't finish the thought aloud. He stuck his hands in his pockets, shrugged. "Maybe you should have just kneed me in the balls."

Nico considered him. "I could knee you in the balls right now."

"No. It wouldn't be the same. It's too late for ball-kneeing. That had to come earlier."

"Well then," Nico said, "fuck you."

Neither of them walked away. They stood in the middle of the chaos staring at each other. It was the moment when most would have parted ways: that moment when two people acknowledged a spark had failed to ignite.

There had been a spark for Ren, but Nico let it fizzle. A silence expanded between them, both intent on the other but neither moved.

Nico broke it. "Is everyone a giant where you're from?" His voice was impassive when he asked it, but the glimmer in his eyes cut back any bite the comment might have had.

It eased the tension in Ren's shoulders. Carefully, he said, "Just me."

The comment made Ren realize just how close they were standing. Nico seemed to be studying his face, and Ren did so in return: long, pale-ginger lashes; serious mouth; sharp-planed, shimmering cheekbones. His eyes, Ren could now clearly see, were a strange sort of brown, lighter than brown had any right to be, tawny in the subdued light. And kind of mesmerizing. God, oh God, he was beautiful. So beautiful it somehow didn't seem fair. They were about to walk away from each other, and Ren would never see him again. The one man Ren hadn't been able to charm. How tremendously unfair. He'd seen others squashed by rejection. It had never actually happened to him, but tonight was apparently a night of firsts.

Someone bumped Nico hard from behind, and he stumbled toward Ren. It was almost too perfect, the way Nico ended up, briefly, in Ren's arms. He caught Nico against his chest, steadied him. Quickly, Nico drew away from Ren. All that registered of the man standing behind Nico was that he was broad, stocky, overly hairy, strangely disproportional, and still standing there in their little moment, ruining it, for no reason.

"All right there, Nic?" the man said.

Nico went very still at the sound of his voice. He didn't answer. The man didn't move, except for the knowing gleam flicked at Ren, who grew a little more confused by the moment. Nico's back remained to the man, his lips a distinct flat line, his cheeks flushed. To Ren, it looked like anger. Or, inexplicably, fear.

It was, in fact, becoming uncomfortable, and Ren was getting the distinct impression he was missing something.

"Are you a magician too?" Ren asked, if only to break apart the moment.

"Of a sort." He laughed.

Ren didn't get the joke and didn't pretend to.

Nico was also not laughing, his expression inscrutable. His eyes were hard as they found Ren's. Ren didn't know Nico well enough to understand the look in them.

"Just checking in," the man said, already walking away. "Someone has to keep track of you, Nico."

He melted back into the crowd.

Nico turned in a slow circle, taking in his surroundings as though searching for someone or something. *Scanning*, Ren realized with unease.

Ren felt he had to ask it. It might explain Nico's furtiveness. "Was that your boyfriend? Or ex-boyfriend?"

Nico gave him a disgusted grimace. "No. And hell no."

"Oh," Ren said on a release of air. He smiled, relieved, as if the fact of a boyfriend mattered at this point. It would make no difference in Nico's rejection of him, but he said it anyway: "Good."

"Someone from my troupe," Nico said, abstracted. The crowd had his attention once again. "No one important."

"Is something wrong?"

A muscle in Nico's jaw twitched. "No."

He was so jittery, fiddling with his hands, lacing and unlacing them as if he couldn't keep his fingers still. It was clearly a lie. Nico was deeply disturbed, worried about something.

Ren played along, though he had no idea what was happening. "Does he do the air acrobatics too?" He was trying to pull Nico's focus back to him, and it worked.

Nico gave him a strange look, hazy with distraction. "Does he seem like someone who capers in treetops?"

"Not really, no." Nico's mercuriality felt like a wave that Ren couldn't avoid. "I don't think he has the legs for it," Ren muttered, helplessly unable to stop himself.

Nico turned all that heavy, focused intensity to him now. "Doesn't have the..."

"Well, I only meant—"

"He has the body of a furry squash," Nico said, and closed his lips on something that squeezed through anyway. He put the back of his hand up to his mouth as if to stop the awkward fart of amusement that leaked out, but he couldn't quite catch it.

"I didn't want to be rude, but he certainly does," Ren said, unsure of what was happening.

"Please," Nico said, "be rude." He shoved his fingers through the stick-straight tousle of his hair, making it fall forward. He dropped his hands back to his sides, his fingers calmer.

Ren had never wanted anything so much in his life than to touch the hair that fell like red silk across Nico's forehead. What would hair that rich in color feel like against his skin?

"I have to go," Nico said and started to turn away.

And so they were back to that. Ren knew he should let him go this time. There was something not quite right about Nico. There was something not quite right about the way he *felt* about Nico—so instantly, intensely immersed.

Ren didn't let him go.

"Wait." He put a thoughtless hand on Nico's shoulder. Nico shrugged away from his touch. And, *ouch.* He probably deserved that.

"I have a show to do," Nico said but didn't turn away or walk off again. He raked Ren with those strange wheat-brown eyes, as if waiting for whatever words Ren might offer this time.

"I only came for..." Embers floated down around them. Ren threw his hands into the air. "Magic. It's always been out of reach for me, in the distance. In my village, we grow up with it right there across the lake, but we never get to experience it. I had to come see it for myself." Softly, he added, "That's all I wanted tonight. I want you to know that I didn't come here to hit on a magician. You kind of just...fell into my arms."

A strange sort of music started up, a beat Ren felt in his bones more vividly than he heard it. It rose languidly, filling the night air as well as Ren's blood. His eardrums told him the amalgam of sound should be a cacophony, but it somehow spoke straight to his body. The tones melted into his skin, suffused his blood. Instruments layered on top of instruments until Ren swore he could taste it on his tongue, sweet and smoky at once.

"Do you feel that?" Ren said softly, afraid he might break the spell. "I think the music is"—he stared at Nico in surprise—"on my tongue."

To Ren's relieved delight, Nico's face brightened slightly. "Well," he said, "you wanted to experience magic."

"Good God." Ren closed his eyes, let the smoke roll over his tongue. "I could listen to this music all night. And savor it too. I don't want this song to ever end."

"The next song might have a different flavor."

Ren came to at that. "Really? Like what?"

"My favorite is the one that's like chocolate and cinnamon." The hint of a smile softened his face into something a bit more approachable, less harsh and otherworldly.

"What kind of magic is this?" Ren asked absently. The song swayed through his body, rippling over each of his senses.

"Mine," Nico said.

"Really?"

Nico nodded.

"All of the carnival, or the music part?"

"The music part."

The best part so far. The sensation of the music made Ren smile.

"Can I take you to dinner?" Ren asked and didn't care how ridiculous it sounded. He might be a country rube, used to nothing but the small candlelit restaurant in the center of town, but he was also a little desperate for the promise of more Nico in his life, if only for a night. He was about to disappear up into the trees, leaving Ren with no guarantee of ever seeing him again. The thought was unbearable. He had to at least throw out a reason for them to meet up afterward and hope Nico might catch it.

Nico paused. He didn't answer right away.

It prompted Ren to rush out the rest. "I had to try. One last try."

"You're tenacious." Nico bit his lip, and Ren's world narrowed to his mouth. "You should stay for the rest of my show."

Ren was having trouble keeping up with Nico's changeable moods, yet warmth spread up his limbs at the invitation. He swirled his drink. Maybe he'd had more than he realized. It would account for the heat tingling just under his skin. Not even a quarter of the mug was gone.

"I'd like that," Ren said, the warmth seeping into his voice.

Nico led him through the crowd to a relatively quieter area that Ren hadn't yet explored. The leaf-crunchy ground was covered with blankets. Dozens of people already sprawled flat on their backs, entranced by the aerial acrobats dancing through the canopy. Ren sat on the brown blanket Nico gestured to, and it seemed to cushion his body as though there were no ground beneath him at all.

Ren looked up at Nico. "And dinner?"

"Gods but you're brazen," Nico said.

"Brazenness usually works for me," Ren said, but then Nico glanced upward into the trees. Not a good sign. "I might never see you again. I know it's likely, but I don't want that to be the case. I thought I might as well just put it all out there."

Nico's face transformed into mock innocence, all big round eyes and an exaggerated frown that made Ren realize he really wanted to get to know this moody weirdo. Nico asked, "Are you sure you want to have dinner with me? The asshole?"

"I honestly can't yet tell if you're a true asshole." Ren really had nothing to lose at this point. "Maybe you're just having a bad night."

"Maybe I'm one of those partial asshole-type people."

"I can't figure you out," Ren admitted.

"We can get something to eat after I finish tonight."

Ren kept it calm, mellow. Inside, he was jumping, fist pumping. He gazed up the graceful length of Nico's legs, up his lean torso, and finally to his face. He was wearing some kind of tight black pants with a black shirt, all of it sleekly streamlined. The clothes hugged the clean, slender lines of Nico's body. For something that completely covered everything, the clothing was astonishingly revealing.

"Perfect," Ren said and wasn't sure if he meant the dinner or Nico's body. Maybe both. Yes, definitely both.

As Nico started to walk away, Ren lifted his mug back to his mouth, ready to dive in to the drink again, but Nico turned before he reached the edge of the crowd. "And you are?" he asked.

Lifting his glass to the sky, Ren said, "Happy to be here."

"That's nice." Unruffled, Nico waited for him to take a long sip of his drink—it didn't burn so badly now. "I meant, what is your name?"

"Oh. It's Ren."

"Ren."

He said it like he was flipping the name around inside his mouth, feeling its edges. Ren liked the way Nico's accent smoothed out his name. The way Nico's lips shaped it, it sounded like a song.

"Good to meet you, Ren," Nico said. "See you around later."

That small gesture, paired with Nico's acceptance of dinner, was all it took. Ren thought he might be damn well glowing.

Ren enjoyed the slinky manner in which Nico walked away. It made the heat rush just beneath his skin like magic.

Chapter Two

REN

There was something glorious about the way Nico maneuvered his body through the air, and it had nothing to do with sexual attraction. Well, perhaps a little to do with it. But mostly it was in the way Nico made every bend and twist into art, using his arms and legs like brushes, the flame his paint. He soared through the air like he belonged in the clouds. He spun through the fire as though he controlled it— Did he actually control it? The ease with which the flames fanned out behind him when he swung between branches made Ren stare in awe. Even on the ground, light seemed to follow Nico like an aura. Ren was more than a little spellbound. He had expected to come to this extravaganza and to be drawn to the magic itself. He had never anticipated being so captivated by a man.

But nothing else mattered when Nico danced up there in the trees, fey and beautiful. He had the ultimate freedom. He could practically fly. Ren's thoughts went to what else he might be able to do.

Ren wasn't the only one taken with Nico. There were two other aerial acrobats in the air with him, but Ren saw how people followed Nico's every motion. *Something in the way he moves so fluidly, so confidently, like he belongs in the air rather than on the ground.* The swirls and rolls and flips seemed to come to him naturally. Despite the flames and the height, he showed no fear in his movements. And, of course, the deep glow of his hair always drew attention back to him. Even when he wasn't focused on Nico, Ren kept catching him peripherally and inevitability couldn't help but be drawn back to him.

It was only once he saw Nico up in the air that Ren realized the strange, tight, coiled tension in Nico's body when he was standing on solid ground was absent when he was spinning through air.

Halfway through the show, Ren had already had too much of the Quavar, but he kept sipping it anyway. The drink was irresistible, much like the entire atmosphere of the carnival and a certain nimble, redheaded magician. It went too well with the shimmery, overindulgent ambience. He touched himself as Nico twisted high above him, indulging in a brief fantasy of flying through the air at Nico's side, catching him in his arms, and taking part in a much more private type show. He came out of that tipsy haze quickly, as if coming awake from a dream. He brought his hands under control and blinked around. No one noticed because they were also staring up at Nico and downing Quavar.

The drink hit him hard and suddenly; he wasn't drunk exactly, but rather soft and dreamy. Half of Ren's mind was up there dancing on the tips of tree limbs. Embers drifted down, never quite reaching the heads of the merrymakers, and fire licked the air in all directions. And in the span of a second—there and gone, just a mere flash between blinks—Ren glimpsed something like a dreamy version of hell. He brought his hands up and rubbed his temples. The world righted itself, and he saw nothing but the beauty of this unprecedented night: magic in the air and acrobats defying gravity with supernatural ability.

He'd probably had enough of the drink. No, he'd definitely had enough of it. On any other night, it would have been his cue to quit. But this was his big night, his one grand adventure. Perhaps the only real adventure he would ever have. He'd wake up in his bed tomorrow morning and go to work as usual. It would all be over.

For now, in this singular moment, it wasn't over.

Ren didn't stop drinking, though he knew he really should.

Ren drank his Quavar and followed his aerialist. Well, not *his*, of course. But he'd probably seen him before these other onlookers, and he certainly had spoken to him more than they had. Technically, he'd seen Nico first. There had to be something to that. Ren took several small sips, one after the other, and watched Nico.

Nico, horizontal to the ground, unwound from some invisible rope—the audience couldn't see it; was it really there?—and rolled smoothly from the top of the treetops all the way to the ground. There were murmurs and then gasps as he spun faster, the ground reaching up for him. Ren's last sip of Quavar caught in his throat. Nico came to a complete stop, his nose nearly brushing the earth, inches from disaster. He hovered there four, five, six seconds and then put his hands out and caught himself against the ground, all as casually as one might push out of bed in the morning and get dressed.

Nico stood to claps and yells, and among them, several loud whistles. His fellow acrobats touched the ground after him, nearby. Many of the onlookers got up from their blankets to surround the acrobats, jabbering over one another. Ren stood next to his blanket, drink in his hand, unsure of what to do next. He took yet another sip. Each one got longer. The Quavar had stopped burning. In fact, he was actually starting to like the drink. In the back of his mind, the part that wasn't floating happily in the golden firelight, he thought that might be a bad sign.

Nico broke away from the cluster, and Ren's heart seemed to dance in his chest when he headed straight for Ren. There was sweat glistening along with his makeup, and his hair fell everywhere, out of its perfect tousle. Ren had a fleeting temptation to tackle him.

"You're spectacular," Ren said as he approached. "I couldn't look away."

Nico didn't smile at the compliment. He was looking around rather than at Ren as he said, "Thanks."

"Do you do this every night?"

Nico's cheeks were red from exertion, and Ren wanted to tumble with him into the trees.

"Different variations of it, and only on carnival nights."

"Are you sure you don't live in the trees?" Ren said, grinning. "I think you might be some sort of pretty birdlike creature."

Nico looked up at him, and Ren's grin seemed to catch a bit and spark a tiny smile onto Nico's face, a sweeter, brighter smile than Ren expected from him. God, it was beautiful.

"Have you ever seen a bird somersault like that?" Nico said.

"Touché. Clearly they've got nothing on your flying prowess."

"Excuse me," said a petite dark-haired woman who suddenly appeared at their elbows. She was all about

Nico. "I wanted to tell you how wonderful I thought you were up there."

"Thank you," Nico said with that glimmer of a smile that was slowly melting Ren's insides. It was clear that some of the tension he'd carried earlier had unwound up in the trees.

"Do you use a rope of some kind?" she asked.

Nico went up on the tips of his toes and then rocked back onto his heels. "Well, that's a secret I can't reveal."

This is Nico the performer, humoring his audience. Even this little show Nico was putting on now was somehow enticing. It made Ren itch to peel away the shiny layers of the entertainer and find the real man underneath.

"I was wondering if you could possibly take me up in the air with you. Just once." Her laugh was as sweet as the delicate fall of sugar granules. "For a ride."

"I'm sorry," Nico said in an easy way that told Ren he'd dealt with this question before, "I can't. I'm trained, but it's too dangerous to take onlookers up there."

"I was so hoping to experience it with you. I just wanted a—" She touched his wrist, glittered up at him. "—small taste." Her fingers slipped under the edge of his shirtsleeve, caressing the skin over his pulse point.

Ren frowned. The heat of the Quavar bubbled in his stomach. How ridiculously obvious. Bold and ballsy, which he had to respect, but kind of also encroaching on Ren's territory right in front of him and that wasn't right. After all, he'd seen Nico first. All right, so he was being ridiculous. But it still stung.

He was too busy being territorial to immediately notice the tension sliding up Nico's spine and onto his face, sweeping away the soft smile. Instead of simply pulling his hand away, Nico stepped back from her, out of touching distance.

Others poured in from all sides, a flood of men and women seeking the star of the show. They'd spotted Nico's distinctive hair shining against the night, and they were closing in fast, eager to get close to the pure allure that was Nico. From the way Nico's body went rigid, Ren knew he'd noticed them too.

"I can't," Nico told her. There was fresh tension vibrating in his voice to match the hardness across his shoulders. "I have something else I need to do." He turned and walked away even as she said something in response.

She and Ren looked at each other. She didn't seem the least bit upset. "Oh well," she said to him. "When you make big moves, sometimes you crash harder." She shrugged and wandered off.

Ren dove into the crowd and spotted Nico a dozen paces away and moving fast. Thank God for that beaconlike hair and for Ren's height.

"Are you all right?" Ren asked, once again walking at his side and letting Nico lead them off to something new.

"I don't like when they touch me."

"I could tell."

"I usually make a quick exit before they can crowd me."

"I think they adore you," Ren said. "You had all of them in the palm of your hand."

Nico was moving through the crowd fast, in a hurry to get as far away from his admirers as possible. "I don't care if they build shrines to me in their homes. I don't want their hands on me. I'll never understand why people are so tactile with strangers."

Ren thought it seemed such a natural thing: a friendly hand on the shoulder, a brush of fingers for attention. Even a stranger's casual touch was usually harmless. It was human nature to touch and to want to be touched. Was his world really that different from the magicians' world?

"Do you deal with that often?" Ren asked, trying to understand.

Nico paused before saying, with a catch of hesitation in his voice, "Yes."

"You don't like it when strangers get in your face. I get it."

Nico was quiet as they swept through the carnival, but then he shook his head, mouth a closed line. "You don't get it. Everyone is desperate. They're hungry for something. I hate it when people touch me as if they think I can give it to them."

"Oh," Ren said because he had no idea how to respond to that.

Nico was right. He didn't get it. Nothing at the carnival made sense. Ren attributed all the unexplainable things to the strange environment that produced someone like Nico. How did one live with magic coursing through their veins?

Through a Quavar-enriched dreamy haze, Ren tried to take in the wonderful, color-drenched beauty of the many carts and stages that lined the path, full of things he couldn't quite fathom, all lit by the golden night.

It took what seemed like a long while of walking through the open market for Nico to say, "You can walk away from me now. We'll pretend you never asked me to dinner."

Alarmed, Ren stopped in the middle of the path. "What?"

Nico stopped as well and faced him. "You don't have to stay with me."

"But...I'm hungry. And you promised me food."

"That cart up there." Nico gestured ahead to a cart so swathed in strings of tiny, multicolored lights that the wood frame underneath was barely visible. "Get some food, and then go home."

It took Ren a moment to understand what he was seeing. The lights weren't just on the cart; they fluttered in the air and over nearby tables and chairs where customers ate. Undulating midair, their vibrant colors ran together and swam in front of Ren.

His mouth flapped open. "The lights..."

"Yes, the one with the lights," Nico said, sounding tired. "Go up to them and ask for the soup and bread. You don't need me with you to get dinner."

Ren came out of his awed daze quickly at that. "You said you'd have dinner with me."

"I'm tired. I'm just going to go back to my tent to sleep."

"Sleep? How can you sleep with all of this going on?" With so many wonders, with so much to see. There was no understanding this man who flew in treetops and yawned at such magnificent displays of power.

Distracted, Nico said, "My tent is soundproof." His attention seemed to be lost to the crowd, though surely he saw similar throngs of carnival-goers every night. He observed the flow of people slipping past them like water.

Ren laughed. "No, no. I meant, how can you sleep when there's so much to do?"

Nico's lips twisted in confusion. "Like what?"

"Like—" Ren spread his arms wide to indicate the bright, sparkling world around them. "—everything." He dropped his arms and let a grin slide across his mouth. "Like talking to me, for example. Talk to me, Nico."

"We are talking."

"You're such a brat." Only after he said it did Ren realize just how fond it sounded, how intimate, as though they'd known each other years instead of a bare sprinkle of hours. It was, perhaps, inappropriate for two strangers, but Ren was full of alcohol, and it made him care less.

Nico was gazing straight at him now, his cheeks flushed. He was sweating underneath the makeup. He heaved in a breath. "I don't—I can't—I don't think I can do this tonight. It was a bad idea. I don't know what I'm doing."

"Breathe," Ren said because Nico seemed to be painfully on edge. "It's just dinner, Nico. That's it. Half an hour at the most."

Nico paused, blinked. "I'm not great company tonight. You don't want to spend time with me."

"The worst thing you can do when you're in a bad mood is to go off alone and mope. I'm great company. I can balance out your terrible company. You should stay with me and explore."

Nico looked as though it took everything he had not to roll his eyes. "Explore?"

"You're so used to living in this amazing world that I guess you take it for granted. But me? I can't brush it off. I can't imagine how you ever could."

"You get used to it," Nico said. "Anything can become mundane when you're around it enough."

There was something sad about that, about no longer being able to see the beauty in beautiful things. What could the world offer if something as monumental as magic failed to evoke emotion? What was more impressive, more important? At the moment, Ren couldn't think of anything.

Ren could already see Nico slipping away from him even as he stood two paces away. He kept searching the crowd, his mind clearly elsewhere. With his arms pulled in tightly to his chest, the sea of people parting on either side of him, he appeared as remote as an island, some place Ren would never be able to reach. He seemed so very alone.

"Please eat dinner with me," Ren said, checking him carefully for signs of flight. "Just a quick meal and then you can be off to bed. I'll even tuck you in. I'll tell you a story if you want. I'll sing you a lullaby. But don't leave me here to eat alone."

"Have I somehow become your guide for the night?"

Ren grinned. "Something like that."

Nico let out a breath that made his hair billow out about his forehead like red smoke. "Fine. A quick meal. Wait here. I'll get the food."

"Thank y—"

He was already gone, lost in the crowd. At least Ren was mostly sure Nico would be back. Hopefully. Maybe.

Several minutes later, he started checking for a bright head in the crowd. Just as he began to doubt if he'd ever see Nico again, he came up behind Ren and dropped a warm, silver-wrapped package over his shoulder. Ren caught it in midair.

"I thought you might not come back," Ren said.

"Why would you think that?"

"Because you're so—" Ren stared down, uncomprehending, at his food. "—*tired.*" Through the thin sheet of silver paper, a bread-like type of food glowed softly. He blinked at it, peeled back the paper from the top.

"I promise, it doesn't bite back," Nico said. He noticed Ren's skepticism and lifted his chin. "Try it."

The bread was thick like a rope, winding in and around itself in intricate knots. And, of course, there was the golden glow. Ren took a bite out of its curved top. Soft and flakey, it filled his mouth with the most comforting warmth, better than sunshine in summer. A hint of cinnamon lingered on his tongue after he swallowed the bite.

"Well?" Nico asked and bit into his own.

"It tastes of spice and sunshine." Ren smiled at him. "It's perfect. How do they do it?"

"Magic." Nico peeled the wrapping completely off his food, held the silver paper up between thumb and forefinger, and blew, his breath lifting and sending it spinning up into the air where the fiery wind caught it and the night swept it higher and higher. It danced across the air, dipping and twirling, a tiny silver dancer, and then burst apart far above their heads, sprinkling the air with a gold mist, the likes of which Ren had only ever seen in dreams. The mist scattered in the wind, a fading dream in morning light.

"Lovely," Ren breathed, delighted. Trash, something so simple and mundane, turned into beauty. Nico loved using magic; it shone on his face, joy dancing there, and Ren thought he might want to stay forever. Was that why his village forbade its people from seeing such things? Maybe everyone who saw it eventually wanted to stay. Maybe they walked dreamily through their days, lost in thoughts of a place in the woods where anything could happen, where some people had the power to create unfathomable experiences. Maybe the humdrum, everyday world wasn't enough after having seen a more fantastic version of it.

They ate under a tree, in a swell of quiet, with the noise ebbing and flowing around them as though it were part of another world.

Out of nowhere, Nico said, "You really need to stop staring at me as though I were some mythical creature. It's unsettling."

"It's just…" Ren didn't quite know how to finish. "Are you all right?"

Nico paused with his food halfway to his mouth, his mouth frozen open. It took him only a moment to shake himself out of it and say, "I'm fine."

"You seem…anxious." When Nico didn't respond, Ren said, "You keep looking around like you're scared something is going to jump out at you."

"I'm—" If anything, Nico seemed more disquieted than ever. He swallowed his unsaid words. He set his food down on his outstretched leg, balanced on his knee, and brushed his hands together. Still, he didn't look directly at Ren. He forced out a laugh. "I get nervous," Nico said, "around men I want to sleep with. I'm not good at flirting."

Ren nearly dropped his food, saved it at the last second. He cleared his throat, said, "And here I thought you were tired." *Thought you were trying to get rid of me.* Nico was absolutely baffling.

"You don't want to sleep with me?" Nico gave him a sly sidelong look through long lashes, another challenge. And, oh, but Ren did love a challenge.

"I do." The golden swirl of the carnival faded into the background. Sleeping with a beautiful man hadn't occurred to Ren when he'd first set out that night, but now he wanted it. He wanted to feel the magic thrumming beneath Nico's skin. Nico's fingers distracted him, pale against black fabric, tightening against his thigh, holding on. Those fingers spoke in an agitated language Ren didn't quite understand. He said, "I'm just surprised."

"Where else did you think this was going?"

"That's exactly where I hoped it was going," Ren said, "but I wasn't sure. Has anyone ever told you that you're incredibly confusing?"

Nico's fingers relaxed against his thighs. He shot Ren a small, shy smile that blinked on and off in an instant. He held his leftover dinner in his palm, in the open where Ren could see it. Ren blinked, and it was gone, gold dust falling through Nico's fingers to the ground, a beautiful, distracting little display. Nico brushed the dust from his hands and shrugged a shoulder.

There was no way Ren was going to pass up the opportunity to sleep with this sublime man. Nico had him. He knew it, and he was pretty sure Nico knew it too. As it turned out, and as Ren was slowly learning, Nico was sly as a cat. He had been drawing Ren in all night.

Ren grinned at him. "Oh, you're good."

"Am I?" Nico asked and blinked.

"I bet you could do anything you wanted."

Briefly, Nico caught his eyes and looked away again. Now that Ren knew his anxious glances were because of nerves, that shy, twitchy energy made Ren want to kiss him. His uncertainty was kind of surprisingly adorable. He'd read Nico all wrong.

"I'm not omnipotent. If I had unlimited power," Nico said, "do you really think I'd be sitting in the middle of a forest and living out of a tent?"

It made no sense to Ren. "You don't love being a part of all this? It's a dream." He paused to follow a flock of birds overhead, as bright as a constellation on a dark night, swoop low and then disappear against the cloudy sky. "It's perfect," Ren said on a happy sigh.

"This isn't what magic really is." Nico said it so softly Ren had to lean closer to hear him. The dusty, gilded air enveloped them.

"I've dreamed about it," Ren said, "but I couldn't have imagined anything like this. This is more than I ever thought it could be."

Nico said, "Magic is raw, organic. It doesn't need to be...displayed like this." He picked at the fallen yellow-green leaves near his leg, stacked them into a crunchy pile. "Magic is usually quieter than this."

"What do you mean?"

"It's everywhere," Nico said. "It's in nature, and we're a part of nature. It flows through the air, pushes up from the earth, bubbles in the water. Our bodies are partially made of magic. It's swirling inside us alongside our blood." With half his concentration on the leaves, he said it casually, as though he didn't realize he'd flipped Ren's world around with the thought of magic being everywhere instead of just a contained entity inside this carnival.

"It's a part of the earth," Nico said. "It's another element like water or air. Some of us have an innate ability to access and use our powers. You call us magicians. This area—your home—there's a large concentration of it here, running through the air currents, gathered in the trees, the dirt, the people. Some choose to come here and steal it."

Ren's mind reeled. "The people? Wait—are you saying there's some of it in me too?"

There was Nico's smile again, humoring, aimed at his leaf pile: quick, small, and sweeter than before. "Everyone has at least a little in them. We're all made of magic, some more than others. It's a natural part of your body." Nico glanced at him. "You're not going to flip out on me, are you?"

Ren breathed in the spicy air, could practically taste it on the back of his tongue. "Why would I do that?"

"Some people can't handle the idea."

Couldn't handle it? Ren was about to fly out of his skin and soar over the crowd with excitement. "Can I use my magic?"

The leaf pile towered, balanced in a way that wasn't quite natural.

Nico said, "Only some can. The ability manifests when you're young. If you can't do it by now, then you're not a magician." He caught the disappointment on Ren's face. Nico's voice gentled. "There's a myth that says wind sprites fly through the windows of some babies at night. When they drift near the sleeping child, their own magic awakens that in the child. They breathe into the child's mouth and stir their power. They say it's how magicians are born. Do you recall any wind sprites in your childhood?"

Ren leaned his head back and laughed, giddy with the energy in the air, in his veins. Somewhere deep in his chest, something marvelous stirred to life. "No. Damn! Do you believe that's how magicians are created?"

"Do I believe there are creatures that awakened mine by breathing on me?" Nico made a derisive noise. "No."

Curious, Ren said, "Magic must come from something ensorcelled. Don't you think? Where else would it come from?"

The leaf tower reached Nico's head, seated as he was on the ground. Nico piled it higher. It quivered but didn't fall. "Not little flying sprites. I think it comes from the earth itself. The air, the water. Maybe over the centuries we've absorbed it. It's seeped into our bodies and become a part of us."

Ren leaned back on his hands and stretched out his legs in front of him. "I'd settle for being able to do only one wondrous thing if it meant I could travel with this carnival as you do. I want to be a part of something grand. To experience it every day. I swear to all the Gods, that would be amazing."

"You don't want to be a part of this. It's not that great," Nico said to the leaves. "Magic doesn't need to be ostentatious or pretty. Or...or *used* the way it is here. It's...depressing."

Sleepy, full of food and drink, Ren was a little mesmerized by the way the light caught on the angles of Nico's face and fell across his hair, a subtle caress. He practically glowed in the night's strange gold light. Or was that Ren's imagination?

Maybe he's cast a spell on me so that I can't look away from him. No, he's beautiful, and I want him so badly. I want this moment to last.

Nico noticed him staring. "But you like pretty things, don't you?"

The moment scattered. Ren leaned into the tree at his back, said carefully, "What's wrong with enjoying something beautiful?"

"Beauty is nothing but a shiny layer on top of something else. It doesn't matter." Nico flicked his fingers at the leaf tower, and it floated apart, the leaves drifting slowly back to the ground.

Ren dropped his voice. "Finding out what's underneath can be enjoyable too." Nico looked up from his leaves and held Ren's gaze until the teasing grin drifted off Ren's mouth in the face of Nico's solemnness. "You're so somber," Ren said softly.

Nico moved fast. He was off the ground and standing in front of Ren in the time it took Ren to blink. He held his hand down to Ren, and when he clasped it, a strange tingle passed through Ren and sparked in his palm, as though he and Nico were electric together. It left him dazzled, blinking at where their hands met, pale ivory against warm brown. Had Nico felt it too?

"Do you want me?" Nico's voice held a sweet diffidence. The fires receded in this area. The dimness shadowed Nico's eyes, turned them wide and dark and unreadable.

Sweet Lord, yes. Who wouldn't? An entire audience that had just watched him dance in the air would answer yes to that question. Every single person who had seen him. Ren was sure of it. Every twist of his body up there had been sensual, and he was no less so on the ground. Even when folded into himself, moody and indecipherable, Nico gleamed crimson and gold in the crowd, inexplicably remarkable. How could he ever be unsure of how desirable he was?

"You even have to ask?" It had to be embarrassingly obvious how much he wanted Nico. The desire was raw and exciting in a way he hadn't felt since his first fumble as a teen. "I've been tripping over myself from the moment we met. And I swear, men don't usually make me nervous. But you... I don't know what it is about you."

"Right," Nico said. He tugged at Ren's arm, and Ren let himself be pulled to his feet. Momentum and alcohol brought Ren straight into Nico. They bumped together, and Ren steadied him by grasping his shoulders. Nico didn't jerk back as expected, and Ren took cues from him. They stood, leaning into each other, hips touching as the magic flowed over them, between them, and people yelled and called and laughed. Ren immersed himself in the brief privilege of having Nico near, relished how Nico's straight shoulders and lissome frame fit just right in his arms.

He feels so real and solid. Warm and rich. Luxurious. Like the way the color gold might feel. No wait. That's ridiculous. How can that be?

Nico's lips pursed. "I suppose that's a yes," he said as he caught something behind Ren.

"Yes," Ren said with a cool calm, which he then ruined in the very next instant by tossing his head back and sending a laugh into the pulsating night. "Holy seasons, yes!"

Nico's shoulder blades shifted beneath Ren's palms.

Something at Ren's back had Nico riveted. Ren craned his neck, but he couldn't spot anything but flowing crowds and air hazy with the frenetic energy of this moment. A fine thread of something jumpy thrummed beneath Ren's hands. Was it fear? Ren imagined it spreading through the muscles in Nico's back where they were touching.

He's scared. The thought, in a sharp moment of clarity, sobered him. He loosened his hold on Nico, canted back to look down into his face.

What's out there? He almost asked it out of compulsion driven by whatever it was haunting Nico. But it made no sense. The night vibrated with shimmery air and dancing lights, music that tasted of smoky cinnamon, fire that glowed but never burned, and loads of exhilarated revelers.

Ren discarded the nonsensical question. It had to be something else, something Ren didn't want to admit. He'd failed to seduce this man. Something about him didn't appeal to Nico. Charm, seduction—those things had always come naturally to Ren. Everyone at home knew this about him, an innate ability he'd had since childhood. He could lure a smile from the grumpiest crone, a free meal from the stingiest inn owner, and a weekly tumble with the blacksmith who claimed he didn't enjoy men. Most of the time, Ren didn't have to try. Things just fell into place for him. *People* fell into place for him. Unused to rejection, this was starting to feel unpleasantly like his first real sour taste of it.

"We don't have to do this." Ren spoke the words softly, reluctantly, and God it hurt. "If you truly don't want to sleep with me, I don't want— Look, I'm not that desperate. I don't want to sleep with someone who isn't interested." He started to ease away, but Nico finally seemed to notice their proximity and tangled his fingers in Ren's coat, held him close.

"I'm interested," Nico said firmly.

"Are you sure you want this or—"

"Yes," Nico said, a hot, fierce breath across Ren's mouth, voice low and rough. "I *need* this."

The light shifted, a glow of warmth momentarily wavered over Nico's face, and Ren noticed freckles sprinkled in with the glitter across his cheekbones. Tender warmth filled his chest. He wanted to spread kisses across those freckles.

"You're a very hard man to decipher," Ren said, but let his arms drop low on Nico's back, nudged him closer so there was nothing but a wire of tension separating them. He touched his thumb to Nico's cheek, swept it over sharp bone and soft freckles.

Nico lifted his face to Ren, turned his head just enough for Ren's finger to slip away from his skin. A streak of gold shimmered on Ren's thumb.

"I really don't get you," Ren said.

"I know."

Nico slid an arm around the back of Ren's neck, tilted into him, dragged Ren's head down, and pressed their mouths together. A scattering of hoots and whistles erupted from some of the people who streamed past them. Nico came at the kiss frantically, barely pausing for Ren to comprehend, diving in as if he wanted to take in all of Ren at once, as quickly as possible.

A hand slipping up under the back of Ren's shirt and a tongue slipping past his lips were all it took for Ren to forget he was at a strange place, with a stranger man, amidst drunk rubberneckers. Giving every nearby merrymaker an indulgent display. There were whistles in Ren's ears.

Nico parted Ren's lips. He tasted of nuts and honey, warm and solid in Ren's arms. Ren brushed wide hands across the small of Nico's back, the tiniest of touches, like running fingertips along an exquisite present yet to be opened and enjoyed, reveling in the anticipation of everything beneath the wrapping. He'd had the same feeling when he held his first hammer all those years ago—that moment of awaited ecstasy, knowing it would be something worth savoring.

He touched his tongue to Nico's. *He's gold, and I'll unwrap him as such.*

Ren slid a hand up Nico's back, up his neck, and into his hair. He cupped Nico's skull briefly and then fisted a handful of that sleek red. The color—the precise shade—of Nico's hair drove him crazy. So good to grasp it, to pull gently at it. Nico let out a little grunt that died between their lips.

The kiss wasn't quite what Ren had expected. Nico wasn't what he'd expected. His mercurial ways threw Ren, even in the kiss. He wouldn't have guessed Nico would have a frenetic, almost desperate energy when he kissed. It didn't quite match the nervy, diffident man who had confessed to being unsure with those he wanted to bed.

Being with Nico was like looking at a crystal and getting a dozen different angles reflected back, dizzying refracted light, never giving away which reflection was real.

But Ren was going to have the privilege of time with this man, if only for a handful of hours. And for now, that was the truth. That was real. They had each other, at least for tonight.

Chapter Three

REN

Nico peeled away from Ren with a hard inhalation, took him by the arm again, and pulled him to the edge of the crowd where he stopped to scan the stream of faces.

"What are you searching for?" Ren asked and jerked in surprise when Nico stuck his hand into Ren's front pocket as casually as if it were his own.

"Rahl!" Nico called to someone passing by, and when the other looked over: "Tell Timon to take my shows for the rest of the night."

The grin Rahl gave them made Ren a little nauseous in its greasiness.

"Well, well," Rahl said, managing to eyeball them both up and down in one encompassing sweep. "I thought you were about to put on an entirely different kind of show in the middle of the walkway. I'm sure we all would have enjoyed that." His laugh sounded like gurgling water, completely at odds with the oil in his voice. "Have fun."

Nico's coworker clearly didn't understand the subtle talent of innuendo.

Nico, already on the move, led Ren into the trees by his arm before Ren could comment on the creep.

They plunged into the trees, fast and desperate. Ren's body, all hot nerves, thrilled at chasing after Nico. Ren thought of all the clothes they needed to shed and wondered how quickly he could free their bodies from so much useless fabric.

Nico slipped between the trees so quickly Ren had no opportunity to talk to him, too heedful of his own step in the velvet black. At some point, they passed out of the carnival's enchanted bubble and into the chilly night. The air shocked Ren, hitting him hard in the face. The sounds of boisterous merrymaking receded behind them, and Ren had to wipe cold rain off his brow with his sleeve. Everything was instantly sopping: hair dripping down his neck, clothes sticking to his skin. Little flickers of lightning flashed above the trees. Nothing like a wet slap to sober him up.

His libido drooped as reality rushed in, dark and miserable. Nowhere in the dark drip of woods jumped out as an appropriate spot for what they planned to do unless Nico had more magic up his sleeve. The trees grew thick around them, yet Nico glided on as though he read the woods by heart, determined and able. Did he even feel the rain? Did his abilities somehow protect him from the weather?

They stopped as abruptly as they'd started, and it wasn't until Nico turned to face him that Ren realized he was just as drenched. Lightning revealed him in flickers. His fiery hair was plastered to his head. Long strips of it streaked across his forehead and temples, the color slightly dulled by the wetness. Black liner smeared dark under his eyes, and the glimmer of makeup had washed off his cheeks. His breath shook in and out of him. The rain transformed Nico into someone a lot less dreamy, less inviolate. And much more vulnerable.

Nico gripped Ren's arm, pinching almost, and got right up in Ren's space. Their exhalations warmed each other's faces.

"You really want to do this here?" Ren said. In the seconds between lightning flashes, the dark outline of trees nearly blended into the sky, swaying gently in the wind. Even the moon and stars were blotted out by the clouds. He had the crazy thought that the only light in the world at the moment was being used up at the carnival, that it had sucked up all the light nearby to power that protective globe.

Maybe he needed to sleep off the drink.

"*Run*," Nico said in a voice whisper-rough with quiet urgency. "Run back to your village as fast as you can. Bar the door. Get in bed and stay there until morning. Don't answer the door for anything. Don't return to the carnival. If someone asks you about me, we had sex and then we parted in the woods."

"Hold on. Wait. *Wait*. What? I thought we—"

"We had sex," Nico said carefully, "and then we went our separate ways. We didn't talk. You don't know anything. Nothing more happened."

Standing before Ren, disheveled and wet, stripped of his glittery shell, Nico still appeared surreal. But now, under the storm-lit sky, he seemed more fey—like some wild forest creature. It was a demented sort of surreal now.

Instinct told Ren to take a step back, but conflicting emotions rooted him to the spot. He wanted to turn away and leave like Nico had suggested, to remember only the beautiful showman seen through a veil of splendor, but Ren also wanted to warm him in his arms, to stop those quivers that made his body shake. It was the idea that the shaking wasn't entirely from cold that made Ren cup the side of Nico's face in his hand. Icy skin. How could he have thought Nico's magic protected him?

Ren brushed back strands of soggy hair from Nico's temples and said, "You're cold and exhausted. Come home with me."

Nico shifted his face away from the light caress. "Are you even real? You're still trying to get me into your bed? Did you hear anything I just said? Forget about it and go home. You need to walk away from me. Now."

When Ren didn't move, Nico was the one who walked away.

Ren couldn't let him go like that. Where was he going in the middle of a downpour? Something was clearly wrong. Something in his life had him ducking through woods on a stormy night. Ren couldn't go home and tuck in cozily next to his fire with hot chocolate and a blanket, knowing a man, for whatever bizarre reason, was shivering out in this weather.

Ren loped to catch up to him. "What are you doing out here, Nico? Did something happen? Are you in some sort of trouble?" Ren walked at Nico's side, but Nico didn't acknowledge him. "Everything will be all right. You can come home with me tonight and then deal with your issue in the morning, when it's not raining." He could already picture the two of them drying out in his living room, warm mugs of chocolate in their hands, legs tangled together, Nico spilling out a sordid tale of mayhem, shining in the firelight, the brightest jewel in Ren's cozy-worn little home. "I promise you'll be safe and warm in my home. No one should have to make hasty decisions in the rain."

"Safe?" Nico glanced at him, his hair a heavy curtain all in his face.

As kindly as he could, Ren said, "If you're running from some ex-lover or something, I'll help you. Won't your family miss you if you leave like this?"

"I don't have *family*." Nico made the word sound improbable. "Are you truly this naïve? Do you even realize what you're doing inviting a strange magician into your home? You have no idea what I could do to you. You don't know me. All you know is that I make you think of gold. Are you that blinded by an empty smile?" He shook his head, wet strands slipping against his skin. "Gods, how are you still alive? Go home and stop inviting strangers into your house."

A hot rush of shame flashed through him at being scolded like a foolish child. And then one word lit up in his mind: *gold*. When had he ever said anything about gold...out loud?

"How did you know about the—"

But Nico was already walking off into the night. Apparently that was what he did: he was the one who always walked away.

Ren hurried to catch up before Nico slipped into the dark and vanished. Coming up behind him, he put a light hand on Nico's shoulder to slow him down. "How did you know? About the gold?"

Nico didn't slow down but said as they walked, "Why are you so trusting? It never occurred to you that a magician might have powers beyond your ken. Beyond sparkly lights and special alcohol." He brushed Ren's hand off his shoulder, and the sting of the gesture made Ren take a step back. "Like being able to read thoughts when in physical contact with someone."

Ren's stomach attempted a complicated backflip. "You can read minds?"

"When touching someone, yes." Nico folded his arms across his chest, hugged himself against the wind that whipped down on them from high above the treetops.

"You witness a show of power like the carnival, and you automatically trust those who created it. Why?"

Ren thought it was obvious. "How could I not? It's beautiful like the stars are beautiful. I don't understand how they sparkle, but that doesn't mean I distrust them. They fill me with wonder every night."

"So, bright and beautiful is all it takes." Nico sounded disgusted. He swiped at his hair, which did nothing but drag more wetness across his face. He blinked it away as his pace slowed. "Is that why you trust me too? Because you think I'm beautiful? You're so damn easy."

"Wait, wait. Stop." This was getting out of hand. At some point, Ren had lost the thread of the situation. He didn't know when exactly it had happened, but it had definitely unraveled away from him, lost in the wet woods somewhere, floating away on the wind. "I came because I wanted to experience something new in my life. I found you, and you're everything I've ever thought magic would be."

Nico yanked his sleeves down over his fingers, as if his sopping shirt might actually offer any warmth. "You really have no idea what you walked into tonight."

Ren shook his head, perplexed. "What do you mean? I went to the carnival."

"It's not a carnival."

The autumn-chilled rain trickled goose bumps down Ren's arms. High above them, wind stirred in the trees, a sudden gust that whistled and rustled, releasing fat drops from the leaves. For a moment, Ren could hear nothing but the slap of rain gusting against trees. "I don't understand. Then what is it?"

"You don't want to understand." Nico touched Ren's arm, the barest brush of icy fingers over Ren's skin. When he spoke, his voice was gentle. "Listen to me, Ren. Your village is right to be wary. Get away from me. Go home. Don't go outside until morning. And in the future, stay away from anything that seems too good to be true."

Nico turned and walked away from him.

Ren hurried behind him. "What's that supposed to mean? Hey, can you slow down for one damn—" He didn't get a chance to finish because he was falling, arms splayed out, flying. The world flipped, and there was the ground. He landed hard, facedown on something wet and lumpy.

"Ren?"

"Shit," Ren said into the thing that had tripped him. He pushed up on one hand, and as he did so, his fingers touched skin. "Oh damn…"

"What?"

"Oh," Ren said again, "*damn.*"

Hair curled against his arm. Muddy clothing squished beneath his hand. Ren came face to face with something.

Someone. Someone not quite recognizable as human. He couldn't scramble to his feet fast enough.

"I think it's a…person. On the ground."

Nico drew closer to Ren's side. "It's a body—"

"The body. Something about it isn't right. We have to—"

"Fuck." Nico sounded desolate, both the tone and the word a shock with his lilting accent.

"We need to get help," Ren said, scrubbing his hands against his thighs, but he couldn't wipe the sensation of a dead body off his skin. "We have to go back and—"

Nico's fingers on his lips pressed hard in warning. Ren shut his mouth. Nico whipped his head to the side, searching the surrounding forest. Inexplicably, the dark night seemed to get darker, to crawl up from the ground in ever blacker patches. Ren blinked, sure he was imagining it.

"No," Nico whispered, so low and so miserable Ren thought maybe he had imagined that too. "No, no no."

It was now the kind of dark that made it almost impossible for him to discern Nico's face, much less his expression. The lightning flashed on and off, a nauseating light show. Though he couldn't make out the treetops, Ren heard them whipping against empty sky. Leaves ripped off branches, lashing through the air with the rain.

"Don't talk," Nico said, low and harsh. "I'll talk."

"I—"

In the flashing lightning, the seconds between darkness, Nico's eyes gleamed, horrified.

"Don't say—"

His mouth hung open, the rest of his sentence falling to the ground with the leaves. Gasping, he crumpled forward into Ren, his fingers catching in Ren's coat.

Ren had not, at that moment, been expecting an armful of man. He staggered, grunted, and caught Nico around the middle. The top of Nico's head banged into Ren's chin. The rain-heavy fabric of their clothes bunched up between them. Briefly, Nico's scent filled his nose. He smelled like evergreens and rain.

As Nico's hair brushed against Ren's chin in wet tendrils, Ren saw them. Two dark silhouettes standing in the bushes nearby, a bare impression of tall men, taller than men should be, backlit by the storm. They stood motionless, but their heads turned toward Ren in unison the moment he noticed them. For a split second, they all stood starkly revealed in the lightning, and Ren had the instinctive urge to cover himself. Then darkness flooded back into the forest. They were gone when the next flash filled the woods. Ren blinked. He was sure they'd been there, sure he'd spotted two men. Or two not-men.

Or maybe he'd seen tree branches, a trick of light, a play of wind.

No, it hadn't been his imagination. He was sure of it.

He swallowed, blinking hard into the night. He tightened his hold on Nico, a warm and very real body against his, security against the dark. When he adjusted his grip, sticky warmth spilled over his hands. That couldn't be. Ren withdrew his hand, rubbed his fingers together.

Blood. A fine sheen of it in the storm's light.

Inexplicably, in the middle of the woods, at the height of a storm, Nico was bleeding on him.

"Nico?"

Nico jerked his head up as if he'd been asleep. Ren cupped his cheek to keep his head upright, and Nico blinked up at him. Reviving quickly, focusing again, Nico turned his face out of Ren's hold. He rebalanced himself with his hands on each of Ren's arms.

"You're bleeding," Ren told him gently because he didn't know what else to say.

Nico blinked slowly. "I know."

"Why are you bleeding? Did a branch get you?"

"No," Nico said.

"We've been waiting for you," said a voice from the trees up ahead, and Ren couldn't help the way he startled, his body jumping at the sound of the unexpected newcomer. Their surroundings only revealed darkness and undulating trees.

Nico sucked in a breath.

Whisper-hushed, Ren said close to Nico's ear, "What's happening?"

The flashing lightning, the low rumbling thunder, the shocking smell of blood in the air—all of it reduced the scene to a hazy, tumultuous nightmare unfolding before Ren. It was hard to concentrate, hard to piece together anything in the dark. The metallic tang in the air, distinct from the smell of wet earth and ozone—that was the worst part: the scent of Nico bleeding.

Ren thought he might be losing it a little at a time with each new sensory overload. The sharp clarity of reality blurred around him.

"What's happening? Oh, that's an excellent question," said a different voice, this one from behind them. The voice circled them as it spoke. "What's happening here, Nico? What are you doing? Where are you going?"

The rain poured down, translucent white sheets in the glimpses of flashing light. Nico lifted his chin to Ren and exhaled slowly, his mouth set in grim resignation. They shared a moment, the smallest connection as the world brightened with lightning and faded yet again. He squeezed Ren's arms hard and said, "I got a dud tonight."

"How strange," said yet another voice. "Because it appears as though you're leaving."

Nico said nothing.

"And by now, you know how we feel about that. It's an insult when you try to leave us."

They materialized out of the night, darker spots softly outlined against trees and bushes. It took Ren's mind a moment to process the new development. The lightning didn't quite reveal them, but seemed to shift away from them, as though they occupied holes in the air. Seven figures glided toward them. They stood before Ren and Nico.

Deep in his gut, Ren knew it was bad. He had no context, and it made no sense, but he felt...pinned. Hunted.

Was he dreaming? He wanted to wake up now.

A tingle washed over Ren, unpleasant, sparking like tiny bites across his skin, the sensation a prickle and then gone. It was so brief he wasn't sure if it was in the air or if it was his nerves doing a panicked dance just beneath his skin.

Nico eased himself away from Ren. He turned toward the others, his back to Ren's front, his body between them and Ren. "I was trying to give him the brush-off, but he won't take a hint." Nico snorted. "He's big, but too stupid to know what goes where. Such a disappointment." Nico didn't spare Ren any further attention. "The moment's gone now anyway." He reached a hand back and shoved at Ren's chest. "Get lost."

Ren gaped at the back of Nico's head.

"You had to walk this far into the woods to get rid of him?"

Nico didn't falter. "The simpleton wanted me to do tricks for him. He's like a child. Infantile but harmless. I couldn't shake him."

"Nico, Nico," one of them said as he stepped closer, his disappointment evident. "You know I would take care of you. You don't have to find strangers for your needs."

"No," Nico said, deadness to his voice.

"I know you. What you want."

"I don't think you do," Nico said flatly. "Do you know how much I want you dead?"

"Of course." Laughter. He came nearer. "That makes it more interesting. You would have killed me a thousand times over, in a thousand different ways. You're creative and vindictive. Such an intriguing combination. You would kill me now. If only. *If only.*"

Up close, in the storm-dark, between the dance of lightning, one would have taken him for an ordinary man, albeit exceptionally tall and willowy. Of course he was a man. Ren didn't know why he'd thought otherwise.

His voice was smooth. It filled Ren with sugar—sweet, sticky warmth in his chest. "But tonight," he said in a low, conspiratorial tone, "you weren't coming into the woods for a bit of fun, were you? No fuck for you tonight."

Calmly, Nico said, "I didn't feel like going back to camp right away. I wanted to be alone for—" He cut off with a gurgle and tripped backward into Ren as though shoved, his arms flailing outward. Ren caught him under the armpits. Blood, warm and too real, smeared Ren's coat when Nico brushed against him as he tried to regain his balance. There was more blood than before. Nico managed to stand, though he took another step back from the other man, bumping into Ren as he did so.

Doubt trickled in, a big solid block of it in the pit of Ren's stomach. This was not an ex-lover, not an abusive boyfriend, not an overbearing admirer. This was power. The air sizzled with their presence—and they were angry. Angry in an aloof, barely controlled kind of way that made the ice in Ren's stomach turn over. How had he ended up here?

Nico's desire for retreat was so evident to Ren that it spilled over from Nico and flooded Ren's senses. They both wanted nothing more than to turn and flee. The fact that Nico wanted to get away from them, had probably already been trying to run from them for whatever unknown reason, was not good. The signs were starting to point toward something ugly. There was a lot of bad starting to add up on what was supposed to be Ren's night of magical discovery.

Whatever this was, Ren wished he hadn't discovered it.

"You put on a decent show, Nico," said the man. "But I'm not one of your gullible human conquests." The others drifted closer, a half circle around the apparent leader. "You know how we feel when you try to leave. I thought we made that clear."

"Then kill me."

Shit. Ren put a hand low on Nico's back, a feather touch, a question.

"Kill you?" A tinkling of soft laughter. "You should know by now that's not what we're going to do."

"I'm done," Nico said, exhaustion thick in his voice. "I'm not doing this anymore."

"After all this time, do you think you have a choice?"

Light burst where the leader stood, and it took Ren a blinding moment to realize it was fire—not a trapped lightning bolt—cupped in the palm of the man's hand. Several brightly blinking seconds later, Nico flinched back into Ren, who instinctively put his hands on Nico's hips and let his own body shift backward with Nico's movements. His body falling in sync with Nico's, their hips moving together—it was a dance Ren had imagined a lot differently.

Light-blind, Ren tried to focus on the newcomers but couldn't clear the flares that wavered before him with every blink. Nico stumbled for retreat. It took Ren longer than Nico to notice the bodies.

The new light revealed crumpled bodies scattered on the ground, strewn like dead logs across the forest floor. Ren sucked in a horrified breath.

No. This couldn't be happening. It couldn't be real. He wanted it to be a trick, an ugly illusion. He knew it wasn't.

They were dead. He knew without focusing on any one body too long that there was no life left in them as they lay bent and broken on the ground. There was something empty about them, a complete lack of everything it meant to be alive.

In front of Ren, Nico shuddered. Ren held on to him tighter, hands locked on his hips. He wanted to crush Nico's bones between his hands, gain his attention, twirl him around, and run away together.

It wouldn't work. There was no running from whatever this was.

"What have you done?" Nico said.

"You knew what we would do if you tried to leave again. We told you that you wouldn't be the one to die." He flung his arm out to the forest. "We did this because of you. It was fun. Slurping up all the people. Just slurping, slurping."

Ren's heart froze in his chest.

Nico swiveled to address the whole group, taking in their glee. "You don't think the villagers will notice all of these bodies?"

The man gave Nico a bored flick of the wrist. "Who cares what the villagers notice." He directed a grin over Nico's shoulder at Ren. He had a lot of teeth. "The villagers don't matter."

"So much strength!" one of the others exclaimed, giddy. "We have it! Wonderful!"

They laughed as one, disgustingly pleasant, the sound of bells tinkling on Winter's Eve, the sound of cool wind rustling in trees. The leader glided closer. Ren tried to tug

Nico back by his hips, sink into the dark of the trees, but Nico didn't move. Possibly, he'd forgotten about Ren altogether, even though the horror of the bodies had flattened them against each other.

"It feels so good," the leader said, exhaling his exuberance into the rain. "All this magic bubbling through our veins. The taste of power on our tongues. Sparking in our fingers. Is this how it feels for you all the time?"

Nico failed to keep his voice level. It shook in the middle. "My power is a natural part of me. You're an abomination."

"Nico, always the charmer," said the leader. "We could take over the world tonight. We could do anything, and you think we would waste that on killing you?"

"No," Nico said, the dread in his voice evident. Ren could tell by the way Nico stood that he knew what was coming, but Ren didn't want to know.

"We're not going to kill you. We're just going to play with you."

Fine tremors ran down Nico's back where his body pressed against Ren's.

Ren's stomach shuddered. He'd walked into a swamp of ugly, and now his feet were stuck in the mud, sinking fast. Maybe he and Nico were destined to go under together.

"Show him, Zeke," one of the others said, speaking up for the first time, her voice honey-smooth and overeager. "Show him what we can do."

The leader, Zeke, gave Nico and Ren a sly leer. Through the haze of rain, as he adjusted to the light, Ren noticed Zeke was just on the edge of too-tall-to-be-normal, his skin smooth as a baby's, with a tall curl of dark hair that stood at a strange angle on his head. His right hand and part of his forearm were missing.

Zeke tossed a flame over his shoulder to the overeager woman, who caught it as easily as though it were a ball. The flickering light bounced over everyone's faces nauseatingly. Ren thought he might be about to vomit.

"We could show even you a thing or two tonight, Nic." Zeke's height grew with each step closer. He stopped a foot away, looming over them. "What do you say? Do you think we're more powerful than you?" A simple flick of his wrist, and Nico doubled over with a cut-off gasp. "Let's find out."

Nico would have sagged onto his knees if Ren hadn't grabbed him by the shoulders and held him upright. They had no chance at all to get away if Nico was on the ground, not that their chances seemed all that great anyway.

Zeke was on top of them, even taller now that Nico was hunched and Ren was half bent over him. A smile glowed across Zeke's face. The smile of a man enjoying sweet satisfaction. It didn't waver when he said, "Your problem, Nico, is you're so powerful you forget you're human. And humans were meant to be ruled."

The ice block in Ren's stomach expanded, shuddered. Any moment now it would explode, the dread too big for Ren to keep inside. Nico's hair stood out to Ren. He focused on that and on breathing evenly. In the indistinct light, that red hair was the brightest thing in the woods, gleaming dark with raindrops. A slice of reality in a nightmare, a snatch of the waking world glimpsed while fleeing a creature dug up from the depths of the sleeping mind. Ren let out a breath.

Zeke put his hand on Nico's shoulder right next to Ren's, their fingers brushing in some twisted pantomime of intimacy. Nico inhaled on a gasp. They stood in a little triangle of tension.

Zeke eased his mouth close to Nico's bowed head and stage-whispered into his ear, "You knew this was coming. It's been coming for so long. Shall I go slowly? I do want to enjoy every moment. Shall I make it hurt like you did for me all those years ago?"

Nico's breathing sounded harsh and wet, but he raised his head.

Involuntarily, Ren's fingers twitched against Nico's shoulder. He wished he were home in bed, soon to wake up from this wet forest, from the cold rain falling like a gold mist in the light, from these loathsome people.

This should be a dream. It looks like a dream.

It felt like a nightmare.

An ugly thought trickled in. Was this magic? Was this its true form? Death and blood and smug laughter? Ren didn't want anything to do with it.

Nico didn't shrink from the threat, though every part of his body that touched Ren's screamed that he wanted to curl into a ball and hide.

"I guess this means our deal is broken," Nico said.

Zeke caressed Nico's upturned face, traced along his jaw and chin. Nico flinched at the contact. Tender as a mother, Zeke kissed the top of Nico's head, his temple, his eyebrow.

It happened so fast but had the indistinct fuzz of a dream about it. Too fast for Ren to follow, too inexplicable for him to understand. Nico made a soft sound, an exhalation of surprise. He recoiled from Zeke, and then he was slipping from Ren's hands without a sound, crashing face-first to the muddy ground. Ren caught a flash of red in Zeke's hand as he turned away from Nico—the silvery shimmer of a short, slim knife tipped with blood. It was there and gone quick as lightning, tucked away in a fold of clothing, or dropped, or vanished out of the air. It didn't matter.

"Bastard," Ren spat, already following Nico to the ground. For an instant, he forgot his urge to run, forgot the fiends in a semicircle. Nothing else existed for Ren but a man bleeding on the ground, balled into himself like an insect trying to survive a boot.

Ren knelt at Nico's back and put his hand on the curve of spine where it bent in a protective curl. He huddled over Nico, briefly shielding him from their sadistic hunger. Softly, he said, "How bad is it?"

At the sound of his voice, Nico winced as though he'd forgotten Ren was there. He focused on Ren with effort, squinted, and then closed down all in a matter of a few seconds.

"Shouldn't be here," Nico muttered. "You...shouldn't."

"Is it bad?"

"Bad—" Nico said breathlessly and couldn't seem to finish, which told Ren it was beyond bad. With a groan, Nico brought a hand up, away from where it was clutched around his middle. His hand was covered in the darkest red Ren had ever seen, like the rubies he'd read about as a child. It would have been beautiful, mesmerizing, if it hadn't been Nico's life pooling on the ground. Nico's lips formed a soundless *Oh*. There was disbelief in the slight way he moved his fingers, a disconnect between his hand, his blood. The red glimmered against his fair skin.

Like a man meeting an inevitability, Nico said, "Oh."

They had to stanch the bleeding. They had to do something. Ren put his hand where Nico's had been against his stomach, and warm liquid seeped over his fingers. Nico gasped, put his bloodied hand on top of Ren's, and pressed them harder against his wound.

"Well, isn't this touching," one of the magicians said. Their bell-like laughter filled the forest, echoing and overlapping, background music to Ren's ears, nothing to the sound of Nico's pained little breaths.

"Nico actually found someone who gives a shit," said another in a voice that strangely resembled a melody. "Isn't that sweet. Most of his lovers probably would have run by now."

"The smart ones," said another, and more laughter ensued.

Nico squeezed his eyes shut, said very low, "Go. I'll...hold them."

Hold them. Right.

They crowded in eagerly, ready to lap up Nico's pain. No way was Ren going to abandon him now. "I can't leave you here like this. With...them."

In truth, he believed it was too late to run anyway. Would they really let him scamper off into the woods without following? He didn't think so. Though most of them simply stood there awaiting the scene to play out, something about them spoke to a primal place inside Ren that said, *You are prey. They wouldn't let prey get away that easily.*

Ren didn't want to think it, but the thought sprang into his mind anyway: *Maybe it was too late to run the moment you entered the carnival.*

"I can—" Nico inhaled the rest of his words on a gasp, drawing inward, tucking into a tight ball of pain. "—give you a chance. Go."

"I say we take his tongue," said one. At the suggestion, the amusement that had been tittering around the circle of magicians ceased. "Just in case. To be safe. Then we can play with him."

Nico's fingers scraped at the ground. His face pinched tight as if he were trying to block out the pain.

Zeke's shock of thick hair waved in the wind like a flag. When he found Ren's focus on him, his mouth twisted up into a bright grin, as impossible to avoid as the sun. Ren wished he could erase that smile from his memory. It left an afterimage.

Zeke said to him, "You can watch us take him apart, pleb. Piece by piece. It'll be fun. Then we'll put him back together and do it again. How do you think we should start?"

Curled against the ground, Nico choked up a terrible gurgling sound. He seemed to be trying to say something, but in place of words, blood oozed from between his lips. Ren lifted Nico's upper body just enough to rest Nico's head on his thighs. Even that small movement dragged a gurgling red cough from Nico, and Ren felt immediately guilty. It was just that he didn't want Nico to die by choking on his own blood. Nico tried to say something again, but only succeeded in a moan of ruby liquid over his lips.

"Is there something you want to say?" Zeke stepped closer. His large bare feet edged too close. In a dramatic gesture, he angled an ear in Nico's direction. "One last thing, perhaps? Anything? No? I didn't think so. Funny how you have nothing to say now that we're as powerful as you."

"Zeke," one of the others said, warning. A new wariness tinged their attitudes.

"What?" Zeke said to his group. "Tonight I could twist his insides without breaking a sweat. Don't fear him."

Ren blocked out everything but Nico. He focused on the tawny eyes, overly bright in an ashen face, already locked on Ren, unfocused but not confused. He knew exactly what was happening to him, and that made Ren sad. The only comfort in a situation like this, for himself at least, would be delirium.

"You're all right," Ren said softly. "Soon you're going to be just fine. You can still escape."

Because soon he would be dead. He wasn't all right, and he wouldn't *be* all right. Ren had seen enough of death to know that Nico was tiptoeing along the rim of death's cliff, about to teeter over its fathomless edge. He hoped the God of endless summer would be there at the end of the fall to greet Nico.

At least there wouldn't be time for them to play with him, as they seemed to think. Ren could feel it in Nico's body: He was fading fast.

Only after he thought it did he remember they were touching, which meant Nico heard everything running through his brain. He cleared his throat, trying to hide his anxiety at having just thought something so entirely discomforting. Nico blinked slowly, sleepily. Blood leaked down his chin, and Ren, without thinking, wiped it away with his thumb.

What a beautiful enigma. Ren's thoughts spun away from him, out of his control. He couldn't keep his mind off the man dying in his arms. *I wish I could have known him.*

"This is just too sweet," Zeke said. "I can't stand it. Take the pleb. Drain him and toss him."

Ren didn't know what *drain* meant, but he was pretty sure it wasn't how he wanted to die.

Against Nico's stomach, where their blood-slick hands pressed together, Nico gave Ren's hand a weak squeeze.

The others were closing in on them, tightening a semicircle around them.

"Tired."

The voice sounded soft and distant, a faraway whisper. It took Ren several long seconds to realize it came from Nico.

That was all it took to send the others into a frenzy. As Ren huddled on the ground with Nico, absolutely bewildered, they devolved into panic.

"Zeke!"

"I know!"

"Stop him!"

"I told you we should have cut out his tongue! I told you!"

One of them, to Ren's bemusement, turned and ran, slipping between the trees.

"So tired," Nico said, his voice rough and on the edge of a whisper, but there was something strange and deep underlying his tone, something Ren couldn't quite place. Nico coughed up a gurgling, wet gasp. Blood painted his lips red, spattered his chin. His eyes were barely open, just slits in his bone-white face.

Of course you're tired, beautiful boy. It's okay to be tired. You can sleep.

"So tired," Nico said again, soft but clearer. "You're tired. You're so tired."

"No!" Zeke yelled.

Behind him, the remaining six magicians pushed their arms toward Nico and Ren in some kind of bizarre pantomime. In Ren's lap, Nico spasmed and vomited out a small pool of blood on the ground next to Ren's leg.

And then it seemed another being entered the forest as a force brushed past Ren's face, swirled through the air in a glitter of colors, so thin and transparent it was barely perceptible. Magic. They were flinging magic at Nico. Ren blinked, and the colors faded, phantom wisps that winked out if he concentrated on them too long.

"Finish him! Finish him now!" Zeke's voice didn't sound quite as honey-sweet when he was screeching. Fear lived on his face, raw and ugly, twisting his features.

Nico let out a wet sob as he struggled to swallow. He choked, coughed, and choked again. Then he spat up a glob of blood that landed on the collar of his shirt. Through a mouthful of his blood, he said, "Your brain is shutting down"—more coughing, more leaking blood—"turning off."

None of them approached Nico, though horror spread across their faces.

"What?" Ren said numbly in the same whisper-soft pitch Nico was using.

"You can't do this!" one of the magicians screamed. They dropped their arms, broke apart in panic. Hysteria tinged the air. Two more ran for the cover of the forest. Another staggered blindly across the ground, oddly slow, with a drunken lean to the left.

"Too tired. You can't stand," Nico said, and Ren gawked at them as they began dropping where they stood, some yelling threats as they hit the ground. The two who ran for the trees didn't make it in time.

"You can't move. Can't talk. Your brain is shutting down. Nothing matters. There's nothing to do but sleep. Sleep."

Nico gurgled up more blood. His whole body jerked and twitched as Ren held him close, held him steady. "You're going to sleep. You can't fight it. Nothing else matters but sleep. Sleep," Nico whispered. "Sleep forever."

On the ground, each of the magicians fell motionless, limp bodies, barely distinguishable lumps in the growing dark.

Ren muttered, "My God. God. Oh God."

"Not God," Nico said, his voice hoarse and thready, the power drained out of it.

They sat there through a dreamy, sleepy stretch of silence, the slow drip of rain through leaves the only sound in the forest. The lightning had stopped, shut off like a lamp.

Above the spatter of raindrops, Ren's heart pounded in his ears, a tremble in his chest. A hot, delicious thrill pumped through him with each hard beat. The dark, smooth finality of Nico's magic, the ease with which he had taken six lives, was completely at odds with the glittery, flying thing that had been Ren's first impression of him. He could barely piece them together as the same person. There was something tantalizing, something seductive about the power Nico had held over those six people.

Nico was still remarkably alert, his focus all on Ren. "You need to go. Go home. Now."

"And leave you here?" *To die alone?* By the way Nico's face screwed up, Ren could tell he'd heard the thought.

"More will come," Nico said and grimaced as Ren's hand shifted nervously against his wound. Nico took in a shuddery gasp of air. "Don't be here."

"I can't leave you here to suffer like this."

"Why?" The pool of blood had spread outward. It reached Ren's trousers, formed a dark splotch on the brown fabric. He only had three good pairs of pants.

"Because you're a human being," Ren said desperately, "and you're bleeding out on the ground."

"Knife," Nico said. "Where's the knife?"

Ren gave the dirt a cursory check. No silvery glint. "I don't know."

Two rivers of blood framed Nico's mouth, smeared against his jaw. He gagged up more of it, more than Ren thought possible for any one body to have.

In a pained whisper, Nico said, "Kill me."

Ren stared at him, at the way he struggled to stay awake. His arm cupped Nico's shoulders, snug. He was tucked into Ren's body as though they'd sat together like that for years, perhaps in front of a lit hearth, with Nico's head in his lap and all of the close contact of comfortable familiarity. Yearning squeezed up the back of Ren's throat.

Ren swallowed, said, "What?"

"The knife. Finish...it."

Already shaking his head, Ren said, "No. I can't. I can't—do that."

Nico closed his eyes. "They'll find me. I don't want them to find me alive." When he opened them again, they were glassy with pain. "Please." One simple word spoken softly.

On the ground nearby, the blaze of light that the others had used quivered as it slowly burned itself out. The wind had picked up, and the red ball dimmed with each gust. The trees and clouds spit rain into Ren's face. Despite how close they were to each other, the encroaching darkness was beginning to paint Nico indistinct.

"You don't want to be here when they come," Nico said, his voice whispery as the wind and as frail as a decaying autumn leaf. He was slipping.

"Then you shouldn't be here either," Ren said.

"They—" Nico gurgled up more blood instead of words, gagging on whatever it was he'd been about to say, leaving more of his life in the dirt.

"Right," Ren said, his mind made up at seeing Nico so small and wet. He'd never been able to turn away from an injured animal, and now was no exception. Gently, he slid Nico's head off his lap and onto the ground. Then he slipped his arms underneath Nico's back and legs, scooped him up into his arms, and stood.

Nico cried out, the sound of it clenching Ren's heart in a way that made his chest hurt. The cry ended in a long, pitiful moan. "Fuck," Nico mumbled, "no."

It came out more like, *Nooooo.* He let his head fall to Ren's shoulder, his face pressed into Ren's neck, his warm breath too fast against Ren's skin. And though Ren had jokingly carried both men and women here and there in his arms, all of them laughing as he did so, the way Nico huddled against him felt much more intimate.

"What're you doing?" Nico asked against his neck and followed it with a groan, deep and raw. "Leave me. Just—Fuck, it hurts!"

Ren began walking. If he'd thought walking through the dark forest in the rain was a pain when he was trying to keep up with Nico, then walking through the forest while carrying Nico was pure hell.

"No," Ren said. Wet leaves smacked against them with every stride, several leaves catching and sticking in Nico's hair as they walked past. Nico didn't even notice.

"Crazy man," Nico muttered without rancor. "Put me down. Don't...don't do this."

"We have healers in our village, a sister and brother. They're very good. They might be able to help you."

"No!" Nico shook his head hard enough to knock the leaves out of his hair. His blood was beginning to seep through the front of Ren's shirt, warm compared to the chill of the rain on his clothes. "No, no, no, no," came Nico's faint voice against his neck, trailing off into a mumble.

"Why not? You need help."

"Don't take me to your village. Nowhere that matters. They'll come."

His last words made Ren's skin prickle. *They'll come.*

"Leave me here," Nico muttered. "With the knife."

"I'm not going to leave you to try and slice yourself to death. Besides, I couldn't even find the knife. All right. So, I won't take you back to my home." Ren considered his limited options. "What about back to yours? Is there anyone there who would..."

He didn't know how to finish it. Did Nico have anyone who actually cared about him? He was beginning to suspect there were no loving arms waiting for Nico back at the carnival. He remembered the way they'd said Nico's name, their enthusiasm for his pain, the way their interest had lingered on his body.

Nico's hands had been folded against his own chest, but at that suggestion, he clutched a fistful of Ren's shirt and twisted. He tried to lift his head from Ren's shoulder but couldn't seem to gather the strength to do it.

"Don't bring me to them." It wasn't pleading or pitiful, just matter of fact. Softly spoken but resolute.

Carefully, Ren asked, "What about your family?"

"Don't take me back there," Nico rasped. "Don't. *Don't.*"

"I won't," Ren said, a quick promise because Nico was starting to sound frantic. Nico's fingers loosened in Ren's shirt, but he didn't let go. His fingers stayed tangled there, holding on to Ren.

"Put me down."

"No."

"You're going to regret this," Nico whispered, his voice growing fainter by the moment.

Ren already regretted the entire night.

The rain fell in big, billowy-white sheets that spread through the trees like translucent banners. The air turned chillier. Ren had never realized just how unpleasant the first night of autumn was. He usually admired the dark glimpses of rain from the warmth of his living room window. His love for the season soured a little now that he was actually out in it, may the God of Autumn forgive him.

In the damp dark, he missed a log. His foot caught under it, and he tripped, barely keeping his hold on Nico even though Nico was all he could think about as he pitched forward. He untangled his foot from the log and rebalanced himself again within seconds, but, jostled so much, Nico let out a moaned cry.

"I'm sorry," Ren said, feeling like an ass. "I'm so sorry."

Nico whimpered against his neck, groaned again, and passed out. Ren stopped walking for a moment just to assure himself that, yes, he could still feel Nico's body rising and falling with breath. With Nico unconscious and insensible to the pain of Ren's footsteps, Ren picked up the pace.

It was easier once he made it back to the shore where he'd left his boat. His arms screamed at him as soon as he spotted it, relief so close. Nico was a lightweight, but in Ren's arms, he felt like a dozen bags of bricks.

Ren laid Nico in the boat and rowed them away from the beach, where the water was still burnt-gold with hot reflections. The fire-wrapped shore faded as Ren speed-paddled them out onto the lake. His arms, as it turned out, didn't get the respite they had been hoping for. Without thought, he plowed through the water and rushed back through the flames that danced across the surface. He scanned the shore for more of the creeps as he rowed away, but it was too dark to pick out anything but the bloom of the carnival's wild light in the distance.

He knew where to take Nico. It wouldn't be his cozy home, full of warmth and comforts and the wonder of having Nico in his living space, but it would have to do.

He just had to make sure they both got there in one piece.

Chapter Four

REN

Even after so many years, the pulley system still worked, a warm surprise on a cold, hellish night. Ren settled Nico's unconscious body into the hammock-like swing, grabbed the rope, and heaved. Once Nico was level with the door, Ren tied the rope to a lower tree branch, checked its sturdiness, and then climbed up the built-in ladder. He swung himself onto the platform and hoisted Nico out of the hammock.

With Nico in his arms again, he ducked through the doorway and surveyed the place. It was the same as he had left it all those years ago. Yes, it was a tree house, but he was proud of it, probably because he'd been the one to build it, with a little help from a friend. Ren never bragged about it, but he could build. He could build anything, and he could build it well. Had been able to since he was a young child. It had only started with small things like tree houses. He'd then progressed to building himself a small house in the village, and once others had seen his home, he moved on to building and rebuilding half the houses in the village and many of the shops, too. After both of his parents were gone, the village soared and advanced, under the skill of his hands, better than ever.

Though the tree house had only been Ren's first usable building, a sort of practice run prior to the real thing, it was sprawling, hidden high in one of the forest's larger trees, taking up most of the tree's branches. It had one large room with vaulted ceilings, a table, blankets and pillows, lanterns, and food so old he wouldn't feed it to an animal. The tree trunk took up a good portion of the room, a regal centerpiece. Leafy green branches poked out of the trunk. It was freezing cold inside, with no source of heat and no hope of warmth, but at least it was dry. After so many years, there were no leaks.

He laid Nico flat on the pile of blankets right next to the trunk. Nico's wound had soaked through the fitted, stretchy fabric of his shirt, leaving a large, darker blotch on the dark material. Skin painted in blood showed through the hole in the fabric where the knife had gone in.

It was bad. Really bad. The rest was beyond Ren's ken. As far as wounds went, he knew what it looked like when you would live, or when you wouldn't. And it looked like Nico wouldn't.

Once he had Nico settled on the blanket pallet, Ren didn't know what to do. He sat beside him and used the edge of a blanket to wipe rainwater and sick-sweat off Nico's cheeks and forehead. His lips were bloodstained. Ren brushed straggling, wet strands of hair away from Nico's eyes. He ran his fingers through Nico's hair to push it back from his face.

Nico groaned, fingers fluttering, and turned his face to the side, into the blankets.

"Nico," Ren said softly, not really to wake him, but just so he'd know someone was there next to him. Some sort of small comfort. If it were Ren, he knew he'd never want to die alone. He said to Nico's slack face, "You're all right. You're safe."

Nico's hand edged out from under the blanket, seeking. Ren took it and wrapped Nico's long, thin fingers between his hands. He might as well have been holding slivers of ice. Nico gasped at the contact. Something sparked where their hands met, a pop against Ren's skin that actually hurt. His hold on Nico slackened. Nico jerked his hand away so fast he smacked his knuckles into one of the smaller tree limbs.

"Nico," Ren said again, soft and soothing, "what are you doing? All right. All right. I'm sorry. I won't touch you. Please don't hurt yourself."

But now that Nico had found the tree limb, he clutched it between his fingers. He groaned, choked on a bubble of blood that popped over his lips, and arched his back up off the floor.

Well, this was new, but all men behaved differently in death. Some called for their mothers, some got angry, others cried. He'd never seen anyone react like Nico.

Nico's back arched off the floor again, heels digging into the wooden planks beneath him. Struggle played out across his face on a stage of blood and sweat, his fine features twisted up with pain and concentration. His free hand was down by his side, fingernails digging into the floor so hard Ren was sure he was going to leave gouge marks in the wood and blood on his fingertips.

A sudden movement drew Ren's attention. A leaf fluttered to the ground, and he followed its course, to see if it might slip through the slight opening in the floor between it and the tree trunk and find its way to the ground. Another leaf floated through the air. And then another one fell—and another, and another. One of the branches from the main tree trunk was dying right in front of him, dropping winter-browned leaves all over the floor. It dumbfounded him, this shriveling limb in the middle of his tree house, a place that had so often meant safety to him throughout childhood.

"What..." Ren said aloud. *What's happening?*

It was the same limb that Nico still held tightly on to, his arm stretched out to reach it. The limb was dying in his hand, one leaf at a time, shriveling and browning outward from the point of contact where he held it. Withered, the leaves turned brown one by one in an instant. The branch grew brittle.

"My God," Ren said under his breath, stumbling back. Even though he'd witnessed Nico's ability earlier in the woods, it still surprised him, made his skin prickle in alarm. This wasn't what he'd always pictured magic to be, what the carnival had promised him it would be: glittering, vibrant, ethereal. So far, most of Nico's power was varying layers of death and dying. This view of it was disappointingly, frighteningly ugly.

Nothing now but fragile little pieces, the limb broke apart in Nico's hand and sprinkled the ground with a crumbly brown dust that had once been a living thing. Nico groaned again, coughed, and reached for something else. His hand groped blindly through the air until it landed on the main trunk of the tree. He clutched at it.

A loud crack somewhere deep within the tree startled Ren out of his trance.

Nico was going to kill the whole tree. Ren was sure of it.

"Oh no you don't," Ren muttered and grabbed Nico's wrist. He pried Nico's hand away from the tree, forced his arm down by his side. But then Nico put his hand flat to the wood floor, fingers tense against it, and Ren sighed.

"You must want to kill us both," he said to Nico's slack face and fitful, unconscious body. "I don't fancy falling from this tree house after you've killed the tree that's holding us up in the air."

One of the floorboards popped. A small crack crawled across the floor, spreading from the place where Nico's fingers dug into the wood.

Gods of all seasons. He's going to destroy the floor right out from under us.

Death hung heavy in the air, but Ren was no longer sure whose death he sensed.

"That's it," Ren said and once again slid his arms under Nico's body. He settled the familiar weight in his arms, the feel of Nico against him strangely comfortable. He walked through the door and out onto the balcony.

The weather was a gut punch. The rain had died down to wet mist and icy spits, but the wind had grown rough, especially up in the tree where they were. He placed Nico back into the folds of the hammock swing. Nico twitched when the wind hit him, his nose scrunching in distaste. The mist made his skin glisten.

"Hold on," Ren told him. He climbed down the ladder. On solid ground again, he grabbed the rope and lowered Nico far enough that he could reach him.

Ren scooped him up and carried him beneath the platform of his tree house, into the relative shelter of the trees where the wind wasn't quite as harsh. He laid Nico on the ground and took a step back to steady his nerves. There was a tiny part of him that was tempted to turn and run home, wash the night away with the whiskey he had stashed in his kitchen. He shoved that ugly little piece of himself away. He couldn't leave a man to die alone. It wasn't right, and he knew it.

Nico sighed at the howl of the wind overhead. By his sides, his fingers dug hard into the ground, clutching leaves and dirt in his fists. He inhaled long and loud, brow crinkling up with strain, back arching off the ground again.

Who dies like this? Ren supposed Nico was a showman even to the very end.

Ren shivered and pulled the front of his sopping shirt away from his body, but that only let in frigid air from underneath. He buttoned his coat up to his neck. Hugging himself with his arms, he hunched down against wind that whipped drenched strands of his too-long hair against his face and neck. He should cut it shorter, and this right here was reason enough to do so. In this weather, it was as if he'd wrapped a sodden blanket around his neck.

On the ground, Nico exhaled a warm plume of puffy white into the ice air. He groaned again, deep in his throat, and Ren couldn't help but think, with his back arched like that, it gave the impression he was in the middle of a sexual act.

That's just wrong. Stop thinking that. Better yet, stop thinking.

The trees swayed and shivered with each passing gust. Ren wished the storm could blow through his mind, clear it of this night.

Nico let out a soft whimper. There was nothing else Ren could do for him except stand witness to his death. Anyone at least deserved that much, even a stranger. Ren moved closer to Nico. Tears shimmered, poised at the tips of Nico's long, pale red lashes.

It's too bad. What a waste.

And not just because Nico was alluring in a way that having the ability to hold fire in the palm of your hand would be alluring, though that was definitely part of it. It was also a shame because he was losing Nico's story. Nico seemed interesting, which was a quality sorely lacking in Klein. He had a story, and Ren would never learn it. Aside from the sheer power, there was definitely something about Nico that would have intrigued Ren in everyday life. He liked hearing people's stories, liked collecting them in the back of his mind. This story, he was sure, would have been a colorful one. And now it would be lost.

He'd never know Nico, and the absolute inexplicable sadness—*wrongness*—of the realization almost brought him to his knees. His gut told him it was never supposed to be like this: over at the beginning.

Nico strained against the ground as though he were fighting its solidity. The forest floor under Nico resembled a disturbing deathbed, a blanket of leaves, curled and brittle at the end of the season, strewn perfectly all about his body in morbid tribute.

The end of the season.

Ren blinked at the ground. It wasn't the end of autumn. It was only the beginning, the very first night. And something was disturbingly wrong. It radiated out from Nico, electrified the air, made Ren reach out because he was suddenly sure, though he couldn't see it, that he could touch it—whatever it was. Something brushed against Ren's extended arm, raised the hairs there, and then swam away from him.

The leaves that had been beaten to the ground by the deluge—fresh green leaves that had most likely just fallen that night—were dying. Ren turned in a circle to take in the small surrounding area that he could see in the dark. Nico was doing it again, this time on a grander scale. Just like in the tree house, the leaves were dying, turning brown and decaying right in front of Ren.

He moved back from Nico, as if it would make him any safer, and said in a hushed voice, "What are you doing?"

And now the nearby weeds and small bushes sagged to the forest floor, shedding their leaves and shrinking toward the ground. Already, within seconds, nothing remained of them but wilted leaves and broken limbs, old dead things you would walk over without noticing on a regular day.

"God, no," Ren said under his breath, and he wasn't entirely sure if it was an exclamation of surprise or a prayer for safety. Maybe it was a little of both.

Leaves continued to fall, floating down as lazily as snowflakes in winter. As soon as they hit the ground, they shriveled and disintegrated with the tiniest crackle, melted back into the dirt. Under the cover of darkness, death crept through the woods, the sounds unmistakable: popping and cracking, periodic *whooshing*, the forest crumbling away. And amid it all, Nico remained a tense little huddle, both hands burrowed deep into the muddied ground.

He was sucking the life out of the forest, right in front of Ren.

This wasn't the bright thing that sometimes left his dreams with a pretty sheen. This was power on a terrifying scale. Did Nico contain magic, or did he control death?

Ren stood in the middle of the forest as devastation fanned out from Nico, no idea what to do.

After an interminable amount of time, the rustlings stopped, the crackling sounds ceased, and the world became very quiet and still. In the dark, Ren waited another ten minutes or so before he dared step closer to Nico. The gloom rendered him indistinct. Ren leaned over him. Nico's rib cage was rising and falling with soft, even breaths, his hands calm, loose, and open at his sides. Ren put a hand to his shoulder, and Nico sighed in his sleep.

Fat drops of rain started plopping. Ren had very little choice, so he gathered Nico in his arms again, put him in the hammock, and hauled him into the tree house. Levering him up and down the tree wasn't all that different from hauling wood and building materials all day. It had such a similar feel.

Back inside the relative shelter, he settled Nico into the musty pile of pillows and blankets. As soon as Ren covered him with a blanket, Nico curled up bonelessly, burrowing into the warmth until nothing showed but the tips of his damp, brilliant hair. Ren pulled out a blanket for himself and sat across the room from Nico, his back propped against the wood frame of the tree house, positioned so that he could monitor both Nico and the door. It hit him as familiar, this staying up on guard. He hadn't done it for many years, when his parents were still alive and he'd stay up many nights to watch over his ma.

He didn't know what he was staying alert for now. It could be to protect Nico from anyone who might find them.

Or perhaps to protect himself from Nico.

He still wasn't sure which it was as sleep grabbed him and yanked him down.

Chapter Five

REN

A gasp startled Ren awake, but not his own. He didn't remember dipping into sleep, but, sure enough, the room glowed with a soft, watery gray dawn. He popped his back as he straightened into consciousness. Nico's blood had dried his shirt into a stiff mess. He was sure he had Nico's blood underneath his nails, maybe even stained into his skin.

Ren yawned, stretched his arms forward, and found Nico sitting in his nest of blankets, apparently back from the dead, his lips parted in confusion as he took in the room.

That wide, uncanny gaze landed on Ren. He blinked several times, slowly, as though remembering how to control his eyelids.

"I'm not dead." His voice was rough as bark. He grimaced, perhaps either at the sound of it or the fact that he was, indeed, very much alive and speaking.

"I can see that," Ren said cautiously. His brain couldn't focus on the fact that Nico was alive—back from the dead, truly—so he focused instead on the curled, dead leaf caught in the absurd tangle of all that silky red hair, hanging just above Nico's ear. It made him appear like some wild, earthy forest creature, just crawled out of the ground. Red stains painted his mouth. Bits of dried blood smeared down his chin. Ren could only goggle at this new being, disconcertingly and wholly unlike the shimmering, graceful one of the night before.

"You're an imbecile," Nico said.

"That's not exactly the thanks I was expecting for bringing you someplace dry to do your dying."

"You saw me take down six of them, and then you brought me with you." Nico's voice scraped over the last words, so dry and raw it made Ren's own throat hurt. "Do you have no sense of self-preservation?"

"*You* definitely don't. You asked me to kill you."

"Did you *carry* me here?"

Ren shrugged. "Partially carried, partially rowed you in a boat."

"Rowed in a— What the hell?" Nico jerked his fingers through his hair and then slid his face into his palms. The leaf in his hair shifted but managed to cling to a tangled strand. From between his hands, Nico said, "I don't get it. Why would you do that for me?"

"Why wouldn't I?" Nico lifted his head with an air of complete incomprehension. Apparently, he was at a loss for words, so Ren said, "If you need water, the lake isn't far."

Nico went completely still. His hands went to the floor, grasped knuckle-white tight in the blankets. "The lake? The one between your village and the carnival?"

"Yes, that one."

Nico took in the room, the deep brown walls, the high-beamed ceilings, the age-worn wood. "Where are we?"

"In a tree house in the woods behind my village."

"We're that close," Nico whispered, but it was as if he was talking to himself, telling himself something ugly as he clutched at the blankets more desperately.

Ren wondered if he'd have been such a mess if he'd woken up, like Nico, on what should have been the first morning of his death.

"Close to what?" Ren asked in the voice he used with newborn calves just entering the world. Nico might startle and bolt any moment. "You're acting like there's a monster under the bed."

Nico peered up at him from beneath his lashes, a cornered animal assessing the situation. Ren had never felt so much judgment in one glance. Pass or fail. Was he deciding Ren's trustworthiness?

Nico seemed to make a decision. Still studying Ren, his scrutiny a heavy, tangible thing against Ren's skin, Nico said, "There's more than one monster under the bed."

"What monsters are you talking about?"

Gone completely still, Nico considered him for a good handful of seconds, so long that Ren shifted, uncomfortable. Had Nico even blinked in the last few minutes? Ren didn't think so. Last night, he'd wanted Nico's full attention, but being at the center of it now felt like baking under the sun.

Nico said, "You truly have no idea what's going on in the world, do you?"

"I know I went to an unbelievable carnival last night expecting something fun and unforgettable, and, instead, ended up sitting in a freezing tree house with you."

Nico assessed him with an intensity that might as well have been a touch, climbed down the length of his body, and took all of him in. "You lead a simple life, don't you?"

"Simple?" Ren couldn't help but bristle. "What do you mean by that?"

"A village life," Nico said, seemingly unaware he had offended. "Do you like the life you lead?"

"Well, I suppose I get along fine," Ren said, discomfited by the sudden focus on his life, on his questionable happiness and the quality of that life. It was everything he'd been pondering lately.

"You need...you need to go home. Forget you ever met me. Forget any of this happened. Live your life and—" Nico's hands finally released the frayed blanket. "And be happy you can put aside everything that happened last night."

"Why would I want to forget last night?"

"Because it was ugly."

"It scared me, but it was an experience—"

"I can make you forget, if you want."

Ren recoiled. "If you try to get into my head, I'll have to snap your neck."

Nico's expression remained impenetrable. It took him a long time to say, "Fine. Block it out on your own. Just go back to your village."

Ren didn't move as Nico plucked the torn and blood-stiff fabric away from the skin on his stomach with a grimace of distaste. "And what about you?"

"What about me?" Nico kept messing with his ruined clothing, the diversion a convenient buffer. Blood flaked onto the blankets with his every movement. "Do you want compensation for whisking me away? You might have already noticed we won't actually be sleeping together."

Nico was a barbed thing, but Ren figured he deserved the benefit of doubt. After all, he'd come back from the dead last night.

"I meant," Ren said, relaxed, "what are you going to do? Where will you go?"

Nico shrugged, his head bent over his shirt, the red mess of his hair falling in front of his face like a mask. He absently rubbed the bloodied fabric of his shirt between his fingers as if he'd given up on getting it clean, as if it didn't matter anymore. His shirt was already hopeless: a stained, shredded, ruined mess. Those tight-fitting trousers of his were hidden beneath the blankets, but he couldn't imagine they'd fared any better.

"It doesn't matter," Nico said. "I didn't get far enough away. They'll find me. They always do."

"The monsters?"

At that word, Nico sneered down at his pale fingers tangled in the black fabric, an ugly little laugh at his mouth. He flicked more little red flecks off his clothes, scraped his nails down his shirt. Such a meaningless task. "Yes. My monsters."

Something about the way Nico was picking aimlessly at himself made Ren nervous. He wanted to get up from his spot by the wall, kneel next to Nico, and close his hands over those slim, jittery fingers. He wanted to pick the leaf from Nico's hair and brush the bright, wild mass of it away from his forehead, as he had last night. It was a lot easier to be tender toward Nico when he was unconscious.

Resisting any affectionate urges, Ren said, "The monsters you're talking about are from your camp?"

"They're not magicians. Not people either." *Flick flick flick.* Another awful laugh, more high-pitched than the one before it. It was full of panic, edged with resignation, like someone tipping toward a meltdown. Ren didn't know what he'd do if Nico became hysterical. Dying, he could deal with. Hysterical was a completely different matter.

But Ren pushed on anyway. He had to know what was going on. He was too close to it now. He had to know the whole story. "Then what are they?"

Nico shook his head. "You don't want to know what they are."

Those pale eyes were wide and luminous and a little wild, and it scared Ren—but not enough. He leaned forward. "Tell me."

"I *am* telling you," Nico said. "Take my damn warning. If I don't tell you, you can still turn back. You can still—" His voice seemed to get stuck, releasing the last words, frayed. "—get away."

Ren stood up. Nico twitched at the sudden movement, a full body shudder. He balled up the bottom of his shirt and crumpled the bloody mess of it in his fist as Ren approached and stooped at his side.

Pointedly avoiding Ren, Nico said, "Don't think I won't drop you where you stand if you touch me. Don't. *Don't.*"

Ren kept his hands folded together. "I'm not going to touch you. But I just can't... You're in a lot of trouble, aren't you?"

Nico didn't say anything at first, but his fingers stuttered, jumbled in the fabric, and Ren caught little flashes of creamy, perfect skin where the knife had sliced through the fabric. As far as he could tell, there was no matching slash in Nico's skin. His brain was having trouble processing that.

Nico's hands went completely still. "I'm not in trouble. Last night was a stroll through the woods."

"I'll help you. Let me do something."

"No one can help me, especially not some simpleton from a backwoods village."

Ren sat back on his heels. "You're quite unpleasant. You know that?"

There was a slight pause, like a tiny rip. "Then why are you still here?"

Absurdly, in that bleak, fragile moment, Ren really wanted to touch him, to make some kind of warm contact. There was something about Nico's skin, about those pale hands, that made Ren want to create a connection with him, to find a moment in which they could hold hands. But he also didn't want to die.

"Because I can't walk away from you now."

"You can. I'm telling you to fucking walk away. Go home."

"No."

Nico squeezed the blankets, twisted them between his hands. Ren thought that was probably supposed to be his neck.

"Have you ever stepped foot outside of this area?" Nico asked him.

"What does that matter?"

That half-hysterical laugh rose between them again. Finally, he lifted his eyes to Ren's, the yellow-brown almost golden in the growing dawn, glistening. The tears came as a surprise, incongruous to the angry-tipped tone of Nico's words. The glimmer wavered, and the fact of those unshed tears churned fear in Ren's stomach, made him lean back farther. He didn't want to know what could make a man with so much power this scared.

"It matters," Nico said in a low, steady tone that belied his tears. "Because you have no idea of the things that walk this world. Last night I killed six of their own. One got away. I know he ran back to them. I know he told them what I did. I'm done. It's over for me. They're going to come for me no matter what. You don't want to be here when they do."

"Why don't you run? Start running now."

"Because I can't outrun them. Last night was supposed to be my head start. I was going to slip away. Instead, I'm still here. I have no chance now. They won't let me get away. And after what I did last night... They'll hunt me down no matter where I go." Nico blinked rapidly, lashes fluttering. In his lap, his hands stilled. "They're good at torture."

Blooming morning light danced across the walls. All Ren could think was, *Torture.* The word felt foreign in his mind, so little had he ever actually used it.

They sat in silence as the harrowing night faded into a foggy morning. Nico's face became more defined in the light: freckles stark across his cheekbones, skin bleached of color, leftover bloodstains on mouth and chin. He might have come back from the dead, but not before rolling in his own grave.

"If you don't leave now, they'll kill you," Nico said.

"No torture for me?" It was meant to be a joke, but it came out sounding morbid. Ren found there was no good way to spin torture.

"No, but I'm sure if you request it, they would oblige," Nico said into his lap. "Go. Please."

Ren took in a deep breath at the way Nico's voice played so softly over that word.

"Listen," Nico said to the play of his fingers twisting in the blankets, "I'm the reason you were out in that forest. I was going to use you to get away. You were my reason to leave the carnival. And I'm the one who walked right into them. I made a mistake, and you were about to pay for it last night. Do you understand? I killed them so they wouldn't kill you. That was for nothing if they catch you here with me."

"All right," Ren said on an exhale, breathing out the words. And quickly, before he could think about what he was doing and what it could mean for him: "If you want me to leave before they get here, then you should probably get up and get moving. I think we can still make it if we go now."

Nico jerked his head up. Dusty gold dawn light caught in his eyes as their wooden room filled with morning. "What's wrong with you?"

Ren stood. "Get up." He held a hand down to Nico. "If you want me to go, then let's go."

"You have a death wish," Nico said.

"According to you, we don't have much time. Are you going to stay here and let me die? I think that would be rude after I went through so much trouble to get you this far."

Nico shoved the blankets away, his cheeks hot with frustration. Ignoring Ren's proffered hand, he put his palms against the floor and eased himself up. On his knees, halfway up, he sucked in a breath. A groan caught in his throat. Ren didn't understand until Nico put an arm against the side that had been stabbed.

"You're still hurt," Ren said, surprised. "I thought you healed yourself last night."

"I did." Nico did nothing but breathe for a moment. Despite the chilled air, his face glistened with the sweaty effort of steadying himself. "Just not completely. Apparently."

"What's the point of bringing yourself back from the dead if you don't finish the job?"

Ren could've sworn Nico's anger momentarily flared gold in the air—a soft pop, a trick of the light.

It lit something low in Ren's belly and had him adding quickly, "Sorry, sorry. I never knew people were so touchy after coming back from the dead."

And Ren truly *was* sorry. Sorry that for some inexplicable reason, Nico, at his worst, could turn him on with a mere look, even an unfriendly one. And it was definitely not the right time. He didn't know what was wrong with him. He'd never before been turned on by waspishness.

Hissing each inhalation through his teeth with effort, Nico said, "I couldn't finish the job." His breathing was uneven, too shallow, and he slumped slightly forward with both arms wrapped around his middle. "I ran out of resources to pull from. Unless you wanted me to drain you."

Ren swallowed. "No thanks. I'm good." At least that had doused the ember of lust.

"That's what I presumed."

"Let me help you," Ren said, moving forward.

"No. I don't need—"

But Ren already had his hands under each of Nico's arms. Nico pushed up off his knees, and Ren half lifted him the rest of the way to his feet.

"We make a good team," Ren said. Out of his vast collection of smiles, he offered Nico his smallest. Each one had a use, a time, and none of them had ever failed him. This one said, *See? You don't know me, but I'm not so bad.*

"We're a disaster," Nico said, his aloofness a shield always between them. There was a pained grimace affixed to his face as he walked toward the door, one arm still wrapping his stomach. He stopped at the door, clutched at the frame, and stood there catching his breath. "I don't know how I'm supposed to make it down from this contraption."

"That's not a problem. I'll lower you in the swing. And it's not a contraption. It's a tree house."

"I don't care what it is."

He'd never met anyone so prickly. Ren followed him to the door, nearly put his hand on Nico's back, but pulled it away at the last minute lest Nico snap it off. Ren brushed past him through the doorway, coming to a stop on the tiny balcony where the swing still lay wadded up near the edge.

Because he was too busy readying the swing for Nico, it took Ren a moment to notice anything different. The emptiness finally tugged at him, made him aware of an unsettling *wrongness*. The world beyond their shelter had changed overnight. The complete lack of a forest froze Ren.

Everything but the tree they were in was dead. Broken, rotted trees decayed into the horizon. Black leaves blanketed the forest floor. Leafless branches lay broken across the ground. Brown brown brown where once there had been greenery, where once there had been a forest so thick the sky could hardly be seen from the ground. The canopy gone, nothing but black dust on the ground, and only a few naked tree limbs reaching desperately for the sky.

As a child, Ren had walked through this nightmare forest in a dream he'd woken from crying. The dream had been so profound that pieces of it remained stuck down inside him even all these years later. He still had wisps of it every now and then in passing dreams, hazy with time, mere impressions of the original nightmare. There had been monsters in that forest, chasing him between the lifeless trees, across the barren landscape, relentless. He had run through a gray world, nowhere to hide. Ren found the forest before him now disturbingly similar, though surely it couldn't be the same one from his dream.

He hadn't been able to go back to sleep that night until his ma climbed into his bed and curled her motherly protection around him. Now, he remembered only tattered bits of the dream, but the feeling of being hunted had stayed with him into adulthood. It had left an unsettling film across his consciousness.

Since childhood, Ren's mind had kept a set of terrifying scenarios it ran through while he slept, the skeletal forest being only one of them. His drowning dreams had much the same feel, often full of fighting dark waters, pounding at a surface that wouldn't break, trapped and consumed by the village lake. Drowning and running. His mother had spent much time trying to comfort him through the sunless hours. Ren's imagination spun out of control every night.

His recurring dreams, so intense, left shards throughout his waking life. Sometimes Ren would be going about his day, and one of the shards would pierce his mind when he came across something that reminded him of his nightly horrors.

The shards shifted and jabbed against his consciousness as he absorbed the grand-scale of the devoured forest.

"My God." Ren turned to Nico, who seemed to care only about the dawn-stained orange clouds blossoming on the distant horizon, as though the decimated forest weren't there, didn't matter. "Did you do this?" There was a shudder of disgust in his voice he couldn't quite contain.

The question pulled Nico back to earth. He blinked at Ren and then finally noticed the ravaged thing that had once been verdant land.

"Yes. I did." No apology, no real emotion at all. Nico sounded half-asleep, as if he'd left his brain wrapped up back there in the blankets.

"You destroyed an entire forest," Ren said, trying to wrap his mouth around the words and his mind around the implications.

Nico focused on Ren, studied his face, said nothing for a long moment in which they simply stood there, testing who would be the first to cave and walk away.

What if I turn and leave right now? Can I take back my loyalty? He probably wouldn't even care. What in the hell have I done?

Adrenaline seeped into Ren's blood, his body readying itself to run.

Neither of them left.

"I didn't do it on purpose," Nico said. His fingers played aimlessly along the frayed hole in his shirt. "My survival instinct tapped into my magic. The magic took over while I was unconscious."

This was not what had been advertised, not the beautiful shimmery mirage of the carnival. This was ruinous, ugly. How strange that it should come from someone so beautiful.

I should have run. Ren had never run from anything in his life. *I should have run last night. This is too much.*

Ren met Nico head-on. There would be no shrinking from Nico, no matter how formidable Ren found him. He got the feeling Nico was not someone to meet with uncertainty in anything.

"So, magic is a farce," Ren said. "In truth, it's an ugly monstrosity." He gave Nico's body a pointed once-over. "Hiding behind a pretty facade."

For the briefest moment, Nico's eyes flared, his shallow breath filling up the little balcony where they both stood high above the evidence of his destruction.

"If you're staying with me because you think I'll swing through the trees and put on pretty light shows for you, you're going to be sorely disappointed. The entire carnival is a farce. Something shiny to lure in the people. People are stupid and easy. They fall for the show every time, and they pay more for it than they realize. Beauty means nothing. Now that all of your childhood fantasies have been shattered, you can run home and drown your sorrows in milk and cookies in front of a nice warm fire."

If Ren had been a lesser man, a man easily intimidated, Nico's hostility might have been enough to push him right over the edge of the tiny wooden balcony. He didn't doubt Nico had chased off many others with it. It seemed like his thing. Perhaps it was even a hobby of his: glaring people away, snarling until they left him alone. But compared to the things Ren had seen the night before, it was only an expression. Nothing more.

No matter how ornery, no matter how frosty, no matter how disappointing Nico was, Ren couldn't leave him alone knowing he was being hunted. He wouldn't be able to live with himself if he left now. Ren had never run away from his father, and he wasn't going to run away from this either.

Ren turned back to the swing, untangled it, spread it out, said, "Get in."

For a moment, Nico didn't move. Then, wordlessly, he limped over, grimacing. He sank down into the swing, and Ren wasted no time in lowering him to the ground. He followed quickly, climbing down the ladder as he had done hundreds of times before. When he reached the ground, he found Nico standing next to the tree that held the house, gently running his hand up and down its trunk. They might have been having a conversation, Nico and the only living thing left in the forest.

They began crunching their way through the forest. Neither took the lead, but they were walking vaguely in the direction of Ren's village, going slowly because Nico winced on every other step. He seemed as though he were barely holding himself together, his shoulders hunched forward. Hard to reconcile this man, bent lines and fragile edges, with the eldritch creature who could take out a forest and a half dozen people in one night. It chilled Ren.

Ren had no idea what he was going to do with Nico once they got to his village. He didn't seem like the sort of man one invited inside for hot tea. And Ren couldn't imagine hiding him beneath his bed or in a closet. Nico also wasn't the sort who should be hidden away. He was too bright for that, a red spark that would stand out no matter where he was.

"A house in the trees," Nico said as they walked through the crumbling, ghostly forest. There was an odd lilt to the way he pronounced words, a strange way he wrapped his tongue over the syllables. It was even more pronounced now that the challenging edge to his tone had softened a bit. He flowed over the words like a stream burbled over rocks, smoothing and polishing them. It made things that Ren heard every day sound softer, almost musical. It made him want the leisure to sit and listen to Nico talk more, in a quiet room with just the sound of a crackling fire in the background and Nico's smooth, deep voice filling the room.

Nico said, "Where did the tree house come from?"

"I built it a long time ago when I was a child."

Nico stumbled a little. "You built it?"

"Yes," Ren said with a shrug that brushed their shoulders together. "I build things." *Unlike you*—he couldn't help but think it as they walked through a pile of fine black powder where a copse of trees had once stood—*who destroys things.*

"How hard it must be for you to realize I'm not some pretty singing thing that magics up rainbows for you and shoots candy out of my ass like all of the magicians in your wet dreams. You should be more careful with your thoughts when you're near me." Nico said it as casually as one would comment on the weather.

Instinct had Ren putting a little distance between them, a bit of safety to avoid hands brushing or shoulders touching again. God of the seasons, but he was unpleasant. It made Ren uneasy because he wanted it to—knew that it *should*—squelch the allure, but all it did was make him want to fuck away that cold, hard exterior until Nico was hot and shuddering in his hands. Really, it made no sense. He always avoided rude, harsh men. He liked well-mannered, nice people as much as the next person, and those were the people he surrounded himself with, in bed and out of it.

But the lure of Nico's bright head so near was like having something shiny and new just out of reach. He couldn't put it down or let it go without getting a chance to examine it more closely.

Nico proved too much for Ren's senses to ignore, and Ren couldn't help but indulge in little tastes of him when Nico was too busy concentrating on other things to notice. He wanted to say, *Why were you a part of the carnival?* But he knew the answer wouldn't be pretty.

They walked into a watery dawn that held only a hint of the sun. Nico huddled further into himself with each step. There was a slight limp to his movements, a favoring on his wounded side. Long, graceful fingers curled protectively against his stomach.

If Ren had thought he was beautiful in the dark, lit by the wild night, he was ridiculous in daylight. Even though worn and exhausted, he was all sharp, elegantly sweeping angles with eyes like the first clear rays of the sun peeking over the horizon in the morning.

He reminded Ren of a fox he had come upon in the woods behind his home once, like a scene from a dream. That bright, early winter morning, he and the fox had participated in a brief staring contest before the fox had turned gracefully and slunk away through the snow. There was something oddly similar about Nico and the fox. They had the same type of aura: sly and elusive and shrewd.

They continued to walk slowly to accommodate Nico's limp. Nico studied the clouds as though they held freedom, and Ren studied Nico much the same way. He made himself turn away before Nico noticed, because he knew that wouldn't go over well. Nothing with Nico went over well.

Ren might have a problem.

WHEN THEY FINALLY reached Ren's village, it was on fire. Smoke was just beginning to curl into the fog. Ren's tiny spot in the world resembled a hellscape. They had a clear view of it from above, where they stood on the hill behind his village. From that high vantage point and down into the valley below, the scene could've been a tiny theater troupe production, all the little people running around the stage while miniature-sized props exploded into flames. Everything he'd ever known was burning.

"No," Ren said, unable to move, unable to believe the bedlam below was his home. "Oh God, oh God, oh God."

Nico stopped beside him, near. "Your village? I thought we were walking in the opposite direction. I told you last night to keep me away from here."

"I don't—I can't—What's happening?"

Nico's breath shook. "They're here. They guessed that we left the woods together last night." Clouds from the fire sprawled across the sky, blotting out the sun. "I haven't seen them do this to a village in a long time. It draws too much attention."

Ren couldn't comprehend the finality of his life burning, but the fear in Nico's voice registered inside of him, in a place he couldn't name.

"I don't—I don't understand. It's stone," Ren said. "Stone doesn't burn like that."

"Their fire can burn anything they want it to burn."

"Why would they—how could they—*why*?"

"They're hunting me, and the last time they saw me was with you."

"But they're...they're burning my village? They're burning...everyone."

How strange. He perceived it happening, but he couldn't feel any emotion. He couldn't feel. He couldn't, he couldn't, he couldn't—

Nico started to say, "We have to—"

Something inside of Ren ignited in response to those flames, and he took off running. Behind him, Nico cursed loudly. Such a foul word from such a pretty creature.

Without a plan, without another thought, Ren ran, and the pulse of movement through his legs began to clear the fog out of his head. Straight downhill he went, flying with the speed that the steepness of the hill offered him, flying toward the wreckage of his home and everyone he'd ever known in his life. Halfway down the hill, the screams filtered toward him. The heat bulged out as he got closer and closer.

Fingers brushed against his back, receded, and Ren kept running. Again, fingers skipped warmly across his neck. He kept running. The third time, a hand closed in the collar of his shirt, the suddenness of it jerking him backward. He flailed, crashed back into Nico. They almost went down, legs tangled together, but saved themselves by clutching at each other and rebalancing.

"You can't go in there!" Nico shouted over the roar of burning wind. The whole world boiled down to these flames, the very air tinted red. Heat and ash blew into their faces, and Ren was momentarily mesmerized by the way the hot gusts whipped all that thick coppery hair across Nico's face, spun it crazily about his head. He seemed part of the inferno, a flare that had licked out at Ren and tightened its fingers around him.

Ren shouted, "I have to help them!"

"They have no chance!" Nico had a good solid hold on Ren now, both of his hands wrapping Ren's forearm.

"Don't say that!"

Everyone Ren had ever loved, fucked, laughed with, cried with, grown up with—they were all in those buildings. When he had so lovingly built those homes and shops, he'd never imagined he was creating their graves. They were dying in those buildings he'd built for them, trapped between the walls he had so carefully crafted.

"You don't understand!" Nico was yelling directly into Ren's face. His inscrutable mask had fallen, his features vivid with a new vehemence. "I'm telling you it's already over!"

It took Ren a moment, through his haze and through the hot smoke, to notice Nico was breathing too fast, gasping in each new breath. There was a little hitch of pain on each intake.

Ren returned his yell. "You should leave, but I might be able to save some people!" He tried to jerk his arm away. Nico's hold was tight with a desperation that Ren didn't fully understand, but he was still bigger than Nico. A hard yank would be all it'd take to free himself and probably knock Nico to the ground at the same time. Ren hesitated between the blaze and Nico.

Smoke and ash dropped a veil over them, closed them up in a sweltering nightmare. Too hot, too close, the flames shimmered across Nico's face. Ren thought he might choke on the claustrophobia.

"Let go of me!" Ren yelled. "I have to do this! I don't want to hurt you!"

Nico's grip tightened. "No!"

Ren started peeling Nico's fingers from his arm, ripping his hand away. "Yes. I have to, Nico. I have to do this."

"They're not magicians!" Nico shouted at him, and when Ren paused, again with a pained exhalation, "They're not magicians."

"What are you—"

"They're wolk."

Ren stared at him. "Wolk?"

"They're wolk. And I promise you, if you walk in there, you'll never walk out again."

Ren knew the word, but it made no sense to him here and now, in the context of reality.

"Those are a myth," he said. Dark fairytales to scare children and keep them in bed through the long winter nights.

Nico's face was wild and grim. "No. They're not a myth."

"Of course they're myths. They're beasts who rise out of ashes. They're creatures of fire and night."

All Nico had to do was merely look at him, and it clicked.

The carnival flashed across Ren's memory, all that strangely beautiful fire. He said, "Oh."—and then, quickly—"But they're not possible."

"Terrible things are always possible. They can burn stone. They can burn anything in minutes. Please." Nico, urgent, dug his fingers so hard into Ren's arm Ren was sure he'd carry an imprint of them there. He drew in, practically stepped on Ren's toes, his features clearer this near, not as obscured by smoke. Something raw and fierce had broken through the cool mask, and the intensity of those emotions on Nico's face dissipated Ren's trance.

"Listen to me, Ren," Nico said.

Believe me, Ren heard.

Nico spoke right into his face. They were standing so close to each other, the breath from his words puffed into Ren's mouth. "When wolk attack you with their power, you don't survive. There's no maybe. There's no rescue. Your people are already dead. It's done." He shook Ren, one hard jerk that made Ren's head snap back. "Don't become one of them."

Ren glanced over his shoulder at his home. Unrecognizable. Though he heard screams and wails, he saw no people.

"They're gone," Nico said firmly. "I swear to you, there's nothing you can do."

"But everyone I know—"

"—is gone. Do you understand?"

Some innate instinct of survival told him to listen to Nico if he wanted to live, to turn and flee. It was the same instinct that had been missing last night in that crucial moment when Nico had told him to run. Now, he listened to it.

Numbly, Ren said, "I understand."

"We have to go. Now."

"Yes," Ren agreed.

The inferno billowed out at them like a large, hungry animal, its heat nipping at their skin, ready to taste. Ren was surprised when he blinked and wasn't on fire. Shapes swirled through the smoke. They coalesced into two people running at them. It took only seconds for Ren's hope at it being someone from his village to shrivel away. No one that he knew could walk through such tremendous heat, could run through a bulging ball of flame as though it were a doorway. No one he knew could move that fast.

Gods of all seasons, but they were moving fast.

They had lingered too long.

"Shit," Nico said.

Ren turned away from the beasts, Nico's magnetism stronger than any demonic spectacle. Besides, if he was about to die, he'd rather drink in the sight of Nico than some mythical monster bearing down on him.

Nico's concentration was skyward, as though he could see through the smoke to the clouds above. What an odd time to gauge the weather.

"We're about to die, aren't we?" Ren asked. The tremendous blaze was creating its own weather. A flash of light overhead whited out Ren's vision for a split second, followed by a low rumble that rose up from the ground and shook through Ren's legs.

"We're not about to die," Nico said as he put his arms around Ren, a move as surprising as the thunder, and pushed himself against Ren into a lover's hug.

Though Ren certainly hadn't expected it, he didn't have to think about it. He pulled him in tighter. Pressed together, with their bodies aligned, Nico in his arms was familiar. Familiar like a dream—nebulous, unable to pinpoint, floating in his mind. *My dream man.*

It hurt how perfectly they fit together and how they'd never get to enjoy that, to explore it. Ren would never get that tangible familiarity, of being warmly tangled in the covers.

It was a stabbing kind of thought, prickling at his mind, and for a millisecond, Nico stared at him as it trickled between them, blatant.

Nico seemed to wake from Ren's thoughts. He pushed the bottom of Ren's shirt up and pressed warm hands against his heated skin.

"Touch me," Nico said. "Touch my skin."

Ren certainly didn't need to be told twice, simply placed his fingers on Nico's jaw. He had large hands perfect for cupping, which was exactly what he did now. He held Nico's face in one hand, traced the lobe of an ear with the tip of his thumb. Fear rimmed Nico's half-parted lips. Ash flecked his hair and the tips of his lashes. His gaze, always so serious, settled on Ren's face. His magician was a solemn man. He was starting to understand why.

Such a strange tenderness to feel for a stranger. It occurred to Ren he would never get the chance to see Nico happy, and what a shame that seemed.

Ren smiled at him, one last emotion to pass to another human being before the inevitable end. The fire bore down on them, red-orange silk in the gray fog. Thunder pounded through Ren's muscles.

Nico took in Ren's smile with a calm steadiness and then pressed himself hard into Ren, his face tucked against Ren's neck, his heartbeat palpable. Ren held him tightly, comforted by the tangible reality of him. He could almost remember the smell of Nico's skin, when they were close and his scent mingled with Ren's—

Nico lifted his mouth to Ren's ear. He breathed words against Ren's skin. "We're half water anyway."

Ren blinked the dream away. It receded into dream dust. Smoke burned his eyes. Oh, how he wished he could have grown familiar with this man. He wanted to know Nico's scent when they were warm and safe in a bed. He wanted to see Nico's face lit with a smile, to learn the exact curve of his smile.

"What?" he whispered. Nico's hair was a tickle across his lips.

The beasts pounded closer, roaring over the thunder, and Ren's heartbeat soared with Nico's.

"We're water," Nico said, "caught in the clouds, falling from the sky. We're as free as rain. We're running down trees and leaves. Sliding through grass. Our bodies are liquid. We're water." His breath flowed into Ren's ear, soaked into his mind. "*We're water*."

And then the world disappeared.

Chapter Six

REN

Water, water, water.

Ren's mind, a feather gently spinning through the air, caught in the current of that one word, though it didn't hold any particular meaning for him.

He was free-falling, tumbling, flying, soaring down. He zipped through misty cloud clusters without feeling a thing. Droplets of rain fell everywhere, in slow motion, practically suspended in the air. Yet he could tell they were falling. Thick and heavy, the surrounding clouds were intimate in a way he didn't understand. They seemed so close; it was as if he were a part of them. He fell through the clouds, or maybe with the clouds. Just falling, falling.

Nothing made sense. Nothing needed to make sense.

So high, he couldn't see the ground, but he felt the height. He could fall forever, and that would be fine with him. He just went with it.

Ren hurtled through the air in free fall, somersaulting, unable to grasp anything about the experience, yet completely indifferent to the possible danger. A bird blurred past him, moving at a slower speed. Where were his arms and legs, the feel of chilled air whipping past his face, his self-awareness? The *ground*? A terrifying, improbable situation, but he didn't care. No panic, no curiosity, no fear—only sky and freedom.

He broke through the cloud base, the landscape spread far below with trees and hills like impossibly perfect, tiny children's toys carved out of the earth. No village in sight, no homes or shops. No people. The land had the hazy feel of slight familiarity, the jarring déjà vu of a dream.

Something was deeply bizarre. Ren was everywhere at once, seeing the landscape simultaneously from dozens of different vantage points. Here, a vast, thick forest, the deep green of it clumped so densely it looked like a rug unrolled across the land. There, gentle hills curved around one another. Here, a field with grass as tall as mountains swaying in the wind, every brown-gold blade the exact color of Nico's eyes. And just there, a silver river trickled through the hills. Over there, the soft hills of his homeland ended where mountains began to lift the earth.

His consciousness spread over the land, taking it all in at once. It should have been dizzying, but it felt natural. He floated toward all of these things at once and was aware of each piece of scenery. The trees, the river, the field—all became more detailed as he got closer. He could make out separate leaves; could discern drops of rain in the river's calm, mirror-like surface; could count the swaying grass. All of the land fit together like a puzzle. He was a piece of that puzzle, and he fell toward all of it to find his place. He slipped past the trees, neared the water, almost fell into the grass, skimmed the mountains. Falling, falling, falling but never quite landing, never actually touching anything.

Then—nothing.

COLD RAIN ON his face like dozens of tiny needle pricks. The sound of it spattering steadily through greenery. Ren groaned and squinted against the drops. He was lying flat on his back, the water pelting him right in the face. He sat up quickly, crashed into awareness, his mind spinning, no ground beneath him. He dug his fingers into the dirt, an anchor. He tipped forward, falling, falling—

But, no. He couldn't be falling. He was on solid land. Strange land. Large blades of grass rose all around him, each the width of his upper arm or larger. They reached dizzyingly high into the sky, bending this way and that with the wet wind, their tips scraping the clouds. He felt the cold loom of surrounding mountains. He'd seen this field at a different angle, a different distance. But that couldn't be—

He turned his head, and there was Nico, supine on the ground nearby. Nothing else seemed to matter as much as that fact. Nico's legs were spread, and he was holding his injured side.

"I can't move," he said with a scrape to his voice that spoke of pain.

Ren went to him, crawling up to his side. He sprawled there next to Nico and leaned over him to shelter him from the rain.

"Did you land badly?" Ren asked into his face. "Did you break something?"

Land? The word echoed in his mind, sounding faintly ridiculous. *I was everywhere... I was flying...*

Nico put a hand over the place where he'd been stabbed. Even his own light touch made him wince. "When I was chasing you down that hill, I think I tore something inside that was only partially healed."

"What can I do?"

"Nothing." Nico's gasp chopped the word in half. His next breath came out as a dry sob.

Ren had no idea what he would do if Nico broke down. He wasn't entirely sure he'd be able to handle Nico's tears as he sat there in the wild wet grass doing nothing and feeling impotent. He could never figure out what to do when someone cried. He'd seen it so often, had grown up with it, but the remedy still eluded him, besides just being there, a solid presence.

"It'll be all right," Ren said as steadily as he could. "Don't cry. You're not alone."

Lines of pain etched across Nico's forehead. "I have to heal it."

"What should I do?"

"It's a deep wound. I have to pull magic from the earth again. Just let me concentrate."

That, Ren could do.

Nico closed his eyes, put his hands palm-down to the ground, slipped them past weeds and grass and shoved his fingers deep into the dirt. Far above them, the improbably long blades rustled against each other with a hushed scraping sound.

Ren thought he had an idea of what was coming. He scanned the area. Fantastical, ethereal, and eerie, he might have dreamed this unknown world. The wind ran cool, moist fingers across his skin. Fog swirled at the base of the blades and curled at Ren's feet. The blades glowed golden-brown in the gray rain-light.

What a shame this land is about to die at Nico's touch. Will the grass wilt on top of us? It's so tall it could drown us.

He didn't particularly relish the thought of witnessing Nico suck more of the land dry. He didn't like seeing beautiful things destroyed. As ghostly as this place was, it was a living thing, a beautiful thing.

Nico breathed in deeply, held it as though savoring the air in his lungs, and then let it out languidly. What a difference from the desperate man of the night before who had writhed on the ground and clutched desperately and violently at the earth beneath him. Lying in the wet dirt and grass, he embodied serenity, red hair twining with green weeds. It struck Ren how godlike he seemed there in the dirt, how fitting, a king of this bizarre world. He belonged here so much more than to the glossy carnival.

Nico's fingers caressed the dirt, smooth petting motions that Ren, with a dry throat, tried to ignore.

Ren gave the surrounding scenery a silent goodbye. All of this might die at any moment. He watched a silver butterfly the color of the rain flutter its wings on a green weed. Time dripped away with the soft patter of rain. Ren grew drowsy waiting for Nico, lulled by the quiet.

Eventually, Nico stirred and pulled his hands out of the dirt. He pressed his palm into his wound and sighed. Ren openly checked out Nico's body, which Nico paid no mind to as he rubbed the spot where the knife had parted flesh.

"Aren't you going to finish?" Ren asked.

"I *am* finished," Nico said and rolled away from Ren to sit up.

"That's it? I didn't see you do anything." *You didn't even kill anything*, he didn't say.

"Good." Nico brushed his palms together to knock the dirt off. "That's the way it should be. Quiet and unobtrusive."

Ren surveyed the field. Nothing seemed amiss—or dead. The grass blades sighed together. The silver-winged butterfly fluttered in the weeds near Ren's leg. Delicate droplets lined its wings.

"Magic done the right way doesn't destroy," Nico added, softer. Raindrops slipped one after another down the length of a long green vine that snaked through the dirt at his feet. He followed the butterfly's lazy path through the weeds. Then he turned to Ren with an intensity that heated Ren's skin. "Magic should never turn things to dust like I did last night. Not if it's used right. I want you to know I don't use my power to kill things. I don't—I don't do that. I don't use it to commit monstrosities."

"Except for last night," Ren said.

"Last night happened because I was dying," Nico said in this new, quiet, steady tone. "I've never used nature like that before. I control myself better than that. But my power took over while I was unconscious. Survival instinct kicked in. It took me a long time to become aware of what was happening. Once I realized, it took everything I had just to keep it from draining you and that tree house of yours."

Ren kept his voice even. "You almost killed me in the same way you killed the forest?" He hadn't realized just how close death had been in that rain-drenched forest. Disquietingly, he remembered a moment from the night before: the feel of something in the air brushing past him but not quite touching him.

Nico bit his bottom lip but didn't evade Ren's accusatory tone. Rain dewed his lashes, more droplets sliding down his nose, and goose bumps sprinkled across his neck. He took his time before saying, "You were too close to me. Bringing a body back from the brink of death takes an extraordinary amount of magic, more than any one person has. My body sought magic in the nature around me. The grass, the trees—you."

The elders in Ren's village warned of magic. As he'd gotten older, old enough to analyze and decide for himself, Ren came to believe certain people in his village were superstitious to an unreasonable degree. Of course, that was before he'd seen a magician take out an entire forest. Even knowing there were people with inconceivable abilities out there roaming the world, he'd never imagined that anyone like Nico existed. His capabilities were terrifying—and alluring. And even more terrifying because Ren found the idea of so much power intriguing. He wanted more.

Ren refused to be frightened by the revelation of his near death. "So there was no other way for you to survive."

"I could have died," Nico said, sighing. "That would have been preferable, but my body didn't give me the choice. It chose to live."

Ren jerked back, his mouth going slack. After a moment, he said, "You can't mean that."

"Trust me, it would have been better for both of us if I had died."

"But death is the ultimate end. Nothing can be worse than death."

Disbelief slowly transformed Nico's face. "Gods, forgive me."

"What do you mean?"

"I've dragged an innocent into hell with me."

"I'm...pretty sure I should be insulted."

Nico pressed fingers to his temple as though warding off a headache. "There are so many things worse than death."

"You would rather be dead than sitting here right now?" Ren plucked a leaf from a nearby vine and touched the silk of it to the underside of Nico's chin, unthinkingly bold. Nico sat very still even as Ren tickled it down the length of his neck. Ren let the leaf flutter to Nico's lap before he pushed his luck too far. "You don't want to be able to sit here and feel? The grass and the rain and—and *life*?"

Nico spoke carefully. "I didn't say I want to die. I don't have a death wish."

"You said you would prefer it."

"I would prefer it to being with *them* again." In the dirt, Nico's hands curled into fists, squeezing the fine grains. "You don't know them. You have no understanding of any of this. Their cruelty—it's beyond your comprehension."

It took a stretch of moments, the rainy quiet pelting around them, for Ren to say, "Our myths say the wolk catch people in the night, in the dark."

Nico paused, thoughtful. "Yes," he said after a beat. "In a way, yes. They catch people at the carnival."

"And they absorb the life from the people they capture."

The first time Ren's father had told him that one, he'd been young and wide-eyed. His father told it to him as a bedtime story, a small smile on his face the entire time. Ren didn't sleep at all that night, or the next one. His ma had to crawl into the bed with him to get him to go to sleep while his father's chuckle drifted to them from the other room. He didn't feel safe in the dark for a long time.

Nico's breath plumed white into the air. "They drain the magic from people because they don't have much of their own. Magic is an inherent part of us. It's not meant to be taken, and it leaves us weak when it is. It can be renewed with sleep, but if they take too much, the body can't recover. It leaves people the way I left your forest."

"Like the people in the clearing last night?"

"Yes. They'd been completely drained." Nico hesitated, indecisive. Eventually, he said, "The next thing after the magic is the soul. If they drain all magic out of a person, there's nothing left but the soul. Sometimes they take that too."

Ren found breathing hard, his chest clogged. "They take—they take souls?" It was worse than any myth he'd ever heard about the wolk.

"Myths are usually based on some sort of reality," Nico said. "The thing with myths is that, after centuries of being told and retold, the truth gets skewed. Obscured."

"So, they're monsters," Ren said. "Why were you with them?"

"You think I had a choice?" Harsh.

Rain misted through the field, drifted between them. Fog frosted the ground.

Nico looked as dangerous now as he'd looked beautiful the night before. His makeup had long washed away. Something about him said the everyday world couldn't quite touch him, despite his disheveled clothes. Maybe it was the new knowledge Ren had that Nico could take down six men while he was dying. That probably had something to do with it. Ren had no choice but to view him in a new light. The makeup had nothing to do with it, the tremendous amount of power did. Ren was sitting next to a thunderstorm that could release a bolt of lightning at any moment. Yet somehow Ren found him more appealing than ever, sitting bedraggled and defiant on the ground in the middle of a foggy field. Gods of all seasons, help him.

Nico tipped his head up and inhaled.

"What is it?" Ren asked.

"Do you smell that?"

"I don't smell anything." Ren took a deep breath of damp air—and there it was. The barest hint of it, but it was there: the bitter, acrid smell of something scorched. It seemed subtle, innocuous, like smoke from a farmer's chimney. Ren knew it wasn't insignificant. He remembered the blaze, something from hell itself.

He'd admired the carnival fire, awestruck by its lack of fire-like qualities. Last night, it was beautiful. Ren had basked in it until it had engulfed his village. How could he have been so fooled? It made him realize he couldn't tell magic from evil, and that was a terrifying thing.

Raindrops chilled the back of his neck. Ren shifted against his disconcertion.

"I thought we were farther away," Nico said. The gigantic grass swayed around them, scraping blades against each other in a way that sounded like fingernails down a wall. "We shouldn't be able to smell it."

"Everyone I ever loved was in that village," Ren said, and something in his chest tightened painfully at those words spoken aloud. It hurt too much to think about right now, a fresh, raw wound he couldn't bring himself to examine yet.

Nico turned to him, his mouth parted around words that didn't come. When he spoke, it was gentle. "Was your family there?"

"No. My family died long ago. I'm not going to talk about the fire anymore," Ren said. "No talking about it. I can't. Just—don't."

Nico gave a single nod. He treated the moment carefully, as though he thought the grief in Ren might burst him apart at any moment, an explosion waiting to happen.

"I'm sorry." Nico seemed as if he wanted to say more, but all he could manage was, "I'm sorry, Ren," again, softer.

If Ren started talking about it, it would all pour out at Nico's feet, and he wouldn't be able to stop it. He needed to contain it, to push it back in before he lost control of it. He said, "They're at peace now. They're—they're not in pain."

Nico said nothing. Abruptly, he stood up and raised his face to the gently dripping clouds. The rain had slowed to a drizzle, mostly a haze of wetness, but the air had acquired a new bite. Their breaths puffed out in little smoky streams. Water dribbled down the blades of grass. Coatless, Nico's black-clad shoulders were soaked with rainwater and dusted silver with mist. His hair was a dark red dampness framing his face.

Ren had been cold and uncomfortable before. He'd worked outside for the past decade. He'd put roofs on in rain, and he'd finished up walls in sweetly drifting snow. But he always had the close promise of a warm blanket and a fire afterward, hot drinks and hotter meals. How lucky he'd been then.

Nico came nearer until he stood directly in front of Ren. He bent his head and breathed into his cupped hands so that the warm breath hit them and spread outward. Except, Nico's breath couldn't feel that warm, be that all-encompassing. Ren blinked in surprise and scanned their immediate surroundings. He couldn't see it, but warmth suffused the air, pushing out the cold. So soft and comforting the way it settled over his shoulders and warmed his feet, like the most comforting hug he'd ever felt. Ren hadn't realized how cold he'd been until he wasn't cold anymore. His fingers began to thaw.

Nico stood before him: slim, average height, hands loose at his sides. Too slight to hold so much power inside that one body.

"How?" Ren asked, the warmth brushing his cheeks as it enfolded them. It was as though he was warming himself at a fireplace, except it was no fire he was basking in. It was Nico's magic.

"The use of reflection mostly," Nico said. "It's my favorite type of magic. Deceptively simple."

"Reflection?" Ren reached out a hand, ran his fingers through rich warmth, and then stretched out his arm. His fingers passed through warmth into cold, misty air. He brought a finger down through the air right where warm met cold. Nico had created a small bubble of warmth for them, free of the dampness that suffused the autumn air.

"I build a reflective wall around my body using magic," Nico said. "When I use more magic to warm the air, it bounces off the wall and builds on itself."

It was there so briefly, but Ren caught it: the sheer joy that flared over Nico's face when he talked about using his abilities. Nico turned away before the expression of delight could form into something more than a fleeting emotion.

Ren found himself staring at Nico. "The things you can do..."

"I told you to run."

A beat. "I'm not sure I want to run."

"You *should* want to."

"But it's too late for running, isn't it?"

Nico licked dry lips. His chest rose with a heavy inhale. As he breathed out, he said, "Yes, it is." He fiddled with the hole in his clothes where the knife had torn through fabric and skin. Every time he did that, he widened it a bit more, though he didn't seem to notice he was messing with it. His fingers worked around it absently. A circle of milk-pale skin peeked out against the black fabric. It was unexpected, and Ren ached to touch him so fiercely the tips of his fingers prickled.

"Do you see those snow clouds?" Nico pointed into the distance where the sky was barely visible through haze and grass. He didn't wait for a reply, just started walking. "We need to make it to those clouds."

Ren was lost in the field, wandering amidst grass as tall as mountains and fog as thick as milk. He could barely see past the forest of grass. There was no sky. Everything above them was white, white, white, an endless blankness. Wind blew wisps of dancing mist above their heads. A particularly large gust spit rain against their bubble. To Ren's delight, the drops hissed and fizzled out when they hit Nico's magic.

"And why's that?" Ren asked, loping easily next to Nico despite Nico's hurried walk. "Why do we need to get to clouds?" The cozy bubble moved along with them, but if Ren leaned too far away from Nico, cold air rushed at him.

"Because we have to get out of this area, and that's our exit."

A part of Ren fancied where this was going, and a hot excitement began racing through his veins. "You use the weather to travel?"

"Not any weather," Nico said. "I use the precipitation in clouds."

"Really?" *The rumors...they're true. They're* true. Ren nearly whooped with delight, barely held it in.

The expression Nico wore was impenetrable. "You don't believe me?"

"Of course I believe you. I've seen what you can do. It's just... I thought it was a myth they told us in the village to scare us away. Do you travel using lightning?" He hoped it was the lightning, because that would be amazing.

Nico tilted his head, searched Ren's face, analyzing. "You didn't get it, did you? You didn't understand what was happening to you after we escaped your village?"

"We..." Ren shook his head. Memories flitted through his mind, strange little wisps he couldn't quite grasp, as ephemeral as fog kissing a mountaintop before dawn.

He'd fallen. Ren remembered that much. He remembered viewing, from an impossible angle, a vast and breathtaking land that went on forever. No fear, no cold, no sense of anyone else nearby. It had been lonely. He knew that now. The memory of loneliness made him reach out his hand, brush it against Nico's arm. He withdrew his hand immediately, even though the memory of wide empty sky and his lack of caring as he flew through it made him hungry for human contact now.

"We were falling," Ren finally said, and it came out hushed, unsure. "It was...far. There was a lot of falling."

Nico, the rascal, actually seemed amused. "Yes, there was." He didn't smile—Ren was learning that his smiles were rare sparks—but his eyes creased at the corners as if he might be considering a smile. "We were definitely falling."

"And then what happened?" Ren asked, lost. "I don't understand how we landed. Were you there?"

"I was all around you."

"I remember I could see everything...from everywhere—"

"We were rain," Nico said, and he made it sound simple, ordinary. "We coalesced back into ourselves once we hit land. Our bodies can't hold the form for long."

Beyond their bubble of protection, the lightest of rains still trickled in rivulets down the blades of grass. Inside the warmth, their hair and clothes were already drying. Nico took in Ren's lack of shock, shrugged a shoulder. The fabric of Nico's shirt moved strangely against his body with the small movement. It was drying stiffly, in a dozen little wrinkles. Strange, the little details noticed in a passing moment.

The thing that surprised Ren the most about this revelation was that he wasn't surprised. Something about it clicked in his brain, completed the memory of falling that he hadn't understood before, soothed his mind as he slipped the puzzle piece into place. It made sense. It shouldn't, but it fit. He'd been falling toward the earth in a hundred different places, uncaring and free. Empty. Only now that his mind realized what had happened did it feel terrifying and exhilarating. Thrilling. He had flown across the sky.

This was magic on a scale Ren never imagined could exist. When he'd gone to the carnival, he expected to see a vanishing act, novelty tricks, maybe some fireworks. Enough to momentarily captivate him. He never expected to find power that reshaped the way he saw the world. He'd never actually known the world until today, until this moment.

It took him a minute or so to realize Nico was intent on him. *He's studying me as if I'm an experiment.*

"You turned us into water," Ren said, picking his way through the words and through his thoughts. "I remember that now. How did we...become ourselves again?"

"A body will always find its way back to itself. It's magic."

Awed, hushed, Ren said, "You have the capacity to take people apart and put them back together."

Nico shrugged, nonchalant, but he was messing with the knife hole again, his fingers as fidgety as ever.

"I was rain," Ren said, just to hear it aloud.

"And you're all right with that?" Nico asked cautiously. "You're feeling fine?"

Nico was handling him with kid gloves, being gentle with every revelation.

No, he's not studying me. He actually cares about my reaction.

Ren was usually better at reading people than this. A smile, a flash of his dimples, a joke, a brush of arms or hands, and he could usually tell he had them. How easy it had been in his village. He definitely did not have Nico. This awe-inspiring man did not make sense.

Ren said, "It makes me want to touch you, and I'm all right with that."

If that surprised Nico in any way, he hid it well. "Becoming an element rips away our emotions," he said. "Sometimes they come rushing back and can be more intense for several hours afterward. It can make us want to use our senses more to reassure ourselves we're human again. Some people, for example, want to touch everything in sight."

Ren didn't want to touch everything in sight. He only wanted to touch Nico. Oh, how he would have loved to put his senses to better use right now. Just being near Nico was a sensual feast. Nico's lyrical accent soared through his veins. The heat in the bubble felt strangely intimate, as if Nico were indirectly brushing against his skin. Nico made everything more vivid, made the world come alive.

"I might not be completely all right yet," Ren said. "Maybe I should touch you to ground myself." He said it with an easy grin, one he thought would make it obvious he was joking.

But Nico shook his head. "No."

"That was a joke. I know you don't like to be touched."

"Then it was a bad joke, wasn't it?"

Maybe it was because he'd seen the things Nico could do, but an irritated Nico made Ren want to take a step back, which was exactly what he'd have done if it didn't put him halfway out of the cozy bubble.

Ren said, "You're right."

When Nico said nothing, just kept walking, Ren continued more softly, "You don't like it when people touch you. You don't like it when people flirt with you either, do you?"

His tone expressionless, Nico said, "There's no point in flirting."

Ren gave a loudly fake gasp that didn't faze Nico. "Flirting is an art form, my friend."

"Flirting is tedious."

Ren made a face. "You're like a creature from another planet."

"I don't want you to touch me because I don't care what you're thinking about me, and I don't need to know." He noticed Ren's frown. "It's not personal. I don't want to know what anyone is thinking about anything, especially if they're thinking about me. It's tiring, *knowing*."

At least it wasn't a full-on rejection, Ren told himself. His pride wasn't completely tromped on. And it did, indeed, make sense. "You can't turn off that power?"

Nico touched things as they walked by: blades of grass, raindrops cupped in crannies. He just lightly skimmed the tips of his fingers over their wet surfaces. It seemed to be a habit, something to keep his ever-fidgety hands busy.

"It's not a power," Nico said as he scooped water out of a strangely twisted blade of grass and took a drink. "It's a part of me. Everyone's skill manifests differently, giving each practitioner certain abilities. Hearing thoughts through touch is another way my mine manifests. Trying to turn it off would be like trying to stop my heart from beating. Impossible unless I'm dead."

How incredibly lonely. Ren couldn't imagine being trapped like that, unable to take pleasure and comfort in human contact. To Ren, it was one of the keenest joys of life. He could hardly get enough of human touch.

"So you can never be intimate with anyone? In a relationship?"

"I can," Nico said, without grand elaboration. Water trickled off his fingertips. "I choose not to be."

"I think I would do it anyway," Ren said, thoughtful. The view of the dismal day from their circle of warmth lulled him into a comfortable reverie. The cloudy mists made him yawn. "I would take hearing their thoughts, as long as they weren't too terrible, if it meant I could have someone to hold and be with me. It would be better than being alone."

"That's easy to say when you don't actually have to hear what everyone is thinking. You'd change your mind if you had to hear what goes on inside people's heads."

Ren shook his head. "I don't think I would."

"People are vile," Nico said flatly. He hugged himself as though chilled. His hair was drying at different angles, the thick red strands messily untamable. "When they touch you, and you hear the constant buzz inside your head, all the ugliness along with the doubts and fears, all of it coming at you incessantly—even you might want to get away from people."

How unfortunate that all Ren could think about doing in that very moment was reaching out and brushing the flyaway strands of hair off Nico's forehead. He wanted to say, *Not everyone has ugly thoughts,* and *Who have you been talking to?*

It was ridiculous. It was too much—far too much for two strangers—so he only said, "It must be lonely living like that, without touch."

"I don't live without touch," Nico said and reached up as they passed beneath a long vine growing between the thick grass blades, hanging like a green banner above them. Disturbed, the vine dribbled leftover raindrops onto their bubble. Instead of falling straight to the ground, the drops slid in a curved path down an invisible wall, keeping the inside of their bubble warm and dry.

"I meant without human touch," Ren said, marveling as he traced the path of a single drop and swept his fingertip through the dewy trail it left behind in midair.

"Oh, excuse me." There was a bitter, mocking undertone there. "Let me assure you, I don't live without human touch."

Ren wanted to ask. God, did he want to ask. That nasty little hitch in Nico's tone dared him to ask, which was why he let it pass. He wasn't sure he wanted to know.

Nico shook the raindrops off his hand, and they walked on. As the quiet swelled, Ren's longing to connect with Nico in some way grew until he could hardly stand it. Nico stood out like a beacon in the monochrome gloom, a gleaming gem Ren couldn't have, always just out of reach. Ren could think of nothing but the man at his side, but Nico might as well have been walking alone.

The sky dragged a wet blanket of clouds low across the field, trailing misty tendrils, the dirty gray barely glimpsed through the tall stalks. Hills rose up, looming ahead of them, and the field began to thin. These weren't the hills of Ren's homeland, those gently rolling things he'd played in as a child and fucked various people on as an adult. He had good memories of those hills. But these sharper ones before him now—these heralded their bigger, colder brothers. Ren often dreamed of mountains, but he'd yet to see a mountain range in person.

They were deep in the field, and the larger the hills grew, the more vigilant Nico became. It made Ren more alert, anxiety flaring as he tried to take in everything at once.

"Do you think they might be following us?" he asked, his voice hushed.

"Of course they're following us," Nico answered, just as quietly. He fiddled with his hands, pinching the skin on his knuckles between the fingers of his right hand. "They still have my trail. I told you they weren't going to simply let me go."

Alarm flickered to life in Ren. "Crap."

"Yes, crap indeed."

"Why do they want you so badly?"

There was a pause. "I'm such a charming conversationalist. The monsters and I, we had many long conversations about books and the state of the world."

Ren gaped at him. "How can you joke about them?"

"I never joke."

Ren's skin tingled with nerves, all of his senses heightened by dread. Nico's unease jumped to Ren until it seemed they were bouncing it back and forth, sharing it. Their little bubble filled with fear.

"What are we going to do?" Ren asked.

"We're going to keep walking. We have to get to those snow clouds."

"Why can't you use the rain clouds again?" Ren asked and gestured toward the sky. "It's socked in today."

"I could, but that would only get us so far. We might land somewhere near your village again. We could land anywhere nearby where it's raining, and it's raining everywhere here today. We need the snow clouds to take us to where it's snowing, somewhere much farther away."

Ren was going to have to bet his life, his very existence on earth, on a hazy understanding of Nico's magic. That fact lodged uncomfortably in his chest.

The crunch of their feet on pebbles and bits of dead grass was the only sound for a while, the both of them too focused on staying alive to make conversation.

When Nico finally did speak, the sudden sound of his voice, even spoken softly, startled Ren. "Are you all right with leaving?"

"I don't have anything left here," Ren said. "No friends, no family, no home."

Their arms brushed when Ren sidestepped a rock. Nico folded his arms across his chest, cutting off the contact immediately.

"I can't offer you anything," Nico said.

"I'm not asking you to."

"You're thinking it."

Damn it. Walking behind Nico was probably safer. "I don't expect anything from you."

Nico nodded. "I want you to understand. We'll be leaving this land entirely, and we won't be coming back. If you can't deal with that, tell me now."

Ren took a deep breath of the warm, ensorcelled air, held it in his lungs while he let the thought of leaving this place settle into the corners of his mind. He exhaled slowly, said, "I can handle it because I have nothing. I need to leave. I need—I *need* to do this."

In truth, Ren had wanted to leave long ago. For years, he'd been dreaming of grand adventures, new places, different people, magical things. He'd dreamed about leaving, of sneaking out in the middle of the night, abandoning the people who had banished his father and then finished raising him after his mother had died when he was eleven. He'd dreamed of leaving and never coming back, with nothing but a goodbye letter pinned to his door. They'd protected him, raised him, and he dreamed of leaving them.

They were only dreams. In reality, he never could have walked out on the village that had raised him, the people who had kept him safe and comfortable. He could never have left his friends, his lovers, his home. They'd sheltered him as a child. As an adult, he'd built shelters for them with his bare hands.

He'd always wanted to explore beyond the hills of his home, but he'd never had an excuse to leave. He'd grown up in the kind of place that people never left. They were born and died in the same area, often in the same house.

It was never supposed to have happened, and especially not like this. No one was supposed to die to free Ren from obligation to his home, to cut his safety net. They were never supposed to burn— *No.* He wasn't going to think about that. He wasn't going to picture their deaths. *Don't think about it. Don't. Don't.*

He felt so light, and he shouldn't. He knew he shouldn't. He didn't want to contemplate the thin, terrible sliver of freedom-relief, or what kind of person that made him.

Now, he not only had an excuse to leave but a real reason. He peeked at Nico. Several reasons, every one of them crazy. Not that Nico was a big reason for him to go, but...he kind of was. Ren was heading down a risky path—dangerous in so many ways. And God, but he knew it. He knew it, and he couldn't stop himself. The moment they'd crashed together, his life had picked up speed. The kinetic energy was inexorable.

There would never be anything between them except death and confusion and secrets. Ren stumbled along the path anyway, knowing this inexplicable feeling for Nico, balling up and growing inside his chest by the minute, was already doomed, a seed that would never breach the surface.

So very quietly, dissipating Ren's thoughts, Nico said, "I never meant to ruin your life."

It was spoken with such softness that the rustle of grass scraping together in the wind nearly drowned out Nico's low tones. But Ren heard.

He slowed to a stop, said, "You didn't. Don't say that."

At Ren's side, Nico also stopped. He faced Ren; his gaze lifted from Ren's collarbone to his eyes, a reluctant slide. "I needed to get away from them." That same soft voice fell as light as snow on Ren's ears. "I couldn't do it any longer."

"Do what?"

Uneasily, Nico rubbed his hands together as though he were still cold. Less than an arm's length of magical air stood between them. Nico said, "Be their prisoner."

There was no moment of surprise for Ren. He'd never for once thought Nico was in cahoots with monsters, and that didn't leave many other options. The night before, it had taken him too long to absorb why anyone would ever want to run away from something so wondrous. Today, he couldn't imagine why anyone would run so hard, so desperately, unless it was to escape something ugly.

"How long?" Ren asked, afraid to know the exact truth of it.

Nico took in a hitched half breath and let it out slowly, but he didn't shy away from the answer. "Fourteen years."

Ren couldn't quite form words. His mouth flapped open. *No wonder. No wonder.*

"Oh, don't," Nico said with disgust, retreating. "Don't look at me like that."

Finally, Ren found a word. "What?"

"Don't look at me like I'm the sorriest creature you've ever seen. I don't want your pity."

"I'll help you get away. Let me help you." He couldn't figure out what to do with his empty arms, because their sole purpose seemed to be for wrapping around Nico, tucking him close and safe. In that moment, it was all he could think about doing.

"Fuck you," Nico said. "I'm not some pathetic boy who needs saving, so just stop. You're not going to win me over by trying to be my hero."

It was, as Ren suspected, no surprise that he wasn't a cuddly type of person. "If you don't need help, why did it take you fourteen years to escape?"

"It—" Nico cut his hand through the air in a sharp motion that either meant he was done with the conversation, or he was about to magically slit Ren's throat. His anger flushed up his neck and into his cheeks, bright on his pale skin. "You don't know what you're talking about." Menace danced at the edge of his voice.

"You don't get to come into the situation for five minutes and act like the solution is simple, like you think maybe I was just too incompetent to walk away from them."

"Why don't you want anyone to help you?"

"Because you can't help me." Pale red lashes swept anger-red skin. "No one can—You don't know what they are. Now stop talking," he said, low, "before I make you stop talking." He turned abruptly and ducked into the fog. Tendrils of mist broke apart and swirled out of place as if shaken. "I have to piss."

Stunned, Ren stood blankly in the middle of the field, his hands loose and useless at his sides. The air felt dangerous, charged, like maybe he had just avoided a lightning strike. With a wall of fog between them, the warm comfort of the bubble vanished with an audible pop. Delicate filaments of gold hung in the air where the warmth had been. Ren blinked, and the strands were gone. He might have imagined them. Damp, cold air rushed to embrace him, prickling his skin. He turned to take care of his own business.

And they were there.

Chapter Seven

REN

A whole clump of them. A group. A mass. A *horde*. They were standing several feet in front of Ren, hazy in the fog, indistinct. Ren stood very still. Vaguely visible through the mist, Nico's conspicuous red head bent forward, distracted, the rest of his slim figure a mere shadowy impression.

Shit.

They spotted Nico too. Ren opened his mouth. One of them looked right at Ren and lifted a finger to her lips. *Shhh.* The sibilance hissed around him, slithered against his ears, curled in his hair. Through the foggy air, across the too-short distance, she smiled at him. Ren shuddered, an involuntary spasm.

Ren didn't hesitate. "Nico!" he shouted. He was not one to be shushed.

Nico's name was all he could get off his tongue before they rushed Nico. Their speed was astonishing, inhuman. Ren felt rather than saw them brush past him, against him, jostling his shoulder. Nico had time only to turn, and then they were on him. Nico was standing, and then he wasn't. He was on the ground beneath them. They piled on top of him.

Ren ducked away, took cover in fog and grass. He panted uncontrollably. Even though they'd hardly shown any interest in him, he was afraid his panicked gasps would remind them he was there. He closed his mouth and tried to breathe through his nose, pressed a hand to his chest and the hard pound of his heart. The rocky ground dug into his hands and knees as he crouched low, palms pressed to the dirt for balance, for an anchor to reality.

Voices and sounds of a struggle filtered to Ren muffled through the thick, miasmal air. Once Ren got his breathing under control, he crept across the damp earth on his hands and knees, keeping low. Sharp rocks in the dirt made each movement painful. He had known of the wolk only a handful of hours, had seen them up close a mere couple times, and they already had him crawling on the ground.

How? How do you fight monsters? No wonder he couldn't escape.

He reached a spot where he could hide behind a clump of grass. From there, he peeked out. Through a morass of fog and bodies, Nico lay flat on the ground, his face shoved into the dirt. The wolk squeezed in close, putting their hands on him, sticking them beneath his clothes, clamoring for a touch of his skin, yanking fingers through his hair to press against his scalp, grasping greedily at him. Like ants on a piece of food, eager and hungry.

Ren gouged his fingernails into a smooth, thin stalk of grass. It took all of his control to stop himself from bursting in an explosion of anger. *But Nico doesn't like to be touched. How dare they. How dare they put their hands on him.*

Nico made a sound, muffled in the soil, and bowed his body, trying to shake them off. It made no difference.

His hands dug into the dirt, clawing as though he could drag himself out from under them. They clung to him as tightly as he clung to the earth. They snatched at his grasping hands, capturing them and shoving their fingers beneath the sleeves of his shirt to reach more skin. Nico let out a strangled gasp into the dirt.

Ren sensed he was about to witness something ugly and intimate, perhaps the reason Nico had fled with such vehemence. He couldn't watch. He couldn't let it happen. He had no chance against them. He had no idea what to do.

Their overexcited voices burbled over each other like a river, the sudden and overwhelming presence of them flooding Ren's mind. They were giggling, laughing. They were excited children with a favorite toy.

"Don't let him say a word."

"Get his hands!"

"Keep his face in the dirt!"

"I never get to try him. He's delicious!"

"They always hog him!"

"Don't let him say a damn word!"

"Drink up!"

"He has so much of it!"

"Why do they never let us drink any of his magic?"

"He tastes so much better than the others! So rich!"

"Finish him! Quickly!"

"We should make him cry. I've always wanted to see him cry."

Nothing that was happening made sense to Ren.

Nico tried to kick them off, tried to roll away. When his feet pounded the ground uselessly, they sat on his legs. They ground his face into the mud.

How can he breathe like that? I have to do something!

They knew Ren was somewhere close by. They simply didn't care about his presence. He was inconsequential to them, a human without the use of magic. Weak. He might as well have been a bug. And that...didn't feel good.

He had to use that misconception. Ren was far from weak. No one had ever mistaken him for weak or stupid or useless.

A rock dug into his thigh. He shifted, plucked it out of the ground to set aside. It was large and jagged in his hand, shiny black, weighty with potential. Running his thumb over its rough surface, without a clear plan, Ren thought, *Yes.*

Yes.

As quietly as he could, he started digging up the rocks within reach, gathering them in a little pile. They came in all sizes, sharpened by time and the elements. Carefully, quietly, Ren straightened up. He lifted the bottom of his shirt into a pouch and loaded the rocks into it cautiously.

On the other side of the swaying blades of grass, in the mud, Nico was trying to buck them off to no avail. He was choking in dirt and coughing out mud, simultaneously struggling to free himself and to breathe.

With one arm holding his rocks close, Ren crouched low and crept nearer. He kept plenty of grass between them and himself. He took one of the biggest rocks in his right hand, balanced its heft, took aim, and hurled it.

Ren had always had good aim, even as a child playing ball with his schoolmates. Years of tossing stones and logs down from half-finished roofs to waiting hands below had only pushed his aim into the category of excellent.

The rock struck one of the squatting wolk on the back of the head so hard he pitched forward. Ren had another rock in midair even as the wolk's head jerked up. The second rock smashed him in the face with a spectacular splatter of blood. Ren did not throw gently. The wolk went down hard.

By the time their babbling-brook voices began to fade and their heads had turned in his direction, Ren was already hunkered down, deep in the grass, where the wide bases of the blades gathered in a dense clump. He rained down a handful of midsized rocks. As the shouts began, he ducked into another lush hidey-hole and threw two of his biggest rocks, one after the other. Two wolk tumbled to the ground.

Yes. Ren's triumphant was fierce and vicious as he crept to another vantage point. *Fall, you fuckers.*

The grassy cluster he'd just vacated exploded. It took Ren a too-long moment to realize his previous shelter was on fire. This wasn't for show. The stalks disintegrated into ash, burnt pieces raining from high above, the fire eating its way up the lengthy blades at an impossible speed.

Ren scrambled over the ground, pummeled them with more rocks, and fled. More grass disintegrated in his wake. He left a trail of fire and ash behind him.

Between the rocks and the flames, chaos infiltrated the strange field.

The grass in front of him burst into cinders moments before he could take cover in it. Ren skidded away just in time, his boots slipping on the damp ground. Around him, the tall, beautiful golden stalks melted like burning candles.

Ren was pretty sure he had a problem.

"You!" came a shout.

He definitely had a problem.

Instinct made him fling himself backward. In the same instant, the place where he'd been standing erupted. He half turned, searching for somewhere else to go, field and fog and fire a trap. He dropped his remaining rocks, and they scattered at his feet, forgotten. The field was catching, flames jumping from one blade of grass to another. Fire rained down everywhere. Ren began to doubt his brilliant plan.

Maybe I'm destined to burn. It was another nightmare of his, one that had not receded with age.

Nowhere to run. He didn't notice the monster until it was standing directly in front of him, a cape of fire at its back.

"Hello," it said to him pleasantly, and then it picked up one of Ren's abandoned rocks and clonked him over the head—

And, oh, there was the ground, opening its dirty arms to welcome him. *Oh. Oh!*

Ren fell into those muddy arms. Nico's monster laughed. The sound of it brought to mind rivers, water gushing over rocks, the gentle burble of a summer day. It was too beautiful.

Ren blinked into a watery world, the weeds near his nose swimming. The laughter echoed in his skull.

"You can't move," Nico said. The words poured through the brume and over the ground, as infinite as water in a river. His voice was hoarse, gritty, powerful.

The laughter stopped. Ren hugged the dirt, closed his eyes against the tipsy world. He wasn't sure his head was quite connected to his body anymore.

"Why did you let him go?" a wolk shrieked.

"I didn't! You're the one who let him elbow you in the face!"

"Useless!"

"You're frozen," Nico said. "Paralyzed. Your body isn't your own. It doesn't obey you any longer."

"You can't even control one little human, you filthbucket!"

Nico said, "You can't move. You can't talk. You can't think. Nothing in the world matters except for how much you hate each other."

The bickering stopped abruptly.

The need to actually see Nico made Ren act. In his mind, Nico was still flat on the ground, helpless. Ren twisted his head around, but all he could see was fading fire and a monster standing over him, unmoving. In the watery daylight, it looked like a man. It could have been anyone, one of a dozen men Ren had worked with or passed on the street in his village. It blinked down at him with blank brown eyes.

"You can't stand the sight of one another," Nico said in a steady, mesmerizing tone, all the more disturbing for the melodious softness his accent brought to the words. Blood and death wrapped in honey. "You know wolk are a monstrosity. You disgust each other. You know you don't belong here in our world. You have to destroy each other. You have to end it. You have to kill every wolk you see. Kill each other."

The man-monster standing over Ren moved, and Ren cringed against the dirt. It turned away from him, flung itself at one of its own, and squeezed the other wolk's throat.

Ren managed to get his legs to work. He sat up amid a bloody brawl. Nico's magic was instantaneous. Already, wolk thrashed each other on all sides. They fought next to Ren, but ignored him. Blood spritzed the air. Grunts and groans filled the alleys between the soft undulations of grass. The field had transformed into ash and blood and smoke. Overwhelmed, Ren finally spotted Nico. Across the field, Nico stood soaking in his mayhem. The gleam of satisfaction that lit his features was visible even from afar.

Ren swayed toward him. He approached Nico with caution, afraid he might be in some kind of magical trance, his eyes bright and dreamy, a stark contrast to the mud smeared down his cheeks and across his mouth. Dirt clung to his hair, brown against red, and muddy wet tendrils of it streaked across his forehead and temples. The entire front of his clothes was caked with mud.

After a hesitation, a bit scared of what might happen when he broke Nico's avid interest, Ren said, "Nico?"

"They deserved it," Nico said, still drinking in the violence Ren couldn't bring himself to witness. The sounds were enough: screeches, grunts, curses, and the low moans of death. Their fires were dying with them, though they'd managed to scorch a hole in the field.

"You're terrifying," Ren said. "Has anyone ever told you you're terrifying?"

"You don't know how long I've wanted to do this." He spoke with a fervent emotion Ren didn't know how to handle. "I would do worse to them if I could. They deserve worse."

That did not comfort Ren. He said, "You're destructive."

Finally, Nico turned that unnerving energy on him. "I'm sorry. Have you been mistaking me for a good person? Let me shatter that misconception for you. I enjoy seeing people and monsters alike get what they deserve. It helps me sleep at night." There was dirt on his tongue. He grimaced and spat on the ground at Ren's feet.

He walked away casually, as though he wasn't leaving death and ruination at his back, saying over his shoulder, "We should go. There'll be more of them coming. These were just the young scouts. The throwaways." He slipped away between fighting, bloody bodies.

THEY WALKED IN the frigid mist. It soaked through Ren's clothes, settled into his skin. It had to be doing the same to Nico, with only his thin black clothes, but Nico showed no intention of putting up another bubble of warmth. Ren didn't ask about it. Considering what had just happened, staying clean and warm somehow seemed less important now. Just being alive satisfied Ren.

Nico gave his face a cursory swipe with the back of his arm, smearing the mud down it. He only got half of it off his skin. Covered in grime, he resembled a fierce, dangerous thing.

He *was* a dangerous thing. Ren could not—*should not*—ever forget that.

Ren walked along uneasily. He wasn't sure if he felt disturbed because he was truly starting to realize how easily Nico could squash him, or if it was because his heart thrilled to Nico's power. Maybe both. God, it was wrong. It was all so wrong.

After a long, dizzy silence, when the sounds of violence lay far behind them, Ren said, "They look human."

He wasn't sure Nico would acknowledge him, but he said, "Not always. There are times—a certain angle, a certain light—when they don't seem quite right. Sometimes they appear *other* in mirrors and in periphery vision."

Ren remembered the split-second glimpse of unearthliness he'd caught in the forest last night during the lightning storm. "It's not right. They should look like monsters. All of the time. How is anyone supposed to know?"

Nico quirked a muddy brow at him, the rest of his expression hard to decipher beneath the dirt. "And you think evil things always come in ugly packages?"

"They should."

"But they don't."

The field stretched out around them, grass on grass on grass that merged into a gold blur. "Life would be easier then. Ugly inside, ugly outside. You'd know who to avoid."

"I'm sure they're not of this world anyway," Nico said. "No rules apply to them."

Not of this world. Ren repressed a shiver. Goose bumps trickled down his spine like a cold drop of water. "So where are they from?"

"I don't know," Nico admitted. "The horde was already here when they captured me. I once overheard them talking about the time they slipped into our world. They mentioned their home. They called it by name, but it wasn't a word. To my ears, it sounded like wind howling on a stormy day."

"They slipped in…"

"Stop," Nico said.

"What is it?"

When Ren halted, Nico came to stand in front of him. "You're bleeding."

"I am?"

"You're hurt."

"Maybe. Probably." A hazy memory of getting clobbered on the head with a rock surfaced in his mind. "Oh. I remember now." Ren sniggered. "Good thing I have a hard head."

"This is some amusing adventure to you?" Nico said it even as he took Ren's face between his hands. His fingers were sure and strong, his nails dirt-caked from clawing at the ground. "Maybe you're delirious."

Nico's warm breath on his face, a pleasant contrast to the miserable drizzle, muted Ren better than any reprimand. Standing close, Nico had to tilt his head up slightly to Ren. He swept shaggy hair from Ren's skin with featherlight fingers and then pressed his palms to Ren's temples. A warm tingle danced through Ren's head like a buzz from the best wine. Swirls of gold spun away from him, over Nico's shoulders.

"Your magic is gold," Ren whispered.

Nico didn't acknowledge his comment, and Ren wondered if he'd even said it aloud. He couldn't be sure. He was too busy dealing with the world dipping in and out. Gold rivers swept past him. Those unspooling rivers might have been in the air or inside his head. He wanted to run his fingers through the gold, like dipping his toes into a sun-warmed river.

This is real magic. The magic I came to see last night. I found it after all.

Nico's fingers edged into his hair, the tips cool against his scalp, and the world stilled. It wasn't until then that Ren realized everything had become unbalanced when the rock had connected with his skull. But when he touched two fingers to his head, he felt nothing but smooth skin. His fingers came away blood-smeared, but the wound was gone. He wiped the blood on his pants.

"The last thing I need is for you to faint," Nico said, his breath soft on Ren's face, his lashes long and absurdly reddish, his fingers sweet and fidgety in Ren's hair. "I refuse to drag you behind me."

"Thanks for fixing my head," Ren said softly.

Nico glanced up at him through his lashes, the lilt of his words curious and cautious. "Thanks for saving me back there. I couldn't have— Just. Thank you. Ren."

Ren snorted. "I almost got myself toasted alive."

"You distracted them. It gave me just enough time."

Unwittingly, their bodies had drawn closer as they talked. Nico's heat spread to Ren, a languid comfort. He wanted to inhale Nico. Hold Nico's scent deep in his lungs, absorb some of that strength.

"I told you we make a good team," Ren said as he wiped mud from Nico's cheeks with his thumbs. "I flap around and nearly get myself killed while you work your spells."

"I—" Nico's mouth hung open.

Kindly, Ren said, "You what?"

"Don't get yourself killed for me. I might not be able to save you next time."

"I bet you could do anything," Ren said, and it came out a little too awe-hushed.

Nico choked off a pained sound. "If I had the ability to do anything, I wouldn't be living with monsters."

"You're not living with them," Ren said. "You got away."

"I haven't gotten away. They're hunting us through this field."

His hands slid from Ren's hair, but Ren reached up and caught his wrists. He wasn't ready to let go of the moment yet. Relenting, Nico let his arms rest on Ren's shoulders. His fingertips teased the back of Ren's neck with the barest tickle of contact, a touch that could almost be called accidental. Ren would have done anything and everything to keep Nico's hands just there, to stand like that for another hour.

"I know you can protect us. You're amazing. Your magic is...it's something I've only ever dreamed of. I never thought something so immense could actually exist."

He thought about easing his arms around Nico's waist, settling them in the perfect dip at the small of Nico's back. This part—slipping perfectly into the moment— usually came naturally to him. With Nico, he had to think about it. He had to measure every touch, every word. He'd never had to work this hard to be close to someone. Would it be too much if he wiped the mud smears from Nico's mouth with his fingers?

"Oh," Nico said quietly.

"What?"

"I have mud on my mouth?"

He'd nearly forgotten how far Nico's ability extended.

"Yes," Ren said cautiously, "here." He trailed a single finger down Nico's cheek, let it graze across Nico's bottom lip, swiping dirt away with his finger.

Nico turned his face from Ren's touch, wiped his mouth against his shoulder several times. "I think I swallowed an entire meal of dirt."

Ren's hand still hung in the empty air between them. He let it drop.

More quietly, as Ren's confidence fell away, Nico said, "I feel a little sick."

"Sick?"

"There's dirt in the back of my throat." Gently, he retreated from Ren, each movement a deliberate step away.

Cold drizzled down Ren's neck where Nico's hands had been, a sorry replacement for the spark of fingertips against his skin.

With a safe, untouchable distance between their bodies, Nico said in a low voice, "You need to stop."

Around them, a *pitter-patter* grew louder and louder as sudden hard rain hit the blades of grass. Ren and Nico were soaked within moments.

"I didn't do anything," Ren said over the rain.

"Stop thinking of me like that."

"I don't—I didn't—" Ren had a mouthful of pathetic lies and denials that neither of them needed to hear aloud.

"Don't think about kissing me when—when I was just forced to eat dirt. I'm tired, Ren. I don't need this. I don't need you...*gazing* at me." Nico started to rub the back of his arm across his face but ended up getting the dirt that had been caked on his sleeve into his eye. "Fuck!" he yelled with vehemence. "I can't—" He doubled forward, scrubbing furiously. "Shit! *Shit!*"

Ren went to him. Couldn't *not* go to him. He put his hand on Nico's hunched shoulder. "Let me see."

Nico's shoulders heaved with a dragged-in breath. "I want to give up. I'm just—I'm *done*. I can't do this anymore."

"I think you can do anything."

"You don't understand. I *can't*. I can't take it anymore."

"Nico." Ren kept his voice steady, his hand solid, firm. "I can get the dirt out." He pulled at Nico's shoulder until Nico finally straightened. Ren kept his hand there on Nico's shoulder, his palm cupped firmly around bone and muscle, but made sure not to touch Nico in any other way. Ren never made the same mistake twice.

When Nico raised his head, his eye was red and watering, and the look he gave Ren was too exhausted to have much force behind it. "I'm a fucking mess," he said.

"I know. Close your eyes."

There were tiny particles of dirt in his fine red brows and specks of it caught in the pale wet clump of his lashes. With the edge of his sleeve, Ren wiped carefully at it. He pulled Nico's face closer and blew the rest of the dirt away. He didn't miss Nico's brief flinch and the way he twitched. He'd allowed himself a moment of vulnerability, and that was enough to agitate him.

Ren gripped Nico's shoulder tighter in emphasis and thought, *I'm sorry.*

Nico squinted at him. He immediately brought his hand up and rubbed. Ren caught his wrist, dragged his hand down and away from his face.

"You'll make it worse," Ren said and held his cupped hand out to let it fill with rainwater. "Here. It needs to be rinsed out." He tilted Nico's face up and drizzled the water into his eye.

Nico jerked slightly and made a sound.

"Better?" Ren asked, withdrawing.

Nico blinked several times. "Better." He gave Ren's arm a squeeze. "Thanks." With nothing more, he put his back to Ren, casually, as though they hadn't been within kissing distance moments before, as though Nico hadn't just veered around a meltdown.

With empty, aching arms, Ren fell into place beside Nico.

The rain seemed to walk with them, stalking them through the field, nipping at their necks with cold teeth. It ran down the grass in rivers and turned the dirt into mud. A small lake grew at their feet.

"Do you know what they were doing to me back there?" Nico asked him, the question harsh and sudden.

Ren felt the words click in the back of his throat, too ugly to say aloud. "I thought they— They were going to—"

Nico waited, but Ren wouldn't finish it. Nico's shoulders sagged, taking his expression down with them. He folded his arms across his chest, shivered. Water dripped from his nose. "They were draining my magic."

Being with Nico, enveloped in his extraordinary world, was like being a leaf, aimless and drifting, controlled by the wind. "But—why?"

"They don't have any of their own, except the ability to control fire." Nico's expression was watchful, studious. "And I have a lot of it."

"You're saying it's a commodity?"

The stinging rain pelted their faces with giant drops. Nico's thin clothes were soaked through and clinging to his body. His hair stuck to his face and neck in wet tendrils. He hunched into his own arms, shoulders curled inward, shivering slightly. "It was never meant to be a commodity. Magic is a part of being human."

"And they're not human."

"Decidedly not." Nico shook his head. "Magic is personal, intimate. It's a part of your body."

"So," Ren said slowly, the horror of it dawning, "they're ripping out pieces of your body when they drain you?"

"They drain it out through your skin," Nico said. "At first, it feels like I'm unspooling into the air. By the time they finish, it's like a piece of my body has been cut out of my chest. They suck the vitality out of you. It's like the wind is blowing and the stars are out, but you don't care. After they're done with you, you don't have the energy to care." Unconsciously, he pressed a palm to his chest as though he could feel the loss now, an ache where an intrinsic part of him had been minutes ago but was now missing.

Ren found himself staring at Nico's hand, where he held it against his body, like soothing an ache deep inside. Nico caught Ren's expression of horror-shock and dropped his hand to his side.

"Magic replenishes overnight when I sleep, for them to do it all over again the next day."

"They do that to you every day?" Ren whispered it. It didn't feel like something that should be spoken aloud. His voice was barely audible over the rush of rain shaking the grass above them. The field shuddered in the storm. High above, golden grass rustled and tangled together in the wind.

"Not...every day. And not so aggressively." Nico hunched his shoulders, bundled into himself. He tilted his face up into the rain. "I don't like to be touched. I don't like to be *pursued*."

"I understand," Ren said quietly.

"Do you?"

Tactile comfort came naturally to Ren. He liked pulling people close, offering them the shelter of his arms and the warmth of his body. It always made him feel better too, less lonely with someone's body pressed into his own, two solid against the world. But he and Nico weren't two solid. Half of their time together was confusion. The other half was picking at each other: picking at answers, picking at the differences that made them unknowable to each other, picking at little scraps of info that helped them learn each other.

"I'm starting to." With aching, empty arms, Ren asked, "Why can't you fight them with your magic?"

Nico's laugh was rough, pained. "Because there are two hundred of them in the horde, and I'm only one man. I can't fight them alone. I would only go against them if I felt like taking a thorough trouncing."

There was water in Ren's ears, in his nose, and in his throat. He shook his head, and his hair flopped wetly around his head. "But you're powerful. You just took down twenty of them at once back there. And you killed six of them last night."

"You don't understand." There were thin threads of exhaustion in Nico's voice, an old weariness, the kind that settled into bones and being. "There's a big difference between twenty and two hundred. The magic I do is called 'telling magic.' You have to hook into the mind. Feed the brain a story it will believe. Convince the mind against the owner's will before they have a chance to physically attack. It's intricate and complicated. Most practitioners don't do it because it takes concentration and an enormous amount of magic, and they don't have enough. Doing it to more than one mind at once is...nearly unheard of."

The glimpses of Nico's skill and its inner workings were mesmerizing. Ren said, "You do it."

Nico considered him. "I have an enormous amount of magic." He stated it with no trace of hubris, simply a fact. "Enough to make them want to keep me, to use me. Not enough to fight them. If I miss one of them when I'm latching into their minds, I'm done. And I would miss more than one if I tried it. It's inevitable with that many. I don't have the power to take on two hundred monsters at once."

Dark patches showed on Nico's thin shirt all across his shoulders and down his back where the rain had soaked through. The back of his neck glistened. The tips of hair at his nape dripped down the collar of his shirt. Ren didn't even have to think about it. In one smooth motion, he took his coat off and swung it across Nico's shoulders.

Nico spun away from him, an elegant sweep that reminded Ren of his graceful fluidity during his performance in the trees. Already shrugging one shoulder out of it, Nico said, "I'm not taking your coat from you."

Ren dragged it back over his shoulder. He stood in front of Nico, tugged the coat lapels together before Nico could shimmy away. It wasn't a great coat, too rough and scratchy, but it was warm and better than nothing. "Keep it," Ren said, pleased to see Nico bundled up in it. "I'm all right."

"I don't need it." But he didn't try to take it off again. Nico's fingers snuck out around the coat's edges, uneasy, torn between ripping the coat off or retreating into the warmth, a moment of indecision on his face.

"You need it more than I do," Ren said. "You look amazing in those clothes, but they weren't made for anywhere outside of that carnival." He made a waving motion with his arms that mimicked swooping through the air birdlike, purposely exaggerated, hoping for a sign of mirth. It didn't work. *It's not a humorous time.*

Ren let his arms drop, feeling slightly ridiculous. He was trying too hard, and he knew it. Trying to amuse, trying to get Nico to warm to him, trying to comfort, trying to find a connection. Trying to understand the man. None of it was working.

He couldn't figure out how to communicate, how to function, in such an inconceivable situation.

Nico wiped rain from his face and said, "I can't create warmth for us right now. They drained too much from me. I have to save what's left to get us out of here." He hesitated even as he stood there shivering. "I know you must be cold too."

"I'll be fine. You already kept me warm and dry once. Now it's my turn. Keep the coat."

Sighing, Nico slipped his arms into the sleeves, tucked his hands up into the warmth, and pulled the coat tight. "Maybe for a few minutes," he said. "Until I can feel my fingers again."

Seeing him wrapped in its oversized folds thrilled Ren in a way he knew well. It was a thing of his, a fetish perhaps. He enjoyed it when his lovers lingered in the comfort of his bed, lazed in his clothes, the fabric of his shirt brushing their skin in the same spots it had brushed against his own body. He liked how seeing his things envelop his lovers made his arms ache with the anticipation of peeling the clothes and blankets off them and using his body to cover them instead. A delicious tease. Seeing his clothes on them always made him think, *Soon.*

Ren didn't think "soon" with Nico in his coat. He thought, *Safe. For now.*

The coat fit Ren well, with a bit of extra room for his shoulders, but it draped over Nico like a small blanket. Ren liked that. If he couldn't hold Nico, at least his coat could. It would do.

They walked on. The soggy ground passed beneath their feet. Ren waited for some unnamable thing to open up between them. Whatever it was, it never came.

Huddled deep in the coat with his arms folded tightly against his chest, the musical roll of Nico's voice was muffled in the wide collar of Ren's coat when he said, "You're too nice."

The field was slowly thinning. The grass was less dense, and the land began to slope upward. The clouds piled high above them, cushioning them between hills and mountains and wheat and rain.

Ren tilted his face skyward and laughed, let the misty rain against his cheeks chill away some of his sparking nerves. "There's no such thing as too nice."

"It might have been fine in your village, but outside of your home it'll get you killed. It only shows how much you shouldn't be here with me. You don't belong in this."

"But maybe I was meant to be here. Maybe we crashed into each other for a reason." Warming to the idea, Ren said, "Maybe I'm supposed to help you escape them."

Nico pulled the collar up even higher around his neck, over his mouth. He didn't speak until he had the lower half of his face burrowed into the coat. "We crashed into each other because you're tall, and I saw you coming a mile away."

Ren's feet slowed. "Wait. You saw me?"

"I chose you." At first, Ren couldn't tell if Nico addressed him or the fog. Clearly the drippy grass and rainy mist ahead of them were fascinating. "I needed an obvious reason to leave the camp," Nico said. "You were big and conspicuous. And I knew you would probably cushion my landing."

Nico might as well have tipped Ren's world off axis. "You planned the collision?"

"I would have let you go if you hadn't shown so much...interest." Nico's voice hitched on the word *interest*, a raw little crack that made it sound far more perverse. "I almost walked away because you looked too young when I saw you up close. I had to find someone who wanted me. Someone who would go into the woods with me." He shivered suddenly and brought his hands up to wipe the rain from his face with the coat sleeves.

Ren blinked, flabbergasted. "And here I thought it was fate." He viewed Nico with a slightly altered understanding. "You're a sneaky one."

"I have to be." Stated flatly.

They had both slowed. The ground, a marshy mix of grass and mud and rocks, sucked at their boots. The heavy air held more unshed rain. "Were you good at tricking the wolk too?" Ren asked.

The air crackled dangerously as the conversation paused, Nico absorbing the question as though he couldn't quite believe Ren had asked it. "No." They walked a long while in the wet air, under tall dripping grass, before Nico said, "They're good at tricking me."

Ren gave him a sideways glance. "You never acted with them?"

"Acted?"

"To manipulate them, like you did with me."

For a moment, there was nothing but the sound of their feet in the wet dirt, a loud squelch on each footfall.

Nico said slowly, "Are you asking me if I flirted with those creatures?"

"I—no." When Nico put it out there so starkly, it sounded twisted and improbable.

Nico shook his head, the raindrops in his hair trickling down onto the coat. "You don't get it," he said, his voice even more potent in the steady rain. "There's no manipulating them. They do the manipulating. They're not people. They don't behave like anyone you know. God, you really—you don't understand at all."

Ren waited, knowing Nico wasn't finished. There was loathing tight around Nico's mouth.

"Do you want to know just how powerless I am against them?" Nico spat out "powerless." His mellifluous accent rolled over the syllables in a strange contrast to the feeling behind the word.

There was no answer to that question. "Make me understand," Ren said.

"Last year," Nico said, "just for me, they brought a man into our camp. They made me come outside and watch while they gang-raped him and then drained the life out of him until they had sucked his soul right out of his body. He was...screaming the whole time." Nico's voice hitched. "And there was nothing I could do."

Ren had stopped walking. He didn't know when he had stopped, just that suddenly he was standing very still in the middle of nowhere. Several feet ahead of him, Nico had also halted. Ren stood staring at Nico's back, at the elegant curve of his shoulders and the tension gathering there.

Ren had to clear his throat, clear away the shock, before he said, "Is that why you were running away from them? Because—they hurt you too?"

Nico's shoulders stiffened even further, but he didn't turn to face Ren. "No."

"No?" Ren said softly.

"You think any of them would dare touch me when I could order them to cut off their own dick? No, they brought that man into camp because they couldn't do that to me. He died because he was a substitute. Because...I wouldn't do what they wanted."

Ren didn't know what to say, but Nico continued over his silence.

"I left because of the things I saw them do to other people. Regular people like you. Like the man they brought into camp last year. I couldn't help him. I couldn't protect...any of them. I left because I couldn't watch them hurt more people while I just—while I just stood there. More and more people kept dying, and *I always just stood there*." Finally, Nico turned, and they faced each other. There was weariness in the line of Nico's shoulders, but his face was a careful blank.

Ren thought he probably made up for Nico's lack of emotion with the pity and revulsion pouring off his own body. "You lived like that for fourteen years? With them...circling you like sharks? And taking out people around you?"

Seeing it all over Ren's face, Nico said, "I'm not telling you this to get your sympathy. Don't pity me. I'm not the one who died. I'm telling you so you'll understand what they are and how—" The words seemed to choke him. "—and how fucking *impotent* I am."

"Sympathetic is not what I'm feeling right now." It wasn't an urge that came upon Ren often—not since he had been a teenager with the fresh-raw loss of his ma—but he wanted to snap someone in half. He wanted to feel a life trapped in his hands. He hadn't felt this way since the last time he'd seen his father. The anger simmered deep in his muscles, hot and useless and *familiar*. He had no one to take it out on. It was only him and Nico staring at each other across a quagmire.

Nico stood very still, the wind pulling at him, lifting strands of hair the color of autumn leaves. He huddled in the coat, crossed his arms inside it. "I don't have any influence or power in this. I'm not going to be able to come to your rescue if things get bad. I'm not going to be able to wave my hands and make everything better. I'm not some kind of magical hero. So far, we've just gotten lucky. It could easily go the other way. Tell me you understand that."

Ren swallowed. There were a dozen things he wanted to say and another dozen feelings he couldn't put into words. He said only, "I get it."

Nico paused for a moment, measuring his sincerity. "If they catch us again, I want you to run. I can't promise they won't come after you, but it's me they want. Once they have me, you might be able to get away while they take care of me."

Take care of me. Ren thought he might throw up right there in the middle of the field, in the midst of a downpour. "You told me they wouldn't kill you."

An ugly sound escaped Nico, something between a laugh and a sob. "They won't."

Ren swallowed the bile creeping up the back of his throat. *Shit.*

Nico said, "I have to be alive for them to drain my magic."

"No way." Ren was shaking his head, couldn't seem to stop. "No. I'm not leaving you to that fate."

Nico took a hasty step forward. He stopped himself from coming closer, but the urgency was in his voice. "You think watching them gang-rape and kill you will *help* me?"

Ren spread his arms wide, let the rain soak through his skin. "I helped you this last time. We worked together, and that's the only reason we escaped. What if I had run away instead of staying? Actually, you're lucky I was there. You're damn lucky, Nico."

"Right," Nico said. "*Lucky.* Do you know how close we were to capture? Do you think we'll keep getting that lucky? Ren, I know you're stubborn, but don't make yourself another one of their victims when you might have a chance to escape." Nico's voice softened, and it was almost too perfect, too showy. "Don't make me live with your death."

Ren recognized Nico's particular brand of manipulation now, could tell when he was using it because he sounded completely unlike the raw, earnest man Ren had glimpsed earlier. Nico might not have been able to manipulate the wolk, but from what Ren could tell, he was brilliant at manipulating people. Ren wondered how many acts he had in his repertoire, how many roles he'd perfected.

"Fine," Ren said. "If it comes to it, I'll run."

Nico gave him a single sharp nod and turned.

Ren was glad there was a safe distance between them then, glad that Nico couldn't brush his fingers against that lie. Ren would never take off and leave Nico behind to be brutalized. What kind of man would that make him? Certainly not one he would ever want to meet, much less be.

THEY WALKED. THE silence ballooned around them. The cool air was full of pent-up moisture, and the towering grass dripped rain from high above onto their heads. Fog hung everywhere. Autumn had arrived on its usual cloud of rain. Ren would have loved it if he hadn't been walking through it.

"I get why you told them to destroy each other," Ren said into the quiet. "They're evil."

"I didn't ask for your approval."

"I don't care. I want to destroy them with you."

Nico snorted. The relentless rain made him squint when he turned to Ren. "How sweet. Do you propose death and ruin to every man you've just met?"

"I'm serious, Nico. They tormented you for fun, didn't they? They tortured that man for revenge. They killed all of those people in the woods just because they could. And they—" The reality of it hooked into his heart, caught in the back of his throat so that he had to breathe in deeply and then force it out. "They destroyed my village. For no reason. Just because they had the power to do it. All of those people...good people."

"Two men against two hundred monsters. What do you think our odds are?"

Ren wiped wetness off his cheeks—rain, only rain— had to clear a throat suddenly closing up. *Everyone.* He'd lost everyone and everything. They were gone. They were dust. Kyle and Syd, Micah and Jens, Sara and— *No, no, no. Don't think of each of them. Don't start picturing their faces, or the last words they said to me, the last hug, don't, don't. Oh God, I wasn't going to think about this, oh God, oh—*

He'd gained Nico's attention. Nico came closer. "Ren?"

Ren shook his head. His heart pounded so loudly in his ears he thought it must be about to burst. *Everything, everything, it's all—gone.*

Hands clasped his upper arms, grip pinching tight. "Ren. Look at me." That lilting voice like a song drifting over the sound of his pounding blood. "Ren. Can you hear me? Take a deep breath."

Breathe? He couldn't breathe. He was going to vomit, eject all of his grief there in the dirt so he wouldn't have to hold it in his heart. His heart beat so loudly. But, no. He wasn't supposed to think about it. He wasn't going to think about— *Sarria and Benji and Willis and Col, gone gone gone, all gone.* Nico wavered in front of him, ghostly. A blur framed Ren's vision, blocking out everything but Nico's face, his pale-brown eyes wide, so wide, so alarmed, Nico had so much to be scared of, they both had so much—

Nico squeezed his arms so hard the pain momentarily cleared the fuzz from Ren's head.

"Concentrate on your heartbeat," Nico said. The deep, dulcet tones of his voice rolled through Ren's body, vibrated in his brain. Nico's voice was smooth enough to get lost in. "Close your eyes, and listen to the sound of your heart pumping life through your body." Ren's mind drifted. "Focus on its steady rhythm. Count each individual beat. Think of nothing else. It's just you and your heartbeat, you and the blood pumping through your body. Picture the blood flowing through your veins, giving you life. You're alive. Nothing else matters at the moment. You're alive and you'll figure out the rest. Just focus on being. Listen to your heart and know that you're alive. You're in this moment. There's nothing else, just this moment."

I'm alive. Nothing else matters right now. I'm still here. Nothing else. Nothing else. Ren took in a deep breath, released it, sucked in another breath. Golden specks flittered behind his lids.

"You know you'll make it through this. You've already made it through a lot."

I can handle it. I can make it. He breathed in and out again.

"You're all right, Ren. Now look at me."

Ren released a sigh that loosened his muscles. The damp light cast Nico's eyes gold as he peered into Ren's face. Ren breathed in yet again. Nico was so close. Ren could smell his warmth. It grounded him further.

"All right?" Nico asked.

Ren's head felt clearer than it had since he'd first walked into the magic-spiced air of the carnival. A numb, dreamy heaviness had lifted.

"You used your telling magic on me," Ren said blinking, gathering his rampant thoughts into something more manageable. His mind had almost scattered in the wind, but Nico's arms were keeping him together.

Though Ren had said it more in surprise than accusation, Nico pulled his hands away, ran his palms down his thighs. "You were having a panic attack."

Ren blinked at him. "Is that what that was?"

"It's not surprising considering what you've been through in the past day. It happens."

Ren stretched his arms over his head, up to the sky. Wiggled his fingers at the fog. "I feel a bit better. Thank you. Things are still...you know. But I don't feel as...bogged down by all of it." It was still in the back of his mind, a big ball of grief, but it wasn't about to engulf him again. Not yet. Not right now.

As solemn as ever, Nico said, "I'm sorry."

"For what? You didn't do anything wrong. Just warn me next time before you use that magic on me."

"Gods," Nico said, withdrawing, "I should stay away from people."

"See this here?" Ren waved a hand up and down his torso. "This is an adult. You're not responsible for me."

Nico checked him out, shrugged a shoulder. "But you do have a baby face." He turned away, saying to the trees, "We need to keep going."

"Is it the dimples?" Ren asked, syncing their footsteps. "People tell me it's the dimples."

"Your dimples are"—Nico seemed to fall over the next word—"fine."

Ren couldn't keep back a small smile, pleased, but Nico was busy carefully studying the rise of land where they stood. Amid the hills, it became a lot harder to see beyond them. The hilly terrain might as well have rolled on forever.

"We have to climb one," Nico said. "I need a better view."

When they reached the crest of a tall one, the field fell away from them. The land unfolded at their feet, laying out more fog-drenched hills. The world Ren had grown up in was gone. There was truly no going back now. Nico paused at the apex. He turned in a slow circle, prey on the lookout for danger.

Goose bumps prickled the back of Ren's neck when he thought he spotted movement below, but it was only the wind playing strange games with the fog.

"Thank you for calming me down back there," Ren said. "Listening to my heartbeat was exactly what I needed. How did you know?"

"It's what I do when I'm having a panic attack," Nico said.

Ren turned to him in surprise. "You?"

Nico was bundled so far into the coat that only his eyes and the red of his hair showed. The more he got of Nico's story, the more he wanted to take him in his arms, ease him into his bed, lie in safe warmth together with the fluffiest blanket he could find. Nico's world was so far from the grand adventure Ren had first imagined.

"I'd have panic attacks too if I lived with monsters," Ren said. "I don't think I'd ever be able to sleep."

Muffled in wool, Nico said, "They're not the ones who give me panic attacks."

"No?" Ren couldn't help it. He had to know. "Who?"

Nico shivered as the wind raked fog over them, a damp caress. He took so long to answer Ren thought he'd abandoned the conversation altogether. But then he surprised Ren by saying, "People."

Ren said carefully, "People. As in regular everyday humans?"

Beneath the coat, Nico rolled his shoulders before he spoke, seeming to contemplate his words. "The wolk want power at the cost of death and destruction. They crave it. It's their end goal. But people—people spend their lives searching and destroying because they don't know what they want, what they crave. They just feel hungry for something they can't name. So they throw themselves into things to try and fill the emptiness. Mostly crap."

Nonplussed, Ren rubbed his forehead. "And by crap you mean?"

"Sex," Nico said.

"Oh." Sex was far from crap in Ren's experience. In truth, he couldn't get enough of it, and he'd never had a lack of willing partners who felt the same. It made him feel good, made his partner feel good. It left them both soaring, left Ren smiling throughout the next day.

Nico let out a sigh full of contempt. There was rain and hair in his eyes, and the expression on his face said he'd rather be anywhere else in the world. "You don't agree. Let me guess. You think sex is all rainbows and sparkles, just like everything else in your life."

"My life isn't rainbows and sparkles. It never was." Ren took a deep, wet breath, let it prickle down his throat. "But sex is the best high in the world. Maybe you haven't been having the right kind of sex."

"Of course," Nico said. An ugly, rough laugh leaked out between the folds of Ren's coat collar. "That must be it."

"If you had actually had sex with me when you took me into the woods—"

Nico turned on him sharply, with a force Ren could actually feel. Ren realized his mistake too late.

"Don't say you could have shown me how great sex can be," Nico said, voice a tightly coiled thing. "Don't you dare say something that absurd to me, you smug little shit."

"I shouldn't have—"

"I swear, I'll leave you here alone."

From the set of Nico's shoulders, the intensity behind his eyes, Ren believed he was, in fact, completely serious. Nico was a prickly thorn that Ren didn't want to brush against too hard.

"You're right," he said quickly. "It's not my place to judge. My life hasn't been sparkles and rainbows, but it's been decent for the last few years. I've lived a safe life for a while now and"—softer, to cushion his boldness—"I know you didn't have that."

A layer of raindrops glistened in Nico's hair when he turned to Ren, dewy silver against red, like a celebration, though their lives were far from celebratory.

"I don't remember what it's like to live without always having to look over my shoulder. It's been...hell."

Ren took a chance. He put his hands on Nico's scratchy wool arms, and it felt a bit like balancing his life on the nose of a lion. Too close, too soon, too quick, and he'd be a goner. By now, he knew Nico could end him with a glance. That knowledge should terrify him, but it didn't.

Ren gave him a squeeze through the thick fabric. There always seemed to be so many layers between them. "You took action. You already changed the course of everything in your life."

"You're so damn sunny," Nico said, wincing, "it hurts my head. You're ridiculous."

Ren opened his mouth, and the hilltop exploded.

It took Ren a long time—minutes, hours—to realize it was an explosion not of earth but of fiery light. Light so dazzling it knocked him to the ground. His world blotted out, nothing but searing red-orange and pain.

He might have shouted at one point. He wasn't sure. Light leaked in around his eyelids. Stunned, one moment, he was lying flat on his back, and then he wasn't. He was standing with an arm squeezing his throat and bodies to either side of him. The clouds swayed and blades of grass were fragile-thin silhouettes against the light. Ren scoured the hilltop. He couldn't find Nico, and that scared him more than anything.

The light faded long before Ren's sight cleared. Phantom spots dizzied him, and the world seemed suddenly darker with the absence of the white light. And there before him, several paces away—thank the Gods of every season—was Nico. He was on his feet, leaning forward, poised as if to pounce. His gaze latched onto Ren's, wheat-gold in the gray light and stricken.

He said to Ren, "Don't move." The hand he held out shook.

"Shut that mouth, Nico," came a voice behind Ren. "One fast move. Try me."

The bodies surrounding Ren put their hands on his skin. Against all instinct, Ren did what Nico told him to do. He didn't move, but the rest of the world did. It tilted, shimmering at the edges, so crisp Ren was sure he could reach out and touch the corners of the mountains, could touch bits of the world he hadn't noticed until now.

"Ooh," said a molasses-thick voice against the shell of Ren's ear, "he's a good one, Nic. Such sweet magic. It's so clear. So pure. There's so much of it. He's lovely. You have excellent taste."

Every sharp, beautiful angle of Nico's body shone in crystalline detail, glowing star-points where bone connected to bone, twinkling lights when he moved. Gods, he was amazing, as alluring and mysterious as a starry sky. Nico made a move toward Ren, and the world receded, dimming out.

A voice on the other side of Ren said, "Don't do it! One move and we'll suck the life right out of him before you can say, 'Oops.'"

"He won't stop us," said another voice. "How much magic do you have left after they drained you back there, Nico? Hm?"

"He can't stop us." There it was again, that incongruous, tinkling laughter of theirs, right in Ren's ear.

"Don't worry, Nico. You're dessert. We'll suck you down next, and we'll take our time with you."

Ren was losing track of the voices, of the world. The corners of reality were fading, the rain and cold ebbing. Nico seemed distant, but he was still an extravagant spectacle of tiny shifting lights, the most prominent thing in the dimming world, the illumination of his body a strange and familiar dream to Ren. Sleepily, he kept his focus on Nico. It was so hard to stay awake, but Nico was glowing gold, and Ren could see nothing but him.

"He's simmering. Look at him. Maybe he actually likes this one."

"He doesn't like any of the dozens of losers he's slept with."

"Dozens? Don't be ridiculous. I'd say he's into the hundreds by now." Their laughter sounded like bells at a Winter's Eve festival.

Nico never took his attention away from Ren, but his eyes flared at their commentary.

"Our Nico does like to sleep around."

Nico crackled with translucent specks of light. A delicate blanket of glimmering gold covered him from head to foot. Ren was too fascinated to understand, drunk on confusion and the lights of Nico's body. The glow brightened.

"Be polite, Nico," they said. "Wait your turn. Let us taste your human first. I think he's going to be a good one."

Ren felt a *pull*, like nothing he'd ever experienced before. He could feel his life quite suddenly, as a lazy river he carried inside his body. Something was stirring it. It rushed through his body, and the *pull* called to it. The world whirled. Ren's head spun.

"What strange magic he has," they said.

"Deeper than usual," they said.

"What a wonderful, untapped well." A delighted hiss in Ren's ear.

Delicate gold strands swirled outward from Nico, as if ready to break free.

"Oh, yes! What a treat. The first sip. Ready?"

"We're going to have to finish off your boy, Nico. He's too delicious. I'm sure you'll find another. Thank you for picking such a ripe one. He's so *full* of magic."

The world dipped and dimmed further. Ren couldn't feel his legs. He thought maybe he should be worried, but the emotion spun away from him.

"How odd," came a voice from behind him.

"I'm lapping at his magic," said another.

"Me too."

"But I can't reach it. I can only get a taste."

"Where is his magic?"

The voices murmured over each other, rising like the burble of a stream over rocks.

The lights limning Nico brightened, illuminating the whole forest in sunset-gold. Nico was the brightest, most beautiful thing Ren had ever seen. The world snapped back into vivid clarity. The gold light shook free of Nico, scattered into the air, a lazy swirl in the sky, where it eventually faded. The forest came back into focus.

Ren was free. He didn't immediately realize the hands and bodies that had been crowding against him were gone. It took Nico's desperate, raw yelling for Ren to come back to himself.

"Run! Run! Ren! *Run!*"

Finally, Ren did as he was told. He ran.

At his back, Nico pounded the dirt hard. They raced down the hill and crashed back into the relative cover of the field. They flew together through the maze of wheat, blades of it whipping at their faces as they flung themselves between the stalks. Minutes went by with nothing but the sound of their breaths dragging in and out, with nothing but their feet hitting the mud. The ground sucked at their boots with each step.

"Stop," Nico panted from farther behind, his breaths ragged.

Ren turned and Nico came to him. He was such a convenient, perfect height for Ren. He leaned his forehead on Nico's shoulder and released explosive gusts of air into Nico's collarbone.

Nico pulled Ren against him, dragged their bodies flush. He tucked himself against Ren's chest, mouth to Ren's collarbone, and wound his arms beneath Ren's shirt to press firm hands—a cold shock—against the bare skin of Ren's back.

Ren didn't have to be told. *Touch me*, Nico had said the first time. *Touch my skin.* Ren remembered that quite clearly.

Instead of buttoning in the warmth, Nico had left the coat flapping open. Ren reached into it, lifted the front of Nico's thin shirt, and ran his hands along Nico's stomach. It was a dream, the slightest glimpse of what he could have if only. *If only.* He couldn't help but indulge himself for four more precious seconds, taking in the feel of warm, taut skin and supple muscles, his thumbs briefly circling Nico's belly button.

The hitch of Nico's breath brought Ren back to himself. He dragged his hands past Nico's hips and settled them low on Nico's back, fingers edging against the waistband of Nico's pants, and held on.

"We're water," Nico said into the skin of his neck, his sweet timbre vibrating in Ren's chest. "Our bodies are liquid gathering in the clouds, flowing from the sky, falling freely. We're liquid." Nico's voice flowed over him like the water he spoke of. "Our bodies are light and free. Our bodies remember how it feels to be water again. We're water in the clouds, sprinkling over the land. We're—"

They came up behind Nico so fast it had to have been magic. One of them hooked an arm under Nico's neck, a hand over his mouth, and bodily yanked him backward with enough force to rip Ren and Nico apart.

"Going to use that pretty magic?" the wolk said, lips against Nico's ear, grossly intimate. He nipped at the shell, and Nico flinched.

The wolk yelped and yanked his hand away from Nico's mouth. It was bleeding.

Ren didn't think before he did it. He launched himself straight into both Nico and the monster, and the force of it tumbled all three of them to the ground in a messy pile of arms and legs.

Nico was sandwiched in the middle. Directly beneath Ren, he reached up, caught Ren's hand, and laced their fingers together as though it were something they had done with each other many times. The tingle of contact went from the tips of Ren's fingers all the way up his arm. He couldn't be sure whether it was magic or the thrill of feeling Nico's hand in his, even in the midst of this calamity.

The wolk clung to Nico's body, clutching at him.

Pressed together chest to chest, Nico nodded at him. Ren knew they had only a matter of seconds. Ren closed his eyes as Nico began to speak, to better feel the words reverberate in his mind, all the way down into his soul.

"It's easy to turn into water and wash away. Our bodies remember," Nico said.

"No!" the wolk howled, tangled beneath them.

"Our bodies remember. We're water, slipping right through your fingers, asshole."

The world evaporated.

Chapter Eight

NICO

This was the easy part.

Nico flew. He sprinkled across the sky. He skimmed over the strange, multicolored land. He soared down toward a dozen different shades of purple and blue and green that rippled below him, the colors a strange shine of neon against the sepia, rain-leached air. He mingled with Ren, melted into him and split away from him, always feeling him near. He wasn't happy or sad. He was content because nothing mattered. Nothing mattered, and that was how Nico liked it. No feelings, no worries. Finally, true escape.

It was easier not to feel.

He glided to earth, landed without pain, lost moments or hours to unconsciousness, blinked, and found himself gazing up into the drizzled-gray sky. He lay there awhile, let his body luxuriate in existence again. Purple grass surrounded him, soft as feathers beneath his hands. It was the first time he'd been to this particular land, and the grass felt good against his skin. He lay without moving, hands tucked into the colorful grass until he heard Ren breathing somewhere nearby to his left.

Nico had always been careful. Cautious. He kept people at bay so that his monsters would never have anything to use against him.

He still saw their hands on Ren, tasting him while Ren sagged between them. They'd used Ren against him. He'd been so close to magicking them into fucking themselves to death on branches, if only to get them away from Ren. If he'd done that, he and Ren would have both been ruined because Nico wouldn't have had the capability to get them away.

Ren should be no one to him, should mean nothing, but it was too late for that. He and Ren were now too far into each other's space for Ren to be another casualty in this. Their lives were enmeshed. There were already too many casualties. They'd all been complete strangers to Nico, but Ren had moved past the stranger stage. And the wolk knew it. Damn them, and damn Ren for weaseling himself into Nico's abysmal life.

They'd gotten under his skin, and it bothered Nico that they could still do so after all these years. He hated that they'd spilled his many dalliances to Ren, and he hated that it made him want to correct the picture their words had painted of him. He wanted to make Ren understand him in a way he'd never wanted to explain himself before.

Into the cold mist of air above, he said, "I've slept with so many people I've lost count."

He thought maybe Ren hadn't woken yet, but finally Ren cleared his throat once, twice, and said, "Why?" with the roughness of something unused, of someone who'd recently been pieced apart and melted back together.

Above, the clouds they'd just ridden raced past. Nico wished he could stay up there with them.

"To escape," Nico said.

"Sex isn't an escape if you don't enjoy it."

"To escape literally, not metaphorically."

Ren hummed softly. "How does that work? Is it magic? Some kind of sex magic?"

Nico would have laughed if he still did that sort of thing outside of the fake stuff he used on his conquests. Sometimes he forgot people didn't grow up in a world of magic and had no idea how it worked. "Sex was the only time they'd let me leave camp."

"Oh." Softly, Ren added, "You don't have to tell me this."

But he did. For some reason, he did. Now that the wolk had said it aloud, he couldn't let it go. He couldn't let their barbs be what formed Ren's impression of him, because their idea of him was that of a pretty, dangerous, insatiable little slut. They had no right to tell Ren anything about him as if they knew him, as if they were intimates, and fuck them. *Fuck them.* They didn't know him at all.

Nico had to take a deep breath. The grass gave beneath his hands when he fisted it between his fingers. "On carnival nights, I would pick some willing person and take them into the woods with me."

He'd often told himself that at least he was saving one hapless person from each carnival. He always sent them straight home afterward, never back to the carnival where one of the wolk could pick them to drain and bag. As if saving one life made him a decent person while he stood by and did nothing as they killed people by the dozens.

"Like you chose me," Ren said. The leaves on the ground crunched with Ren's movements. Nico could tell from the new angle of Ren's voice that he had sat up.

Nico sat up too, only because he didn't like someone—anyone—hovering over him while he was flat on his back. Ren gave him a tiny, unsure smile that managed to bring out his dimples. Bits of fuzzy, purple grass were stuck on his damp shirt and in his hair, the color vivid against the dark muss of it. How fresh, how untouched. How unfortunate that Nico had dragged someone so wholesome into this ugly situation. He couldn't handle the rumpled, sweet innocence on Ren's face.

Nico folded his knees against his chest and clasped his arms tightly around them to keep himself from fidgeting. He enjoyed Ren's fingers threading through the grass over and over, purple splitting and weaving between strong, calloused hands. It was distracting, mesmerizing. God, those fingers...

"I wanted them to see me going into the woods with a random someone all the time," Nico said. "I wanted them to think it was becoming a habit."

The fingers paused in the grass, mid-sweep. "You wanted them to know you were going to have sex?"

Nico made sure to be succinct. This topic was not something he wanted to dwell on for long. "It needed to become something they expected me to do. I wanted them to get used to seeing me leave with someone."

Ren bunched his hands in the fluff of grass, held on. "Oh. *Oh.* One night you would go out there with someone. They would think nothing of it because it was something you did often, and you wouldn't come back. I was that night, wasn't I?"

Nico let his head fall forward onto his knees, his face hidden, thankful for Ren's astuteness.

"You saw how well that plan went," Nico said.

Because Zeke had been waiting, Zeke, who'd always been near, always watching him, always harassing, always salivating, always following him into the woods to enjoy the show from nearby. Zeke, who'd made his life hell.

Nico had chosen the night so carefully. He'd waited a year for them to come back to this land, where he knew the wolk would be the most distracted with what the nearby villages had to offer. There was such an unusually large concentration of magic in Ren's area. The wolk loved it there, the saturated earth and the enchanted people. They absorbed gigantic, disgusting amounts of the stuff from the locals. They gorged themselves on it once a year.

That night, Zeke was supposed to have been with six other demons doing a draining party, getting their fill. That was how it always went in Ren's region. Take enough magic from each to fill themselves, but not enough to kill the locals. A bunch of dead locals didn't look good. Other villages might become as superstitious as Ren's village. Word might spread. People might stop coming to the carnivals. The wolk found it easier and safer to take a bit from several dozen hapless humans. They would awake confused, thinking it was all because of the odd drinks they'd consumed the night before.

It was never the drinks.

The night near Ren's village, that one night a year when the wolk overindulged, was the only time Zeke ever detached himself from Nico's side. This year, inexplicably, instead of being off slurping from the villagers, Zeke had been waiting for him in the woods.

Nico should have known it wouldn't work. Zeke was his constant shadow. For the last fourteen years, Zeke had made sure to always be within sight of Nico, not daring enough to actually touch him, but ever there to make Nico feel watched and gross.

Nico didn't quite feel like himself when their eyes scraped over him—a little bit too exposed, his skin too raw. Their heavy presence made him too aware of his body, because he knew that was what they reduced him to: his body, his magic, how they could use him. If he didn't control his discomfort, he'd become nothing but a panic-fast heartbeat and a dry throat when they came too near. Over the years, he'd become good at suppressing his fear. He'd become good at suppressing a lot of things.

And so a year and a half of crappy, dirty, voyeuristic sex in the woods had led to nothing. It was supposed to have been a clean break: Zeke off getting drunk on power and Nico slipping away through the woods. It was supposed to have given him several hours' head start before they realized he wasn't coming back. It was supposed to have freed him.

It didn't work. All his planning and all his hope, and it didn't work. He'd schemed for a whole year, and then he fucked it up. Now he was left sitting in this strange grass with Ren, and they were probably both done for.

Ren felt sorry for him. Nico felt it in the shift of Ren's posture.

"You slept with all those strangers to get away from your captors?" Ren asked.

Sure enough, pity dripped from Ren's voice, oozed across the ground, and pooled at Nico's feet. God, how he hated it.

"There was no other way to get out," Nico said gruffly, hoping his tone would end the conversation.

It didn't.

"I get that," Ren said. "But it's sad. It's so damn sad. You're too—you're *too much* to waste yourself like that."

Nico laughed into his knees, muffled. It was either laugh or scream. Ren must have picked up the thread of derision in his laugh.

"Forget I said that. It's none of my business, all right? It doesn't matter what you did. You're free of them now."

The scream waited in the back of Nico's throat, gathering force. "Stop talking. Just. Stop."

"I'm only trying to say—"

"How am I free of them? They're still there at every turn, right over my shoulder."

"And you keep getting away."

The incongruity of Ren's muddy boots in the untouched grass, brown against purple, comforted Nico. "For how long? Eventually I'm going to make a mistake." He was so painfully, numbingly exhausted. He could have slept there, sitting up, with his knees as a pillow. He got this way when they drained his magic down too far, so tired he could hardly move.

Ren's fingers lifted from the grass. "This area feels far away. Maybe you lost them now."

"We didn't." Nico breathed in the stale dampness of his clothes, breathed out, breathed in. *Calm down.* "Powerful magic leaves an imprint hours after it's used. It might take them some time to pick it up, but I might as well have left a trail of breadcrumbs for them to follow. Once they latch on to it again, they'll come."

Ren's regard was a heavy weight along Nico's shoulders. No way was he going to face that head-on. "They're going through a lot of trouble to get you back."

"My magic is valuable to them." Nico braced himself for the next question.

Ren let it slip away, sighing. "Well, maybe staying here isn't a good idea. Can we move faster? Should we leave now?"

"I can't get us out of here right now," Nico said, straining his hands together, anger tingling all the way to his fingertips. There it was again, the familiar helplessness that came when he was without magic, like a warm, clammy hug from an unwanted relative, suffocating and enveloping. He hated being weak. That was how they liked him. "They drained me." His loathing was there in his voice, unavoidable. "I used too much to get us here."

Technically, he could take from the surrounding grass and trees, but it wouldn't be enough to get them out. He'd need to take half this gem-colored forest for that, and it had scared Ren when he'd done it before. Truthfully, he didn't like it either. He avoided sucking magic from the natural world. It was a bad habit for any magician to form, and what he took felt foreign and wrong in his body. He'd have to leave destruction behind him if he went that route. He wasn't willing to become that person.

"We're stuck here?" Alarm gave Ren's voice a deeper pitch. It made Nico lift, not his head, but at least his eyes.

Ren couldn't hide a thing with that face. His wide mouth was twisted, his big brown eyes even rounder. Fear flashed across his features in waves before he shook himself out of it.

"My magic won't refresh until I sleep," Nico said.

Ren waved a hand at him. "Then sleep. I'll be your—" He cleared whatever he'd been about to say out of his throat. "I'll stand guard."

It wasn't that Nico didn't trust Ren. It was that he didn't trust anyone but himself to have his back while he was unconscious and vulnerable. He'd spent many nights in his tent going in and out of a light sleep, jolted awake by nothing more than shadows. It was always worse on nights after they'd deeply drained him, when he was weak and they knew he was weak, and he didn't want to leave himself vulnerable in sleep.

Like now.

But the only way to recharge and become strong again was to give himself up to sleep.

He had only the tiniest bit of magic left. And he was tired. So tired. Tired enough to sink into the purple fluff and tumble into sleep.

"I can tell you want to sleep," Ren said, a smile soft around his mouth. "You nearly died yesterday. I think you deserve rest. I promise, I'll wake you immediately if anything happens."

Nico found himself nodding and couldn't figure out why, except he was more tired than he'd ever been. "We need to at least find a place with some cover."

"Like a house with warm beds?" Ren's gentle smile grew into a grin, dimples on full display.

Nico bypassed that grin as he stood, turned away from the easy genuineness of it. He led the way to a dense clump of trees with overgrown red-and-green grass crowding the space underneath. The undergrowth grew so closely packed it formed a small cave of sorts, with the red and green grass piled like a stack of pillows against the tree trunks. Nico crawled in first, scooted over as Ren squeezed his much larger frame inside as well. It put them close, their shoulders and legs inches from touching.

This might have been a bad idea. Nico was not good with prolonged close proximity to...anyone.

Though it wasn't raining anymore, everything was damp. Nico's crappy aerial performance clothes were soggy and useless. They'd been alternating between wet and damp for hours. He was sure he probably smelled sour. He lay back against the varicolored grass, and his body sank right down into it, cushioned.

Between Ren's coat and Ren's body nearby, it was like being surrounded by him. Ren's scent wafted to him every time he moved, the soapy musk pressed into the coat's fabric. It wasn't unpleasant.

"That actually looks snug," Ren said. All of his interest zeroed in on Nico as he settled in for sleep.

Ren was always watching Nico with a sweetly amused expression on his face, as though Nico might pull a magic trick out of his ass at any moment, and he didn't want to miss it. Nico was no stranger to being watched all of the time. And, in such a closed space, it proved impossible for the both of them not to be aware of each other's every motion.

From the depths of the grass-fluff, Nico shrugged. "It could be worse." But it really wasn't bad. Surprisingly. The grass expanded to support him, protective, while also giving him a nice little shield. He'd had a pillow this soft, once, long ago—at home.

Nico shifted, burrowed a bit. "Do you want your coat back now?"

"No, I'm fine. It'll keep you warm while you sleep."

Nico was a little relieved he didn't have to give up the warmth just yet. "Wake me up at the first sign of anything."

"I will."

"Wake me if you get tired and want to switch."

Ren smiled at that. He was so free with those smiles, and he had so many different ones to share. A whole collection of smiles, each one as startlingly refreshing as the last. This smile crinkled his nose a bit and—no. *No.* Nico averted his eyes.

"I will, Nico."

Nico pulled Ren's coat more closely about him and let his body relish the soft grass. He thought he'd sleep lightly, keep his usual ear out. That was his plan. He didn't remember closing his eyes on Ren's smile. Most of the time, it took him hours to fall asleep, alone in his tent with nothing between him and the wolk but a flimsy layer of fabric. But something about Ren's presence soothed him. For once, someone else kept watch.

Nico went from wakefulness to a...

When he finally woke, he woke as usual: fully, senses heightened, heart pounding. It was dim in their little grass cave, edging into night. Ren sat against a tree trunk, legs crossed, an indulgent, tender expression on his face the likes of which had never before been directed at Nico. There was a fresh, nascent emotion blooming behind his eyes that Nico couldn't quite place.

Nico was used to being ogled—by monsters, by carnival goers, by magical hangers-on, by an entire lifetime of creeps. Ren's attention felt completely different, less assessing. Nico had no idea what to do with that expression, how to react to it, what to say to it. It filled him with a wonder he feared to explore.

For a moment, they held each other's gaze and said nothing until Ren blinked, smiled, and said, "I don't think you moved once while you were asleep. I've never seen anyone sleep that deeply."

Nico brought his hands to his face, rubbed sleep-blur from his eyelids, and scrubbed at his stubbled cheeks. He needed those brief moments, a slight respite from the warmth in Ren's expression that he didn't know how to handle.

The heavy air held the combined scent of their sweat. In such close quarters, Ren's presence enveloped him.

The strangest sensation of Ren inside his chest, stirring his magic into a rising tingle, panicked Nico a little. His power didn't respond to people the way an organ would. It didn't work that way.

Except, apparently, it did now. Nico didn't like it. He couldn't afford for this to happen.

From behind the safety of his hands, Nico said, "I've never slept that soundly before."

"You looked like you were dreaming."

Nico let his hands drop to his sides. A dense ceiling of leaves cocooned them. Everything was static and quiet. "I don't know. I never remember my dreams. I might remember small pieces here and there, but that's it."

"Really? Never?" Ren's sigh was gusty. "That must be nice. There are some dreams I wish I could forget."

What could a villager possibly have nightmares about? He'd thought Ren's life probably consisted of the comfortable simplicities of small-town life. Nico viewed him in a slightly new light. "Why? What do you dream of?"

"Oh, don't get me wrong. They're not all bad. I've had a lot of good dreams. But there are some... I used to have some really vivid, ugly dreams as a child. The kind of dreams that leave you raw, that leave an impression long after. Some of them have stuck with me. In the bad ones, I was running from something, or trapped, or trapped *and* trying to run simultaneously. There always seemed to be something just behind me. A lot of them were recurring. It was like they had themes I couldn't escape."

Shivers tickled down Nico's arms despite the warmth of Ren's coat. "Do you still have them?"

"Not often."

"Maybe I don't dream." Nico let the world go soft, unfocused, blurring the leaves above. "Maybe that's a good thing."

"Maybe you don't have nightmares because you've been living in one."

Nico swallowed. The leaves wavered. "Maybe you're right."

"It feels like nightmares don't have a place here. The trees and plants are too calm."

"I don't think trees and plants dream." Nico couldn't help a small, teasing smile aimed not at Ren, but at the protective leaves and branches overhead. At Ren's sudden answering laugh, Nico said, "What do they have to dream about anyway?"

"Sunshine."

"That's something I'd like to dream about." Nico yawned. Their grassy hideaway grew dimmer by the moment. If he stayed put any longer, he'd be tempted to turn over and curl into the soft grass for the entirety of the night. He scrubbed his fingers through his hair. "How long did I sleep?" It had been a while. He could feel it in the way his magic, in some unnamable place deep down inside his body, felt warm and ready, almost completely renewed.

Ren let out a long, strangely comfortable sigh. "I would guess five or six hours. It's just now getting dark out."

"You should have woken me up so you could get some rest too."

"I think you needed it more. Besides, when I close my eyes, I see my home and I—" Ren's voice stuck. "I really don't want to close my eyes right now."

"Fine," Nico said, "but know that I won't be carrying your ass if you collapse from exhaustion."

Ren's laugh was soft, muted. "You mean the way I carried yours?"

Nico dropped his hands into the grass and snorted. "Completely different. I was dying."

"That didn't make you any lighter to carry."

"With all the blood I spilled out on the ground?" Nico gave him a look. "Maybe a small amount lighter."

He sat up to Ren's sweet, gentle laugh filling the small space.

"Feeling any better?" Ren asked, warmth in his voice.

"A lot." Nico rubbed his palm against his chest as if he could feel his magic with his hand, through flesh and bone, though it didn't work that way. He could feel his magic from the inside, not the outside. "Most of it's renewed. We can leave immediately."

"I guess we should go," Ren said on a sigh. "But it's actually not that bad here."

"It'll get bad when they come." In the cramped space, Nico couldn't help but notice the long stretch of Ren's legs spread out before him, so close to brushing against his own. "Are you ready?"

Ren abandoned his languorous lean against the tree and sat up straighter. "If you are, then yes. Uh, I—" There was hesitation in the slight pucker of his mouth. "I'm sure you know what you're doing, but I was wondering where you plan to go. You have a plan, don't you?"

Nico exhaled slowly. He only half knew what he was doing, but he couldn't say that. "We're going to a city in the north—Vellen. To my father's."

Ren's shoulders relaxed in easy, unknowing relief. He smiled at Nico so brightly it almost made Nico forget what lay ahead. "I'm glad you have someone to go to. That makes a lot of difference."

"I see," Nico said, and he did. He saw that when Ren pictured family, he envisioned safety, security, assistance.

He had to get away from the sweet hope on Ren's face.

Nico squeezed out of their grassy cave first. He emerged into the night sky. Hundreds of little white stars hung in the darkening air to the horizon. Nico turned in a circle to take it in. Ren joined him, his lips parted in awe.

"What is it?" Ren asked. "Magic?" He tilted his head back to the lights above them. Pure glee shone on his face. "It's like floating in space among the stars."

"Not magic," Nico said. "I've never seen anything like it before, but I think it might be some kind of...bug." He reached out to one that hovered nearby, put his hand underneath it very slowly, and raised it until the star rested on his palm. He brought it closer, and Ren leaned in, their foreheads nearly brushing as they both studied the speck of light between them. It was small, the size of a pearl. Up close, it changed colors so subtly it was hard to notice—white, to pale blue, to pale gold, and back to white. Nico could discern no wings, no eyes, no actual insect. There was only a tiny ball of light.

"Nature's magic," Ren said in a hushed voice on the edge of a whisper. When Nico glanced up, Ren was looking not at the bug cupped in his hand, but at Nico. He lingered over Nico just long enough for the both of them to get caught up in the moment.

Nico cleared his throat. "Maybe it's not a bug," he said, turning his hand to study it from another angle. "It could be from a plant. A seed of some kind."

"Whatever it is, it's spectacular."

Ren bent forward. His lips were so close to Nico's hand, Nico thought he might be about to kiss either his hand or the light. Instead, Ren pursed his lips and blew out a gentle puff of air that floated the speck back into the night. He touched Nico's hand where the mote of light had rested, traced the lines of Nico's palm with a single featherlight fingertip. It tickled. Every nerve in Nico's body zeroed in on that one small touch, on the sensation Ren's touch aroused.

Oh no.

Ren laughed at Nico. "There's one in your hair."

"There's one in yours, too."

Nico raised his hand and plucked the light out of Ren's hair. Between his fingers, the speck was warm and solid like a polished pebble, but without the weight. He let go of the light, let it slip through his fingers and float away from them. He wasn't sure what he was doing. He never voluntarily touched people. Yet—yet he stood there with his hand in Ren's hair, and he didn't pull it away.

Ren's hair curled around Nico's fingers. In turn, Ren curled his fingers around Nico's, a loose hold, his palm hot against the back of Nico's hand. His thoughts danced through Nico's mind, sweet and teasing: *You can touch me anytime you want.*

Out loud, Ren said, "I wish we could stay here for the night." —*wish I could stay here with you.*

Nico pushed the tips of his fingers through Ren's hair. It was boyish hair that didn't help him come across as any older: floppy, wavy, a bit long and unkempt, and as deep brown as the rich chocolate his mother used to make and sell in their candy shop. Heavy silk against his fingers. He scratched his nails lightly against Ren's scalp and took satisfaction in the way Ren's eyelids fluttered downward in response.

Ren's thrill at being with Nico trickled warmly across Nico's mind, the unfurling of instant infatuation. So many tender thoughts, delicate like new buds, fresh and unexplored. Dangerous. His infatuation would bloom out and die when he found out what Nico had done, what he had caused, what kind of person he was.

"I think you're some otherworldly creature," Ren said, soft as a secret, "standing here with all these lights glittering around you."

"I'm just a man." Nico dragged his fingernails against Ren's scalp, pulling a sigh from Ren. He should back away. He knew he should. But he didn't. He stole this single, indulgent moment.

"I know, but you feel special."

"Only because you've seen me do magic."

"No. That's not it. There's something about you that— I don't know what it is. You feel different to me."

While other people's thoughts were often dark, ugly jumbles, Ren's were playful and direct, like a clear note of music on a quiet evening. Ren skimmed his index finger down Nico's nose, thought, *I want you*, which came as no surprise to Nico. It had been one of Ren's first thoughts when they crashed into each other, and he had been radiating it off and on ever since with his glances and his loose smiles. Ren wasn't exactly a subtle man.

"I slept with half the men in my village," Ren said. "I like the closeness I get from being near people, with people. Being with other people—having sex and talking and eating and laughing—it's exhilarating. It's a lot of fun. Then it's over, and I'm alone again, bored. But being near you feels..."

He paused, and Nico filled it with a wry "Not fun?"

Ren didn't laugh, his face so serious now as he searched for words. "More satisfying. Just being near you feels indulgent. I could lie down with you here and just drift in the lights and enjoy being beside you, learning about you." He sounded a bit puzzled at all of it, but went on anyway. "That would feel good. I think...really good."

That wasn't what Nico had been expecting, the earnestness of laying it out there so bare.

"You know we can't do that," he told Ren. "That's never going to happen."

"I know." Ren gave Nico's fingers a squeeze, though his features were shadowed in resignation. "But if all these other things weren't happening, if things were different, I think I could end up liking you. Quite a bit actually."

Nico made sure not to inhale sharply, his first instinctive reaction. He breathed evenly, said, "Don't like me. People don't live long around me."

Ren tilted his head. "Too late."

Shit.

"You don't even know me." It was probably time to take his hand back from where it was currently wound in Ren's hair.

Ren smiled. "Maybe one day when all of this is over, I'll get that privilege."

"No one knows me," Nico said. "There's nothing good to get to know."

"That's not true," Ren said. "It can't be." —*not after the beautiful things I've seen you do with magic.* "No one with magic like yours can be ugly inside."

Nico shook his head. "People don't get close to me, and I don't get close to them."

Ren appeared honestly and endearingly baffled. "But why?"

"I've found that people are a constant disappointment."

"So you don't think anyone is worth knowing."

"Knowing me isn't worth it."

"We'll see."

It was like trying to offend a tree limb. It merely swayed in the wind when you batted at it.

Nico said, "We haven't talked, we know nothing about each other, we've spent less than a day together—and half of that time was spent nearly dying. You're just drawn to danger."

A frown settled across Ren's lips. "No."

"You can't know that for sure."

Ren's arm slipped around Nico, fitted against the small of his back, drawing their bodies closer—and Nico was in trouble. So much trouble. Ren bent forward, his mouth at Nico's ear, lips warm against Nico's chilled skin. More breath than words, he said, "I know you feel great in my arms."

Nico's breath dragged out as he tried to steady his heartbeat, which had suddenly jumped into a hard pound. "Is—is that what you tell all the men in your village to get them into your bed?"

Ren's laugh was a warm huff in Nico's ear, a rumble deep in his chest. "I don't usually have to put forth this much effort."

Nico didn't know what to do but slip his other hand into Ren's hair, feel Ren's skull between his hands, brush his mouth against the smooth-rough stubble of Ren's cheek, and say, "Our bodies are water, liquid falling through the sky..."

He had nothing to give Ren but another day to live.

Chapter Nine

NICO

The world they landed in was a much different one than the dark, starry world they had left behind. Nico woke with snow on his lashes that dripped down his face as soon as he blinked.

He immediately knew where they were—in his blood and in his magic. They were just outside of Vellen, in the land of the Winter God where the air frosted the world in white all year long. Nico wanted to shout his emotions into the sky—release. His mind thrummed with so many conflicting feelings.

Snow meant he was that much closer to home. Of course, it wasn't home anymore. It hadn't been home since he was a child, a different person. It hadn't been home since...before.

Nico sat up, wiping melted snowflakes off his cheeks. A thin, translucent white layer covered the ground. Ren lay nearby, curled into himself, unmoving. Nico went to him, knelt at his side, and put a hand on his shoulder. Ren didn't move. His thoughts were the blank static of sleep that Nico had never been able to penetrate. If there was a talent for reading dream-thoughts, Nico didn't have it. And he didn't want it. The last thing he wanted to hear was other people's dreams. Their waking thoughts were already too much.

He shook Ren gently, and when that didn't gain a response, Nico sat on the frozen ground next to him. He pulled a handful of magic from his well and began spinning a warm bubble into the air, gently displacing the cold air and replacing it with warmth, letting the warmth bounce back against his conjured shell and expand. More went into creating the shell that kept in the precious warmth and was just thick enough to keep out the mixture of icy snow. It sealed them into a safer world. Or at least, a warmer world. It took less than a minute to complete. The snow on the ground melted quickly, marking the boundaries of their little circle.

It wasn't unusual for it to take a while to waken. Once, Nico had been out for half a day after traveling the clouds in a desperate, headlong flight. And he hadn't had someone to warm the air for him as he slept. That had been fourteen years ago, his first and ugliest attempt at escape, immediately after he'd been given to the wolk. Back then he hadn't known about magical trails and how easily his monsters could follow him. He had learned.

He took off Ren's coat, folded it, lifted Ren's head, and placed it under him.

Nico lay on the ground, spread out next to Ren's supine body. The grass here was nothing like the soft multicolored grass from before. Dry and crackly, it was the dormant grass of a much colder land, rough against Nico's skin, poking through his clothes. It grew green in Vellen for only a brief period in midsummer. Greenery didn't last long in the land of the Winter God.

He blinked up at the snow falling around the bubble. Until he was lying down again, he hadn't realized how exhausted he was. Another blink was all it took for him to pass from consciousness into sleep.

He woke to Ren leaning over him in the dark. The dimmest outline of his shaggy hair was the only thing that held Nico back from sending him flying with a harsh blast of magic.

"Don't do that," Nico said over the pounding of blood in his ears.

"I wasn't sure if you were unconscious or asleep."

"Don't loom over me while I'm sleeping."

In the dark, Ren nodded. "Sleeping then. And I don't loom."

Nico sat up, rubbed sleep from his face. "It's like you're daring me to mistake you for someone else and blow you up."

"Like who?" Ren asked.

Nico just stared at him. "Who do you think?"

Ren didn't reply right away, though his unspoken words seemed to build up in the air. Eventually, gently, he said, "Understood." He let the awkwardness of the previous moment disperse. "You can blow people up?"

Nico let out a mirthless laugh. "Life would be a lot easier if I could."

Ren sat back on his haunches, a measured amount of space between them. "Can you conjure food?" he asked, voice teasing but hopeful. "Like you conjured this warm air?"

"If you walk in the woods with me, I might be able to conjure some berries from a bush."

"That's not as exciting as I imagined," Ren said.

As though any of this was meant to be exciting. Nico stood and, with a thought, the warmth dissolved. Ren followed him up, turned in a circle, and waved his hand through the places where the magical seal had been, as though he were trying to catch it on his fingers. It was too dark to see Ren's face, but there was that familiar childlike wonderment in the sway of his arm, in the waggle of his fingers.

"You can't hold on to it," Nico said. "Magic is intangible."

"I want to."

The cold seeped back into Nico's bones. The snow fell over them freely, a quick dusting. He scooped up Ren's coat from the ground and handed it back to him.

"No," Ren said despite the shiver in his tone, "keep it."

"Where we're going, there'll be plenty of warmth and food." Nico pushed the coat against Ren's stomach until Ren reluctantly gathered it in his hands. "My magic is completely replenished. We're leaving now."

"Where?"

Nico didn't bother with an answer. They were so close to Vellen, Ren would see it for himself soon. He had only to press against Ren, and their hands drifted together, lacing almost automatically. Nico let his head rest on Ren's shoulder. He closed his eyes, pictured the expanse of glass and snow, clear images lifted from his memory. He said the words aloud, reverently, like a prayer to the God of Winter. The snow clouds welcomed them, and they flew.

NICO NEVER TIRED of this: the airy free fall, the grand vistas, the safe seclusion. The *freedom*. Nico shook out over the land, drifted toward its pure expanse. The moonlight caught in the low-hanging clouds and reflected blue-white on the snow. In the distance, the city of Vellen picked up the cold moon-glow, the glass walls glinting.

Nico had forgotten how beautiful his homeland was—aloof, sumptuous, and inviolate.

It was all glass castles etched into the sides of mountains, delicate and glimmering between the folds of the land, soaring and slender, spires and turrets seemingly fragile enough to snap in a strong wind. All of it a distant jewel dripping with magic, an untouchable dream. The magicians were what made the harsh, sloped land viable. Without magic, the northern peaks were nothing but ice and snow. Harsh and remote, they produced some of the world's strongest conjurers.

Nico had walked the cobbled streets and played in the delicate buildings of the place currently unfolding below him in glimpses between clouds.

Vellen. A dream that had once been home. A frosty glass city, always covered in a soft layer of snow and magic. Nico had spent many long, warm days wrapped in the blanket rooms kept specifically for the children, where mattresses and pillows covered the floors and fireplaces heated the air, where the warmth smelled like sugar and chocolate. He'd had an early childhood of bouncy pillow fights and hot chocolate while his mother sold confectionary items and traded recipes with other nearby cities and his father helped to run Vellen.

Nico had thought he'd never come back. He didn't want to be back.

The lake glimmered behind the buildings, iced in shimmering black. It appeared now just as it had on that last day.

Nico floated toward the earth, toward that blanket of snow that waited so far below. He spun lazily through the air with hazy images of childhood and home, but no worries of how he had lost all of it. In the midst of all those memories, he landed, and then he dreamed through his unconsciousness—one long fuzzy stream of cold air and warm homes, days of laughter and nights of comfortable safety, and one wide lake with black water and sheets of ice thick enough to drown beneath.

Memories of the lake intermingled with Zeke's dark voice in his ear whispering in detail exactly what they would do to him if he ever escaped. He was sinking beneath the water, but somehow the wolk were still with him, enveloping him. He was suffocating as they drained him, choking on water even as they stripped him in underwater slow motion. He had shattered their fragile truce by killing their own, and now they were going to make good on their promise and use him over and over until there was nothing left but his screams. Their laughter was so clear beneath the ice, so gleeful. They'd been eagerly waiting for this day, for him to give them the excuse to finally destroy him. He'd never get the chance to escape them again. There was the beginning of a scream in his chest. He opened his mouth.

The dream-screaming woke Nico.

He woke on a gasp, inhaling snow. Someone loomed over him.

Still wrapped in the cold black waters, sinking down, hands all over him, Nico's panic sent him past magic. All primal reflex, he thrashed against the arms that came at him, rolled away into the snow, tangled up in something heavy. The soft fluff enveloped him.

"Oh God," someone said, and it took long moments of huddling low in the snow for Nico to recognize Ren's voice. It took him even longer to realize he was tangled in Ren's coat, which had been spread on top of him as he slept.

Nico didn't move. The snow soaked into his clothes, into his skin. He let his hands unclench one finger at a time as he gasped and shuddered like a cornered animal.

"I want to come over there and check on you," Ren said, "but I'm afraid you might roll down the side of this mountain if I get any closer. And possibly take me with you."

Nico uncurled from his fetal position and sat up, the left side of his face numb from resting in the snow. The snow fell thickly, rendering Ren nothing but a vague outline, soft at the edges. The fluffy snow, light as feathers, sent him right back to childhood. He'd played for hours in this same snow.

A strange phenomenon happened only in the northernmost mountains around Vellen. When the whole cloud layer caught the bright moonlight from above, it diffused into a blue-white glow that lit the snowflakes and sent the world into a hazy, swirling, perpetual twilight. The distinctive silver-blue covered the ground, a color Nico had seen nowhere else. He'd almost forgotten its exact shade.

The clouds hung so low it seemed he could reach up and run a finger through them. This corner of the world gleamed.

Nico was home.

He shuddered, plucked Ren's coat from the snow, and pulled it tightly around his body.

"I told you not to hover over me like that," Nico said, brushing snow off his cheeks with the back of his hand.

"Are you...all right?"

"No." He was very much not all right. Nothing about this was right. It had been better from the sky when Vellen had been tiny with distance and he was snow—uncaring, indifferent. Though he couldn't see it now, the city towered large and heavy at the edge of his senses.

"Please tell me," Ren said. "Let me do something. I want to do something. I want to—" He cleared his throat. "I want to help you."

Nico squinted at him through the falling snow. There was no point in hiding it. Ren would find out soon enough and better if it came from him. "I came here for help, but I think they're going to turn their backs on me."

Ren went very still. "Why would they do that? You're trying to fight a bunch of monsters."

"Because a long time ago I killed one of their children."

Through the whirling blue curtain of snow, Ren recoiled. It didn't hurt him, because he didn't care what Ren thought of him. Who was Ren to him? No one. It didn't hurt him.

It didn't hurt.

It didn't.

Nico flicked the collar of Ren's coat up around his ears. He turned away from Ren, out into a forest alight with moonlight and snow.

Ren's voice sounded distant, strangely hoarse. "You killed...a child?"

"You've seen what I can do," Nico said, as blandly as he could. No emotion. It was all about showing nothing and revealing even less. His chest tightened with restraint.

Ren didn't run like Nico expected him to do. He said only one word, clear and steady through the storm: "Why?"

"Does it even matter? I—" Nico nearly choked on the word, but pushed it out anyway. "—killed." A human. He'd killed a person, which was a world away from killing monsters that were giving chase.

"It matters." Ren came to him, half crawling across the snow-soft ground. "Did you mean to do it?"

He knelt directly in front of Nico. Even on his knees, Ren was tall.

Nico let his head droop and said, "I planned it beforehand."

The snow swirled between them like a translucent veil. In a whisper that barely rose above the wind, Ren said again, "Why?"

Concern wrinkled Ren's forehead as he waited for Nico to open up his heart and pour the whole ugly contents out into the snow. That guileless face nearly undid Nico's resolve.

Nico couldn't do it. How could he turn himself inside out and share with Ren the things he'd been carrying for fourteen years when he could barely stand close contact for more than a few minutes? Snow gathered on the ground between them, a growing pile of drifts at their knees.

"It doesn't matter now." Nico shook his head. "Why do you care so much?"

Ren hesitated. Thoughts flickered across his face, unreadable in the half-light. "I've always been curious. My ma called it my curse. She said one day it'd get me killed."

"She was probably right."

"I guess...sometimes I care too much. I like to know things. I like to know people." Stark earnestness brightened Ren's face. It sent a pain through Nico.

Nico shook his head once sharply. "You don't want to know me."

"I'll decide that. Tell me about the child, because I don't think I believe you." Ren nodded once, his mouth firm, challenging.

"You don't *want* to believe me. You want me to be a good little magician who squirts glitter out of his ass."

A gust of snow briefly turned Ren into a hazy silhouette. "Is this another put-on, like the flirting at the carnival? But this time you're trying to chase me away?"

Nico ran a hand over his face. It was cold, and his fingers were even colder. "Do you want to sleep with me so badly that you'll ignore me when I tell you I've killed someone?"

"I'm not ignoring it," Ren said. "I'm calling it a lie." The set of his mouth was resolute.

Nico wished he'd chosen someone else to crash into at the carnival. Someone easier. Anyone would have been easier. Probably.

He said, "Why would anyone lie about something so atrocious?"

"I don't know, Nico." Ren sat back on his haunches. "Why would they?"

It was too cold to think. His mind was exhausted. Nico imagined bits of his brain growing icicles, shutting off one section at a time. He thought warmth into the air. He drew on his magic to create the skin of their bubble. The trapped heat gathered around them, visible for a moment as a frosty white swell. Just for them, the snow stopped falling. Snowflakes melted in Ren's hair and across his cheeks, the drops a sprinkle of glitter against his skin.

Ren inhaled the radiance, held it in his lungs. "Thank God. I think my nose was getting cold enough to snap right off my face." He touched his fingers to his nose as if to make sure it was still in place.

The snow at their feet had melted into the dirt and grass. Ren settled into the toasty grass, leaned back on his elbows. He tossed his head back, his throat exposed, and said, "Do you mind if we relax here a few minutes? I just need a rest."

Nico found it impossible to understand how anyone could relax so easily next to someone who had just admitted to murder.

"That's fine."

Nico stayed seated, legs crossed. Beyond their warm cocoon, frosty blue swirled. Now that they were so close to their destination, Nico was in no hurry. He could feel rejection heavy ahead. The clouds shifted, taking the blue brilliance of the moon with them. He squinted into the night, aware of every branch that creaked in the wind.

"Are you going to sleep any?" Ren asked, yawning.

How could Nico sleep knowing what was probably coming? They were going to reject him, turn him away. After what he had done, there was no way they would help him. He was dangerous. What had he been thinking? He never should have come back.

Into the snowy night, Nico said, "I'm not lying. About the child."

Ren's head turned in his direction, indistinct in the gloom. He waited a beat before he said casually, "Tell me more if you want."

"I got into a fight with another boy." Nico rushed it out of his mouth, low, half hoping Ren wouldn't hear him.

Ren sat up. "How old were you?"

"Fourteen."

"You were a child too," Ren said hesitantly. "Just a boy."

"I don't even remember what Jones and I were arguing about." Nico had to keep talking, had to push it all out there at once. If he stopped talking, he would never get rid of it all. The whole ugly thing would slither back down his throat and sink into his chest, where it would stay dark and curled.

"It was after school. A bunch of us were hanging out in the woods behind the school. I think it'd been coming for a long time, and all we needed was a spark to set us off. There'd been years of buildup. We'd been picking at each other since we were young. Kind of circling each other. Finally, one day Jones and I got into a fistfight. It got ugly, and some of the others had to pull us off each other. Two days later, I was walking home when he and two of his friends jumped me."

"Crap," Ren said softly.

"Yes, crap. He was the leader of our group. They decided to teach me a lesson. They beat me down and then dragged me to a lake that was frozen over. They shoved me onto the ice right at the shoreline. The ice cracked under my feet. I broke through and went under."

Ren leaned toward him, drawn in by the tale, so clearly completely caught up in it. His eyes were wide and horrified. "What did you do?"

Nico almost couldn't go on. He'd never told anyone this part. No one had ever asked. He peered over Ren's shoulder, out into the dark. *It doesn't matter now anyway. None of it matters anymore. It's done.*

Nico said, "I slipped in farther and got stuck under a sheet of ice. I tried to break through the surface, but it was too thick. Everything was dark underwater, and I couldn't see. I was struggling too hard to come up with a way to use my magic to get out. I couldn't breathe. I forgot I even had magic. I just wanted to breathe. I was panicking."

Ren held his breath as if he, too, were reliving the sensation of frigid water. He seemed stunned. He let his breath out slowly. "It's just like the nightmare from my childhood. I used to have these recurring nightmares about drowning. I'd wake up screaming, and my ma would have to climb into bed with me to help me go back to sleep. Trapped underwater, unable to breathe—that would be the worst way to die. The absolute worst." He shuddered and then said softly, "Oh, Nico."

Nico tried to ignore the pity in his voice, but it bubbled between them anyway, sticky-sweet and overwhelming. The clouds danced in a way that pushed the moonlight down onto them again. The illumination highlighted Ren's empathy, his lips soft and downturned. Just for a moment, Nico had to turn his head away from Ren. The rest of his story clogged his throat. All that compassion reached toward him with arms of its own. He needed to swat it away, or he would sink into it and drown. Momentarily blinded, all Nico could see was warmth, firm shoulders, strong arms, big brown eyes. He fought the inexplicable, visceral urge to climb into Ren's arms. He could get lost in those arms. In the clean lines of Ren's body. In that sweet mouth. It would be too easy to lose himself in Ren's comfort—in Ren.

Nico shook his head, shook away the thought. Ren was a distraction he couldn't afford. He said, "Don't look at me like that."

Ren frowned. "Like what?"

"Let me finish," Nico said.

Ren waved a hand that said, *Fine. Finish.*

Nico swallowed, continued. "I was beating the ice with my fists and breathing in water before they finally used magic to break the ice so that I could make it to the surface. They wouldn't even pull me out. They stood on the shore laughing while I dug my fingernails into the ice and clawed my way out. I kept sliding back in."

"Little bastard brats," Ren said. "They were magicians too?"

"Everyone in the northern lands is a magician."

"I didn't know that was possible." Ren ducked his head. "Sorry. Go on."

There's a lot you don't know, Nico didn't say.

"Once I made it out of the water, they dragged me off the ice and then played it off as a big joke. Remember when you were dying a minute ago? What a laugh." He could hear Ren gathering breath to say something, so he pushed the words out faster, rushed. "I went along with it. I even laughed. I pretended for weeks. I still spent time with them in the woods after school. We'd all been around each other for so long we didn't know what it was like not to spend every day together."

"But they were never your friends?" Ren shook his head. "Of course they weren't. They almost killed you."

Nico hesitated. It was hard to explain the glue that had held them together even though they had not all been good friends. They'd stayed together their whole lives, a solid group, because it was natural, a habit, not because they'd all enjoyed each other's company.

"We were childhood mates," Nico said. "We all grew up together, went from grade to grade with each other. In my hometown, children were always grouped by age. We were encouraged to be together often as we grew up."

Ren hummed but said nothing.

"I waited in the woods one afternoon for Jones to pass through alone," Nico said. "Then I used my telling magic to make him walk out into the middle of the lake where the ice was thin. I stood on the shore and shouted at him to jump in."

There was a long silence of whirling wind and powdery blue, the cold pushing at their sanctuary with a howl. Above, the clouds tore apart and reformed in plays of dark night and half moonlight. The wind blew puffs of snow through the air like sparkling dust. Shadowy moonlight tinted Ren's face bluish and emphasized his hesitancy.

Nico pulled his knees to his chest, wrapped his arms around them. Into Ren's quiet, he said, "He was a little tyrant. His father ran the city's council. He was used to having power. He'd always been a monster to everyone. He just didn't expect me to be a bigger monster."

Ren took a long, cool moment before he asked, "Do you regret it?" He sounded careful, picking through his words. Ren shifted, leaned back a bit. Moon and cloud shadows played strange tricks with his expression. Nico couldn't quite read him in this light, and it unnerved him.

The words felt explosive in Nico's mouth, a buildup of so many years of keeping quiet, of no one ever knowing.

"I regret what happened next. I was going to have him splash about in the cold for a few minutes. I wanted him to feel the panic that I'd felt under the ice. But someone came through the trees behind me while I was shouting my magic at Jones. He grabbed me, and it distracted me. I turned and started trying to explain. By the time we got to Jones, he was gone, deep under the water. It was only a matter of thirty seconds, but it was too late. That was all it took."

There was no movement from Ren, so Nico laid the rest of it out on the ground between them, bare and twisted. "We were never to use our magic on each other. The man who caught me reported me. There was a council meeting, and they decided to banish me. They were aware of the wolk because they passed near our area every year. Three days later, they dragged me out of Vellen and gave me to them."

The steady rise and fall of Ren's chest calmed Nico. There was no other sound but their soft exhalations and the wind beating against Nico's magic.

When Ren's voice did come, low and steady, Nico barely kept himself from flinching. "So you did get a boy killed," he said, words that overflowed their little bubble. "I didn't believe it."

Nico swallowed louder than he meant to. He suspected he wouldn't hold Ren's infatuation for much longer. It would be better that way. "You've seen me kill," he said.

Ren swept his fingertips against the seal, and the sensation echoed in his body, as though Ren had jiggled Nico's arm or leg.

"I saw you kill monsters," Ren said, "not a child. I thought you said it to try to scare me off, to get rid of me."

"I wouldn't need to make up a lie to get rid of you."

Ren snorted. "Comforting." He considered Nico like one might a newfound insect. "Do you feel remorse for it?"

"Yes." *Yes.* Nico dreamed of reliving that day, of walking past that lake and simply going home, of not having someone's death in his heart, of growing up safe and living a life without this constant terror.

"Your punishment," Ren said, hesitating over the words, "was cold. Really cold."

"So was what I did." Nico sank further into Ren's coat. Every time he breathed into the collar, he got a whiff of the earth and sweat scent of Ren's neck.

Ren said, "Monsters for death."

"I would rather have had death," Nico said into the coat. He turned his head to rest his cheek on his knee. "At least death is relatively quick. At least death doesn't last a lifetime."

"Did your parents fight for you?"

"No one said goodbye to me. No one wanted to see me. No one was on my side."

Something brushed against Nico's hair, a touch as light as wind, and he got a flash of intense, overlapping emotions, too jumbled to piece apart. By the time Nico lifted his head, Ren had retreated.

"No one," Ren said with certainty, "deserves what you got."

Nico held his breath. The strong lines of Ren's profile stood out against the snowflakes and gloom, a pillar of support Nico could so easily cling to. "Ren, I got someone killed."

"I know, and it was a terrible thing to do. You deserved some kind of punishment, but not that. Never that." Ren turned to him, and they were suddenly, unexpectedly, staring at each other. The strong connection made Nico's fingers twitch. "Do you think you deserved it?"

The clouds shifted again in a way that bathed them in another wave of lustrous blue. In the snow-light, Ren's expression was tight, intense. The silvery falling snow reflected in his wide, dark eyes.

"No," Nico said, swallowing. "I— No."

Ren sat back, his shoulders relaxing. "There, then." He sounded satisfied, like he had proven something.

Unsure of Ren's reaction, Nico said nothing. The clouds raced past. Snow fell like tiny stars around them, caught in the moon's strange light. It was easy to understand how this land produced long generations of magicians, the strongest in the world. There was something extraordinary about this air, these mountains.

"Nico," Ren said and touched his fingertips to the back of Nico's hand as Nico looked up at him.

The thought came clearly, fiercely, spreading between them: *You do have someone on your side.*

Chapter Ten

NICO

"I don't want to go home," Nico said.

It was a little late for that sentiment. They stood at Vellen's entrance, beneath a great white arch that spanned the space between two mountains. The jagged peaks of Nico's homeland soared over them. Fog hung crystallized in the air, glittering in the dawn light. Tiny white lights spilled from the curved apex of the arch, nearly touching the ground, undulating in each sway of the wind. Beyond the arch, the city slept behind frosty white mist.

Nico wondered if they already knew he was there, if they were watching him through the winter haze. Combined, their magic was vast. He knew more than anyone that anything was possible with powerful enough magic.

Ren tore himself away from the arch and its lights. He said nothing, but when he moved closer to Nico, their arms brushed, and Nico got a very clear picture of Ren pulling him close. ...*feel your shoulder blades beneath my hands...run my hands up and down your spine until you vibrate...quiet your loud fingers—*

They bent away from each other at the same time, a synchronized step back, and Ren quickly returned his attention to the arch as though he hadn't just shared an intimate thought with Nico.

Nico's fingers itched. He slipped them up into the sleeves of Ren's coat.

Ren put his hands to the arch and studied it with his palms. "If you can handle monsters," he said as he ran his hands up and down the smooth white column, "you can handle your family."

"You would think so," Nico said. Ren's hands were large, nimble, and mesmerizing. Dark against the ivory marble. The easy, capable way those hands moved made Nico's throat go dry.

When Ren turned to Nico, the swaying lights from above danced in his dark irises. "Are you going to ask them for protection?"

Nico paused. He wasn't quite ready to tell Ren everything yet. He didn't know how Ren might react to the news he carried, so he spoke with care. "I'm going to ask them for help."

"Do you think they'll give it to you?"

"I think they'll make me beg."

Ren's hands fell away from the arch. "That's disgusting." He hesitated before asking, "Do you think they might hurt you?"

"They already have," Nico said.

Ren threw his hands up in the air. "Then maybe we shouldn't do this."

"But I have nowhere else to go. I'm desperate. They'll like that." Nico ended the conversation by walking beneath the arch and into the city.

IT WAS JUST as Nico remembered it from childhood: a dream city. And no matter how hard he had tried to push this place from his mind, he'd certainly daydreamed about it enough since his banishment. He'd walked these ivory-and-gold cobbled streets day after day in his dreams, snow and magic floating down the street with him.

The streets were empty this early in the morning. No one in the city would be out in the predawn cold unless they had to be, and no one had to be. It would be long lazy hours before anyone appeared.

The fog began to lift with the dawn sun. The glow of morning gilded the city, drawn to the elaborate spires like a bee to a flower. The translucent buildings reflected the snow and the sunrise, the walls a glimmering swirl of white and burnt gold. The peaked roofs were covered in thick layers of white snow. Receding fog licked at the tops of the tallest turrets, holding on with pale, wispy fingers.

The play of light throughout steep mountains seemed to hold a magic of its own. Dew from the fog left droplets on the cobblestones and the tops of streetlamps. It glittered when the light hit just right as Nico and Ren walked amongst hundreds of tiny argent jewels. In Vellen, light and shadow converged in elegance, effortless beauty everywhere.

Nico had never wanted to see any of it again. There were memories everywhere. They had walked him down this same street on the way to the main hall after he'd been caught in the woods. That night was a dusty blue with soft snowflakes catching in the light from the streetlamps, everything fuzzy and muted. People lined the edges of the street, but no one would look directly at him. He would never forget the way they'd turned their faces away from him as he walked to his sentencing. A shudder skittered up Nico's back, and he pulled Ren's coat closer to his body.

When Ren stopped walking in the middle of the street to admire the buildings, Nico had to turn to him.

"Is this a dream?" Ren asked, whisper-soft.

No, it's a nightmare.

"It's real," Nico said. He wished it weren't. He didn't gander at the buildings or the beauty of what had once been his city. This place made him ache.

Wonder bloomed pure and sweet on Ren's face. As the fog lifted, he turned in a slow circle. "The architecture... I would never have been able to even imagine anything like this. Glass buildings shouldn't be able to stand on their own."

"They don't," Nico said. "Magic is infused into the glass. Each building is reinforced with the magic of a dozen magicians. I don't think there's any force that could topple these buildings."

Ren nodded. "It's smug—all this fragility. They're like delicate figurines on the mantel, gone with one brush. But I suppose they don't need sturdy buildings for protection. They don't have to huddle in wood and stone like the rest of us. They have the power to perch in glass on the sides of mountains. It's like they're daring nature and enemies alike to touch them." He made a face. "Very smug."

Nico blinked at the accuracy. In a single glimpse of the city, Ren got it. "Nature stands no chance against them, and they don't have any enemies," Nico said.

Ren's focus shifted from the shimmer of the city back to Nico. He considered Nico from across the cobblestones, a small stretch of street between them. Nico's skin prickled with the renewed attention.

When Ren moved toward him, hands flexing as though itching to grasp, Nico said, "I can't be as interesting as a dream city complete with fairy-tale castles."

Ren closed the gap with four long strides and came to stand in front of Nico, his expression soft and pensive in the dawn light. He said nothing, but the back of his hand brushed against the back of Nico's, knuckles against knuckles.... *You in this light...like a piece of something I've dreamed... I dreamed of you like this... There are yellow sunrise sparks in your eyes...*

Nico didn't move. He stood and soaked in Ren's thoughts, their hands touching, their gazes level. Quietly, in a voice as soft as Ren's thoughts, Nico said, "What? You dreamed about me?"

Ren blinked like a man coming out of a memory. *Did I?* He seemed surprised for a moment, but then his mouth quirked. The impish smile it produced made Nico's stomach dip. Ren lifted his other hand, caught a lock of Nico's hair between two long fingers, and pushed it away from his forehead.

"If anyone's awake," Nico said, "they could be watching us right now."

Does that matter?

"It matters," Nico said.

Ren took his hands away, and Nico flexed his fingers where their skin had touched.

Nico said, "I can't—I can't do this right now."

Ren gave him a short, wordless nod. Nico wasn't sure if Ren fully understood what he was saying, but they didn't have time to stand in the street discussing a future that would never happen.

They were several streets away from the house Nico would have one day inherited had he not been tossed aside. There were no words to describe how much he didn't want to be here, how much he didn't want to see someone else living in the place he could have called home, how much he didn't want to walk through this world of faux safety and false comfort.

Safety was only an illusion anyway. Nico knew now that he had never been safe in this city. He had always been one fatal mistake away from ostracism. He would never be safe, because safety didn't exist.

Nico didn't pay the city any attention, didn't reminisce in the memories Vellen's shimmering gold-white beauty held. Being here hurt more than he could ever put into words.

So he said nothing.

THE WHOLE CITY scintillated: streets, buildings, lamps. Many of the buildings had spires so tall they disappeared into the low clouds. Nico saw the city anew, through Ren—the frosted walls, the delicate spires, the curving lines, the silver streets. A sumptuous dream perched amongst mountains.

The arrogant, casual opulence of Vellen hadn't diminished in Nico's absence. After having seen the world, having passed through the villages scattered across the land, the wealth of his homeland was more apparent than ever. There was something appalling about this ostentatious place.

The farther into the city they walked, the more anxious Nico became. Dread built in his stomach, skittered all the way down to his toes. In the folds of Ren's coat, he laced his fingers together tightly. It felt as wrong as he had imagined it would, walking these streets again. They were no longer his streets. It was like every dream he had ever had about this place since he'd been banished. His chest was heavy with the feeling of walking into someone else's home, roaming through their rooms, scuffing his feet across their floors, peeking into their wardrobes. There was the sense that he'd be caught any moment now.

Their boots made the lightest tapping on the cobblestones, the only sound in the whole city.

Into the dawn silence, Ren said, "We could turn around and leave. We could keep running."

"No," Nico said, "we couldn't."

He stole a glance at Ren. In such a grandiose setting, he stood out like a vision, clearer and more real to Nico than ever before. His hair dried in peculiar clumps that poked out every which way. His clothes, ripped and dirty, hung raggedly. A blotch of Nico's blood marked his shirt, conspicuous against the gray fabric. None of that mattered when the pale light of dawn filtered through the crust of clouds and limned him in sunrise gold, turning him dreamy, reshaping him. The light caught in the waves of his hair, kissed his medium-brown skin with gold, and gilded the strong lines of his face.

Looking at Ren was a bad idea.

Ren's question came gently. "Why not run?"

The dew-jeweled road spread out before them, drawing them farther down a path Nico dreaded. "Because there'll be nowhere to run."

Ren spread his arms wide. "There's the whole world. We'll just keep running if we have to. I've always wanted to travel the world."

"You don't understand." He had to explain it. He had to expand Ren's perspective, make him comprehend how massive the situation was. Nico's hands broke apart, and he shoved them into the pockets of Ren's coat. "The wolk want power and death. They'll travel the world eating up life until they've spread death everywhere. They want to own this world. They want to own us. There were two hundred wolk in my camp, and I couldn't fight them. I don't know how to fight them, but I know that I have no chance alone."

Ren was nodding, a slow, thoughtful motion. "I've been living in ignorance."

"That's how most people live."

"Cuddled up soft and remote," Ren went on. "Now the blankets had been thrown off my bed, and it's damn cold out here."

"That's one way to put it." It was, indeed, damn cold out.

"What's the other way to put it?"

"The world is shit."

"Not all of it," Ren said. "Everything isn't shit."

"I didn't see it either, until I was kicked out of my home." At one time, he'd thought everyone lived with glittering snow, soft luxuries, and accessible magic. A world of ease. There were no words to describe how wrong he'd been.

Ren was quiet for a minute before saying, "You don't think you're going to find help here."

"No."

"What about your father? Maybe he'll help."

He's never helped me.

"It's not just that he didn't make any attempt to defend me." Nico's swallow was audible in the quiet dawn. Even that soft sound gave away too many of his feelings on the matter. "He was ready to give me to them."

Ren turned to him in surprise. "You think he wanted to get rid of you?"

Nico folded his arms across his chest. Ahead, the high peaks of the buildings gathered cloud wisps. His father worked in one of those sparkling spires.

"My father didn't like to have contact with me. He hated it that I could read his thoughts. So he made sure we never touched, never played. We were never close." Ren's bright attention distracted him, and he almost lost his thread of thought. "One of my first memories as a child is my dad swinging my sister into the air and carrying her out the back door to play with her in the yard. When I tried to follow, he blocked me with his leg and shoved me back inside. It got worse as I got older. He was—he was a completely different person with me than he was with everyone else."

"And your mother never questioned him?"

"She got sick with the cold fever when I was seven. She had chills for days. Nothing warmed her. Her blood froze in her veins. Her whole body shut down. Magic was useless against it. She died within a week."

"I'm sorry," Ren said. "I've only ever heard of it in passing. I don't think our area gets cold enough to harbor it."

"He treated my sister well, so I knew he was capable of kindness. But he never had any kindness for me."

"This is not going to be the family reunion I pictured. So we don't go to him at all."

"He's on the city council. I can't avoid him if I want the council's help."

"That's...unfortunate."

Nico, keenly aware of Ren's contemplation, walked faster, trying to outpace Ren's next thought. He didn't want to get caught up in whatever Ren was seeing in him at the moment.

It came anyway. Ren was not one to hold his deepest thoughts safely inside. It was a dangerous way to live.

"How could he not want you?" Ren asked in his smooth, mild voice. There was genuine puzzlement there. "You're perfect."

Nico's laugh came unwittingly. It sounded like a low, bitter scrape in his ears. "That must be it. I was too perfect for him. Clearly, I don't belong with mere mortals."

"You didn't belong with a parent who didn't love you. I know that much."

Nico carefully didn't respond to that.

"So what are we going to do?" Ren asked after another quiet stretch of wet cobblestones were behind them.

Besides pause to possibly upchuck on the street?

"We go home," Nico said, "and let him reject me again. He'll enjoy that. But I have to tell them what's coming."

Nico couldn't avoid the deep frown on Ren's face and how wrong it looked on him.

SO EARLY IN the morning, Vellen was nothing but a colorful mix of clouds and reflected sunrise, a swirl of gold and white as they turned down the alley to his sister's home. Crystal icicles hung overhead between the buildings, clinking softly with every shift in the air. There were a dozen different lights trapped in those crystals. Their rainbow reflections danced along the alley walls. As Ren and Nico walked beneath them, the crystals stirred into a gentle musical chorus. It was a familiar sound. He'd run down this alley many times on his way to play in the snow, that same tinkling skipping with him down the walkway.

Beside him, Ren grew thoughtful. "Magic tricks," he said with a shrug. "It's child's play after what I've seen you do."

"Jaded already?" Nico asked him. Their pace slowed beneath the crystal icicles.

"They're beautiful, but they're too showy. Almost... silly." Ren was heedful of Nico's reaction. "Sorry."

"Don't apologize to me. They're not mine."

As they walked, Ren ran his fingers along the smooth pellucid walls of the surrounding buildings. "But it was your hometown at one time."

Swallowing hurt. Nico's throat was suddenly too dry. "None of it's mine anymore."

Ren gave a wordless nod.

Halfway down the alley, Nico stopped at an elaborate archway covered with a strange pearly flower that reached outward. Snowflake flowers, named for their delicate, gossamer petals, each one an intricately different shape and design. The petals melted a few minutes after being touched. In all of his travels across the world, Nico hadn't found them anywhere but Vellen. Apparently, they grew nowhere else. At one time, he'd rolled in a field full of these flowers, wrestling and laughing with other boys until they were all covered in the diaphanous, melting petals. That had been so long ago.

Several steps and two more flower-covered archways later, they stood before a beautiful frost door that shimmered at them in the morning light.

The height of the tall, narrow house was hard to discern craning a neck up at it from below, but Nico knew it was nine stories. It all would have been his, this slim, lofty castle that reached into the clouds. But with him gone, it would have passed to his sister.

Nico's hand shook when he reached up and pressed a button on the door. Ren stood slightly behind him, their shoulders close but not quite touching.

The door opened on a figure, lanky and awkwardly tall, outlined by soft light from behind. Warm air poured toward them. He stood a step above Nico and Ren. Nico forced himself to face the man head-on, a slow process of gathering courage scraps. Silhouetted by the light from the house, the man's features were dim and indistinct, but he seemed uncomfortably familiar.

For a moment, none of the men moved. The tinkle of the rustling crystals filled the cold silence, and the rainbows spun crazily over their faces. Everything Nico had come to say fell out of his head.

An interminable time later, the man in the doorway said, "Nico."

It was not said kindly. But Nico recognized that voice, the nasal whine of it.

At the sound of his name in that gruff manner, Nico leaned back, bumping into Ren. It took him a long moment before he said, with some uncertainty, "Davvon."

A startling gleam of white teeth shone in the dark—a smile. Maybe. "You recognized me," Davvon said.

In the doorway, Davvon tilted his head at them. His green eyes stood out in his shadowy face. They had always unsettled Nico. Like a forest at night, eerie and waiting.

He barely noticed Ren, too busy taking in Nico's body with one long up-and-down sweep. He lingered on the folds of Nico's thin clothes, roaming over the hole where the knife had gone through and pale skin peeked out. Behind Nico, Ren's hand brushed the small of his back, the briefest contact that gave Nico a bare glimpse of his tumbled thoughts.

...looking at Nico like that...making me queasy.

Nico eased slightly away from Ren. His own thoughts were confusing enough at the moment. He didn't need Ren's as well.

"All grown up," Davvon said, the words a slow slide across his tongue. "Oh, I bet they enjoyed having you around."

Nico felt the angry shift of Ren's body at his back. "Aging tends to happen." He didn't dare back down from the challenge in Davvon's stance. "That or death."

"Isn't this glorious," Davvon said. "You look like you were dragged through a gutter. But now that I think about it, I suppose you were."

Though Davvon stood in dimness, the full state of their scruffiness was spotlighted by the sunrise that streamed through the alley. Having lived and traveled with the wolk, Nico had been sweaty and dirty over the years. But he was keenly aware of how he and Ren must appear, standing on the front step of wealth and privilege, each rip and every dirt smudge visible. Ren had a smeared glob of dirt down the leg of his pants and Nico's blood splashed across his shirt. Dirt streaked Ren's face and probably his own as well. Standing before people who held so much power, the grime made Nico feel even more vulnerable. He yearned for a hot bath. He couldn't remember the last time he'd had one.

Nico resisted the urge to reach up and pick at his hair. "So you married Thea," he said with flat impassivity.

"I easily became a part of the family after you left." Davvon's teeth were flashing again. "I was like the son he'd never had."

It hurt more than it should have, like a gut-punch he'd known was coming but couldn't avoid. Though it was exactly the reaction Davvon had been hoping for, and though he'd had years to accept his father's lack of affection, Nico stood on the front step staring at Davvon, his lips parted around a response that didn't come.

Ren cleared his throat, snapping him out of it. Nico asked, "Where's Thea?"

"She's not here."

"Not here? This is her house."

"She'll be back," Davvon said. "In the meantime, you can tell me how your little trip was. I want to know what it was like for a pretty fourteen-year-old boy living with monsters. You must have been popular." A rough chuckle followed.

Nico couldn't shut down the vulnerability of his stunned reaction fast enough. It was already out there, evident on his face, and he knew it. He'd expected rejection. He'd expected disbelief. He had not expected vicious and gloating. Then again, he hadn't expected Davvon.

In the aftermath of that moment, Ren came out from behind Nico and moved past him. Nico didn't anticipate Ren in time: his intention or his speed. It took half a second for Ren's fist to materialize in midair. Nico got it then, but it was already too late. Davvon was mid-chuckle. Ren's fist connected hard with Davvon's laughing mouth and sent him reeling back.

"Shit!" Nico said, already in motion. He put his hands on Ren's arms and jerked them behind Ren's back, restraining. Ren didn't resist the handling, though he easily could have knocked Nico away. The anger ebbed from his thoughts and his body as quickly as it had surged. Against the shell of Ren's ear, Nico hissed, "Are you suicidal?"

Davvon was flattened against the door, mouth bleeding into his hand. Nico didn't need any warning. He knew what was coming.

Nico threw his magic into the air. The seal formed around them quickly, years of practice behind it. The impact of Davvon's magic struck hard against his own, and Nico felt the pressure of it almost as a force inside his body, though it was only his protective seal that Davvon's magic actually hit. The wave of magic lasted no longer than a handful of seconds. Nico felt it in his blood, in his bones: the precise moment Davvon's magic fizzled against his own and died out with a spark that tingled in his chest.

"Oh," Ren said in a faint voice, like a man coming out of a dream.

Davvon could only glare at Nico and Ren, at where they stood untouched. He staggered back a step before he caught himself, a bony hand clutched on the frame of the door. "You're stronger than you used to be."

Nico loosened his hold on Ren's arms. As they pulled apart, their fingers brushed. Briefly, Nico's blood flared with magic and adrenaline and Ren's blazing thoughts, the combination dizzying.

When Nico didn't respond, Davvon blasted Ren with a nasty scowl. "You dare," he said, voice low, "come to my house and attack me?" He'd mostly ignored Ren at first, but he definitely took notice of him now.

"Ignore him," Nico told Davvon. "It won't happen again."

"I should peel the skin off his face." Davvon's own face looked a little rough, the blood from his busted lip leaking between his fingers over his pale skin.

"He's a plebeian," Nico said. It was hard to speak calmly against the racing of his heart. Magicians never used against other magicians, but the rules regarding outsiders were hazier. Outsiders rarely ever visited Vellen. "He's not worth it."

If he had to disparage Ren to keep his skin on his body, then Nico would go with it. He preferred Ren in one piece.

"That's why we don't bring gutter rats here," Davvon said from between his blood-wet fingers. "They're basic. What is he—" A heavy, uncomfortable pause. "—your boyfriend?"

"He's an acquaintance I met along the way."

Ren smartly kept quiet.

Davvon's disgust nevertheless emanated from the doorway. Nico thought he could feel it as an oily residue on his skin as soon as he let his magical seal dissipate.

"I bet you find many *acquaintances*."

"I didn't expect such a salacious welcome at my sister's house," Nico said.

Davvon's lip curled. He leaned into the light, and a gaunter version of the teenager Nico remembered came into view. He was no more than five years older than Nico, but his skin was rough, his dark hair wispy-thin, his cheekbones painfully stark. The swaying crystal rainbows caught on his rawboned features.

"You," Davvon said to Ren. "If you come into my house and attempt to assault me again, I'll make sure you leave this city with one less limb."

Nico pinched the inside of Ren's wrist, and Ren's revulsion in the face of Davvon's demeanor poured through his mind.

"Understood," Ren said, meeting that forest-dark disdain.

There were the white teeth again, perfectly straight and more than a little disturbing when Davvon's lips peeled away from them in a slow grimace. There was blood on the white.

"And no fucking Nico under my roof." The grinning grimace widened.

With deliberate care, Nico said, "That won't be a problem."

Davvon gave a high-pitched laugh that grated on Nico's nerves. He stood aside. Nico trailed Davvon into the house with Ren close behind.

Warm air enveloped them. Nico took a deep breath of it. Nothing smelled the same. Throughout his childhood, this had been his great-aunt's house. Back then it had smelled of fireplaces and melting chocolate. He and Thea had chased each other up and down its nine stories.

Having no cousins, Nico would have inherited his aunt's house. Thea was to inherit their childhood home when their father passed. Now it would all be Thea's one day. Better not to dwell on a life he might have led.

As they moved through the soaring entryway, Nico carefully shut himself off from the house's splendor—from everything he'd lost. He found Ren, who gawked at the grandeur and made no attempt to conceal his awe, far more interesting. Of course, Ren would be taken with the architecture. He built things like that improbable, wonderful tree house Nico had nearly destroyed.

He couldn't blame Ren for his blatant awe. Everything about this place screamed magic. Every crystalline wall was delicately balanced atop glass floors and over even more fragile walls. The only thing holding all of it up was the magic woven into the structure. Nico remembered the entire house, its opulence and comfort stamped into his heart.

They paused near a staircase. To their right, delicate frosted steps curved upward. The ceiling soared beyond sight. Somewhere above, sunlight glinted through the transparent ceiling, and the stairs seemed to curve endlessly into the golden half-light.

"I guess they don't have homes like this in the lowlands." Davvon basked in Ren's wonder, slurping it up like the greedy asshole he was. Nico figured Davvon would probably wallow in it later, like a pig in the mud.

Davvon hadn't changed at all. For him, life was about status and riches, about possessing beautiful things others didn't have.

"No," Ren said, "they don't."

"It's easy to create a place like this when you have magic," Nico said, studying Ren's face. "It's a lot more magical to create something from nothing with your bare hands."

Ren shared an intimate smile with Nico, the intensity of it as tangible as a touch.

Oblivious, Davvon moved toward the stairs. "Why would you toil in the dirt making some dinky thing with your hands when you could create this?" He swept his hand over the curling pearl banister as if to indicate the whole grand spectacle.

Behind Davvon's back, Nico mouthed, *Blah blah blah,* and Ren had to suppress a laugh into his shoulder. The past day was catching up with both of them. They were running on exhaustion and emotions, all of it ready to spill over in an alarming variety of reactions.

As they ascended the stairs, Davvon said, "Please bathe first, before you soil anything. Some of my old clothes are in the wardrobe."

As if Davvon hadn't already soiled Nico's family home.

As they spiraled higher into the clouds, Nico's sense of dread increased. Something was wrong. Thea was nowhere to be found, and there was no reason for Davvon to let them in without Thea here. He should have turned them away at the door. Nico folded his arms close to his body and fantasized about flinging Davvon down the stairs.

The climb to the eighth floor took forever. Davvon went slowly so that Ren wouldn't miss a thing. Finally, they reached a landing where an arched doorway led into yet another fragile dream. Davvon ushered them into the room.

The space was the delicate color of an eggshell. Ivory gossamer fabric hung in waves from the ceiling, brushing the floor along the walls. A low bed took up the length of one entire wall, piled with pale, fluffy pillows and a blanket shot through with flecks of pearl. A fluffy white rug covered most of the floor, like something you could drown your feet in. Morning light filtered through the walls in a way that lit the room in soft silver.

God, it was everywhere, Nico realized. Growing up, he'd never noticed the blatant affluence. Wealth and riches swam in Ren's wide eyes as he stopped in the open archway to take in the room.

Ren entered the room gingerly, his entire focus on the fine opaque floor beneath their feet. He leaned his weight on one foot and then the other, as if that would make a difference between safety and death.

"You don't have to worry about the floor," Nico said. "A lot of magicians have reinforced it. Nothing in this city will break."

"No one can shatter it," Davvon said, leaning against the arched doorway, arms crossed, "especially not some peasant."

"Fine," Ren said and stepped with care to as far as the rug.

"Shower before you touch anything," Davvon said. "You know where the bathing room is, Nico."

Nico and Ren stood in the middle of the floor, at the center of delicate riches. Ren turned in a slow circle. Ivory streamers from above floated around him, swaying with his movements.

"Where's Thea?" Nico asked again.

Davvon shrugged against the doorframe. "I told you, she'll be here soon. She's hardly ever home anymore. I'll bring some food up later." Thankfully, with that, he left them alone.

Nico turned on Ren. "What is it with you?"

Ren blinked at him as though he were coming out of a daydream. "What?"

"The first thing you do is take a swing at him? I thought by now you'd have learned not to anger someone who has magic. What's wrong with you?"

"Nothing."

"Oh, there's definitely something." It was cruel. Nico knew it was harsh. But he didn't understand why Ren didn't value his own life more.

Ren stood his ground in the face of Nico's harangue. "I've never met anyone who needed to be punched as much as that man."

Nico felt like he could take a swing of his own then, right at Ren's head. It wouldn't be fair, of course. Ren could take him with pure physicality, but Nico had more power at his will than Ren had in his whole body.

Nico balled his fists against his stomach, calming himself. Time stretched between them, their raw connection the only thing in the room.

"He could take you out with one swipe," Nico said. "Do you understand that?"

"My arm was moving before I realized it." He said it like a meager offering, like he already knew it wasn't enough. "I'm not usually so hotheaded. I don't know what— I usually don't jump into fights. I try to control myself better than that."

"Really?" Nico kept his frustration balled in fists. "Because you did a pretty good impression of a macho dimwit today."

"I'm exhausted. That's the only reason I—"

"So you start punching people when you're tired."

Nico regarded Ren with a new slant. He needed to reassess his impression of Ren as innocuous. Ren caught Nico's expression and seemingly absorbed the situation.

More softly, Ren said, "That was the closest I've ever come to being like my pa. It didn't feel good. I don't lose my temper like that. I don't go around punching people. The last man I hit was—" He stopped himself, changed course. "The last man I hit was a long time ago." Ren faced Nico helplessly, his empty hands spread in the air between them. "The vulgar way Davvon was talking to you—"

"—had nothing to do with you," Nico said firmly. "Stay out of it."

"You don't deserve to be spoken to like that. No one does. It's not right. I only—"

Nico jabbed Ren in the chest with his finger, a move that shocked them both. "Don't make me have to fight him to protect you. Don't look at him. Don't touch him. If he defends himself with magic—and he will—I'm going to have to jump in again. I don't need that right now."

"I won't do anything else." Ren held up a hand. "I swear."

"If you do," Nico said, "I'll take you out myself." And he meant it.

"I don't want to make this worse for you," Ren said. "I can control myself."

Nico deflated quickly. He'd spent the last bit of his energy on that surge of anger. Getting physical, even if it was only his finger in Ren's space, depleted him. Before Ren could open his mouth again, Nico dropped onto the mattress. Its soft cushions curved around his body, such delicious support. His muscles began to relax. He hadn't felt a bed this soft in years. Having a ceiling overhead shocked him. It had been so long. The room above was a mystery, nothing but dark shadows of furniture, indistinguishable through the frosted glass.

"You must have found all of the villages in my area primitive, after living in this place." Ren's voice floated to him from across the room. It held the same sleepy weight Nico felt in his own limbs. "The rest of the world must have paled in comparison to your homeland."

Nico dropped his arms to the bed, stretched out against the silk of the coverlet. He felt like a man caught in free fall, like the bed might drop out from under him at any moment and he would plummet, arms spread wide.

"The rest of the world surprised me at first," Nico admitted. "I thought everywhere was like this."

"You look like you belong here," Ren said, "with all of these beautiful things."

Nico snorted. "I never belonged here."

"Do you ever wish you did?"

"Not when I remember the people who live here," Nico said into the fine, silvery air. "None of the beauty matters once you know who lives inside the buildings."

Ren sat on the bottom edge of the bed next to him, and it dipped Nico slightly toward him. "Are you all right?" Ren asked, caution in his tone.

To the ceiling, Nico said, "I didn't think he would be here."

"Davvon?"

"He and my sister were together a long time ago when we were young."

"Was he as charming back then?" Ren's grin curled around the words.

"We've always disliked each other," Nico said. "He hated that I came from a prominent family. He hated that I was more powerful than he was even though I was younger. He hated that Thea and I were so close." His voice softened as the memories trickled through his mind. "But then he changed her."

"Changed her?"

"She was an eighteen-year-old girl completely in love. He became her entire world. I don't know what that's like but—" Ren's brows rose. "But we were close before Davvon entered the picture. Her attitude toward me changed when she was with him. She started—she started treating me a lot more like my father did. She was the only reason our house was livable for me. Until Davvon showed up."

"So he had a lot of influence on your family."

"My father welcomed him with open arms. By the time I was tossed out, he was practically living at our house. It was a bit like they both fell in love with Davvon."

"Gross," Ren said and languidly stretched his legs out over the floor.

"My father had always hoped for a different son anyway. I suppose it worked out for him."

The mattress jiggled a little with every little movement Ren made. "Talk about a downgrade."

Nico folded his arms beneath his head and felt Ren's focus shift to his body. "What?" He dared Ren to voice what he was thinking, even though he had a pretty good idea what Ren had in mind.

"Nothing." Ren cleared his throat. "You have freckles on the underside of your chin. Just a few."

Apparently, he had no idea what went through Ren's head. Nico swallowed unwittingly, the moment dangerous, so close on a bed and the both of them so exhausted. Sprawled comfortably, Nico's legs hung off the end of the mattress. He let the coat fall open and flare out on either side of him, mindful of the way Ren skimmed his body. Nico's villager was too polite for an outright ogle, so he indulged in what he thought were furtive glances. He'd been sneaking little peeks the entire journey.

Too tired to shower, too tired to discourage Ren's infatuation, he just wanted to sink into the bed and sleep.

Ren's hand rested close to Nico's thigh. Also dangerous.

Nico said, "I shouldn't be surprised that she married him but...I am. She deserved someone better. Someone *more*."

Ren went along willingly. "Someone who isn't an asshole?"

"Yes."

"Love makes people blind. At least when it's fresh."

"Right." From his comfortable sprawl, Nico regarded Ren with solemn curiosity. "Been in love a lot, have you?"

Ren's grin dimpled. "A few times."

Nico turned away, safer. "Of course you have."

"It's fun," Ren said. "Dizzying, fast, thrilling. None lasted long, but I don't think I would want to trade any of those times." There was a pause. "You don't know what I'm talking about, do you? You haven't been in love?" Ren noticed Nico's frown. "Ever?"

Nico kicked his leg against the bed's frame, an idle tick. *Bump bump bump.* He couldn't seem to keep completely still, no matter how tired he was. "Who would I have been in love with? One of the wolk? Zeke, perhaps?"

Ren shifted uncomfortably. "Who's Zeke?"

Nico lifted his hand from the bed in a lazy gesture. "The one missing an arm. A real charmer."

"How lonely," Ren said softly. His hand on the bed next to Nico's leg remained very still. Nico, keenly aware of how motionless that hand was, had an incredible urge to nudge his leg into Ren's space. He resisted, though one lift of Ren's finger and he would be brushing along Nico's thigh.

Dangerous.

"He wasn't lonely," Nico said. "He still had the other arm." He let his hand flop onto his stomach. *Bump bump bump* went his leg. "But now he's dead, so it doesn't matter."

"You know what I meant."

Nico got a little lost in Ren and came to only when he realized their conversation had paused. Ren was all solid, golden-brown lines against the pale white room, a beautiful contrast. He was refreshingly disheveled against the meticulous order, impossible to ignore. Currently, he was focused on the spot where his hand lay next to Nico's leg. For a moment, they both contemplated that hand.

Nico sat up suddenly, and Ren snapped back into the moment with a little jerk.

"You can have the bath first," Nico said.

"We could share," Ren said with a shrug. He read the expression on Nico's face. "Never mind."

"Being naked, wet, and vulnerable together while that asshole lurks outside the door sounds like a fun time to you?"

"I always manage to choose the wrong thing to say to you." Ren let out a short, self-deprecating laugh.

"That's not—" With a deep sigh, Nico ran a hand down his face. "I can't do this now, Ren."

"I get it." Ren stood up to grab some clothes from the wardrobe. He hesitated with a pair of thick black pants between his hands. "It's only that— Well. I know I angered him. Do you think he might come after me while I'm in there? You know, with his magic?"

Nico got up from the bed and stood in the doorway where he could see if Davvon came up the stairs. "I'll watch the door."

Ren passed close, brushing by Nico in the open archway, and Nico went still. It was unprecedented, the way his magic stirred deep in his body when Ren came near. It had happened before with Ren, only once, but this time it left Nico pressing his back into the frame of the arch to keep upright. The shock of it jolted him. His magic surged in his bones, in his blood, almost as if it wanted to reach out to Ren. Nico grasped the doorframe at his back and dug his fingernails into the smooth glass. It offered no comforting grip.

That wasn't how magic worked. It didn't ebb and flow depending on who was near. It didn't *react* to people.

It happened in an instant, and then Ren passed into the hall, and Nico's magic settled.

"I've never had a guard before," Ren said on his way to the bathing room. "I guess if I have to have one, I'm glad it's you. At least I get a gorgeous guard, right?" He laughed as he ducked into the room.

Nico could barely stand. He stared at Ren's retreating back.

What in the hell are you?

Chapter Eleven

REN

Ren's muscles felt wonderfully loose and melty. Exhausted but much more relaxed, he floated out of the bathing room on mint-scented air. The cakes of soap had smelled of fresh herbs, and there were lavender hair cleansers. He smelled like a garden.

From the doorway of the bedroom, Nico followed Ren's progress down the hallway. He leaned against the arched entryway, arms crossed, mouth its usual serious line, gleaning unknowable things from Ren's every movement. Ren had never been analyzed so closely.

"What?" Ren asked as he walked up to Nico. "Did he come up the stairs?"

"Only to bring a tray of food." Nico swept a look up and down Ren's body, a slow roving. "His clothes don't fit you at all."

Davvon was Ren's height, but he was a weedy man. He had nothing on Ren's width. The borrowed shirt strained tight across his chest and shoulders. The pants, thankfully, had some kind of stretch to them, but none of it felt right on his body.

Ren crossed one ankle over the other and leaned against the curved entryway opposite Nico. They were close enough he could taste Nico's magic, a warm, lush, earthy tingle on his tongue. The longer he was with Nico, the more he sensed his magic all around them, like another piece of Nico akin to hair or scent. He loved Nico's magic, the power of it so near, the growing familiarity of it.

He smelled the woods in Nico's hair. It made him want to lean in, but he didn't. He said, "Should I take them off?"

Nico paused. It took him a beat to say, "No."

"Because I will if you want me to."

"No." Nico's voice was firm, but his fingers were light when he trailed them across Ren's skin where the stretched neckline of the shirt revealed his collarbone. Ren stood frozen, too afraid to shatter the moment, but Nico withdrew anyway.

Nico touched him as though Ren might have an answer—and stopped when he realized Ren didn't even know the question.

"I left you half of the food he brought," Nico said.

"I'll guard the door for you now."

Surprise flashed across Nico's face. "Why?"

Ren thought it was obvious. "Because I don't like the way he talked to you. I don't like the way he looked at you. I know I'm no match against his magic, but I can at least stand here and holler if he's about to come in there and harass you."

"I—" Nico searched Ren's face. "You don't have to do that."

"You did it for me."

Nico stayed in the doorway, an uncertain figure. "Don't you want to eat and rest?"

"I can watch your back and eat at the same time." Ren grinned at him. "I'm multitalented."

Nico leaned toward him. "Are you?"

That piqued Ren's interest. From anyone else, it would be flirtation, but Nico said it with a straight face and his usual reticence. From him, it could just as easily be distracted small talk.

"Hey," Ren said. "It's fine. Truly, I don't mind." Nico's surprise that someone would do something so simple for him tightened Ren's stomach. It made him wonder when the last time was that anyone had had Nico's back. Ren started to slip by him to grab some of the food. As he turned, he put a light, brief hand on Nico's shoulder in reassurance. "You're good. Go bathe."

Nico hesitated another moment. He got caught up on Ren's lips, his neck. Then he ducked into the room, grabbed some of Davvon's old clothes from the wardrobe, and rushed past Ren toward the bathing room.

Ren let his head thunk back against the arched doorway. With any luck, it would knock all of the jumbled thoughts from his mind.

NICO EMERGED FROM the bathing room with a trail of fresh steam in his wake.

Ren's mind had been drifting as he leaned against the wall, but he flung sleep aside at the sight of Nico. Drowsily, unthinkingly, he said, "You look—"

"Don't," Nico said. He sounded spent. His arms were full of his bloody, torn clothes.

"—fresh."

Even from down the hall, Nico looked like he would smell good, of clean soap and warm skin. Free of product and forest dirt, his hair fell softly straight into his eyes. His pale skin, still flushed from the hot water, set off the red of his stubble.

Ren went into the room and climbed into bed. Nico followed him through the archway. Davvon's too-long pants dragged endearingly around his feet.

Nico dumped the clothes on the floor by the wardrobe. The sleeves of his shirt, Ren noticed, hung down past his fingertips. A strange flutter passed through Ren's stomach. They sized each other up across the silvery elegance of the room.

Nico pushed his sleeves up to his elbows. "What?"

"Nothing." Ren's heart pumped desperately. *You. Why do you get to me?*

It was overwhelming, the urge to gather Nico in his arms, to press kisses into the bright shock of red hair that swept across his forehead until the tension ran out of his body and he melted against Ren. He wanted to see Nico like that—loose and carefree and happy. He wondered what kind of person Nico was without all of the heartache and worry.

Nico ran a hand across his mouth. "We're in my sister's house."

Ren blinked at him. "I know that."

"This is hell. I'm in hell right now. Stop looking at me like that in hell."

"Like what?"

"You want to fuck me right now. I can tell."

"No," Ren said. Nico looked at Ren, and Ren stared right back at him. "Well, yes. But—"

"Nothing's going to happen between us, Ren."

Ren's stomach ached. Maybe he'd eaten too fast. He'd scarfed down the cheese, cream, and bread. "I know that."

A single red brow lifted. "Do you?"

"Yes."

Nico sighed and walked across the floor toward him. Even the way he moved got to Ren, all sleek grace.

Ren lay back, stretched out, and let his spine sink into the mattress. It was the most comfortable bed he'd ever been in, and that included many of the beds in his village and some of the neighboring village beds as well. He was welcome in many bedrooms, but none had ever been as nice as this one.

Nico crawled into the covers. For someone who'd been living in a camp with demons, apparently sleeping in a tent most nights, Nico spent an inordinate amount of time plumping and arranging his stack of pillows before he lay down. Ren had to hold back a laugh as Nico meticulously smoothed wrinkles out of the bedding.

Though the mattress took up one entire wall, they lay close. Close but most definitely not touching. The bed moved beneath Ren with Nico's restless shifting. He wished Nico would stop moving. It was distracting.

The whole room was distracting. Ren didn't know how these people slept with the subtle, swirling lights in the walls and in the floors. Tiny opalescent sparks of color melted into new colors behind the frosted walls. It wasn't bright, but the movement was enough to catch in Ren's periphery. He wanted to reach into the walls, trace his fingers through the melting swirls. And that was the most distracting thing of all. More than anything else in the city, the sinuous colors trapped in the walls looked like pure, raw magic, and Ren wanted to feel it, hold it in his hands. It was so close. *Right there.*

Ren supposed it was something you just got used to— this dazzling, delicate world of magic.

"What happened between you and Davvon?" Ren asked.

In the glass floor above them, lights danced in dozens of colors and poured down the walls, yet Nico in bed beside him tempted him more than anything else.

The fidgeting stopped. "Nothing."

"I don't know how you ended up surrounded by so many creeps."

Nico's head turned toward him on the pillow, a bright spot in the room, an enticement. "What do you mean?"

"I mean the wolk. Your father." Ren waved a hand at the doorway. "Your charming brother-in-law. I don't know how you managed to get all of them in your life. That's unlucky."

"I didn't choose them."

"That's the unlucky part," Ren said. "They ended up in your life anyway." Nico went quiet. Ren glanced at him without thinking, caught sight of one arm bent comfortably above his head, of red hair against an ivory pillow, of loose shirt and bare neck. "But you got me in your life. Maybe you're not so unlucky after all."

Nico made a disgusted noise that had Ren laughing. "God, what a line," Nico said. "It's hard for me to believe you charmed your way through your whole village with that kind of stale stink."

"Hey now. I'm usually quite charming, except when I'm with you. Nothing works on you, and I know it won't work, so it all comes out badly from the beginning."

"A convenient story. Right. Of course. It's just because I'm so *unique*."

Daylight seeped through the frosted walls, far from the sweet dark of night that allowed for sleep. The filtered light bathed the bed in a dim, lazy silver glow. Ren fidgeted on his pillow, cleared his throat. Magic swirled in the walls around them. Ren forgot about it. Every sense zeroed in on Nico.

Nico sighed sleepily. "This house has been in our family for years. It's been passed down through generations. I was supposed to inherit it."

Forgetting himself, Ren turned to Nico. "This was going to be your home? Really?"

"Davvon never liked that either, on top of already disliking me. He thought it should go to Thea. He said I already had too much. Big inheritance, powerful magic, prominent father."

"Jealous little bastard, isn't he?"

Nico snorted. "I wouldn't call my father a golden prize. It was like growing up with a cold fish as a father."

"So that little weasel managed to steal your position in your family and take your home."

Nico took a long time to reply. He had the blanket pushed down to his waist. Ren caught a hint of pale skin where the loose shirt had bunched up in the covers.

Finally, blinking up at the ceiling, Nico said, "I don't know why he would despise me now. Our positions are flipped. I have nothing."

"Well," Ren said without thinking, "you're gorgeous. There's that."

Nico's gaze drifted to Ren's face. "What does that mean?"

"I saw the way he was leering at you. I don't know what other issues he has, but that's definitely part of it. Maybe he wanted you to have that taken away too."

"I—" Nico closed his mouth, his thoughts seeming to build like a thundercloud, and Ren realized he stood out in the open, exposed to Nico's growing anger. "Listen, I know you like me, but don't project your—"

"I'm not," Ren said, insistent despite the danger. "Just the sight of your face tees him off. It's obvious. He can't stand it. It kills him that you're strong *and* attractive."

"That's ridiculous."

"Is it? He stole so much from you, but he couldn't have everything. It probably eats at him. Actually, he really does give the impression of being a little chewed at the edges."

"What is there to be jealous of in appearances? What in the hell has being attractive gotten me in life?" Nico swallowed loudly and twisted the blankets viciously in his hands. "Besides the daily harassment of a monster horde. Beauty is damned useless. An empty, subjective, fleeting concept. None of these people would know that, playing house in their protected towers, in their sheltered city. They're too busy throwing parties and sleeping until noon. They haven't seen the way our world actually works." He jammed his hands into his hair, clenched his fingers in the damp strands, and grimaced. "They haven't had to deal with anything but parties and privilege. Fuck. *Fuck*. Fuck them all."

Ren reached for him across the bedclothes. As his hand made contact with Nico's shoulder, another thoughtless bit of unwanted comfort, Nico said, "No, *no*, don't touch me."

That was all Ren needed to hear to lift his hands in the air: surrender.

Nico said, "There are monsters out there sucking humans dry, and the only people who could stop them are sitting in this useless city worried about who's prettier and who has the bigger seat on the council." He squeezed the strands of hair between his fingers. "It's sick. It's fucked up."

"I shouldn't have said anything about Davvon. It doesn't matter what he thinks."

"For a month, Zeke killed one person every night I didn't sleep with him."

"What? Good God," Ren whispered across the pillows. "I don't—"

"He brought one to me each morning and slit their throat in front of me. Thirty people died because of me. That was only one month out of fourteen years. And Davvon is *jealous* of me?" Nico spat the words out. He dragged his hands over his face, fisted them over his eyes. "I couldn't do it. It was the last thing I had left. I knew—I knew if I let them over that boundary, I was gone. It was over. I lost count of how many innocent people died because of me over the years. Because I wouldn't capitulate. I got—I got so many people killed." His voice hitched. "There was just—a pile of bodies growing around me while I did nothing."

"No," Ren said. "No way were those deaths your fault. You weren't responsible. Nico, you can't actually believe that. Tell me you don't actually believe that."

Nico shook his head. "I could have done something to stop them."

"You couldn't have. No matter what you gave, they would have asked for more. That's what monsters do."

Nico let a long silence seep across the bed.

"Just go to sleep," he said eventually, voice tight, his frustration hidden behind his fists.

Chapter Twelve

REN

Ren blinked awake to the comfortably dim room. He sensed Nico's magic in the air—a wonderful thickness, warmth he could breathe in and hold briefly in his lungs. The longer they spent together, the more sensitive he became to Nico's magic. Even now, he recognized it in bed with them, gathered close to Nico's body, spread across the blankets and hanging languidly in the air. It wasn't like a third presence in the bed, but more like being under a favorite old blanket, or cuddled against a lover—a layer of safety against the dark. The air held a faint gold dust, gone when Ren turned his head or blinked. He knew that was Nico's magic too, the same way he knew the warm tingle on his tongue was also Nico's magic. Ren was surrounded. It was exquisite, a brush along all of his senses.

Nico. I'm in bed with Nico. The heat, the solidity of Nico nearby was a comfort in itself. Ren turned his head.

Curled on his side, Nico was heavy-lidded and sleepy, hair a tumbled mess in his face. Helplessly, Ren smiled at the mussy sight of him and then shuttered it quickly. It was not the time for smiling.

Nico had slept like a thunderstorm. He'd tossed and turned so much he'd churned the bedclothes into a storm. In the center of the chaos, he lay curled inward, with the wild beauty of the eye of a storm.

"Hello," Ren said, his voice sleep-scratchy.

Nico didn't respond. In the absence of a reply, he didn't return Ren's smile either, which didn't surprise Ren at all. Nico wilted toward sleep, his features relaxed in the drowsy glow of the room.

"I'm an oblivious twerp," Ren said softly. "You must have hated it."

Nico stirred back to life. "Hated what?"

"Every time I called you beautiful, or implied it, or teased you about it. I thought I was being smooth, but I was actually being a jerk."

"At least," Nico said, "you didn't say it like a threat."

Ren had to close his eyes, shut out the meaning of those words for just a moment. The whole time, he'd thought he was flirting. He'd thought it was a game. "I thought you were playing hard to get."

"No," Nico said sleepily.

"No," Ren agreed.

"I can't figure you out."

"There isn't much to figure out."

Nico started to say something but then seemed to change course. "I didn't mean to tell you any of that. I shouldn't have told you. You're just a man I dragged from a village."

"You don't have to apologize for anything."

"I'm not apologizing. I'm telling you. It's bad enough you're here. I keep pulling you in further. You don't need to know the whole story. You shouldn't have to hear *any* of my story. You shouldn't have to hear about all of the death and violence."

"Maybe I need to hear it now. I'm a part of this. I'm not a regular man anymore," Ren said, turning it over in his sleep-slow brain. "Not after what I've seen. Not after I saw my people—" *No. Not that.*

Perhaps it was the sleepy light or the warm bed, but Nico's countenance softened. "No, you're right. You're not a regular man."

"But you? You're up there with the strongest person I've ever known. And that's saying a lot, because my ma was a strong woman. She survived my pa, and he was a nasty bit. A monster in his own way."

Nico blinked drowsily. "Your father? What was wrong with your father?"

Ren hesitated. This was the part he always had trouble explaining. His pa had been a charmer and an amazing actor. He'd come to the village in a traveling theater troupe. Ren's ma, barely out of her teens, had fallen for him.

"He was a harsh man," Ren said as he gathered uneasy memories that didn't want to be stirred. "She put up with a lot and still managed to raise me to be a better man than my pa ever was."

Nico smoothed his fingers over the sheet between their bodies. "Did he hurt her?"

"Every single day."

"Did he hurt you?"

"Not—not in a physical way. It was all emotional. There are so many ways to hurt a person without ever laying a finger on them."

Nico's thoughts remained shuttered behind the tangled fall of his hair, but his fingers stuttered in the wrinkled bedsheets. "I know." He fiddled with the wrinkles between them, flattened them back out, and then crinkled them again. "She couldn't leave him?"

"She had nowhere to go." Ren shook his head, remembering how trapped she'd been in the situation, how resigned. "He would have found us. He had the town on his side. He was so good. Such a brilliant actor. So adept at fooling people. We wouldn't have been able to get far enough away. But she stayed calm, mostly. She kept me happy and comfortable. She got up every day and lived in spite of him. He never touched her, but he was verbally abusive. He beat her down mentally every day. He always had something ugly to say to her. And to me if she wasn't in the room to shield me. An environment can be abusive even if there's no physical abuse involved."

The sleepy eyes widened slightly with understanding, the gold in them alight. "Are you trying to equate my situation with your mother's?"

Ren tilted his head.

"It wasn't—I wasn't—" Nico closed his mouth, swallowed the rest.

"No?" Ren said softly.

It came as a whisper: "No. They didn't hurt me." It sounded worn, familiar, like something he'd told himself often.

"Put in your situation for so many years like that, a lot of people would have broken down." Ren dipped his head a little to peer beneath that screen of hair. "Hell, I would have broken down. I never would have been able to make it through all of that. Day in and day out. Alone... At least Ma and I had each other. Ma shielded me so that I didn't take the brunt of his abuse."

Nico's fingers moved across the bed, fiddled with more wrinkles in the sheet, and then found the loose edge of Ren's sleeve to twist back and forth between his thumb and forefinger. He toyed with the fabric as he spoke, not quite touching Ren. "Why didn't the village help your mother?"

"She didn't want to tell them," Ren said. "They all thought my pa was a good man. The whole village loved him. She didn't think they would believe her. He was this truly horrible creature who was so good at pretending not to be. After she passed away when I was thirteen, I told them about Pa. They believed me, and I think they felt guilty for not seeing it for so many years. I realized later that I should have told them sooner, but for so many years Pa had me convinced that if I said anything, no one would believe me either. He told me they'd banish me from my home. When I finally told the rest of the village, it was him they banished. But for all those years, I was so young, and he had my mind so...muddled. I didn't get the courage to tell anyone until I was older. My whole view of the world was warped until I was free of him. The village helped raise me for the next four years until I was old enough to live on my own."

"Is that why you never left the village? Because they helped you after your parents died?"

It caught Ren by surprise—the immediate understanding, the empathy that transformed Nico's mouth as he said it. With that tenderness, with that tone of voice, this Nico was a completely different man to the somber, cool one Ren had first encountered. This Nico felt like a genuine human being instead of a remote fantasy.

"Yes," Ren said. "My father tried to come back years after they banished him. I caught him in the vineyards, and I lost it. I hit him. I knocked him into the dirt. I would have gone further, but they were suddenly there." Ren had to stop, clear his throat, clear the vivid memories out of his head. "They stopped me from doing something I would have regretted for the rest of my life."

Something in Nico's expression shifted, newly alert. "You would have killed your father?"

"I don't know," Ren said honestly. "I might have."

Nico was very still. "Could you really have killed your own father? With your bare hands?"

Ren shook his head, though he didn't know for sure. "They made sure I didn't do it. They took care of it. They kept him away from the village and away from me. After that, they were my family. We were solid."

"Family comes with a lot of obligations," Nico said, his voice a thoughtful murmur. He snorted softly. "Not my family obviously, but some families. Or so I've observed."

"That," Ren said, "and because I became their builder. I think the village would have fallen apart without me there to constantly repair and rebuild. There was one other builder, but I was the best they had." Ren hesitated. He had never said it aloud to anyone, but he said it now. "I dreamed of leaving every night. I daydreamed about it all day."

Nico let out a little sigh. "I'm sorry you didn't find something good when you finally did leave."

Ren let that settle in his mind before he said softly, "Who says I didn't?"

Nico's fingers on Ren's shirt faltered. He licked his lips, said, "You didn't."

Ren studied his face in the soft silver light leaking in from outside. "Do you think of yourself as a bad person?"

"No, I—"

"You what?"

"I'm a coward. All of the people I saw killed..." Nico squeezed the fabric of Ren's shirt between his fingers. "You don't know how many there were, Ren."

"Do you think I'm a coward for letting my pa hurt my ma?"

"You were young."

"So," Ren said carefully, pointedly, "were you. You got out when you could."

Nico let out a long breath. "The wolk and I formed a delicate balance. I didn't harm any of them. I didn't use my magic against them. I let them drain me and use my magic. I didn't try to escape again. They didn't force me to help them drain people. And they didn't hurt me. They didn't touch me except to drain me. I was scared to tip that balance. So I did nothing. One slip, and I was done." His voice tightened. "So I let them hurt other people instead. For years."

"You're doing something now." Nico's hand was too close to resist. Ren brushed the tips of his fingers over the back of Nico's knuckles.

Much to Ren's relief, Nico didn't pull away. His fingers stopped fidgeting, and he went very still under Ren's touch.

"If I were as strong as you seem to think I am," Nico said, "I would have done something years ago. I would have found a way to escape sooner. I would have found a way to end it."

"You can't blame yourself for the things they did while you were their captive." Nico opened his mouth as if to protest, but Ren didn't pause. "No. You didn't have any control over the situation. You can't live with their wrongdoings on your conscience. Eventually, it'll tear you apart if you keep thinking that way. If I blamed myself for not doing anything about my pa all those years, I never would have managed to live my life. But I realize now that I couldn't have done anything about him. I was just a child, and he had me under his control."

Nico sighed into the blankets. His voice came out hushed. "I don't think I can get past it. Any of it."

Ren slid his fingers over the grooves of Nico's knuckles, slowly traversed the bumps and valleys between bone. "You do what you can now." Their hands transfixed Nico as he followed the path of Ren's fingers. "They can't hurt you anymore."

Nico spoke in a whisper. "They can."

"No. That part of your life is over."

"But it's not over." With quiet desperation: "You don't get it, Ren. It's never over. They always find me."

Ren covered Nico's hand with his own, said quietly, "Did you try to escape before?"

Nico hesitated, and Ren realized he was fighting against a deep-seated fear that had probably haunted him for years. How much easier it must have been for him to keep it sealed up inside, to never talk about it. Nico's reluctance curled around them in the quiet blankets. Then he nodded against the pillow. Ren was learning that Nico always paused before giving away a piece of himself, always had to deal with those fragments of fear in a way that wouldn't splinter him.

Ren wanted to absorb some of that enduring strength.

Nico said, "Right after I was first given to them. I used the snow to come back home. I didn't know anywhere else to go. It wouldn't have mattered." Nico stopped, cleared the catch out of his voice. He had a faraway expression, his thoughts clearly tangled up in a memory. "They caught me in the mountains an hour later. That's when I learned they could follow my magic trail. They can't use the weather to travel like I can, but they can move fast over the land. Inhumanly fast." His fingers were still beneath Ren's palm, his bright head a chaotic red gleam against the ivory-gold room. "I floundered for years after that."

Ren kept his voice low, secluded in the tumble of blankets. "Anyone would have." He couldn't imagine what they might have done to Nico after catching him in an escape attempt. He didn't ask, didn't want to know.

There was a new tremor to Nico's voice, as fine as the musical thread that bound his accent. "I floundered every night when they drained me and then circled me until morning. I floundered when I had to get up every morning and face them again and again. I floundered when one of them would look at me too long, and I had to retreat into my tent before they saw me shaking. I floundered when they lured people in with the carnival and I couldn't scream at them to run. I floundered every day I was with them."

"But you survived them," Ren said, squeezing Nico's hand. "Because you're a survivor, like my ma."

Without responding, Nico focused on the fold of their hands together the way one would regard a new creature.

"Do you mind when I touch you?" Ren asked as he lifted his hand from Nico's and grazed a fingertip along a tendon on the back of Nico's hand, a slow explorative journey to his wrist.

Nico swallowed. "I told you, we're not doing anything. You and I aren't— We can't..." Ren encircled Nico's wrist loosely with his fingers, and Nico's breath stuttered. "Ren..."

"We're just talking." Ren leaned in, brushed the words across Nico's forehead. "I want to know you." Ren pulled back with a smile. "You know, something good came out of my pa being a dickwad. I had to do something to get my anger out, so I got some tools and started hammering away at wood scraps I found. It's what got me started building things."

"I'm picturing you out in the woods flailing away at a log."

Ren laughed. "That's actually very close to reality."

Nico's eyes were brilliant in the dim light. "What was the first thing you ever made?"

"A dollhouse for my neighbor, this little girl I used to play with who was a year or so younger than me." Ren smiled, remembering. He could still picture the little doll mansion—all of its windows and turrets. He'd made it three stories tall. "That thing was magnificent." Her face when he presented it to her had been pure joy, more magnificent than the dollhouse itself. That had been the best part. The joy, the pure pleasure—that was always the best part.

"I didn't have a hammer to bang away at things," Nico said, voice thoughtful. "But I had the air."

Ren said, "The air? Oh, you mean the acrobatics you did in the trees?"

Nico nodded against the pillow. "I started playing around with it shortly after I arrived. It was the only time I felt free. Teaching myself how to do it shortly after they got me was my only way to escape them for a little while."

"Well, you're damn good at it. Does it take a lot of magic?"

"Some magic. The movements are mine, but I use magic to keep myself in the air longer."

Wondrous. Ren wanted to see Nico dancing through the air again, this time as free as a bird.

Nico gave him a small smile, a secret shared only with Ren. "And your tree house was impressive. I don't understand how it stayed in that tree on its own."

"A different kind of magic." Ren wanted to laugh, giddy with the feel of Nico near—the scent of him, the feel of him crawling into Ren's heart.

Nico made a careful study of Ren until he squirmed. "Many of the people I left camp with had this empty yearning that exploded in their thoughts when they were with me, like there was something inside their chests that could never be filled. Thoughts like that always seem stronger in the middle of sex. The carnival had a way of drawing all kinds of desperate people. I think it was the promise of seeing something bigger than themselves. They wanted to forget themselves, to indulge, to be less alone. They were so desperate to get all they could out of the sex and out of me, to make themselves feel better. I hated it when we were in the middle of sex and I realized I had someone like that, because I couldn't get away from their thoughts. All of that desperation scraping at my mind and digging in. They filled me up, and there was no pulling away from them. They all wanted something, and I couldn't escape their hunger when I was with them."

It piqued Ren's curiosity. "Men and women both?"

"Men and women both," Nico said. The hand beneath Ren's flexed briefly. His nervous itch was always just under the surface.

"Were there really many people like that?" Ren asked.

"You wouldn't believe how many people are unhappy. I think everyone is unhappy in some way."

Ren rubbed his thumb over the pulse in Nico's wrist, said carefully, "Are you unhappy?"

Nico licked his lips, considered the question for a bit. "Right now? This second? No. I wish we could stay here in this bed."

That brought a grin to Ren's face. "Do you now?"

"You're a strange comfort to me." Nico drew closer to him, and Ren instinctively put an arm around his back, felt sharp shoulder blades shift beneath his touch. Nico's lashes were pale-red fans against his cheeks as he studied their hands, an unexpected vulnerability to them. "I haven't felt comfortable in a long time," he said, voice pitched low. "I knew I would have to come back here for help, but I didn't think I'd have anyone by my side when I did."

Ren tipped his head closer. "Well. I'm here."

The lashes lifted. "I thought I would be alone. I got used to being alone."

Daringly, Ren kissed him above his right eye, the soft, messy red hair against his lips, and then did the same above his left, even as Nico kept talking.

"Maybe I find you comforting because I've been alone for so long," Nico said. Tentatively, he reached a finger out, ran it along Ren's jaw, a warm slide across skin. "If only you'd had this stubble at the carnival. It would have at least made me feel less like I was taking you straight from your mother's bosom."

Ren grabbed Nico's hand, kissed up the tendons to his wrist, an unfurled laugh on his lips the whole way. "You must be half-blind to truly have thought I was so young."

"It was dark," Nico said. "I couldn't be sure."

"I'll grow a beard only if you do as well. I like you scruffy. And it's the most delicious red color." Ren lowered his voice. "Bit like a flower."

He knew what that comment would do, and Nico didn't disappoint. He squinted. "You must want to wake up with flowers growing out of your backside to say something like that to a magician."

The laugh broke free no matter how hard Ren tried to subdue it, just a release of relief, this small comfort of talking. Ren let his head sink into the pillow to better enjoy it. "Could you really do that? Make my ass grow flowers?"

"No. Probably not. Maybe." Gold glimmered in his gaze. "Would you like me to try?"

"I'll pass, thanks." Ren rolled onto his side and skimmed his fingers up the back of Nico's hand, reveling in the way the long, slim fingers fit against his own.

"Which one were you at the carnival, Ren?"

Thrown by the question, Ren leaned back. "What?"

It was unnerving to have that shrewd focus so intently, completely aimed at him, but Ren was riveted by the concept of finally having Nico's full attention.

It wouldn't surprise Ren if Nico didn't even need the ability to read thoughts through touch. Just that keen regard alone could probably lift the thoughts right out of people's heads. Nico didn't just look at a person. He picked up every nuance in the shifting emotions that crossed a face. It was disquieting, that uncanny ability.

"Did you come to the carnival because you were desperate for something?" Nico said. "Most people do."

"I— No." But the thought rose in his mind, unbidden, and that was all Nico needed.

Nico nodded as if he'd known all along why Ren was drawn to him from the first moment, as if he'd always known how badly Ren needed someone.

As long as they weren't talking about him, Nico seemed calmer, his fingers still. "Is that why you slept with so many people in your village?"

"Cheater," Ren whispered, glancing down to the spot where their hands kept soft, cautious contact in the tumble of blankets. "You don't play fair."

Nico raised his brows unapologetically—dark-red, they were more expressive than the rest of his face put together. How had he not noticed that before?

"You know I can read thoughts through contact," Nico said, "yet you touch me anyway. That's not my fault."

"Fine." There would be no secrets kept from Nico, not if Ren wanted the luxury of touching him. That was becoming clear. "I suppose I don't like empty beds." Ren traced between Nico's knuckles with his index finger. He found a vein and followed the elegant curvature of its path across Nico's hand. "I don't like that empty kind of quiet when you wake up in the middle of the night and no one else is there. It's an ugly sound."

"Loneliness," Nico said softly. Haltingly, he touched his fingers to Ren's arm, brushed over the dark hair on his forearm, the barest of contact. It sent a shiver up Ren's arm through the rest of his body. "You were lonely even when you were with all of your bedmates?"

Ren's path across Nico's skin stuttered. "I don't want to sound insensitive, but weren't you lonely when you were with someone out in the woods? It's easy to be lonely, isn't it?"

When Nico didn't respond right away, Ren feared he'd offended.

But Nico only bit his lip, thoughtful. "I didn't want to be with any of those people. Being with them made me feel worse."

Ren nodded. He carefully traversed the bones of Nico's wrist. "I didn't feel worse when I was with someone. That part was amazing. I felt worse when they inevitably left, and my home was empty again. I could never keep anyone."

"Why not?" Nico's voice gentled. "You're a good man. Why wouldn't anyone stay?"

"There was never..." Ren swallowed, gathered his thoughts. "I don't know. There was never anyone I wanted to spend my life with. I mean, I did have many friends and a lot of lovers, but I was never close with any of them. I suppose none of them ever stuck. It was just for fun. Eventually, in a small town like Klein, you exhaust all of your marriage possibilities."

Twisting the edges of Ren's sleeve around and around his finger, Nico said, "It's too bad you couldn't have left your village. Met new people."

"I wanted to. I wanted to see the world. I almost left after Ma died, but the village came to depend on me."

"So you never got to interact with anyone else outside of your area? It was the same people over and over?"

"I spent time with people in neighboring villages, but there were only so many people close by. I didn't meet anyone new until I went to the carnival."

"Meeting me," Nico said, "was the worst thing you could have done. You should have stayed home that night."

"Don't say that. It's too late for that anyway."

How could Ren ever say he regretted meeting Nico? Regretted having this easy, personal conversation with someone? He couldn't say it. It was more than he'd ever had. Nico's mere presence in the same bed with him was a marvelous event, something Ren felt he'd been flying toward all his life. He didn't regret Nico. But he mourned all of the people he'd lost because he had gone to a carnival he'd been warned about since childhood. He couldn't have one without the other, so he didn't say anything. He let Nico soak up his confusion through touch.

"Is this fine for you?" Nico asked. "Lying together like this and doing nothing?"

"Nothing?"

"Nothing intimate."

"This is intimate."

Once the sex was over with the pick of the night, Ren always found himself yearning for something else. Maybe this was what he'd been longing for—this quiet closeness, sweet simple touches, and talks about more than the weather and how much Mr. Cront was charging for milk. This was exactly what he'd been craving—the intimacy, the warmth between them, the sweet simplicity of being completely comfortable with another human being. In that moment, he thought he could tell Nico anything about himself with no self-consciousness.

"Uh," Nico said eloquently as Ren's thoughts trickled into his mind. He went still but didn't pull away.

Nico's fingers rested on his arm so lightly, a feather touch that made Ren's stomach flutter. "Sometimes, after I'd finish work for the day and go home and sit in my little living room, the emptiness would swell. Press against me until I thought I might drown in it. I went to the carnival to be near other people. And to see magic, of course. I wanted something new. But that night, I mostly wanted to be in a crowd. All those exuberant people, just as excited as I was to be there. Then you crashed into me and it was— it was hard to let you walk away." Ren gave him a grin. "I felt like you would be interesting."

Nico's mouth quirked. "Interesting?"

"Well, for one thing, I'd never had a redhead before." Nico's hesitant touch along his arm turned into a pinch. "Ow—ow! Sweet Lord!" He grabbed Nico's hand, half playfully, and squeezed Nico's fingers in his own. His magician had quite the grip.

"If monsters and getaways aren't interesting enough for you," Nico said, fingers flexing against Ren's, "I can show you interesting."

Ren was sure he could feel the magic pumping through Nico's veins, sizzling between them. "Oh?"

They were in each other's faces now, kissing-close, hands tangled together between them. Nico's breath warmed his face when he said, "If you're really that desperate for something interesting..."

"Maybe..."

"Maybe we were both desperate." Nico lowered his voice even further. "That night. And many of the days before that. A commonality."

"I think so."

"On the days we didn't have a carnival, I used to lie awake in my tent stretching my magic out to test how far I could push it."

"Stretching it?"

"I practiced with it. Over and over. I could feel my magic growing as I got older, like a widening lake." Nico cleared his throat. "Magic was all I had. There was—no one."

A miniscule strip of space separated them. Warm breaths mingled in the blankets, fingers twined. How different their lives could be now. Together.

Ren nodded. Though it was a complete world away from what his situation had been, he got it. He'd felt that emptiness, clinging to the bright spots in life. God, if only he'd had magic too. Somehow, his life would have been much different.

"I dreamed," Ren said. "Those nights I was alone. During the days, I daydreamed about traveling the world and having someone by my side." He laughed, a little self-deprecating. "And then I went to sleep and dreamed of magic and adventures, like a little boy with an imagination too big. I couldn't stay in my body. My mind was always out exploring the world even into adulthood."

"When I could feel my magic expanding," Nico said, "I used to lie in my tent and pray to the Gods that I could contain all the magic in the world, just for a few moments, so that I could take out all of the wolk in one sweep." Nico let out a harsh breath. "The inane daydreams of a captive."

Ren brushed a single finger down Nico's nose. "That's not inane."

"It's impossible."

"Maybe nothing about magic is impossible."

"No?" Nico's gaze was on Ren's mouth. He raised his hand to the collar of Ren's shirt, bunched the fabric in his fist, and slowly pulled Ren closer. He paused there, his breath coming faster.

Ren's world tilted. "What are you doing?" he whispered.

"I want to see," Nico whispered back, wisps of air against Ren's lips.

"All right." Ren leaned in the half breath it took to press their lips together, but Nico twitched his head back. It took only seconds for Ren to take in the hitch to Nico's breath, the jitteriness coursing through his body. Ren stilled, the tender pause of a man who didn't want to further alarm a wild animal. He smiled into Nico's face, languid and gentle. Nico might have been tense, but Ren had never felt more at ease than in this borrowed bed with his magician. "What is it you wanted to see?"

"I don't—" Nico crushed the crinkled ball of Ren's shirt in his fist. He was making a nice wrinkly pattern out of the fabric. "I don't often kiss people."

Ren watched him carefully. "The people you brought into the woods?"

"No," Nico said with the hint of a grimace. "I don't kiss strangers."

"Bad breath," Ren said. "Bad teeth. Obscure oral diseases."

"It's too intimate."

"It is intimate." Ren paused, unsure. Sometimes he couldn't tell where Nico was going with his thoughts, but he was willing to follow him down the path anyway. "You kissed me at the carnival."

"For show." Nico released Ren's shirt one finger at a time. He smoothed his palm over the creased fabric, across Ren's collarbone, down his chest. "I need to know if I even want to kiss anyone. For real."

Ren let that sink into his heart. It was a foreign idea to him. He couldn't imagine not wanting the sweet anticipation a kiss brought, couldn't imagine never having the delicious burn it ignited.

Nico paused, as if taking in Ren's thoughts.

"You don't know?" Ren asked.

"I've never wanted to know." Nico traced back and forth across Ren's collarbone with his index finger. "There was never anyone I wanted— Not like this."

Surely Nico caught the pleased thoughts that flooded Ren's mind. He would do anything Nico wanted. *Anything*, Ren thought to the pounding of his heart, *anything*.

Nico drew back, studied Ren's face, solemn in the half glow of light. "Anything?" He lowered his voice as though giving Ren advice. "That's a dangerous thought."

"You're already dangerous."

"I thought seeing me kill a handful of monsters hours after we met was a giveaway."

"That's not—" Ren took a breath, let his words out softly. "That's not the kind of dangerous I meant. I like being in bed with you and talking, and that seems dangerous. I don't usually have a lot of conversations in bed." He enjoyed the feel of their heat mingling in the blankets. Nico was intoxicating. Ren just wanted to breathe him in, hold him there in his chest next to his heart.

Nico's eyes widened as Ren's thoughts poured out across the pillows, his lips parted slightly, and the warmth of his breath spilled across Ren's mouth.

"Fuck," Nico whispered, a hotter huff of air right into Ren's face. "You're not supposed to like me. Don't like me."

Under the covers, their legs brushed together. Neither pulled away.

"Too late," Ren said. Far, far too late.

He tracked a heavy swallow down Nico's throat. The movement brought Nico's Adam's apple to his attention. Ren touched a fingertip to Nico's throat, and Nico shivered. Ren slid his finger up Nico's neck, circled his Adam's apple, followed the line of Nico's jaw, and brushed his fingers over Nico's sharp chin.

The lengths of their bodies aligned, the delicious spark of first close contact. They both moved forward at the same time, slow and easy, and met in the middle. It was the gentlest beginning Ren had ever experienced, a sweet press of lips, trying each other out, testing the fit of their mouths together.

Nico grazed his tongue over Ren's lips and made a sound in the back of his throat when Ren opened to him, and then they were learning each other's taste, mapping teeth and tongues, so deep in the kiss Ren forgot where they were, what was out there. He only remembered the most important part: who they were, Ren and Nico, together, *together finally*. Even though they'd only known each other hours, he felt like he had waited forever for this. For the *together finally* part. Nico put an arm around Ren's waist. In response, Ren wrapped a leg around Nico, pulled Nico's body snug against his own. It was impossible to get close enough to Nico. It was a marvel how perfectly their bodies fit, all easy litheness pressed into hard muscles.

It was so unlike their first kiss—this seductive, quiet confidence and curious exploration. Nothing like the panicked, frenetic energy of the carnival kiss. Now, intrigue thrummed between them instead of desperation.

His strange, wonderful awareness of Nico's magic increased. He could sense, somewhere in the back of his mind, Nico's magic brushing against him, suddenly there with them in the kiss, entwined, inextricable. The kiss spun out in gold, phantom banners of magic in the dark. He tasted the fizz of magic on Nico's tongue; felt the tingle of it on his lips; breathed in the warm scent of magic in the air, something like woodsmoke but more subtle. He was afloat in Nico's magic.

Ren's thoughts melted into Nico. His fingertips scraped through Ren's hair, his magic sweeping over Ren's senses. The reality of his body, warm and tangible, moving against Ren. *He's real. He's alive. This isn't a dream. He isn't a dream. Why would he be a dream?*

They took their time, a languid first discovery, tangled there in the covers, in the city where Nico's nightmare had begun. A horde of monsters could have exploded down from the mountains and blasted through the door, and Ren wouldn't have noticed any of it. Nothing could have spoiled the moment for him, this precious second of having Nico in his arms and against his lips.

Ren was drenched in the moment, in Nico's magic, in Nico's skin and the supple solidity of muscles beneath his fingers. The perfect, effortless way his body cradled Nico's made him giddy. Gold dust floated like stars against the black of his eyelids. Ren pressed his fingers into Nico's hips and sank into a dreamworld. *But it's real. It's real. Not a dream.*

He's so very real.

It was Nico who pulled back, finally. Ren had forgotten they still needed to breathe. Nico tucked his face into the curve of Ren's neck, his hair a wild red tickle against Ren's chin. His lips trailed tingles over Ren's skin, aimless wandering.

Against his collarbone, his voice a warm laugh, Nico said, "You have a big imagination." His breath heated Ren's skin, a hot temptation. His bold fingers twirled in Ren's hair.

Ren did indeed have a big imagination. He was imagining all of the things they could do together, all of the scenarios this moment could open.

Ren rubbed his thumb down Nico's spine, enjoyed the shiver that followed it and the sizzle of Nico's magic sparking against his fingertips. Magic crackled the more he touched Nico.

"I do?" Ren murmured. He'd definitely never imagined it would feel quite like this, this sweet and intimate. The joy of physical contact bubbled up Ren's throat, came out as a laugh. Touching Nico was a decadent, delicious treat. He slid his fingers down Nico's sides, explored the graceful sweep of his torso, slowly familiarizing himself with Nico's body, savoring the privileges of intimacy.

Nico lifted his head from the curve of Ren's neck. "Imagining you can see my magic. Does that turn you on or something?"

"I *can* see your magic."

Nico's breath caught. "No. Wait. What?"

"It's like having another part of you here. Your magic is beautiful," Ren said, trailing the words along Nico's shoulder, "like you. It's gold, made up of all these little streaming specks of light. Breathtaking. That's how I always imagined magic, not at all like the fire at the carnival." It was a handful of jewels he wanted to reach for, hold in his hands, keep close to his heart. His desire for it was as strong as his understanding that he would never be able to have it.

Nico stopped him with a firm grip on his shoulders. He pushed Ren away. "What are you saying? You actually saw my magic?"

"When we kissed." Ren raised a hand, swirled it through the air to mimic the banners of Nico's magic he'd seen during the kiss. "I see it now too. It's always near. I can feel it on your skin. In the air. I guess it's in the walls too, where there are lights. It's everywhere."

Nico's magic was so thick in the air that Ren imagined he could drink it. If only he could gulp it down and keep a little of it for himself, deep inside.

"Lights in the walls? What lights?" Nico searched the room. His hands flexed on Ren's shoulders. "Ren, that's not possible."

Ren was too distracted by the little crinkle between Nico's brows when he made that face. He wanted to lean in and taste it. Abstracted, he said, "What do you mean?"

"No one can see magic," Nico said. "The actual particles of it aren't visible. Only the results of magic are visible. People only see the tricks."

"I see it." Ren stared at him. "I feel it too."

The tension stretched out between them for a long, confused moment before Nico said, whisper-soft, "It can't be. You're some kind of—"

"Nico."

At the sound of the new voice, they fell away from each other, startled. The moment broke apart as easily as gossamer. Nico sat up quickly, and Ren followed. The blankets and sheets glided down and clouded in their laps.

In the sleepy gloom of the room, the light weak with bronze shadows, Ren thought Davvon stood in the doorway. But then the man stepped past the open archway and fully into the room. Definitely not Davvon.

The unmistakable familial resemblance hit Ren immediately. Nico was there reflected in his face, in his sharp cheekbones, in his elegant stance, in the similar height and slim lines. His faded red hair—nothing like the coppery rich hue atop Nico's head—fell in a similar thick sweep across his forehead. Their solemn, narrow, unsmiling mouths competed for deepest frown as they regarded each other with twin expressions. Ren felt suddenly invisible.

"Father," Nico said, one simple word with nothing and everything behind it. There was a pause. Then, pointedly: "*Martin.*"

Nico received no greeting from his father. His name didn't pass Martin's lips. Nico made to get out of the bed, but Martin held up a hand. "Don't move."

Nico paused, the blankets thrown to the side, one leg out. "Where's Thea?"

"Don't speak, either."

Nico ignored him. "This is her house. Where is she?"

At the sound of Nico's voice, Martin took a wary backward step in the direction of the exit. "She's not here. She hasn't been here in a long time."

Nico's body was suddenly alert with tension. "What is that supposed to mean?" He slid his feet to the floor and grabbed his boots from nearby.

"I told you not to move," Martin said, breathy and insubstantial. The thread of hesitancy in his voice was obvious. "You haven't changed at all. You still never listen."

As close as Nico sat to Ren on the bed, Nico's anxiety radiated between them, a vibration of his magic that echoed in Ren's chest.

"Put your boots on," Nico said, and it took Ren a moment to realize the steady command was directed at him.

"Nico," said Martin, "you're not leaving."

Disaster hung crisp and imminent in the air. Ren slid to the edge of the bed next to Nico, slung his legs over the side, and jammed his feet into his boots.

"Did you give Thea away too?" Nico said as he slipped the boots over his feet with slow finesse, deft fingers tightening the buckles. Ren gave him a sidelong glance. Anything that might have been revealed by Nico's eyes was hidden by the rumpled fall of his hair as he bent forward.

There was a long pause, the clink of Nico's boot buckles the only sound in the room.

"She left of her own free will," Martin told him. "Because of you. You managed to splinter my family without even being here."

That brought Nico's head up quickly. He straightened his back. "You haven't changed either," he told his father.

"You still strive to blame me for everything. You must have missed this hobby while I was gone."

"I didn't miss anything while you were gone." The simple statement, the easy delivery of it, hovered in the air for a long time. "She went to find you."

The slick performer's mask slipped a little. Nico's lips parted with the vulnerability of surprise, but then he firmed his jaw. "How long ago did she leave?"

His father remained still, several paces from the door. "Years ago. Davvon woke up one morning, and she was gone. I take it she never found you."

"No," Nico said, his voice fainter, "she didn't."

"Last I heard, she was living with a group of magicians on the Summer Shore like some bohemian." Martin's sour expression made his distaste clear.

Nico smiled as if remembering something from long ago. "She always wanted to see the Summer Shore. She used to dream about it."

"I thought she would come home one day. Instead, here *you* are. You never should have come back here."

Nico stood, and Martin startled back another step. Ren recognized the slight tremor of his lips, the shake in his hands as he flexed them, the heightened alertness. The signs of dread inked across his face in bold, sweeping letters. He didn't even try to hide it. He feared Nico. He backed up farther and braced a hand on the smooth frame of the glass arch that led into the room, his knuckles white.

"I didn't come for a reunion." Surely Nico noticed his father's reaction to him. The apprehension was unmistakable, but he ignored the unease in the room. "I came to tell the people of this city that the wolk are planning to take over our world. I thought," he added carefully, "you might want to know."

The words floated through Ren's mind, sank into his new reality. *Planning to take over our world.* Ren studied his profile—the sharp curve of jaw, the long sweep of lashes, the unexpected tumble of red hair around his ear. He was as beautiful and distant as the mountain range Ren used to gaze at from his window.

Ren wanted to shake him. *Why didn't you tell me?*

There was a painfully telling, complete lack of reaction from Martin. Father and son stood motionlessly at opposite ends of the room, distorted reflections of each other.

Nico spoke first, flatly. "You already know."

"We know."

Nico's hands spread, questioning, and Martin tensed. Every little new movement from Nico drew an unwilling reaction from him. He stayed perpetually on edge.

"You're the only ones with enough power to stop them," Nico said. "So what are you doing to stop them? Do you have a plan?"

"Nico." Martin still clutched the archway, his fingernails scraping against the glass. He pressed his fingers against it so hard, so violently.

They stared at each other across the expanse of fluffy white carpet and glass.

"No," Nico said finally, his voice pained. "You're not doing anything about it, are you?"

Martin gave no answer, but he tracked Nico's every move.

"We're talking about the end of our world as we know it," Nico said. "You're just going to sit back and let them do it?"

Martin said, strained, "You've been out there. You've seen how it is. People are scattered across our world, all of them living in a dozen different ways. There are no leaders, no laws, no control. Our world needs order if we want to advance as a civilization."

"Oh." It was spoken so softly, with such disbelief. "God no. *No*. Tell me you're not in league with them. Tell me that's not what you're saying. *Father!*"

Martin didn't hesitate. He stood straighter. "We're the two most powerful forces on the planet. We need to take control of the people to build up our world. It only makes sense to—"

"They're monsters. I know. I've been living with them." Nico's breath gusted out, as though he'd been running. His hair stood up in a staticky, wild red sweep of silk where the pillow had pressed against it. The reality of the moment settled across his face, altered his features with shock. "Whose idea was it to work with them?"

"It doesn't matter. It was a group decision made long ago."

"They're going to take over the world." Disbelief threaded through Nico's voice. "And you're going to let them."

The tension in the room grew so thick Ren could swim in it. He could scarcely breathe through it. Or maybe he sensed the wave of his own rising panic about to drown him.

Martin's knuckles clenched on the doorframe. "We will take over the world *with* them."

"Why do you want to subjugate the people of our world?"

"That's not what we want."

"If you're working with the wolk, that's exactly what you want. That's what the wolk have been striving to do for *years*."

Martin pursed his lips. "They know that isn't our goal."

"Why would they give a shit about your goal? Why not get rid of you once they have power over our world? They won't need you."

"They will always need our magic." Martin's voice grew louder, slightly hysterical. He took a deep breath. When he spoke again, he'd tamped down his nerves for the moment. "We offer them access to the magic of our realm, and they offer us the secrets of theirs. They're going to advance us."

"They're going to destroy us."

Martin shook his head as though Nico were a dimwitted child. "You have very little understanding of this."

"I have more understanding of them than you'll ever know." It was rough and bitter.

"We know them," Martin said, as though Nico hadn't spoken. "We've been working with them for decades. They're powerful, but in a different way than we are. They have access to a world we can't imagine, but in our world they need a constant source of magic."

His soft sigh was the only sound in the room. "So we promised them one of our strongest magicians."

Chapter Thirteen

REN

Nico stood statue-still. It didn't seem like he was breathing, but then Ren realized *he* was the one holding his breath.

Trepidation clogged Ren's throat, and dread made bricks of his feet. No one moved.

Let's go. Let's go now.

Martin turned his head the slightest amount. "Come."

Too late. Too late. Too late.

They're here.

Movement on the stairs and in the hall. A gentle shuffling of feet. A small group of people emerged in the hall behind Nico's father. For a moment, Ren was sure it was the wolk, ready and eager to take Nico back right away. But these people appeared a bit too normal. Something in the way they stood screamed *human*.

Ren turned to Nico, saw the slow horror of realization come over him.

There would be no stroll out of this glass castle. Ren thought they might die in this pretty place.

"You," said Martin in the same soft-spoken manner he'd been using since he'd entered the room. "You were always powerful. So terribly powerful. Even as a young child, you would do things with magic that astounded me. Things I had never seen even an adult achieve. A *magical virtuoso*, the council called you. You could do things no single magician should be able to do. You scared me. You've always scared me. From the time you were a young child, you did impossible things. You're unnatural."

Nico's cheeks brightened with anger. "*I'm* unnatural, but you're willing to work with the wolk? They're uncaring *abominations—*"

"Nico," his father said tiredly. He was already done with the conversation.

And Nico got it. "You're going to give me back to them." His whisper shook and broke apart. His swallow was loud in the waiting hush. "You're going to do it to me again."

"No one should possess the amount of power that you do."

"All that time I was with them, I thought—I thought it was my punishment. That you gave me to them because I killed someone. But that wasn't it, was it?" When Martin failed to answer, Nico's voice rose. "Say it! Say it to my face! I want to hear it aloud. I'm a commodity for you to trade."

His father gave him the words gently, like an offering he was passing into Nico's hands. "You're too strong. You have to be kept. I had no other choice."

Ren's chest tightened. *Kept.* It was a horror show, a tragic performance that should be played out on a stage.

Across the shimmering stretch of floor, Nico regarded his father, really contemplated him, like he knew him now in a way he never had before. "I've openly defied them. Do you know what they're going to do to me if you give me back to them? Do you even care?"

Softly, his expression mild, Martin took in a breath. "It's none of my business what they do to you."

It became evident Nico was not good at masking his feelings—not when it truly mattered. He gasped in a breath as if he'd been gut-punched, all of the air knocked out of him.

In the quiet aftermath, Nico said faintly, his voice hoarse, "None of your business."

A menacing stillness settled over the room in the wake of the revelation.

Something tugged on Ren's body, inside his chest, the tide pulling away, sucking at him. His stomach clenched up in a tight ball of alarm as magic rolled through the room, rolled through him, thrumming with a force of its own. It dragged at his body and mind so strongly, with a familiar thrill, Ren thought it had to be Nico.

"None of your business," Nico said again, louder and clearer. "*None of your business. You're such a fucking asshole.*"

There was no looming wave, no crash of water. There was only Nico and his low voice, a deadly undercurrent ready to yank them all out to sea. Calamity rose in the air. Ren didn't know what to do, where to hide. There was nowhere to go in the pretty glass room.

Whatever Martin saw in Nico, it scared him. He reeled back against the archway, nearly stumbled into the hall, his face caught in a cringe.

"I knew you were capable of killing," Martin said from just outside the doorway. The group at his back rippled as many of the magicians nodded in agreement. He stood partially huddled behind the entry wall, only half his body visible around the frosted glass. "I was afraid one day you would get angry at me or Thea." He shook as he spoke, his voice shuddering with his nerves. "I thought Thea and I were lucky when the day your wrath came out, the moment you finally lost your temper, it wasn't at one of us. I knew it could have just as easily been my daughter or me. I could feel it coming for years. I knew one day you would explode at someone. You're dangerous. You don't belong with people. The wolk can keep you under control."

Martin startled when Nico turned to the wardrobe and grabbed a coat of sleek black fabric. He tossed it to Ren, said, "Put it on," and grabbed a coat for himself.

The group in the hall stirred, a ripple of unease whispering through the magicians in response to Nico, though they were utterly silent, wary and riveted by his simple, mundane motions. Every eye seemed to follow the precise, pale fingers as they slipped the first button into place. There was something chilling, something absolutely dangerous about the measured, methodical grace with which he did it.

With care, Nico went down to the second button. His focus was on his hands, but he said, "When I was fourteen, three weeks after you gave me to them, some of them cornered me, came at me while I was bathing in a lake." He reached the next button, looped it through the hole as though it were the most important task in the world. "Is that the kind of control you think I need, Father?"

Nico took a moment to pause. "What? No comment?"

No one reacted. No one breathed loudly. Ren couldn't move, was too scared to turn away. Nico held the room captive with nothing but the threat underlying his quiet words, and the reality of it fascinated Ren. The air tasted of spices and lightning, at the back of Ren's throat a tingle, not quite electric.

"One of them touched me," Nico said, the simple play of his fingers across the fabric elegant, like a tiny dance.

Mesmerizing. "He told me I'd learn to like it, but I knew I wouldn't. So I told him to chop off his own hand. The one he touched me with, of course. I let him keep the other one."

Someone made an indecipherable sound. It was Nico's father.

"You see," Nico said in his smooth, hypnotizing voice, the one that made you want to lean in and listen, "I knew I had to set a precedent. I had to show them I wasn't the meek child they thought I was. After that incident, none of them seemed inclined to take any chances on losing a body part. We came to a tentative understanding." Nico finished off the last button and reached up to straighten the lapels of the coat. His fingers smoothed them down.

Zeke, Ren thought, remembering the slow, euphoric way he had traced the angles of Nico's face before he slid the knife into Nico's body with his single, remaining hand. He remembered how efficiently Nico had killed him, the way they had left the bodies crumpled on the forest floor like dead leaves. Ren hoped they turned to dust and sank down to hell, Zeke especially.

Nico turned to his father. "I suppose you think I'm terrible for that."

"You," Martin said, "were always terrible."

Nico let his hands fall to his sides. "So were you. That scene I just described, that one example out of fourteen years, that's the life you consigned me to. I'm your *son*, and you sent me to a life of torment and terror and subjugation. And you don't even care."

"We couldn't dictate to them exactly what they did with you," Martin said. "It wasn't our intention—"

"It wasn't your intention to whore me out? Well, as long as that wasn't your *intention*, you might still be eligible for father of the decade. You'll probably have to hand in your pimp card first."

A soft wave of murmurs trickled through the magician's at Martin's back.

Martin grimaced, soft and delicate, as though he'd just smelled something unsavory. What an unpleasant conversation for him, this reminder of what he'd done to his son. His lips puckered. "It was a business deal between magical beings. They took you for your magic, nothing else."

"Bullshit. You knew exactly what they would do to me. How I would live the rest of my life." Nico walked forward. He didn't raise his voice; he didn't have to. As one, the group in the hall moved away from him.

An entire room full of magicians, Ren realized with growing awe, and they all feared the slender man trapped in the middle. He didn't come across as particularly formidable in the overlarge coat, his hair a silken mess rumpled around the collar, his skin pale against the red of his stubble. Dark circles smudged his eyes, and pillow creases hadn't yet faded from his cheek. Any fear of Nico that Ren might have had—perhaps *should* have had—was washed away by the sense memory of Nico's lips against his, of the bare brush of what could be, of the idea that he could have this terrifying man, that he could be a part of Nico's life.

Ren didn't think, didn't hesitate. He followed closely behind Nico as they moved toward the door and the filled hallway beyond.

"You can leave this room," said Nico's father, his voice quavering. He'd inched out of the room completely and now stood with the other magicians at his back, a wall of magical support. "But the wolk are at the entrance, waiting for you."

Nico stopped so suddenly Ren fetched up against his back, and they both stumbled forward an inelegant step.

"No," Nico said. "I'm not going to be a part of this. If you want to take over the world, you're going to do it without me. The wolk are going to do it without me. You're not going to use my magic to destroy the planet."

Halfway across the length of the room, they stood much closer to Martin now, near enough for Ren to see the sweat on his upper lip. His body strained back against the magicians behind him. They seemed to be holding him up.

"You're already a part of it," his father said. "Don't make us carry you out again, like last time. This doesn't have to get ugly."

The world cracked.

The sound came from everywhere, two quick seconds of some object screaming under pressure. Long after it split the air, the sound echoed against the walls, bouncing off of them. It reverberated in Ren's chest, his heart thumping with the unfathomable noise rocketing above them.

Ren's heart fluttered with one thought. *They're here. The wolk are inside the house.*

It was over. It was all going to end in this absurd fantasy of a palace, in this perfect trap.

Nico's inhalation was loud, air sucked between teeth. "It's already ugly," he told his father, and Martin cowered, as though he sensed a blow coming. "Last chance."

Then Ren saw it. Little specks of gold sparking, coalescing at the edges of the room.

From the clump of people at Martin's back, someone muttered, "I knew we shouldn't have handled him this way."

"Nico," said another voice from the hall, "calm down."

"I'm calm," Nico said in a perfectly calm voice that sounded like a threat. He studied the magicians who surrounded his father, skimming the faces turned toward him. "So they're at the gate. Work with me to go out there and rid our planet of them. Right now. With our combined magic, we can end this."

Specks of gold fluttered through the air like dust caught in sunlight, like a languid Sunday morning dream. And that was when Ren recognized the beautiful spinning gold, and he knew. The same magic had enclosed him in a safe, warm bubble in the cold. The same magic had brushed their kiss earlier.

Not the wolk. Not the end. Ren's released breath was ragged. *Not the end. Not yet.*

"I told you he was unstable," Martin said, and mutterings of ascent followed his statement. "Imagine the things he could do."

"He wouldn't be talking right now if we had slammed his head into a wall and dragged him out like I suggested," said another voice that was quickly shushed.

"I guess that's a no," Nico said, his shoulders straight and resigned. He'd already known what their answer would be.

Although Ren had only known Nico a day or so, a handful of hours, he could tell Nico was done talking. Nico didn't waste time with angry threats. Nico never threatened. He just did. Without laying a finger on you.

A series of loud cracks startled everyone but Nico. It sounded deep and raw, new, as if something that shouldn't be was waking up and stretching for the first time, popping joints and shaking loose foundations.

In the painful, swelling quiet after the noise, no one moved.

The rest of it was a swirl of light. Unexpectedly, Martin moved first and fast, a trembling ball of meekness until he became resolute. A brilliant white-blue ballooned, swelled to fill the hallway and roll into the room. So all-consuming, so blinding, it took over Ren's senses.

The magic swept into the room, a wave heading straight for Nico and Ren. Nico flinched, staggered back several steps, and nearly tripped. Ren squinted, held his breath as one about to go under water. It should have engulfed them. Nico regained his balance. The light rebounded a foot from them, spewed outward, and scattered into thousands of glowing pale-blue dots that hung like a mist for several moments before dispersing. They had only seconds before another wave of magic rolled into them, this one an amalgam of varied glowing colors in what Ren assumed must be the combined power of everyone standing in the hallway. The abilities of several dozen people bent around Ren and Nico and fell in torn tatters.

Ren couldn't help but stare at Nico, who stood motionless, his face unstudied. There were no grand gestures, no thunder and lightning, no indication at all that he was wielding such power. Only his arm clutched across his middle as though he felt the force used against him inside his body rather than outside.

When Nico used magic, he got quiet. No dramatic hand movements, no furrowed brow of concentration, no strained shouts. He simply stood there with his shield enveloping them, seeming all the more powerful for his lack of showy effort. The finest spun gold, thin as a snowflake, poured over them. It twinkled in and out, beautiful, translucent, and deceptively fragile. When the full force of their attack hit the shield, it rippled like a sheet in the wind, but didn't break.

Ren tasted Nico's magic—like lightning right before the strike, an ineffable combination of electricity and potential—before it flooded the room. Gold light filled the air, filled Ren's mind. It popped and fizzled on his tongue, on his lips. The brilliance of Nico's magic starkly outlined the world: the golden glow of a sunset before it sinks below the horizon, little glimmers of it on every reflective surface. His light suffused the walls, the ceiling, the floor, a sun trapped behind glass, and they were the people burning in its core. The gold of it overwhelmed everything until the whole room shimmered incandescently. Nico's power took up so much space it pushed all other magic from the room.

A distant clamor grabbed Ren's attention. It took him a moment to realize dozens of people pounded the stairs in a frantic scramble to escape the house. They had nine flights and limited time. Would a head start save them? Had Davvon and his big talk already fled?

Was it already too late for Ren?

He didn't care. He couldn't leave Nico. Maybe it'd been too late for Ren long ago.

Martin stood in the hallway, just outside the door to the bedroom. "How," he said, one word spit out. He had an arm out in front of himself, another braced against the splintering glass wall of the doorway. Against the overwhelming swirl of light, an ugly emotion darkened his countenance. "How are you so powerful?"

Nico remained immobile, a wrecked reflection of his father. Though he said nothing in return, horror spread across his mouth and twisted around his eyes. They were far past talking. They'd been past talking for a long time. Nico stood unyielding, strength in his silence.

"Nico," Martin said, despairing. "If you bring this building down, you bring them all down. The magic connects them. Vellen will fall."

Still, Nico said nothing, but his hands shook at his sides.

He knows. He knows exactly what he's doing.

The glass began to spiderweb, the soft splintering it produced like someone breaking apart a cookie one tiny piece at a time.

There won't be anything left but crumbs. Nico was going to bring the place down. He was going to crumble it with them inside.

Ren couldn't fathom the infinite horizon of Nico's capability, the vastness of it. It staggered him to try and wrap his mind around it.

"Ren." Nico spoke his name softly over the sound of dying glass, like an apology. The skin on Ren's arms prickled at the despair in Nico's voice, at the fizz of Nico's power saturating the air.

"I know," Ren said. *I understand.* There was no other path but capture, an unthinkable end.

Nico's magic swelled. Walls and floors groaned. Golden light heaved.

"I knew you were ruinous," Martin said, staring at Nico.

They were both fixated on Nico as intricate cracks formed and splintered under their feet. How could anyone not? He was thrilling. He was terrifying. Ren couldn't look away. The dangerous, intimate urge to lay his hands on Nico now when his magic was surging, to reach inside him and feel its flow coursing through Nico's body, was suddenly overwhelming. Nico's strength on such a grand scale was sheer intoxication. When they'd first met, Nico had spoken of that place inside, a reservoir of magic. Ren wanted to dip his fingers into Nico's deep well, trail magic over Nico's bones with his fingertips, acquaint himself with every part of this body that could contain so much power.

Ren shook his head and came back to the moment with a crash.

The crumbly crackling turned into a series of pops. Lines snaked across the floor. He'd wanted to see magic so desperately. He saw it in his dreams. Always had. He daydreamed about it while hammering at a roof or fitting a door into place. It came to him when he closed his eyes. Now the grandest power in the world was splitting open at his feet, and he couldn't escape it.

Magic is real. Magic is so very real and so very fucking enormous.

Something in a room below them broke, and the floor tilted drunkenly. Martin clung to the edge of the doorframe that led into the room. As if that one doorway would save him.

Ren tried to brace himself. He flattened his feet against the floor but pitched forward a second later when the ground tilted at a different angle. The new direction tripped him into Nico, and the force of their bodies smashing together nearly sent them both to the floor. They caught each other, grasping arms and coats.

It was only a handful of seconds, the last moments of Ren's life, but it stretched into forever. Above them on another floor, something shattered—a wall or a ceiling. It didn't matter. The sound of breaking glass grew into a cacophony that clawed at Ren's eardrums. He'd never realized glass could shriek. The wall behind the bed shook beneath the force. It rippled, wavelike. Then, a second's shocked hush before crystal shards exploded into the room. The colorful motes inside spilled out, poured into the space. They slammed into Nico's golden magic. Like the glass, they exploded, hanging for a single moment, a rainbow of little specks, before fading against Nico's light.

The world spiraled after that. Everything transformed into a chaotic, glitter-sharp mess of shards, magic, and screams. Ren's face stung with little bits of glass, like tiny bugs biting at him.

Where was the damn door? Remotely, he wondered if the others had made it down the stairs and out of the house. The shattered rain of walls and floors created a piercing brume. The world narrowed to his death grip on Nico's coat and the shifting of Nico's body beneath the clothing, the slip-slide of fabric over solid muscle. A nightmare swirled over Ren, but Nico felt like reality.

Ren lurched to his left when the floor gave beneath his feet. Someone screamed. A moment later, he realized it wasn't him. And then he was in midair, dropping with the furniture and the screams, the house coming down on top of him as he flew by all of it, fragments of wood and metal and sprinkles of gold shooting past him like falling stars, twinkling in the eerie winter light. Ren's legs dangled in emptiness.

They fell forever. Much heavier than they were, the bed they'd been sleeping in plummeted past them with its sheets and blankets aflutter like a giant butterfly.

Disaster shouldn't be so beautiful. But, God, was it beautiful—this glowing gold fog of bedlam Nico had created, full of sharp, glittering doom. Ren pressed his face to Nico's shoulder, hid from the sting of light and death, from the beauty of Nico's devastation.

Through the screams and the ruin, someone was yelling Nico's name, ripping it apart in the middle in a broken tone. *Ni-co! Ni-co!* It sounded like Nico's father, and it was awful. Ren didn't want to hear it anymore. It was too late.

There were other screams: furniture, walls, floors. So many things ripping apart. There were the screams of people too. It sounded like the magicians hadn't made it out of the house fast enough. Ren took shelter in Nico. He didn't want to see them.

Ren needed the solidity of someone else's body. He encircled Nico's waist with his legs even as Nico wound his arms around Ren's neck and clutched at him. Nico put his mouth to Ren's ear, and over the roar of the disaster, his words tickled Ren's skin.

"We're snow. Our bodies are light as we drift on the air currents, high in the clouds."

For the first time, Ren could clearly feel Nico there, brushing against his mind, a gentle caress as real as the warm breath against the shell of his ear. Ren blocked out the calamity, felt nothing but Nico, let the poetry of Nico's words flow through his body, slip deep into his mind, coax him into tranquility. Behind his eyelids, he could see the sky in Nico's voice, infinite blue-gray freedom, clouds forever.

"We're water and ice. We gather in the clouds, sprinkle over the land. Our bodies know how to fly."

It was rushed—but it worked. Ren went from falling to his death, glass and air roaring past his ears, to drifting through an endless gray sky full of white flakes. The moment went from raging thunderstorm to complete hush.

He spun lazily in a hundred different directions, saw the heavy clouds from a dozen different viewpoints. He felt fine. He felt soothed. The silence was the sweetest thing.

Chapter Fourteen

REN

Off to his left, someone was vomiting noisily against the backdrop of a distant roar. Light-headed, a part of him still spinning, Ren sat up. His head might float away from his body any second now. The ground was at a crazy downward tilt, which definitely didn't help at all. He wobbled where he sat, dug his hands into the long, rimy grass, and took in what felt like a lungful of ice. The air bit down his throat, into his chest, and woke him up as quickly as cold water to the face. He pushed himself off the ground. The ground didn't feel too steady, and his mind didn't quite believe there could be solid earth beneath his feet. A part of him believed there was no way he wasn't still falling through fathomless air, past endless debris.

They had landed on a mountainside, one of the smaller ones that led to the larger range behind it. On one side, a slope of dormant grass dipped at an alarming angle. The other side was the source of the roar—a steep waterfall. It was so high there was nothing to see below but a white blur of snow and churned water. Deep in the distance lay the silver unspooling of a wide river. Its unsettled rapids ribboned away into the cordillera.

Ren turned in a slow circle, taking in this slice of the world. Nico's childhood home, distant and tiny tucked into its alpine folds, was a glittery cloud of shattering glass, the bits and pieces trapped in snowy half-light. The toppling castles sent shards high into the clouds. At first glance, stars seemed to shimmer and burst over the city, a strangely beautiful display of the heavens.

They were too far away to hear the screaming—of buildings and of people. They were too far away to hear the collapse of a society.

Ren had to consciously lift his jaw, tighten his lips to keep the jittery exclamation on the back of his tongue from escaping.

He brought down a city. My magician. It dizzied Ren.

A safe distance away from Ren, Nico was on his knees, almost hidden in the tall, brittle grass. That red hair blowing against the cold white grass gave him away.

Ren approached him, his footsteps loud and crunchy in the frost. Doubled over, Nico's face practically touched the ground. Ren crouched at his side, careful to avoid the vomit. There were bits of broken glass stuck in Nico's hair, glittering like small jewels. Nico heaved again, making sure to twist his body away from Ren and turn his head in time. Ren cringed in sympathy. His own stomach muscles tightened. When the wave eased and Nico was releasing nothing more than dry heaves, Ren put his hand on the curve of Nico's back. Such a light touch, the barest of contact, but it pulled a little gasp from Nico. Ren didn't take his hand away, and Nico didn't move away from it.

Head bent low, his hair a screen between them, Nico whispered, *"Fuck."* The misery in his voice splintered the word.

"I know." There was nothing else to say, so Ren just knelt there beside Nico, rubbing tiny, aimless circles into his back.

Unseeingly, Nico ran his fingers through the grass near his thighs, fisted his hands in the cold blades, and let out a sob. He turned his head away from Ren and smothered another sound against his arm, but Ren recognized it building up inside him.

It hurt more than Ren would have thought, surprised him how much it ached in his hands and in his chest to see Nico on his knees, sobbing on the side of a mountain and to know there was nothing he could do to make things right.

Ren murmured, "Nico. *Nico*."

"I had to do something," Nico said, muffled against his arm, quiet and desperate. "All of that power and magic... They were going to support a bunch of monsters with it. They would have helped destroy us all." Tightness in his voice made it seem taut enough to snap.

"I know," Ren said and slid his arm firmly over Nico's back. "I was there. I heard what they were going to do. What they were planning for the world."

"Oh God." Nico sounded like he was in pain. "Oh God. I killed them. I killed all of them."

Ren made a soft sound but didn't reply. There was nothing to say. They were beyond gentle reassurances.

"There were children in that city. There were innocent people. My father—I killed—I killed my own father." That muffled, choked sob again, a wrenching sound. It echoed in Ren's chest. It *hurt*.

Nico sucked down breaths and heaved them back out. Beneath Ren's hand, he was shaking. The sound of his breathing grew louder, harsher. Ren knew, quite intimately, what was coming.

"God, my father—my father. No. *Noooo*."

"Hey." Ren pressed his hand firmly against Nico's back, Nico's spine beneath his palm. "Listen to your heartbeat." The words came back to him. "Close your eyes, and listen to the sound of your heart pumping life through your body. Count each beat. Don't think about anything but the blood pumping through your veins. Feel your heartbeat. Concentrate on its steady rhythm."

Nico's breath hitched, but then he gradually began breathing slower. Ren knew he was counting, focusing. They sat there as Nico's panicked breaths progressively morphed into hushed tears.

Ren drew Nico closer. A surprise—Nico came to him without resistance. He tilted into Ren at a sideways angle, his head just under Ren's chin. His hands brushed Ren's stomach, and then Nico froze, as if just realizing what he was doing and where it had put him. But before Nico could think about it, Ren enfolded him in his arms. He wrapped one arm around Nico's back and the other around his shoulders, the response as natural as breathing, as instinctive as turning over in bed on a chilly night and pulling the blankets close.

Tension seeped out of Nico's muscles, melting him against Ren as though he'd been poured there. He curled into Ren's chest, buried his face against Ren, and that felt natural too. He was practically in Ren's lap, the whole slim line of him huddled against Ren, shaking out anguished breaths onto Ren, steadying himself against Ren. Nico kept his hands balled in Ren's shirt, beneath the open flaps of his coat.

Ren sat quietly with Nico in his arms, with Nico's tears warm on the bare skin of his neck, leaking toward his collarbone. Ren held him tightly.

Low on the ground as they were, the ice-crusted grass enclosed them in its willowy white sway, cushioned them for a moment in their own little world. Ren had forgotten it was barely autumn, that it had been only a sprinkle of days since he'd stepped into the carnival. The Summer God had only recently passed. It was even harder to believe it was autumn here in this strange, cold land with tiny white flakes falling, flecking the ground. The Winter God ruled here.

"I never," Nico said, his voice wet. He gasped his words out between inhaled sobs. "I hated him... God, how I *hated* him for so long. But I never wanted to kill him. He might have wanted me dead, but I never wanted him dead. I didn't want it to end like this." Ren rubbed up and down Nico's back in warm, firm comfort, massaging his thumb into Nico's nape each time his hand swept back up. "I can't believe it. I can't believe what I've done."

"Was there any other way?" Ren asked softly.

"There was...surrender."

"Then there was no choice," Ren said gently, firmly.

In Ren's arms, Nico collected himself. He swallowed his tears, steadied his breathing. He pulled himself back from the edge of whatever he had tripped over, because there was no time for more. Ren pressed his lips into Nico's hair, a kiss to the crown of his head. He inhaled the scent of expensive soap Nico had used at Thea's house, lavender and vanilla still lingering in the strands.

"We need to—" Nico made a *go* motion with his hand.

They unwound and stood. Nico was a messy crier, all swollen red eyes and blotchy red cheeks and red runny nose. He wiped the back of his arm across his wet nose, wetting his coat sleeve with snot, and it was gross and oddly endearing, and Ren's heart pumped hard at the sight of him.

The ground beneath Ren's boots cracked open with a sigh. It was only a tiny splinter that snaked between his feet, but it made him jump sideways and bump into Nico.

Nico crouched to the broken ground and put his hand over the crack, smoothing his palm over brittle grass and hard-packed dirt.

Deep below their feet, the earth groaned. The sensation hummed up Ren's spine, reverberated in his bones.

Ren glanced at the wintry grass that rustled around them. "Nico? What's happening?"

"It's absorbing the magic," Nico murmured in awe.

"What is? The ground?"

Nico dragged a finger through the dirt. He stood. "I'm not sure. I think...maybe the earth is absorbing Vellen's magic. Those walls held an immense amount of magic. I've never actually seen it happen, but I've heard that strong magicians are often drawn to each other. Power finds power. As far as we know, earth has a limitless well of magic. It's the ultimate magician. I think it might be acting as a gigantic, strong magnet, and all of the magic that was just released from Vellen is attracted to it."

"Oh," Ren said slowly, "that's a bad thing?"

"It's a natural thing. But we don't want to be here to witness it. It's never a good thing when the ground under your feet is unsettled."

The grass swayed strangely in the wind, heavy with snow and ice. Ren parted the strands, and their soft winter world opened. Ren made an involuntary sound.

At the base of their mountainside, the wolk rose out of the grass. They were silent and smiling—and there were hundreds of them.

Chapter Fifteen

NICO

"No," Nico whispered, because it was all he was capable of thinking.

His monsters stood below them, still as statues. They were done playing with him, done teasing, done with their game of chase. They were here to end it. They had come to take him back. It was the finale, and the entire horde had shown up.

"Shit. *Shit.*" Beside him, Ren's dark eyes were huge with the innumerable size of the group on full display.

Maybe they had escaped the glass castle only to fail on a winter-swept mountainside. Nico couldn't believe it would end here, where the raw wind tasted of freedom and the waterfall whipped up the feel of adventure. The entire world was *right there*, so near, and Nico couldn't grasp it. He could never hold on to anything but fear.

From somewhere in that crowd of horror, one of the wolk murmured his name so gently, so carefully. A caress. *"Nico."*

He could almost feel the phantom touch of the wolk's too-sharp fingernails scraping down his spine as it rolled his name off its tongue. Goose bumps skittered across his neck, down his back.

"Nico," whispered another.

"Nico," said two more, until the entire horde was murmuring his name en masse and smiling at the sound of it in the air.

He knew what they were doing. It was a ploy to terrify him, to freeze him in place. He knew their modus operandi because they had used the same sort of tactics to haunt him day and night. After so many years, he should be immune. But torment and terror didn't work that way, and it still made Nico want to crawl somewhere dark, curl into a ball, and hide. His stomach churned, but he had nothing left to eject.

Nico's lips parted, but he said nothing. His breath stuttered out of his mouth.

Ren bumped his shoulder against Nico's, jolting him back into the moment.

"I don't know what to do." They were his doom, and he would never escape. "I was actually starting to believe I could find a way out of this. But they always find me."

Ren brushed his fingers down Nico's palm. He touched each of his fingertips to Nico's. It drove away the sensation of the wolk skittering across his skin.

"You're magic," Ren said. "You can do anything."

Nico's fingers twitched against Ren's. "Don't say that right now, Ren. Don't."

"I know what you can do. I've seen it."

Desperation roughened his voice, hard to get words out past it. "You think I can fight two hundred monsters?"

Ren touched Nico's wrist. *Yes.*

Nico grimaced and shook his head. "You crazy, ridiculous man." He couldn't fathom Ren's unwarranted faith in him. "I'm sorry. I'm so sorry."

"Don't say that right now, Nico. Can we run for the cliff and jump into the waterfall?"

"They move too fast. They would be on us before we made it that far."

"I wish the wolk had been in that glass house with us," Ren said vehemently. "They'd be dead now, and we could leave this place together. That's all I want. I just want to leave with you."

"They'd never walk into Vellen. They avoid entering human-made structures if they can. They prefer solid ground."

Solid ground.

Something clicked into place. Hope bloomed in Nico's mind.

"Niiiicccooooo." Their voices swayed together over the curves of his name, licking into the grooves. He heard their feet shuffle, but he closed his mind to it.

"*Nico*," Ren said warningly. "They're moving."

"It's not solid right now," Nico muttered. In his mind, he could picture the shifting dirt, the unsettled rocks deep underground. This land had just soaked up an unprecedented amount of power. What if he pushed a little more magic into already uneasy ground? The earth was still full from its last meal. Maybe it was the perfect time for dessert.

"They're coming," Ren said.

Nico glanced at him. "Get ready."

"For what?"

"Magic."

The expression on Ren's face was so full of anticipation and yearning he practically glowed with it.

Nico poured magic into the dirt at his feet: resistance and then a satisfying give. He wound his magic through little tunnels and deep into the granules of soil, drenching every particle he could reach and coating them with magic. As he pushed and pulled blindly at the dirt, the earth seemed to relax a little and invite him in. The strangest sensation.

Dozens of tiny fissures formed under his boots, spreading, racing downhill. His magic rolled away from him, picking up speed underground, the tug of it on his body immense. His magic snowballed, gathering more and more dirt. Above ground, the grass shivered. The earth creaked as dirt and rocks moved at his will, grumbled because of him. Their planet was cracking open for him, and Nico wasn't sure how he felt about that.

The wolk sensed something happening. They rushed at Ren and Nico, and the fissures opened wider and rushed back at the wolk, rumbling with each new crack. The earth pounded with two hundred pairs of feet—and magic. It hummed through Nico's body in a chaotic jumble.

Nico flinched as the wolk came nearer. *Too close. They're too close.* How familiar that feeling. It had practically become his mantra in that camp of creatures.

Dirt and grass fell away. The earth shifted to make room for Nico's magic. The mountain groaned, trembled, and a chasm opened between them and the wolk. Several of the monsters in front didn't stop in time and ended up tripping into the hole.

"NICO!" No gentle whispering now, no creepy smiles, no more games. The rage in that voice, bellowed across the chasm, was enough to give Nico a headache. "You're making it worse for yourself, Nic. You'll pay for every one of us that you kill."

It was Uio, Zeke's right-hand goon. Nico had once watched Uio pull the legs off a spider one by one, the whole while running his eyes over Nico with as much slow deliberation as he was using to torture the creature. The meaning was evident, and Nico had never forgotten. It had been one of those times of complete unreality, when what he was witnessing was so gruesome he couldn't move, couldn't ignore it, couldn't turn away.

Nico folded his arms across his chest as if he could hold in all of his terror, as if he could contain it for just a little while longer. Ren touched a hand to his back, a quick connection of strength, there and gone. Only Ren was close enough to see his shattered composure, how fast he was breathing, how he was holding his arms tightly to keep the shaking hidden, how wild his face probably looked. Shit, he had to keep it together.

He would slit his own throat before he ever became that spider.

Uio smiled, and it was a horror Nico knew would haunt him later in the dark of night. "Niiiccco, we're going to split you open and suck out—"

"Fuck you," Nico said evenly, just to cut off the rest. Anger churned hotly in his stomach. Heat rose up the back of his throat. Sweat prickled at his nape. He dropped his arms to his sides, stepped dangerously close to the edge, and screamed across the chasm the words he'd wanted to scream a hundred times over the years. "Fuck you! *Fuck you*! You're never going to touch me! I'll melt your fucking arms off your body before I ever let you touch me! I'll implode the damn planet and take out all of us before you ever get—"

The earth collapsed. Uio's smile seemed to hang in the air a stunned second before it plummeted. The ground beneath the wolk crumbled and caved. Ren yelled something.

For a dazed moment, Nico didn't understand what was happening. Someone had wrenched a rug out from under him. But it wasn't a rug, only the ground, vanishing before he could move. He was going to end up stuck with the wolk forever in some dark place, falling endlessly...

A shout ripped out of Nico's mouth. Just as the ground disintegrated beneath him and he dropped—

—a hand gripped the back of his coat and yanked him bodily away from the edge. Nico tripped backward in surprise, going down hard on his ass.

He clutched at the shaky ground. It took only an instant for the earth to swallow the wolk and most of the mountainside in a single loud rush of devastation, nothing but a gaping sinkhole now in front of him. His feet dangled over an abyss.

From somewhere behind him, Ren let out a strangled sound.

Nico stood up slowly. He peered over the edge. The side of the mountain had been sliced off. He couldn't see the bottom of the crevice, only a fathomless pitch-black. The other side of the sinkhole stretched far into the distance. Not a single wolk in sight anywhere. The planet had wiped itself clean.

He backed away from the edge and turned to Ren, who was doubled over with a hand over his mouth. Nico's magic swirled at his back, billowing up from the abyss.

"They're gone." Nico's voice was strange in a way he didn't recognize. He bent forward, hands braced on his knees, and just exhaled into the frosty grass, his huffs of breath rustling the blades. His shoulders shook with an unknowable emotion. His eyes watered. He let his head hang down between his shoulders. "They're gone, they're gone." He had to say it again to make it solid, to get his mind around it.

His magic surged warmly through his body as though rejoicing, but his mind couldn't catch up to the reality of what just happened. *Oh God of Winter! Oh God! Did that really happen?* He was loose and shaky. He didn't know what to do with himself, so he stood there sucking down mouthfuls of frigid air.

Ren came to him cautiously. Nico straightened, the ground still unsteady—or maybe it was his body. His stomach tilted. The world tilted. His entire reality had just shifted, a bizarre sensation as if his whole body was floating up into the sky, weightless with release. He threw his arms around Ren's neck and pressed his body to Ren's. He needed to feel something solid, and Ren was wonderfully solid.

Ren made a startled sound, but he immediately enfolded him in an embrace, pulling him even closer. He smooshed his chilly nose against Nico's temple and simply breathed deeply as they held on tightly to each other.

Nico turned his head and said into Ren's neck, *"Thank you."*

"Of course." Ren gave him a squeeze. "I'm just relieved I didn't have to go in after you."

How did Nico get lucky enough to have this man in his life? He'd never thought of himself as fortunate—until now.

He laughed against Ren's skin. It poured out of him as smoothly as his magic had. Once it started, he couldn't contain it.

Ren let out a laugh, too, as though it were contagious. "What are we laughing about?"

"I don't know." A little delirious. "I just have to let it out somehow."

"I didn't know you could laugh like this." Ren said it against the shell of Nico's ear.

"I don't think I can stop."

"How does it feel?"

Nico closed his eyes, savored the flavor of laughter. It was the most joyous thing he had ever tasted.

"It feels momentous."

Chapter Sixteen

REN

The ground shuddered, a gentle nudge reminding them they stood on the edge of a cliff. It was only a small jolt, but it felt like the beginning of something bigger.

"That's our cue," Nico said. "We have to get out of here."

Reluctantly, Ren released Nico, though it was the last thing he wanted to do.

Nico leaned into his side, and Ren caught those strange, solemn eyes. They gleamed. "Trust me?" he asked Ren softly.

After everything? Ren didn't have to ruminate. "Yes."

"Run," Nico said and took off tearing through the grass up the side of the mountain toward the waterfall. Ren didn't pause, didn't hesitate. He ran.

He was running away with a man who had crushed a city. He was putting his life in the hands of someone who had manipulated the structure of a planet.

It came unbidden, the thought he shouldn't be thinking, the inappropriate rush. *How wonderfully terrifying.*

It was terrifically unseemly, as dangerous as an addiction, but his feet pounded with the thought. *You wanted adventure. You wanted it.*

Ren ran, freedom an exhilaration in his lungs, the wild blast of it all like a window opening to fresh air, like a familiar dream he had run through over and over, like a gust of dream-memory blowing through his brain. It blew through his mind too fast for him to catch.

Ren had felt this grass. He'd heard that waterfall. He'd ridden this particular high.

As his feet pounded the grass, the realization hit. *I did dream this. I remember.*

Barely. His mind snatched at pieces of the dream. The air had been misted with gold. The gilt tips of grass had brushed his legs as he ran, leaving streaks of gold across his pants. There'd been gold stars twinkling in the dream clouds. The sun had been setting into the mountains in molten tones, gilding the world as it took the last light with it.

In reality, the scene wasn't gold, and there was no gem-ball sunset. But the thrill of racing to the edge of the cliff was the same thrill he'd felt in the dream. Dream-Ren had chased hazy swirls of gold straight off the cliff, that exultation filling him even as his feet ran out of ground. Now it was Nico ahead of him. It was Nico he ran after.

Ren remembered having no fear in his dream. He remembered the cold mist of water as it slapped him full in the face. He remembered rushing down a river, carefree, over and around rocks, infinite and flowing. He remembered being everywhere and nowhere at once. He remembered having someone always by his side, never seen but ever-present in nearly every dream he'd ever had.

Ren remembered that instant draw he'd felt toward Nico the moment they first touched. Nico had seemed like a treasure to him, something he'd been chasing for years but had never been able to grasp, like the unattainable gold in his dreams he could never quite hold. Now, in stark reality, he watched Nico's legs pumping ahead of him, his hair flying. *It was you. I was always chasing you in my dreams.*

Impossible. And yet—Ren had lately learned that nothing was impossible.

Snatches of long-buried dream-memory tumbled in his mind. He was catching bits of something familiar yet far away, something he'd once held in his mind but had slipped away with consciousness and time.

There had been so many nights in his life when he'd woken up restive with foggy, gold-tinged dreams still clouding his mind. On those nights, he got up and made himself hot tea, sat by the window with a tug in his chest he couldn't name.

The cold air burned down his lungs, cleared his head. Ren breathed deeply as he ran, and his mind churned.

As a child, he'd wake up in the middle of the night, heart pounding, everything still gilt-edged from another magical dream. He'd never been scared on those nights. He loved the feelings that lingered from the dreams— adventure and freedom, familiarity and closeness. The dreams had been so much better than his real life at the time.

It was dawning on Ren now as he raced through winter-kissed grass. Gold had been running through his dreams all his life, a familiar thread that went as far back as childhood. Though he never fully remembered his golden dreams, he was often left with impressions, pieces—and yearning. Always a deep yearning.

He had always thought of himself as a dreamer, head in the clouds, imagination somewhere off on the horizon where possible adventures lay. But were they only dreams? Gold had saturated his dreams for so long, the thought that it might be abnormal had never occurred to him. It had become a part of his life. It was just something his subconscious clung to.

They neared the waterfall's edge where an endless river waited far below. The river had been a misty liquid gold in his dreams, full of light and magic. Nico's magic, Ren realized now, after having seen that same golden magic in person. In reality, the river was a deep gray, a reflection of the low clouds. Wide and tumultuous, it disappeared into the rise of mountains.

Mist from the waterfall rose up to meet them. Nico didn't slow. He caught Ren's hand in his and held tightly enough to hurt Ren's fingers. They ran straight for the edge.

Ren stole a glance at Nico, at the red hair whipping across his face, at the color in his cheeks, at the plume of breath puffing in front of his face.

I know you. I think I've been dreaming of you all my life. I've dreamt this moment over and over.

Nico turned to Ren in surprise. It was all he had time for as the edge of the cliff rushed toward them.

Over the crash of water that was getting closer, louder with each step, Nico yelled, "We're water flowing across the land, vast and free, always slipping away!"

They leaped. Together, they flew off the cliff. Swirls of white, snow a cold sting, water a harsh spray, nothing above or below. But Ren's hand was in Nico's, and he knew they would survive.

Chapter Seventeen

REN

Ren floated in a dark night sky. Clouds of gold drifted around him, tendrils warm and tingly on his cheeks as they brushed past him. Every little particle of gold that made up the clouds stood out in crisp focus, each one a tiny bright spark. Gold glinted everywhere. His eyes filled with it. He reached out and ran his hand through the specks. They parted for him. His hand, his fingers, his entire arm emanated gold.

A distant part of Ren's mind knew immediately: *I'm dreaming.*

He'd had these dreams so often, for so long. Being amid the gold felt like coming home.

Nico drifted nearby, unseen, always out of reach, the warm comfort of him at the edge of Ren's senses, also afloat in the burnished clouds. Ren caught a brief flash of pale limbs, ethereal and trailing through the clouds, strangely bare. There. Gone. Lost in the spectacular mist. Nico was there with him. Of course it was Nico, and of course he was with Ren, as he should be—as he had always been.

Ren spun in the gold, free of gravity. The rippling warmth passed through his spread fingers and strands of his hair, wonderful against his skin. He could never hold it, but he could feel it as it touched him, as it spun away from him, little flares all over his body. He could see its beauty. And those things were enough. It had always been enough, just to dream it.

The clouds of magic spread out as far as Ren could see. The gold was limitless.

Ren stretched out his arms and legs into the magic of the dream and woke seamlessly.

He lay on a pearly shore, curled comfortably on his side, the sand a silk pillow beneath his cheek. The river water gurgled gently at his feet, kissing the soles of his boots. He noticed these things first before he recognized the feel of Nico at his back, pressed against him, an arm and a leg slung casually over Ren's body. One of the same elegant hands he'd seen in the dream hung down over Ren's chest, slim-fingered and almost the same shade as the pearl-pale sand.

The dream still dangled over them. With the distraction of Nico warm and languid at his back, it took Ren even longer to recognize the dream-gold still wafting through the air. In Ren's sleepy perception, dust motes danced in sunlight.

He knew it wasn't dust, in the same way he knew the stars weren't holes in the sky.

Against his back, Nico stirred awake and then froze. He pulled his loosely sprawled limbs carefully away from Ren's body.

Ren turned over and came face-to-face with Nico. He curled toward Nico, both on their sides. The sand cushioned their bodies.

There was nothing but the sound of the water and the quiet indrawn hush of their shared gasp. Ren saw his surprise mirrored in Nico's widening eyes.

Nico was glowing faintly, a soft, sweet gold. Ren's tiny dream specks soaked into Nico's skin.

It seemed too unbelievable to say aloud, so Ren whispered the question. "Do you see it?"

"No," Nico said after a shocked moment. "I feel it."

Ren brought his hand between their bodies, palm up, and Nico mirrored the gesture. Their fingertips brushed. Magic hovered in the air above their upturned hands like a lingering dream. The gold drifted around Ren, blew gently toward Nico, and faded into his skin. His body absorbed the magic.

Through the gold, their gazes locked above their outstretched hands.

"What are you doing?" Nico whispered. Beneath his coat, he was taking short, nervous breaths.

"Nothing, I swear."

Nico stared at him. The water *shooshed* at their feet, the sand cool and dry beneath their bodies.

"I swear," Ren said again, emphatically.

"You told me you've never used magic."

Ren opened his mouth. Closed it. Opened it again and whispered back, "I haven't. I've only ever dreamed it."

His voice hushed with wonder, Nico said, "I was in your dream." He had the look of someone seeing a lot of impossible things.

"I—I was dreaming about magic before I woke up." Inexplicably, it was hard to admit. Ren had never shared his dreams with anyone.

"I know," Nico said, magical golden motes reflected in his irises. "I was there."

"We were sharing a dream?" The enormity of the possibility slowed Ren's thoughts. "How could that be?"

"Why was I naked?" Nico asked in a puzzled voice.

"The magic was all over us in the dream. We were in clouds of it."

Magic brushed across the skin at Nico's throat, gilding him briefly, and then settled there. Nico rustled, brought his hand up to his throat, chasing an invisible touch. He rubbed uneasy fingers back and forth across his collarbone.

"What does it look like?" Nico asked Ren.

Ren studied the magic a little more closely. "It's a bit like...glowing pollen. It's blowing from me to you. It's dusted across your skin. There's a layer of it on you that just kind of...melts into you." Nico slid a hand up his neck as if he could feel the caress of the magic. "What's it like?" Ren asked, fascinated by Nico's fingertips touching his own skin.

Fear tightened the muscles at the corners of Nico's eyes. "It feels like...my own magic."

"What does that mean?"

Nico shook his head. Fine bits of pearl sand shone on his cheek, in his hair. He was covered in the fantastical dust. "I don't know. God, *I don't know.*" He squeezed his hand into a fist. It was shaking. "I don't know this magic. It should feel foreign in my body, but it doesn't. I don't understand."

"I don't know either," Ren said helplessly.

Magic spun over them, between them, swirling in a sudden wind, caught in the currents. The air was gold with it.

"Of course we shared a dream," Ren said as magic swept over the sand and out into the water. The shards of all his dreams were shifting, piecing together at the back of his mind. "I met you in my dreams. Don't you remember?"

Nico shook his head, mouth open in the shape of confusion.

"It's like our subconsciouses reached out to each other. I think you've been in my dreams for a long time, since I was young. I can't remember the details, but I think we were always together."

There was disquiet on Nico's face, and Ren didn't like it there.

"It'll be all right." Ren reached up. Gold swirled outward from his hand as though flung into the air. Ren smoothed his thumb over Nico's left brow and then his right. He brushed his finger between Nico's brows, down his nose. More gold melted into Nico's skin with each touch.

Hesitantly, Nico put his hand on Ren's arm and then gasped at the contact. Light swelled where skin brushed, and Ren wished he could feel the sensation exactly the way Nico did. He wanted to experience every side of this phenomenon.

Nico swallowed heavily, took in a deep breath of golden air, and said, "No one in your village ever used magic?"

Ren tried to restrain some of his eagerness, though his body was coming alive, thrilling to a glimpse of a brand-new future. "You're the first magician I've ever known."

"No," Nico said carefully, studying him across the sand. "I think *you're* the first magician you've ever known."

Ren caught one of Nico's hands, slid his fingers between Nico's. The magic sparked where their skin met, bright flickers. Nico jolted at the sensation but didn't move away.

Though Nico was clearly unnerved, Ren's chest was hot with excitement. He couldn't help it. He didn't know what any of it meant, but there was magic in the air and anticipation in his muscles. He wanted to jump to his feet and shout. A new world awaited him, unfurling at his feet, full of unknowns and possibilities. Adventure. Promise.

Magic.

Chapter Eighteen

A LONG-AGO DREAM

Ren rolled over in bed and woke up in snow. He sat up. He wasn't warm in his bed, with his ma nearby. Snow fell thickly, slid off of his shoulders and head. Fluffy drifts covered his legs. The world was a flat, endless white plane in every direction. The air was cold enough to snap, but Ren wasn't cold.

Directly in front of him, a figure huddled in the snow. Through the swirl of snowflakes, all Ren could make out was shocking red hair blowing wild against the infinite white. Everything else about the figure blurred at the edges, indistinct, half blending into the snow. His skin, the bare glimpses of it that Ren could make out through the storm, was as creamy as the endless expanse. He seemed disconcertingly unclothed in the cold. Ren wanted to see him, but it was as if the universe said, *No, not yet. Not quite yet.*

Something lurched slightly in Ren's chest, the smallest of tugs. He put a hand over his heart to keep it in place.

Hello, Ren said. No sound came out, though Ren's mouth moved around the shape of the word.

The boy raised his head from his knees. Red whipped across his face. The snow smudged his features. Ren thought the boy might be a little older than himself, but he couldn't be sure.

Hello, replied the boy.

Again, no sound came to him, but Ren tasted the vibration of the boy's voice in his chest and on the back of his tongue, like mint and song. He instantly wanted more of it.

Where did you come from? asked the boy.

My bed. Ren marveled at the dizzying blizzard. *Oh. I'm dreaming. I must be dreaming.*

The boy nodded. *Probably.*

What is this place?

It's... The boy paused. *A safe place. It's the only place I'm safe.*

Really? Ren was interested. *Can I be safe here too?*

Only as long as you dream. He hesitated before he asked Ren, *Are you running from monsters too?*

Ren shuddered. *One monster.*

The boy stood up. He was skinny, a hardly visible sapling in the gusting snow except for that conspicuous bloom of deep red on top. He took a single step toward Ren but then halted. *I have a lot of monsters.*

Are you scared? Ren wanted to move closer, but the boy kept the snow between them like a shield.

Always.

Ren nodded knowingly. *I don't want to be scared anymore.*

The boy swayed a little in place. *Neither do I.*

We could be not-scared together. Something bloomed in the dream-space between them. A beginning.

Will you stay with me a bit? The boy sounded hesitant, hopeful.

I don't know how long I can stay. I might wake, but I'll come back. Ren could make that promise because now that he'd seen the boy, he knew he would find him again. Somehow. Somewhere.

Ren wondered why it wasn't time for them to meet in person and how he knew it wouldn't be time for a while. He wanted this dream boy in his life *now*. They could play in the woods together. They could build tree houses. They could fight each other's monsters.

Here, I think you should have this. For the monsters. Maybe...maybe it'll help? Ren spilled golden specks across the air, intermingling with the snowflakes. They rushed to the boy, a flood of gold, until the boy's body glowed with them.

The boy's voice was faint with surprise, though he didn't make a move to run. *What are you doing?*

I have no idea. I just feel like you might need this. To protect you from the monsters.

Ren had the boy's full attention, and he kind of liked that. Experimentally, he thought, *More gold.* The specks multiplied until the air itself seemed to turn golden. Ren reached out his hand, but it went right through the flakes.

Are you giving me magic? the boy asked, his voice rising. *How are you doing this? I already have magic.*

Ren's chest expanded with the boy's blossoming astonishment; his heart fluttered at the mention of magic.

Magic?

Ren woke up. For a moment, he couldn't figure out where he was. The reality of a chilly bedroom faded the dream quickly. *How strange.* He blinked sleepily up at his dark ceiling, but he couldn't pinpoint what it was he found odd. *Strange...* His mind drifted. He turned over, curled in tighter against his pillow, and fell asleep again.

And the dream, like so many dreams, was forgotten.

About the Author

Emme C. Taylor can be found wandering stormy beaches with a pen and notebook in hand, waiting for inspiration or lightning to strike. She believes the atmospheric environment helps her to write the grittiest parts of her stories. Crochet and dark chocolate ease her mind when her characters aren't cooperating. Emme will happily talk about almost anything to avoid having to talk about herself. How about this weather, huh?

Email (public address): emmectaylor@gmail.com

Twitter: @emileewrites

Instagram: www.instagram.com/woolgatheringgirl

Also Available from NineStar Press

Connect with NineStar Press

www.ninestarpress.com

www.facebook.com/ninestarpress

www.facebook.com/groups/NineStarNiche

www.twitter.com/ninestarpress

www.tumblr.com/blog/ninestarpress